Eye of the
Storm

Also by Hilary Jones

Frontline

HILARY JONES

Eye of the Storm

WELBECK

First published in 2022 by Welbeck Fiction Limited, an imprint
of Welbeck Publishing Group based in London and Sydney.
www.welbeckpublishing.com

Copyright © Hilary Jones, 2022

Hilary Jones has asserted his moral rights to be identified as the author of this Work
in accordance with the Copyright Designs and Patents Act 1988.

A CIP catalogue record for this book is available from the British Library

Hardback ISBN: 978-1-78739-777-4
Trade paperback ISBN: 978-1-78739-778-1
Ebook ISBN: 978-1-78739-779-8

Printed and bound by CPI Group (UK) Ltd., Croydon, CR0 4YY

10 9 8 7 6 5 4 3 2 1

To Noreen, whose wisdom, knowledge and generosity know no bounds.

'One of the great liabilities of history is that all too many people fail to remain awake through great periods of social change. Every society has its protectors of status quo and its fraternities of the indifferent who are notorious for sleeping through revolutions. Today, our very survival depends on our ability to stay awake, to adjust to new ideas, to remain vigilant and to face the challenge of change.'

– Martin Luther King Jr,
Where Do We Go from Here? Chaos or Community? (1967)

'No society can surely be flourishing and happy, of which the far greater part of the members are poor and miserable.'

– Adam Smith,
The Wealth of Nations (1776)

Prologue

Queen Mary Convalescent Auxiliary Hospital, Roehampton, London, February 1919

Will entered the hospital's magnificent grounds with its expanse of manicured lawns and beautifully tended gardens. He was earlier than usual, and besides the birds it was peaceful and quiet. He'd woken with the dawn and he thought he'd give his pregnant wife, Grace, a lie-in and get a head start on his rounds.

As he turned a corner towards the steps, his eye caught something out of place – grey, large, in a tree at the edge of the gardens. It swung lightly in the morning breeze. Will dropped the folder in his hands, his papers splaying out across the stone path. He made an inhuman sound as he ran towards the figure, leaping up on to the fence and lifting with all his strength the man wearing a noose around his throat. He was still warm.

Will screamed for help. He couldn't fight gravity and untie the man at the same time. An orderly came running and climbed up on to the fence beside Will – almost losing his balance.

'Can you scramble up into the tree?' Will said.

The man looked desperately at the coiled rope.

'You!' Will yelled at a gardener entering the grounds. 'Shears!'

The gardener dropped his wheelbarrow and ran over with the cutting implement.

They cut the man down as an assortment of nurses and patients — several of them hobbling on crutches — began to file out towards the noise.

Will pulled the rope from the man's neck. A livid cicatrice. Choking gasps as the man took in oxygen. He was injured, but alive.

'You're going to be fine, Calvin,' Will said. But the man refused to make eye contact with Will.

A couple of nurses dropped a stretcher on the ground by Calvin Darke as he pushed himself up with his one remaining arm.

Will wondered at the planning and effort that went into the attempt. To get up there and kick himself off with only one arm and one leg.

Just then, Will's wife Grace arrived. He saw the shock and concern on her face when she saw him on the ground. She rushed over. He stood and pulled her close to him.

'What happened?' she said.

'Darke, he . . .' He pointed at the remaining rope coiled around the tree.

Grace involuntarily lifted her hand to her own throat.

'Oh, Will. You saved him?'

'For now.'

They walked a little way from the crowd and Grace insisted Will rest against the fence.

'How desperate must a man be to want to take his own life, Grace?' he asked. 'And after all he's survived.'

She thought about it for a few seconds. He watched it play across her gentle, heart-shaped face, her green eyes.

'I suppose that carrying on living in his present circumstances seemed, to him, even worse.'

'Then I hope I've done the right thing. Am I wrong to think that we can help change anything? Give a man back the will and desire to live a good life despite what has happened to him?'

That's the work they'd been trying to do at this rehabilitation hospital. It was about much more than limbs. It was about restoring men back to some sense of purpose, even joy.

'Of course you're not wrong. You've helped so many, Will. So many who are just as badly damaged and who are now leading contented, fulfilling lives.' She took his hand in hers. 'You may be a budding surgeon and understand a quick fix — an incision here, a dissection there, stitch them up and hey presto! But rehabilitation from war wounds isn't as simple. You of all people know it's the injury to the mind that's the limiting factor. And that takes time to heal . . .'

Will clasped her hand. He still had adrenaline coursing through him. 'You're right, I know.'

'You've given him another chance. Another day to turn it all around. Sometimes that's all it takes.'

Though Grace was trying to get Will to focus on the good, a litany of faces passed through his mind — the men on the fields of war, his beloved Captain Daniels who had been unfairly shot, his fellow stretcher-bearer Arup Nur, his mother who died giving birth to his sister, and his father whose mind sometimes slipped away before his eyes. An intense feeling of helplessness came over him, despite the act he'd just performed.

'I want to do *more*, Grace.'

'Will,' she said, looking deep into his eyes. 'You can't save them all.'

3

PART ONE

1

Parish of Putney, London, March 1919

The modest accommodation in Barnes that had been provided for Will and Grace was cramped and bare, but it was clean and dry and only a short distance down the hill from Roehampton village. Unfortunately for Grace, who was already thirty weeks pregnant, there was no omnibus service on that particular route and the uphill journey to work seemed to have become increasingly steep.

When their duties began at the same time, Will would walk beside her. He would carry whatever bags she needed for work, take her by the hand and thoughtfully reduce the length of his stride to keep in step with her. She insisted he was making far too much fuss.

She also realised that, in view of his own mother's untimely and tragic death giving birth to his sister, accompanying her was more about allaying his own anxiety about her pregnancy than anything else. So, she acquiesced.

Besides, the walk from the little terraced house on the edge of Richmond Park to the Queen Mary Convalescent Auxiliary Hospital was a pleasant one. Today the sky was blue and cloudless and a fresh spring breeze from the south-west gently shook the branches of cherry blossoms and budding leaves of oak and elm trees either side of them. As they strolled along Priory Lane, they looked at the sweeping heath-land to their right. Unfurling fronds of spring bracken peppered the grounds of the 2500-acre Royal Park in dense clusters and day by day slowly changed the colour of the landscape from orange-brown to a vibrant leafy green.

Red and fallow deer meandered and grazed under the ancient woodland trees and a small group of children flew box kites on the ridge of Richmond Hill. Their excited voices carried all the way down to their expectant parents.

To their left, they could not help but admire the splendid private mansions with their sweeping drives, shiny new motor cars and magnificent topiaries. It reminded them of Grace's parents' wonderful estate at Bishop's Cleeve, which they had promised to visit again as soon as they were granted the privilege of some well-deserved time off.

That might not be until after the baby came, given the peripatetic nature of both their work. Unlike many others after the war with no work or stuck in mundane, low-paid jobs requiring slavish adherence to tedious routines, Will and Grace's roles were spread out.

Grace had already made a reputation for herself at Roehampton as one of the best operating theatre nurses in London and such was her exemplary post-infection record that she was in great demand from orthopaedic surgeons who wanted to secure her services. She made their own results and reputations look better.

Specialist surgeons would visit Queen Mary's on a regular basis to supervise the rehabilitation side of the work but whenever surgical revision of an amputation or any acute procedure was required, the surgery would be performed at the specialist's own hospital and Grace would be invited to assist. It was an arrangement that suited everybody. The hospital's goodwill in lending out one of the nurses meant that the services of the consultant were retained, a handsome contribution to her salary was made and her experience and knowledge was developed further. And despite her pregnancy, the London teaching hospitals she visited were all on the major omnibus routes.

Will was content with the four days' work each week the hospital could afford to offer him and although he had made his presence there indispensable, the hospital was largely charitably funded and its meagre budget could stretch no further. But this too suited him. It meant he could devote three remaining days, as well as occasional evenings, to the role of Dr Forrester's assistant. The man who had recognised Will's medical potential five years previously while he was just a lowly hospital porter in Chiswick and the man who had come to his sister Kitty's rescue at home when she was poleaxed by the Spanish flu was now determined to be Will's mentor.

Ahead of them on the walk was the portion of land that had been earmarked for development by the London County Council to build homes 'fit for heroes' after the war. Yet despite them being desperately needed and promised, there was no sign whatsoever of construction having started.

The whole area between Roehampton and Barnes in the Parish of Putney was still open and undeveloped and as they turned into Clarence Lane, the handsome profile of Roehampton House in all its Edwardian splendour hove into view.

They reached the gate and entered the hospital's lush grounds. Grace gave Will a peck on the cheek and set off towards the main building, while Will headed for one of the newly built huts where new patients were admitted to be registered and assessed.

As they separated, Grace was flooded with memories of their lovemaking from the prior evening. Ever since their honeymoon spent in a small clifftop farmhouse overlapping the sea just outside Le Tréport in northern France, Will and Grace had made love almost every day. Reaching for each other as they lay in bed together was as natural and life-giving as breathing itself. It was as elemental to them as the dawn of each day, and perhaps especially because of what they'd survived. War had taught them both that life was short and unpredictable.

Their courtship had been gradual, at the front, almost coy to start with, but that was not surprising as both of them had been young — Will only sixteen and Grace just two years older. And the opportunities they'd had to consort with one another without emergency duties getting in the way had been few and far between.

For the last few months, they had made up for lost time, and despite Grace's pregnancy they still could not keep their hands off each other. Will was strong, muscular and athletic, and now at nineteen was physically indefatigable, but never demanding. He was also a tender, unselfish and considerate lover, which made Grace adore him even more. He was cautious and encouraged Grace to take control over the tempo and scope of their passion. And despite being thirty weeks pregnant, Grace still felt healthy, lithe and agile enough to satisfy both her own and her husband's physical desires. In fact, it was more enjoyable for her than ever.

Overall, their physical bond, cemented as it was by the child Grace was carrying, was incredibly strong. Grace found the concept of the three of them joined together so closely, so intimately and inseparably in the act of love unutterably beautiful. Each day, as she met the challenges of her work, she carried within her the flame of another evening's intimacy to look forward to.

Will approached a motley group of men outside the registration hut, gathered together under one of the giant cedars. He recognised several of the faces he had seen on his rounds over previous days.

All were double amputees: three of them in wheelchairs and the other four sitting on benches or standing with the help of walking sticks or crutches. They were neatly dressed in light blue or grey buttoned tunics with shirts and ties underneath. Their trousers were baggy and uniform in colour and some of the men had rolled them up and tucked them under the stumps of their missing limbs. Their hair was neatly parted to the side or in the middle and all but two had impressive and carefully trimmed handlebar moustaches.

Around them stood several Voluntary Aid Detachment nurses in their long grey gowns, white pinafore aprons and nun-like head coverings and all seemed engaged in quiet conversation.

'Could've done with your services last night,' said Martin, leaning on his crutches and standing behind one of the other men in a wheelchair. 'Darke, he went berserk again . . . Shouting and screaming he was. Thrashing about and throwing things. It took four of your orderlies just to hold him down,' he said. 'The RMO hadn't a clue what to do. A rookie straight out of medical school. Don't know why they bothered sending him here. Too young to have served in the war. Too stupid to imagine how we feel.'

Will had seen the recently appointed junior doctor struggle with his new role. Formerly, the convalescent hospital only concerned itself with rehabilitation. Any surgical revision would be done at London teaching hospitals where the visiting orthopaedic surgeons usually worked. Now, with the appointment of a resident medical officer, minor treatment could be handled in-house. At least that was the theory.

The new doctor had already missed one obvious case of appendicitis, which Will had dealt with himself, and he'd also made himself scarce when inpatients had succumbed to the Spanish flu, which still circulated. There had been ten deaths in all from this: six soldiers, two nurses and two orderlies, with many more laid low for days or weeks. Will had attended and treated all of them. He had learned much from his experiences in the military camps and hospitals in France that had been overwhelmed and devastated by this terrible pandemic. And because of his frequent exposure to the virus, he was without doubt now immune to its persistent threat.

The young medical tyro had seemed scared stiff of coming anywhere near someone harbouring the infection and had left all those patients' care and clinical management to Will. Will could not really blame him. The Spanish flu had already killed nearly two hundred thousand people in Britain and was only gradually beginning to peter out. The death toll had unexpectedly been greatest among the youngest, fittest and healthiest, like the RMO.

'It's not always easy dealing with meltdowns like that,' said Will diplomatically. 'Not when you can't understand what people have been through.'

Martin nodded. 'You're different. Bloody stretcher-bearer at the front for two years. You've seen a thing or two. People respect you for that, Will. And you know how to talk to us an' all.'

'That man, Darke, though,' said another chap, 'he's still in a right bad way. You wouldn't want to leave him on his own.'

'The men are right,' offered one of the nurses. 'We had to have someone watch him all night. The poor man seems to be in dreadful pain.'

Will nodded. 'I'll go and see him.'

'Thanks, mate. Tell him to come out here and join us later if he fancies. The nurses are getting a bit frisky and keep flirting with us.'

'That's right, they won't take no for an answer,' said his neighbour, laughing.

'I can quite believe it,' grinned Will, walking up the ramp to the hut and opening the door.

He glanced back at the VAD nurses, whose arms were folded across their chests and their faces screwed up in mock indignation.

I'd better get in there and send out reinforcements, he thought, smiling. His trip to the library would have to wait.

Secretly, without Grace knowing, Will had been assiduously reading every medical textbook he could find on the subject of obstetrics in the library at Queen Mary's. He was well acquainted with the facts and they did not reassure him in the slightest. Quite the opposite.

He had discovered that it was not so long ago in Britain that one in every thirty women died after unassisted delivery. Even now, one in every two hundred did not survive, especially among the poor who could not afford medical care. Even though Will could just about afford to pay for a midwife and Grace's father, Arthur, had offered to help, their skills and abilities were limited.

He was only too aware that the complications of labour were many, unpredictable and often irreversible. A little knowledge, Grace had often told him whenever the subject arose, could be a dangerous thing.

But there was more to it, of course. His darling mother, Evie. His beautiful, carefree, devoted, fun-loving mother. She had not survived the birth of his sister.

There was also the fact that Grace had been badly injured in France when her field ambulance had taken a direct hit from a German shell only a few months ago. The surgeons had removed a large sliver of its casing from her lower abdomen and carried out emergency surgery to preserve as much as possible of her left ovary and fallopian tube. Her intestine was repaired and her contused uterus had to be patched up. She had lost copious amounts of blood and had fought the infection and pain for several weeks afterwards. The doctors had warned her at the time that, provided she recovered, she could not take her fertility or ability to carry a child for granted. Grace had been concerned in accepting Will's proposal of marriage that it would be unfair to do so if it meant he might be sacrificing a chance to one day become a father. But Will reassured her it made not a shred of difference. He loved her for who she was and loved her unconditionally.

He did not know what he would do if the birth did not go well.

But first, he had to find Calvin Darke, the man in trouble.

2

Chiswick, London, March 1919

Clara peeled carrots, onions and potatoes for the evening stew, looking through the kitchen doorway at little Kitty as she sat at the table in the lounge. Her curly blonde locks tumbled on to her shoulders, framing an oval face with wide cheekbones and a button nose just like her mother's. Her round blue eyes were cast downwards at her book and she mouthed the words that she was silently reading. Clara's heart melted. She looked so utterly sweet.

Clara was proud of her niece. She was only nine but she had the maturity and vocabulary of a girl twice her age.

Clara had become Kitty's surrogate mother – and Will and Jack's – on that fateful day when Kitty's real mother, Evie, had given birth and then succumbed within days to childbed fever.

Her brother, Robbie, had struggled to come to terms with the enduring grief caused by the loss of his beloved wife and he had been absent from the family home throughout the war, oblivious to the risks of trench warfare and totally insouciant of his own survival. The letters he had sent had been as rare as they were brief and were never encouraging. Robbie's soul had died along with Evie's on that dismal day nearly ten years ago.

The two boys, Jack and Will, in defiance of her resistance and protestations, had also enlisted, despite being underage. Mercifully, both had survived. What horrors they might have witnessed in the meantime and what mental scars they still suffered, she could only imagine. Jack was still out in Flanders taking the King's shilling, busy with the unenviable job of clearing the battlefields of unexploded ordnance and identifying rotting corpses. Ghastly work, Jack had told her in his letters, but at least it paid well.

Will was living with his lovely young wife of a few months, Grace, in Barnes, only a few miles from this little house in Chiswick, and they were looking forward to the birth of their baby in just three months' time.

Clara was proud of all of them. Will, the future doctor. The wayward and impetuous Jack. And especially Kitty, who had responded in ways Clara could never have dreamed to her love, guidance, mentoring and teaching. It helped that they attended the same school, of course. Clara as an experienced senior teacher and Kitty as a pupil. Together they walked to Belmont School, two blocks away, in the morning and returned home together in the evening, even when Kitty had activities or games, such as gymnastics or rounders, after classes.

Kitty would regale Clara with everything she had learned that day and then bombard her with further questions in her relentless quest for knowledge. Clara gazed at her now in the other room, slowly turning the pages of her book and making notes and annotations.

'When will Daddy be home, Aunt Clara?'

'Any time now,' she replied, glancing at the carriage clock in the centre of the mantelpiece. 'You'll have time for a game of dominoes before tea.'

PART ONE

Clara was delighted by the question. That special word: 'Daddy'. It was only recently that Kitty had started using it again. It was testament to the growing bond between father and daughter that had begun to rekindle. After having been incorrectly reported dead – missing in action – Robbie had finally returned home, but markedly a changed man.

Now, his moods, although still occasionally dark and bleak, seemed less severe and frequent. He'd got his old job back at the dockyards by the river with a rival company to the one that had sacked him five years previously and he was coping with the work. He took a much greater interest in his children, from taking them out on the river with him in a borrowed rowboat to playing football with them on Turnham Green. He would read to Kitty and she to him. They talked about Jack in France and Will working at the hospital for the men who had no legs or arms. They talked about their excitement at the prospect of Kitty soon having a little niece or nephew to play with and they wondered what Will and Grace might call the baby.

'I want to learn Spanish, Aunt Clara,' Kitty suddenly said.

'Spanish, indeed? And why is that?'

'I just want to.'

Clara smiled knowingly.

'Is it anything to do with that Spanish boy in your class? Thiago?'

'No,' said Kitty rather indignantly but blushing slightly. 'It's nothing to do with him at all. I just want to learn another language.'

Kitty had been spending lots of time with the olive-skinned, brown-eyed, dark-haired Thiago and the two of them now always sat together in class and appeared inseparable.

'Of course you can, then,' said Clara. 'You already speak English very well, so why not? It can only be advantageous to speak more than one language. It will help you discover even more new words and phrases.'

'*Estupendo*,' said Kitty out of the blue.

'*Maravilloso*,' Clara answered back.

'So we've started then?' smiled Kitty without looking up, turning another page.

'It would certainly appear so,' said Clara as she grinned and threw a handful of chopped onions into the pot on the stove.

Kitty jumped up as she heard the sound of Robbie's key in the lock and the front door opening.

'Daddy!' she cried and leapt into his arms.

'Hello, my little kittycat,' he said. 'Do you fancy a game of dominoes?'

Kitty screwed up her eyes in concentration and looked at her father squarely.

'*Si lo hago y te amo*,' she said, saying each word slowly and pointing her index finger at his face to emphasise each one.

'What?'

Kitty giggled and buried her face in her father's neck.

'She says, yes she does, and she loves you,' translated Clara. 'Sometimes it's easier to say things like that in a different language.'

3

Queen Mary Convalescent Auxiliary Hospital, Roehampton, London, March 1919

Will sat next to the man who lay in the hospital bed with his back turned, facing the wall.

'You're thinking about Captain Ahab on the *Pequod*, aren't you?' Will said. 'You're thinking about the white whale that bit his leg off and the artificial one he wore afterwards made from whalebone.'

There was no response.

'Or maybe Captain James Hook with the iron hook that replaced his severed hand?'

There was no suggestion at all that he had been heard.

'Or even Long John Silver with his wooden leg and that parrot perched on his shoulder?'

Nothing.

'We've come a long way since then, Mr Darke. My father-in-law had his thigh bone shattered by a Boer marksman's bullet at Stormberg. The army blacksmith fashioned him a workable copy of a prosthetic limb created in 1863 by a New York inventor who went by the fanciful name of Dubois L. Parmelee.'

Silence.

'It wasn't perfect, but it was better than those old peg legs.

More comfortable and adjustable. It made him independent again and restored his dignity. Still wears it today.'

Will was not going to give up. This man had been on his own for too long. In constant pain from the phantom limb, helpless without his right arm, reliant on crutches, unemployed and ostracised from his own community, he had given up on any chance of not only practical rehabilitation, but of life. Though Will had pulled him down from that tree, he knew the terrible danger that Darke would try again. He had to get through to him.

At the start of the war, prosthetic limbs were still very rudimentary. Heavy, cumbersome and painful to wear. Calvin had previously told Will that he'd tried one and it supported his weight all right, but it was so awkward to use, difficult to balance on and uncomfortable, he had thrown it away in disgust and swore never to try one again. But that was in 1915. Back then there was very little call for artificial limbs. The few being made derived from a fledgling cottage industry that rarely fitted the devices themselves or tailored them to the specific needs or comfort of their clients. One year later, following the terrible events in Belgium and France, demand was vastly outstripping supply. Over forty-one thousand men and officers survived after losing limbs during the fighting and now nine hundred of them were resident at Queen Mary's, with 4321 soldiers still on the waiting list.

It was a depressing statistic. Yet the sheer scale and necessity to produce greater numbers of prostheses had resulted in greater innovation, better design and the use of more lightweight materials. It meant their functionality and quality had improved dramatically.

Will regarded the broken man in front of him.

'You can ignore me if you want. You can tell me to go to hell. But things have moved on, Mr Darke. Limb-makers from all over the world have come to Queen Mary's and brought with them their skills and expertise. And they know their stuff. Take Desoutter Brothers Ltd as an example – one of the Desoutter family lost a leg above the knee in a flying accident. The company worked out of a small aircraft factory in Hendon and designed a metal leg made out of Duralumin. That's the stuff extensively used in the construction of their aircraft.'

Calvin didn't move, just sighed deeply as if exasperated.

'You've lost an arm and a leg. There are men here who have lost all four limbs. We get visitors from Queen Mary's in Sidcup. They've had half their faces blown away. No eye or socket, no cheek, no nose, just a big hole. Two thousand men suffered disfiguring facial injuries in the Battle of the Somme alone. Major Harold Gillies does extraordinary surgical reconstructive work. But these men will never look the same. You've still got your looks, Mr Darke. Some of their mothers can't look at their sons.' He paused to let that sink in. 'Men from St Dunstan's come over too. They've been blinded in the war, so they can't even see how many arms or legs you still have.'

Calvin sighed again and turned on to his back, looking up at the ceiling.

'I understand,' he finally spoke. 'There are men much worse off than me. I should be grateful, yes? Grateful to be regularly woken in the night with pain like a red-hot poker being thrust up my thigh to the groin. To be a shadow of the man I was. An empty shell. Well, let them get on with it. I'll find no solace in the fellowship of the disabled. I want to get away from it, not embrace it.'

Will looked down at the wooden floorboards and back up again.

'There was a bloke called Billy Isle who came here three years ago. He was the Kansas City branch manager for the JF Rowley Company and had an artificial foot himself because his own had been crushed by a train and amputated. He said something that every man here remembers to this day.'

'Enlighten me.'

'He said, "I know it's hard, but it's not what you've lost that counts, it's what you have left."'

'Profound.'

Will ignored the sarcasm.

'Most of our patients wear artificial limbs provided free by the Ministry of Pensions. Many of them are playing sports again, working as paid members of staff at the hospital, learning new trades or finding employment. There are further operations that can be undertaken, too, to help with the pain.'

Using his left arm and good leg to help himself, Calvin slowly turned towards Will. His face was grim. He had already told countless do-gooders to sod off, in no uncertain terms. But one of the other men had told him that Will had fought in the trenches and served as a stretcher-bearer for two years before the armistice. The average life expectancy of a stretcher-bearer at the front at that time was six weeks. So rather begrudgingly he felt he at least owed the fellow some respect and an acknowledgement for giving him the time of day. Even if he had ruined his attempt to end it all.

'You're wasting your time. The leg is one thing. Anyone can stick something on the end of a stump. But the arm is useless. I was right-handed. Now I have trouble even wiping my arse.'

'Glad you mentioned that,' said Will, encouraged at least by a response of sorts. 'Because you're right. For almost everyone, lost lower limbs can be replaced these days with a fair degree of success. But arms have always been more of a challenge.'

'They gave me some contraption with a leather socket and a clapper claw on the end. Worse than bloody useless.'

'It would've been. But now you're here. You're going to meet men with a similar disablement to yours. You're going to see how they've progressed.'

Calvin appeared unmoved.

'Look, if you do nothing else, will you take a walk with me? We can go anywhere you want in the hospital or around the grounds. You'll see armless men at work. Digging, hoeing, using a pitchfork, wheeling a barrow up a steep slope, swinging heavy hammers, collecting hens' eggs from the coops, raking out the pigsties. All without effort or discomfort.'

Calvin looked at Will in clear disbelief, yet the young man kept talking.

'We'll visit the workshops. We'll see men without arms doing carpentry, using planes, chisels, spokeshaves and the like. Right now a group of them are rebuilding a 12HP Darracq Type V touring sedan from the ground up. Beautiful car.'

For the first time, Will saw a flicker of interest in his patient's eyes.

'With men who have lost their legs as well as their jobs, their prosthesis is the most important thing. Their limb takes precedence. With men who have lost their arms, the opposite is true. Their employment, their trade, comes first. Dudley Myers is working miracles here. He's found employment for hundreds of men, either in their old jobs or brand-new ones.'

'Such as?'

'You name it. Architecture. Tailoring. Art and design. Bakery. Basket- and boot-making. Cinema work. Confectionery. Diamond polishing. Draughtsmanship. Engineering. Photography. He's offered twenty-five trades to learn at one time or another. That's probably more than you get in civvy life,' Will said. 'Tell me, Mr Darke, what did you do before joining up?'

'Groundsman at the sports club. Used to play cricket and golf myself. And call me Calvin, please.'

'All right, Calvin. You know, you will play again. In fact, there is a cricket match here in the grounds this weekend. There are eleven in the team and only fifteen arms between them.'

Calvin managed a rueful smile.

'We'll also go down to the games room. How about a game of billiards later?'

Will noticed the slightest upturn at the side of Calvin's mouth.

'Do I get a handicap?'

'A handicap? You're kidding me. Why the hell should you?'

Will sensed the long-lost competitive spirit in the man beginning to resurface.

'Look out this window, Calvin,' he said. 'You see those two fellows over there by the hedge talking to that lady who is taller than the both of them?'

Calvin sat up on the edge of the bed and reluctantly did as he was instructed.

'That's Mrs Gwynne Holford. The hospital's founder. On her left, the man smoking – that's Private Frank Chapman. The inspiration for the hospital. With a record of more than

24

twenty-one years' service and at forty-six years of age, he chucked in his job and rejoined his regiment at the very beginning of the war. He went one better than you, though. He lost not just one arm but both of them. In 1915.'

'He's not using,' he remarked, amazed.

'No, he's not. I'm told that back in January 1915 he was sitting at a table at the Millbank military hospital with a look of utter sadness and hopelessness on his face, having gone through what he did. What the government had given him as a substitute for those arms was totally inadequate. Mrs Holford was passing by and asked him to tell her his history. She listened and was appalled. She resolved right there and then that those men who'd had the misfortune to lose a limb in that terrible conflict would be fitted with the most perfect artificial limbs which human science could devise.'

'And that's how the hospital started?'

'Yes. And before you know it, she had persuaded Queen Mary herself to become patron, raised the money and persuaded Mr E. Kenneth Wilson of the Ellerman Wilson shipping line to lend Roehampton House and its grounds for free.'

Calvin was quiet as he took all this on board.

'So that man on her left, Frank Chapman . . . he is pointing to something in the distance using one of his artificial arms?'

'That's right. Frank Chapman also rides a bicycle, is a keen gardener, has learned to write in an elegant albeit artificial hand, and pretty much does everything else.'

'The other man?'

'Sergeant Arnold Loosemore. Survived Gallipoli and was then sent to the Somme. He was awarded the Victoria Cross for bravery under heavy enemy fire and later the Distinguished Conduct Medal for helping to get his unit back to the safety of their own lines. As bad luck would have it, just before the end of the war in October 1918, he lost his leg above the knee. He's a damn fine man. He reminds me very much of another courageous man I served with, who was also a born leader and twice decorated. Captain Jacob Daniels.' Will paused as he reflected on the gross injustice of that man's death by firing squad for desertion when his misadventure was only due to being incapacitated by shell-shock. 'But he didn't make it.'

Calvin had been without hope or expectation for so long so depressed, isolated and withdrawn that life until this moment had all but ended for him. But something was stirring within him. An emotion he hardly recognised and could not immediately understand nor express. He could not find a word to accurately describe it. The nearest he came to it was guilt. Guilt about his recent indulgence in his own self-pity.

'You're not alone, Calvin,' said Will.

'I'll give it another go then, you persistent bugger. I can see there are men worse off than me.'

'Many.'

'Holford, Chapman and Loosemore. I'd like to meet them. I'd like to shake their hands.' Then he broke out into the first proper smile he had produced in months. 'With my left hand, obviously.'

4

Royal National Orthopaedic Hospital, Shepherd's Bush, London, March 1919

Grace picked up the sterilised bone saw from the theatre trolley and handed it to Mr Arthur Sidney Blundell Bankart. The surgeon had already excised the inflamed and knotted scar tissue covering the existing bone stump from the patient in front of him and preserved as much of the remaining healthy skin as he could.

Grace had spent four long years in Belgium and France as part of the First Aid Nursing Yeomanry and had seen so many men mutilated and killed during the conflict. She had tended thousands of soldiers, assisted in hundreds of emergency surgical operations and often been left to sterilise the guillotines used for amputations and to stack up the severed limbs in the operating theatres or mortuaries.

Now she was involved in the reconstructive work. She was helping put men back together, rebuilding their shattered bodies and coaxing them out of their gloomy mental state of despair and despondency, along with Will.

The war was over and the future was brighter. Death and destruction were behind them. Their focus now was on repair and healing, on hope, renewal and optimism.

At the same time, the lives of these men were irrevocably changed. Physically disabled, the young men were conscious of how they were regarded by the people of the country they fought for. The trajectory of their rehabilitation was a long and uphill one.

'Swab please, Mrs Burnett,' said the surgeon as Grace simultaneously mopped up the blood spurting from a number of tiny arterioles with a gauze square. 'There are one or two small bleeders here. Let's tie them off.'

Grace duly passed the suture material and the Spencer Wells haemostatic forceps over to him.

'Now, if you would be so kind as to hold this retractor and protect the bulk of that remaining quadriceps muscle, I'll have a little nibble at the femur.'

He took the serrated blade in his right hand and gingerly sawed through the bone a good 4 inches above the original skin incision.

'What a difference these improved anaesthetics have made, Mr Bankart,' Grace said.

'Indeed. Not long ago, before we could safely render the patient unconscious for protracted periods of time, we had to work as quickly as possible. It was speed rather than skill that used to be paramount. Now it's the other way around. We can take our time. And hopefully get it right.'

Grace nodded. 'Smoothly rounding off the bone and using the muscle as a flap over the end has changed everything.'

'As has your diligence and expertise in antiseptic technique, Mrs Burnett. Our post-operative infection rates put every other surgeon's in the shade. Well, those that don't employ your services anyway.'

Grace felt herself blushing slightly beneath her surgical mask.

'That's very kind of you, sir, but as everybody knows, it's your surgical skill which is responsible for the patients' good fortune, not me.'

'Nonsense. It's teamwork. You can't have one without the other. Anyone can hack off a limb. It's glorified carpentry. But to do it in a clean surgical field without worrying about abscesses, putrefaction and blood poisoning, that requires a multidisciplinary approach.'

'It certainly seems to be improving the results.'

'You're the one improving the results, Mrs Burnett. My colleagues are not doing anything we haven't always done. It might embarrass you to hear this but your name is sometimes mentioned at meetings of the Royal Society of Orthopaedic Surgeons.'

'Well, only because the last one was held at Queen Mary's.'

'Nonsense. You're like a Florence Nightingale mark two. And a lot easier to work with from what I've read about her.'

Grace laughed. 'I think she had more to contend with. She was a lone pioneer in a world dominated by men who weren't used to ever listening to a woman, let alone being told what to do by one. They were also set in their traditional medical ways and many had never even heard of the germ theory of disease.'

'I'm not sure it's changed all that much.'

The surgeon was rearranging flesh and dissecting tiny nerves away from fibrous muscle tissue as he spoke.

'Maybe not everywhere. But it *is* changing, and I certainly feel listened to here.'

'Our reputations depend on your work too. It's just a shame about . . .' He indicated with the instrument towards her rounded belly. 'I mean, really, you should be resting by now. You have the most important role of your life ahead of you.'

Grace sighed internally. She had been enjoying this conversation about medical advancements and, if she was honest, her own capabilities. But pregnancy marked her, it seemed, as a different kind of woman than a Florence Nightingale. Motherhood was perceived as a role in and of itself – one that would alter and apparently subsume her and all her interests from before.

She chose not to reply.

'How is morale back at the convalescent hospital?' Bankart asked. He was checking that the muscle flap had a viable blood supply and was now wrapping it over the rounded bone end and suturing it on the inside of the thigh.

'Improving, but there is a long way to go. For men like this one, this operation could change his life. He's been in agony.' Calvin's leg had been blown off at the knee.

'Surgery in the field? Guillotine, it seems.'

'Like so many others. There was no time to be wasted then. The result meant that the stump was just under the surface of the skin, excruciatingly painful and ulcerated, unable to bear weight with all the nerves tangled up in the scar tissue which have been screaming at him ever since.'

'Phantom limb pain?'

'The whole ghastly syndrome.'

'Well, this should make him more comfortable. I've transposed some of the nerves and placed them to one side where they won't be subject to further physical insult.'

'And tailoring the surgery to the best type of prosthesis available, rather than the other way round, is proving revolutionary. The men can achieve so much more this way. More mobility. So much less pain.'

'We aim to please.'

There was a silence between them for a while as the surgeon applied the last few sutures.

'Well, I've done what I can. It's all down to the rehabilitation now. And you're all working wonders over there. I see it.'

'Slowly. It took some persuading for Calvin to go through with this.' She didn't go into any more detail, but she thought of Will getting the poor man down from the tree. 'And there are many more waiting.'

'But the numbers will fall in time. The terrible influx has stopped at least. And the mood is better, I sense? The workshops, the camaraderie?'

'There is plenty of horseplay all right,' Grace laughed.

'And I'm sure they adore you.'

'I don't know about that, sir,' she smiled. She didn't need the patients to adore her. She just wanted to help give them a better quality of life.

5

North-eastern France, March 1919

Jack Burnett's war had been much like that of most of the other sappers in the 183rd Tunnelling Company of the Royal Engineers. It had been brutal, bloody and barbaric. He had dutifully played his part, digging the underground mines and laying the explosive charges under the trenches of thousands of now deceased German and Austrian soldiers and had done whatever ghastly deeds were required of him by the military machine to help defeat the enemy.

He'd had several narrow escapes, just like his younger brother Will, and lost many good mates and comrades during the two years of fighting in which he was involved.

Jack sat now in front of the bar at Chez Maxime's and felt a stab of regret when he saw Amandine at the far end of it, arm in arm with a tall, handsome-looking young Australian officer.

He and she had spent several romantic months together since the ceasefire, Amandine helping her father out on the farm and Jack carrying out his duties retrieving unexploded ordnance from the battlegrounds and rendering it safe.

She was a lovely girl with a buxom figure and a genuine, good-humoured nature and there had been times when Jack had even wondered whether they might get married and start a little family right there in north-eastern France. Yet Jack had remained restless and unsettled. Always one for the main chance and looking out for the next opportunity, he just could not bring himself to commit to her and the promise of wedded bliss. He was not ready to pledge himself to her or to marriage. Perhaps he never would be ready to wed her or anyone else.

The work he was involved in was dangerous and unpalatable and the thought of settling down in a place that held such dreadful memories for him did not appeal. He would be surrounded by the still undiscovered bodies of thousands of his dead but not forgotten comrades. Their identity tags still in the mud. Their uniforms buried deep in the trenches. Their corpses beneath the new cowshed behind the farm. Skeletons almost in the closet.

Despite their closeness and Amandine's understanding and willingness to accommodate Jack's reticence, she had finally realised that he would never be entirely happy in that place, or with her, and had taken the decision herself to call it a day. She had already lost one husband at the start of the war and was determined not to lose another as a result of him not loving her enough at the outset.

She had cried and agonised over the decision, but she knew it was the right one and had tenderly told Jack in her soft French accent that it was over between them. She had looked into his eyes, kissed him on the lips and held him closely one last time.

'C'est pas ta faute, Jacques. Je comprends. Ta liberté est la tienne.' She had told him she was married to the farm anyway. And duty-bound to help rebuild it with her ageing father. She was impatient to start a family. To raise children who would one day take over the farm themselves. She knew Jack wasn't ready for that. And, for that matter, he'd make a lousy farmer. 'Au revoir, Jacques,' she had said finally with a genuine smile. 'Tes bêtises vont me manquer.'

He hadn't understood what that meant initially. He had never bothered learning the language. It was only afterwards that his Canadian mate Tyler had translated for him.

'She'll miss all your nonsense is what she said. Your jokes, your craziness and stupidity.' He had grinned at him knowingly.

Now as Jack sat there with Tyler, the corps burial officer with the 2nd Canadian Division, he looked over at Amandine with her new beau and could not help wondering if he had made the wrong decision. He certainly had never stayed with the same girl so long before without straying. And she was lovely.

But no, he would not allow himself to feel jealous. Jealousy was a useless emotion.

He picked up his beer glass and drained it.

'Thirsty?' asked Tyler.

'Very,' Jack replied. 'Had to drag a 75 millimetre French cannon and a Little Willie out of the ground today. With only a dozen men.'

Tyler raised an eyebrow.

'Yes, don't say it. Little Willie was a Mark I British tank brought in in 1915. Piece of crap, by all accounts. Top speed 3 miles per hour. Forever breaking down. You?'

'Parched.' Tyler waved at the girl in a red Chez Maxime beret behind the bar and gestured at their empty glasses. They were thirsty from the physical nature of the work, but sometimes the men needed a drink to calm their nerves, too. Picking up piles of human bones and clumps of chalky white maggot-ridden material in tattered uniforms all day, sealing them respectfully in bags with identity tags – it took its toll. 'It's been getting harder and harder to locate and identify the bodies of men reported killed or missing in action lately,' Tyler said.

'That's a good thing, right? Job nearly done then?' said Jack.

'We thought so. Until today.'

'What happened today?'

'Well, after the torrential rain last night, the deluge had nowhere to go because the original watercourses, streams and canals that once drained the fields before the war still haven't been repaired.'

The barmaid placed two more beers in front of the men and sashayed away.

'It poured down the slope in a torrent, taking the top two feet of mud and soil with it.'

'And?'

'It washed away the mantle and cloak. It uncovered all that we've missed. Helmets, rifles, gun belts, boots, ID tags, spectacles, cigarette cases, you name it. And, of course, evidence of the poor men who once owned them.'

'Jesus.'

'We didn't need to look for the usual subtle clues and hidden signs for a change. We could see the bones and skulls and the remnants of muscle and cartilage still holding joints of limbs together with our very own eyes.' Tyler shook his head, took a deep sip of his beer.

They were able to talk like this because of what they'd both seen, and still saw every day.

'Do you ever wonder,' Jack said, voicing something he normally kept inside, 'why them and not us?'

'Of course,' Tyler said quickly. 'But it doesn't bear thinking about for long.' He slapped his friend on the back, raised his beer. 'To life.'

'To living,' Jack said.

6

Bishop's Cleeve, Gloucestershire, March 1919

Dorothy Tustin-Pennington walked down the stairs of the house at Bishop's Cleeve to the sound of her children's voices in the parlour. After the years of silence, the hubbub was almost grating on her ears, but perhaps it was more that, in the symphony of voices, there was one key missing – that of her son, Charles, who'd been killed in action on a reconnaissance flight over Verdun. He'd been barely nineteen.

But she knew that she and Arthur were the lucky ones. Five children had gone to fight or help with the war, and four had returned. Another two children had remained safe and at home. And none had perished of the terrible flu, though it was still rife enough for her to remain worried.

She reached the parlour and looked in: morning sunlight streaming in, her grown children relaxed over tea, books and games.

Amy spotted her mother in the doorway. 'Morning, Mother,' she said languidly. She had prepared the tea tray herself; given her parents' current finances, they could no longer afford live-in help. And, surrounded by brothers, Amy found herself playing maid. She didn't mind it for the moment – delighted as she was by the presence of the boys after all this time. Though she knew her tolerance would wear off. 'Would you like some tea?'

'I wouldn't mind a cup,' Dorothy said.

Fitzwilliam, the youngest, sat right in the corner, almost facing away, but catching the light from the window on his book. His current read was Oswald Spengler's first volume of *The Decline of the West*. He looked over his spectacles to bid his mother a good morning. He'd been a wonderful companion to her through the war years, as they'd read together by the fire and walked a little way around the estate — as far as he could go without putting too much strain on his heart and becoming breathless. But now his brothers were back, Fitzwilliam knew he had to concentrate on moving on. He wanted to work, but he didn't want to take any work from the brave men who had returned, of course. He'd been contemplating Oxford, though it'd take some convincing of Dorothy so she wouldn't worry for him living away.

Rupert, Henry and James sat around a card table. Dorothy sipped her tea standing up, almost unbelieving. That they were here, but also that these *men* were her sons.

'Mother,' Rupert, her oldest, said. 'Sit!' He stood to offer his chair. He was dark-haired and wiry like his father, though more tanned, from working on the sea. Rupert had worked for the Navy during the war and retained his position even now. The family had been holding their breath even after the armistice, knowing Rupert was at the Navy base at Scapa Flow. The last German ship had been interned on 9 January and they were being guarded by the Battle Cruiser Force. Rupert was due to report back, to help guard while the Navy decided the fate of the Germans and their ships, but he'd thankfully been allowed to take leave.

Dorothy took the chair Rupert offered, smiling at her eldest, wishing he didn't have to leave again, but also grateful that he had ongoing employment.

For James and Henry, it was another story. Henry, twenty-three, had been stationed near Arras, and then in Belgium, dealing with prisoners of war. But superior officers continued on with that work and he was here, jobless but upstanding and optimistic — sleeves rolled back and hair slicked always in readiness. He carried none of her worrying nature. James, now twenty-two, carried Dorothy's fairness — he'd seen plenty of battle in the Balkans, and his light hazel eyes beneath his soft eyelashes were like an old man's looking out of a young face. But he was here, Dorothy thought. In one piece. They would both have to find work. Arthur, their father, was doing his best to put the word out to his contacts, while keeping the estate afloat.

Arthur's beloved 1910 24HP Series A four-seater Alfa pulled up now in front of the house. Arthur tried not to notice, as he walked through the front garden and the hall, all the things that needed fixing, replacing, repainting. Not to mention the car itself. If only Grace and Douglas, his old gamekeeper, could still be there to service the vehicle, it would not be so much of a worry. He did not look ahead to the large living room, where there was a gap on the wall where the pre-Raphaelite, that he'd been devastated to sell, used to be. What was important now was the small window of time when his children were back here, back together. He wished Grace could be here, too. His adventurous girl. But she and Will were so busy with their important work at Queen Mary's and other hospitals, as well as preparing for the new arrival.

He stood at the entrance to the parlour, taking in the happy sight of his children. The joy was mixed with guilt that they would not enjoy the kind of life he and Dorothy had done. Yes, he had fought as well, in the Boer War, and been injured, but he had lived beyond that in comfort and luxury – with staff, plentiful quality food and surrounded by beauty: art, furniture, clothing and gardens. He'd been able to put his mind to political work, not take whatever middle-class position might come his way, as his sons might have to do.

For Amy, his sparkling daughter, he hoped she'd find a good husband. Unlike Grace, she had no intention to follow any kind of cause or passion. He wasn't sure she *had* any, except gossip and fashion. She'd had invitations and callers already, since the war ended, and she indulged in the attention but was dismissive of it in the same breath. Arthur was not sure he'd ever quite understand her.

It was sad that, for the boys, Rupert was the only one with a sweetheart – Emma – but was also the only one who would have to remain away for his work. Arthur hoped they'd find time to marry. James and Henry hadn't had a chance to meet anybody.

'Boys,' Arthur said, as Dorothy smiled at him, clearly happy with her children around her. 'I need your help with a project.'

'Of course, Father,' said James.

'Your mother and I have discussed letting out the west wing for hunting parties. We may have lost most of the horses to the war effort but the hounds are healthy and if the Duke thinks they're good enough to breed with his hounds, then we can breed them ourselves.'

The children looked uncertain.

'Have things become so dire, Father?' Amy said.

Arthur sighed. 'I would not say they are dire, my dear. We simply have a lot of land and I would rather do what we can to keep this, our family estate, in one piece—'

'But *strangers* in our house, Father. Won't it be a terrible bore? Won't it be hard work?'

'About time you learned something about that, sis,' Rupert joked, standing by the window with a pipe in hand, as though peering from a porthole on one of his ships.

'Now,' Dorothy said, again throwing a little smile towards her husband, 'everyone has had to make sacrifices in recent years, and the world has changed, and your father and I — on the whole, we've been lucky. But it's become time to make some changes, and we'll do what we have to do.'

Amy groaned.

Fitzwilliam put his glasses down. *'We are in the becoming and the changing, not the set-fast . . .'* He pointed at his book by way of explanation.

Rupert gave his little brother a friendly scruff of the head.

Henry stood and stretched out like a cat. 'Let's make a plan,' he said to his father. James stood to follow.

As they walked down the hallway to Arthur's office, James said, 'Father, I've been thinking about what to do some more . . .'

'Yes?'

'And I thought: it has to be either an old profession that never wanes, or a role in an entirely new industry.'

'That's smart thinking, James.'

They entered the office, which had a superb view of Arthur's favourite redwood tree. Arthur went to sit behind the desk and the boys pulled up chairs to the back and side.

'The lack of traditional education and experience' — James said this in inverted commas, referring to the intense experiences recently had — 'means I can't take up a profession like law or politics. So, I'm considering emerging industries.'

Arthur felt that squirm of guilt again. That it wasn't easy for his sons, that they had to think about how to live and survive.

'There are new motor car companies popping up every day, Father. And I love to drive. I know I might only start out in a lowly sales position, but I could work up to managing or perhaps be the person who visits international offices — something still with a bit of flexibility.'

Henry was nodding along. 'Would suit you,' he said.

Arthur felt overcome. He had to swallow a burning in his throat. That wasn't like him. Maybe with his daughters, but not his sons. He cleared his throat.

'To be surrounded by beautiful motors all day — that sounds wonderful.' He smiled at James, then pulled open a drawer for the paperwork he'd started on the hunting lodge budget and plans.

7

Putney, London, April 1919

It was always worse with children, thought Will. Especially ones you knew. Freddie was a lovely little boy of six who lived just a few doors up from Will and Grace's terrace near Richmond Park. He and his older brother, Terry, would often be seen pulling one another along on the little wooden cart that their father had made for them out of discarded pram wheels and planks of wood.

Freddie always had a beaming smile and an enchanting and insatiable curiosity.

'Why have you got a metal leg under your arm?' he would ask Will on his return from work at the rehabilitation hospital. 'Who is it for? Why do they need it? How could they be so clumsy as to lose their own leg? How does it fit on? Can you play football with it?' And so on.

Freddie's father, George, was a carpenter and his mother, Briony, worked in the haberdashery shop on the corner. They were a kind family that Will and Grace had come to know quite well and they often spent time chatting over the picket fence at the front of their modest property. Kitty played with Freddie and his brother when she came over.

Freddie now lay prostrate in his bed, grievously ill. His skin looked pale grey in colour, blood trickled from his nose and his curly blond locks, usually so beautiful and springy, were stuck to his scalp and forehead with dried sweat. His neck, which was usually slender, was grotesquely swollen with enlarged lymph glands, and his breathing was shallow and rapid. When he coughed, it was a shrill yelp, a bit like a seal barking for fish.

In between coughs, the sounds of inhalation and expiration were reedy and coarse. At times, he would open his eyes, but when he did, the signs of a newly acquired divergent squint — where an eye begins to turn outwards — were apparent.

Grace, who was now into her thirty-third week of pregnancy, had been urgently summoned to the house by Briony, who knew she was a well-respected and highly experienced nurse. Experienced enough to know exactly what they were dealing with. After a very brief but thorough assessment, she had promptly sent George over to the limb-fitting centre at Queen Mary's with a hastily scrawled note to fetch Will. He had turned up less than thirty minutes later, perspiring and breathless.

Over the last few months, thanks to his tutelage from Dr Forrester, he had already attended many sick children within the community exhibiting a wide variety of ailments. These ranged from the dreaded Spanish flu, which was still circulating and claiming lives, through to erysipelas, tonsillitis, rheumatic fever, pneumonia and tuberculosis. Will had learned just how susceptible small children were to dangerous infections by dint of the immaturity of their immune systems.

George had led him upstairs to the boy's bedroom and placed a rickety wooden chair by Freddie's bedside for Will to perch on.

He took the boy gently by the hand now and spoke softly to him.

'Hello, Freddie,' he said. 'It's Will. I'm sorry you're poorly. Would you mind if I had a little look at you?'

Freddie opened his eyes and tried to speak but the words would not form in his throat. But somehow he bravely, almost imperceptibly, nodded his head.

Will stood and bent over the boy. Within moments he confirmed without doubt the diagnosis.

The breathing and the racing heart could signify many things. But the grey, adherent pseudomembrane covering the boy's throat and obstructing his airway, together with the bulbous congested neck, could only mean one thing. The dead cells lining the respiratory passages only formed a solid sheet of tissue like that as a result of one particular infection. An illness that had a worryingly high mortality rate. An infectious disease known as diphtheria.

Will looked to Grace in the corner of the room and lightly shook his head to signify the seriousness of the situation. She was carrying their unborn child and was at increased risk of infection due to the pregnancy. Grace understood, blew him a kiss and left the room, seeking Freddie's brother, Terry, to get the young boy out from underfoot and to distract him while his parents were busy worrying.

Will urgently sent out for Dr Forrester with instructions as to what he should bring with him. Dr Forrester trusted Will's judgement enough by now to put his faith in him and do as instructed.

Here they both were, standing solemnly on either side of Freddie's bed. Will watched the kindly face of the doctor, peering through bifocals, fully stocked medical bag at his feet, as he carefully but swiftly examined the boy from head to foot.

Forrester was conscious of the worried parents who paced the room and wrung their hands in the background. He instructed and explained to Will what he was doing, as had become their custom, but at the same time hoped it would help the parents understand the status and gravity of the situation.

'Your conclusion is correct, young Will,' Forrester said. 'The temperature is 102.4 degrees Fahrenheit and the pulse irregular and thready at 150.' He did not need to refer to the fob watch buried deep within his waistcoat pocket and attached by the golden Albert chain to his jacket. Years of practising medicine had enabled him to mentally assess the patient's heart rate as precisely as any Patek Philippe or Rolex timepiece. 'The respiratory rate is sixty per minute. The thoracic excursion shallow. There is marked stridor, a sign of obstructive breathing in the upper airway.'

Will glanced at the poor boy's father, whose honest, open face was wracked with concern and fear. His eyes were red and puffy. Briony was unable to watch or listen to anything further and she swept from the room to collapse and weep downstairs.

'There is a sixth cranial nerve palsy affecting the left eye and the lad is not moving his right arm spontaneously,' Forrester continued.

Will knew that advanced diphtheria could lead to neuro-logical involvement and muscle weakness.

'Look. The feet and ankles are swollen. Will? You will be aware of the reason?'

Yes, thought Will, nodding . . . Heart failure. But please don't ask me to say the words in front of the father. They always sounded so . . . alarming.

'There is some petechial haemorrhage under the skin, can you see? Denoting early spontaneous bleeding. Do you know about the fluid balance?'

'George?' said Will, looking up at the father. 'When did Freddie last have a wee?'

George looked bewildered by the question. He put his hand to his temple.

'I can't remember, Will. He's been in bed like this for hours and obviously not been downstairs to the toilet outside. He hasn't wet himself, though. We can't get him to drink anything, however much we've tried.'

'Let's look at the throat,' said the senior doctor. Gently, he palpated the bull neck with both hands and the swollen glands behind the nape and above the clavicles as well. Then he inserted the smooth wooden tongue depressor into the boy's mouth and brought the candle on the bedside table nearer to the boy's face. 'Look,' he said, shifting the flickering light so his apprentice could see better. 'The membrane is like a curtain of white velvet extending from one side of the throat almost to the other.'

'It's a wonder he can still breathe at all,' whispered Will.

'The toxin released by the bacteria peels the dead tissue away from the airways, forming a glutinous shroud every bit as tough and as unyielding as the calloused skin over a labourer's blistered hands.'

Straightening up again, the doctor opened the boy's eyelids with his finger and thumb to examine the conjunctiva and pupils. Then he squeezed an earlobe with increasing pressure, but the boy scarcely stirred.

'He's not responding to painful stimuli and is semi-conscious already, Will. You know what we have to do. There is little choice. Would you talk to the parents while I prepare? Quick as you like?'

Will turned and took the boy's father by the elbow. What the two medical men were about to do was going to be hard

46

enough, but explaining to the loving parents why and how they were to do it was almost harder.

'Come downstairs with me would you, George? I'd like to speak to yourself and Briony.'

George hesitated at first but soon complied, looking back uncertainly at his son before descending the stairs.

In the sparsely furnished lounge downstairs, Will sat the parents down quietly and explained the situation. They listened, Briony soundlessly weeping and George staring at the threadbare rug on the floor with his head in his hands.

'I'm afraid it's diphtheria,' he said, 'and it's already quite far advanced.'

'No! Surely not,' cried Briony. 'Not diphtheria. Couldn't it just be tonsillitis? It can't be diphtheria.' The mere mention of the word pierced her heart like a dagger. She knew full well how serious it was and what a large proportion of otherwise healthy children it disabled or killed each year. 'He was fit and well just a day or two ago. We thought it was a sore throat, that's all. He's hardly been anywhere. He's hardly seen anyone.'

'Like many infectious diseases, Briony, diphtheria can be caught from someone else who doesn't show any symptoms themselves and isn't unwell. It can also be contracted from objects we touch. Just randomly like that.'

George went over to his wife and put his arm around her heaving shoulders. A moment's silence passed.

'Freddie is very sick, Briony. I'm so sorry. If he is to have any chance of surviving, this thick membrane obstructing his breathing has to be overcome. And it has to be done soon.'

The parents blinked at him uncomprehendingly. Will needed them to understand and formally request that Dr Forrester take the next step. The necessary treatment was not without risk and certainly not something any doctor wanted to volunteer for or suggest themselves without a parent beseeching them to do it in their child's best interest and as a last resort.

Still they said nothing. The only sound in the little front room was the ticking of the clock. Each second seemed like an hour to Will, yet time was of the essence.

Diphtheria, he thought. From the name Dr Pierre Bretonneau had given it in 1826. Diphtherite, from the Greek word *diphthera,* meaning leather. Without doubt, that word accurately described the typical appearance of the membrane that developed in the airways. Will also remembered reading about the epidemic of the disease in Spain way back in 1613, the year that came to be known as *El Año de los Garrotillos*: the year of strangulations.

His reverie was cut short by Briony, who had suddenly found her voice.

'In God's name, Will, is there anything you and Dr Forrester can do to help?'

'We're going to lose him otherwise, aren't we, Will?' added George.

'He is grievously ill. We need to help his breathing and the only way we can do that is to open his throat and put a hole in his windpipe to breathe through.'

Briony started weeping again. It sounded so brutal. George, however, because of his occupation perhaps, seemed to grasp the reality of the situation more readily. The carpenter's work is practical, precise and involved finding solutions. If something cannot be done one way, it can often be done a different way. The process of breathing, he surmised, was no exception. A question of mechanics. Like drilling another hole in a wind instrument like a flute or clarinet to change the musical note, or the holes made at different levels in a bookcase into which pegs could fit to raise or lower shelving.

'Is there any alternative?' sobbed Briony.

'I'm afraid not. Not if he is to have any chance now. Sometimes it's possible to put a breathing tube over the tongue and into the throat — past the membrane. But it's too late for that. The membrane has extended further down and the tube won't reach beyond it.'

She closed her eyes and dropped her head.

'And if you do it, Will,' asked George, 'will he . . .?'

'There is no guarantee.' He swallowed, but his mouth was dry. 'His condition is grave. But it's his best chance. His only chance. If he can breathe through the tracheostomy tube . . . that's what we call it . . . it might just give his body enough time to overcome the infection naturally. That's our hope.'

He looked from one parent to the other. 'I have known it to happen.'

Briony looked at him expectantly.

'Please ask Dr Forrester to do it,' she said firmly, much to Will's surprise. She had rallied from her place of despair and grief. 'Doing nothing is worse and I could never live with myself for not trying. I trust you. May God guide the good doctor's hands. You have my blessing.'

George left his wife's side and followed Will to the foot of the stairs and paused.

'How likely is Freddie to survive, Will? Tell me the truth.' He looked directly into Will's eyes.

'The truth?' Will looked down at his feet and then up again to meet his neighbour's gaze. 'No more than fifty-fifty. But we will do all we can. As if he were our own son.'

Will found Dr Forrester with his tools carefully laid out on a clean sheet and the signs of iodine solution already drying on the front of the boy's neck. Initially, when Will had re-entered the room, he feared the boy had already died. But although barely discernible, the chest was still rising and falling and a weak but desperate respiratory effort was still apparent.

'We'll need to be quick,' said Forrester. 'To restore ventilation and help keep pain to a minimum.' He handed Will a retractor and a swab. 'Although I don't think in this case the poor lad will feel very much anyway.'

They rolled up a pillowcase behind the boy's neck and extended the head back over it to expose the windpipe and larynx, stretch it and pull it forward. Freddie stopped breathing completely.

Forrester's scalpel passed lightly over the skin and his minimal dissection gently pushed the isthmus of the thyroid, that bridge between the two lobes of the gland, downwards out of the way. He then stabilised the larynx, with his left hand placed Will's retractor in position to hold back the muscles from the field of operation and made a swift horizontal cut through the windpipe below the vocal cords. He then deftly and quickly inserted a child's narrow tracheostomy tube into the aperture and inserted three or four stitches into the tissues around it.

Immediately, the life-giving sound of a healthy volume of air passing in and out of the tube could be heard and Freddie's skin colour began to change from grey to pink.

Within moments, Freddie opened his eyes and tried to reach for his neck and speak.

'Shush, shush,' whispered Will into the boy's ear. 'Don't try to speak. We've done something to make your breathing easier, but you can't speak. And keep your hands down here by your side. I'll fetch your mum and dad.'

Dr Forrester was now at the bedroom door, preparing to leave. He always had other patients to see and was confident about leaving his patient in Will's capable hands.

'A word in your ear before I go.'

Will joined him at the top of the stairs.

'Diphtheria is a contagious disease. You know the proto-
cols. Others need to be kept away as much as possible and
I'll inform the local public health authorities. As far as young
Freddie is concerned, this is what I would expect to happen
next . . . and you will need to be prepared.'

When finished, he patted his protégé on the shoulder,
took one final look at the boy, his crow's feet crinkling with
a concerned frown, and traipsed wearily downstairs.

Will sat at Freddie's bedside throughout the night, never
once allowing himself to close his tired eyes and sleep. Briony
and George would come into the room either together or
one by one at regular intervals with a cup of tea and a McVitie's
biscuit for Will, but they were in a daze and, understandably,
could be of no practical help. Will had assiduously tepid-
sponged the boy every few minutes to reduce the fever but
not so much as a single sip of water had passed his lips and
obstructed throat. Despite that, the fluid surrounding his
feet and ankles had inexorably accumulated. The heart and
respiratory rate were still galloping and the boy's skin was
bone dry and had lost its youthful elasticity.

Try as he might with swabs, suction, pipettes and other
instruments, Will's continued attempts to clear the tracheostomy tube from the thick adherent pseudomembrane forming
around and below it were proving inadequate. The velvety
white curtain had spread lower and lower, deeper and deeper
into the airway and extended into and beyond the tliache-
ostomy tube itself.

Once again the boy's skin looked slate grey and devoid of
blood. His eyes were deep in their sockets and immobile.

The whistle of what little air was passing in and out of the narrowed breathing tube was becoming quieter and more shrill.

Will had seen many men die during the war from wounds, blood loss, sepsis or poison gas. He had seen men drown in cloying mud, blown apart by shells and bayoneted through the heart. He had never got used to it. It was always harrowing and ghastly.

But it was so much worse with children. Will wiped the tears falling from his eyes with his sleeve, rose from the bedside chair and kissed Freddie tenderly on the forehead. He was distraught. He had been unable to save him. George and Briony had put their trust in him and he had let them down. He had let Freddie down.

'Sleep well, darling boy. I'm so sorry I failed you.'

Dreading it, he turned and slowly padded downstairs to tell Briony and George to come and say their farewells.

Grace knew as soon as she saw Will's face. It was six-thirty in the morning and the sun was rising over the trees in the park as the front door opened and her husband came through the hall and into the small dining room and kitchen. She could tell by the bags beneath his deep-set hazel eyes that he had not slept a wink. He took his hat off and held it in both hands, looked at her steadily and slowly shook his head.

Grace peered at the eight-year-old boy nonchalantly eating jam on toast in front of her at the table and wondered how they were going to tell him. Or would they leave it to his mother and father? She wondered if they would be in any fit state to do anything.

Will came over to her and kissed her on the cheek, setting his hat down on the bench. Then he went over to Terry and stood behind him with a hand perched lightly on each shoulder.

'What are we going to do with you then today, young man?' he said.

Terry looked up at him and continued chewing. How do you tell a boy so young that his brother has just died? The younger brother he was playing in the road with just a few days ago? It would break his heart, Will knew. It would also leave a lasting scar on him emotionally for the rest of his life. It was something no child could ever forget.

It was also at times like this that Will felt most impotent. And angry. He was dog-tired, of course. He hadn't slept for twenty-four hours. That was nothing new for him, but it did sap his optimism and his resolve and it was always at times like this he questioned whether his battle to overcome infirmity and disease would ever be won or even prove worth the struggle. Human beings lived and died side by side with the germs that teemed around them and pervaded every part of their environment. They were in the soil, in the food they ate, on their skin, in their guts and even in the air they breathed. For centuries these dreadful microscopic killers had taken a continually cruel toll on humanity, causing misery, pain, disability and premature death. Would there ever be a time, he wondered, when doctors would gain mastery of these invisible harbingers of doom that could strike so randomly, unfairly and unpredictably?

Now they had claimed the life of poor little Freddie and Will felt sick to the stomach.

At that moment, Grace felt a sudden stab of pain in her lower belly and a crescendo of tightening in the involuntary muscles of her womb. The contractions had become more frequent in the last day or two but she knew it was to be expected at her stage of pregnancy and she certainly was not going to worry Will with it at this precise moment. He had enough on his plate, and he was already beside himself with worry about her pregnancy and forthcoming delivery. He was forever asking questions about how she was feeling, how many kicks was she experiencing, how many twinges she was noticing – which might be the result of the abdominal injury she'd sustained in France last year. And then he would be fretting over the amount of work she was still carrying out at the hospital.

Now he would be worrying about her exposure to Freddie's diphtheria.

She understood. His mother. He still talked about it a lot. At least to her. That was a good thing, she supposed. The experience had been deeply traumatic, but at the same time it had created that resolve within him to become who he was today.

'This jam's really scrummy,' said Terry suddenly. 'It's black-currant and it's Freddie's favourite. Can I take some home for him?'

Grace looked at Will. Forlorn.

'You can take the rest of the jar,' she said, 'of course you can. But first Will is going to go up to bed to get some sleep and you and I will go for a walk in the park and find the deer.'

'I love the deer,' he replied excitedly, 'especially the stags with their giant antlers. They're scary! Can we go to the waterfall in the Isabella Plantation? I want to dam the stream and make a pond.'

'You can do whatever you want this morning,' said Grace. 'And when we come back, we'll see how your mummy and daddy are getting on.'

Will raised an eyebrow as if to ask Grace if she was really up to it. He did need to get some rest before going to work in two hours' time. Grace smiled, eased herself out of her chair and went to grab coats for the two of them from the hook on the back of the door.

'There's tea in the pot, Will. And fresh bread in the pantry.' She opened the door to let Terry run past her and, ignoring the new contraction just coming on, she smiled at Will, blew him a kiss and set off for Richmond Park.

In the park, Grace began to worry. She knew this should not be happening. The baby's expected date of delivery was the sixteenth of June and today was only the twenty-eighth of April. She was only thirty-three weeks pregnant, and she knew that the final weeks of a baby's safe incubation in its mother's womb were vital.

The powerful and enduring contractions were becoming more frequent now as Grace watched Terry picking out large rocks to dam up the stream. Poor Terry. This was too much at once. She slumped against a tree, still on her feet, worrying that if she sat she might never get up. Her overriding concern was how a premature delivery of her baby would play out with Will. She had spent the entire pregnancy trying to convince him that everything would be all right — that the pregnancy would pass uneventfully and that the outcome would be assured with the arrival of a beautiful, perfectly formed, bonny baby.

As another wave of vice-like spasm began to build and an unfamiliar pressure became apparent lower down, Grace wondered how she would get the message about what was happening to her husband without him panicking and losing his head. Even now, in early labour, her thoughts were almost entirely for him.

8

Putney, London, April 1919

Grace was now in the second stage of labour. Will felt terrible that he'd had to leave the boy with Grace while he ran for the midwife — no doubt this day would be burned on Terry's memory forever — but he couldn't risk leaving her alone. When he returned with Kirsty, he sent the poor boy off home to receive the bad news about his brother. The cycle of life and death.

Kirsty had instructed Will to pour Grace a brandy in the hope of reducing the strength and frequency of the contractions and staving off full-blown labour. But it was not working. The neck of the womb was fully dilated and the bulging membranes had ruptured, meaning delivery of the baby was now inevitable. Since it had reached this stage, Kirsty knew there was no turning back and the faster the delivery, the better.

Will was doing quite well disguising the panic and apprehension he felt inside. As he held Grace's hand and calmly talked to her through the contractions, he was simultaneously distracting his own mind from the possible catastrophes he imagined.

With a few more pushes from Grace, the baby's head crowned, and with a gush of amniotic fluid and one more squeeze, a tiny baby boy was brought into the world and placed in Grace's welcoming arms. Will was ecstatic. Relieved, and in awe of this little miracle of nature. He gazed at the baby and put his arms around Grace to kiss her. She turned her face to kiss him back and tried to ignore another strong contraction in her belly. She realised the afterbirth now had to be expelled.

'He is gorgeous, isn't he?' said Kirsty, still down the business end of the bed. And then, rather strangely, she added, 'Are you intending to have more children in the future?'

'We've always talked about having two,' answered Grace, still focused on the newborn in front of her. 'But didn't dare hope because even this one seemed a miracle.'

'Well, you won't have to wait long,' said the midwife rather excitedly. 'Because you've got twins!'

Grace and Will stared at her. 'Excuse me?' they said in unison.

'You've been pregnant with twins,' she said. 'And the other one is coming now.'

Will looked terrified and confused.

Grace could hardly believe what she had just heard.

'Twins?' she asked. 'How can it be twins? How could I not have known? I'm supposed to be a nurse!' She did not know whether to laugh or cry. The next contraction made her wince.

Three more contractions were enough, however. A perfectly formed but also tiny girl was duly delivered, pink and bawling and full of life. Kirsty quickly wrapped her in a towel and blanket and gave her to Will, whose chin was almost on the floor.

Grace was laughing and crying at the same time.

'A boy and a girl,' she said incredulously. 'A pigeon pair. I can hardly believe it, Kirsty.'

Kirsty, who was attending to the third stage of labour, looked up with a huge grin and nodded.

'I had my suspicions, but I couldn't be sure and I didn't want to alarm you. It all makes sense. Women carrying twins normally go into labour and deliver early. And even though you're usually so slim, you were carrying your baby higher than I would've expected you to at thirty-three weeks.'

'And you didn't want to worry Will.'

'And I didn't want to worry Will.'

The two women smiled at him.

'But if they are low birthweight and premature . . .' he said.

'No, don't start that,' cut in Grace. 'They are perfect, and will be fine. Between us all, we'll make sure of it.'

Will blinked back at her. His eyes were still rimmed with dark.

'Now go and make yourself useful. Get some blankets, boil some water in the kettle and leave us in peace to finish up.'

Will walked across the room on shaky legs and opened the door to go and do what he had been ordered.

'And Will?'

'Yes?'

'Get me another large brandy, would you?'

Kirsty was true to her word. She had promised to overwhelm the four members of the Burnett family with professional and personal love and attention. She had visited every day since the birth. This was the fourth day post-partum and she knew this day was especially important since Will had lost his mother on the equivalent.

'What are you reading, Will?' asked Kirsty as she came downstairs after talking to Grace and looking at the babies.

He seemed a little agitated.

'It's a medical paper summarising the immediate stormy postnatal period for premature twins throughout history,' he replied.

'And no doubt it's full of scary statistics about horrendous complications with gloomy prognoses.'

'Well, since you mention it, yes.'

'May I see?' Kirsty took the journal out of his hands and rapidly scanned it. 'I know this author,' she said. 'And in my humble opinion, he is a general surgeon and apothecary who only dabbles in obstetrics and loves to put the fear of God into people to encourage them to pay for his so-called expertise.'

'Really? Isn't that somewhat unethical?'

'Oh, Will!' she laughed. 'For someone who's been through what you have, you're so naive sometimes. Medicine is a noble profession and I know you want to join it. But don't make the mistake of thinking all doctors have every patient's best interests at heart like you do.'

'But the twins are smaller than average. According to the Finnish paediatrician Dr Arvo Ylppö, babies that weigh less than 2000 grams only have a fifty-fifty chance of surviving.'

'Will!' shouted Kirsty, grabbing him by the shoulders and shaking him. 'Stop reading this gibberish! Please? As your wife's midwife, I forbid it.'

Will, feeling a little like a naughty child, put down his reading materials as the midwife sat opposite him.

'Do you know how much the babies weigh?'

'Tell me.'

'The boy weighs 4 pounds 8 ounces.'

'And the girl?'

'4 pounds 12 ounces.'

'So small.'

'And yet they are a healthy pair of babies. Pink and screaming from the start. They have only lost a mere 5 per cent of their birth weight.'

'They've lost weight? But they didn't have enough to lose in the first place.'

'It's usual for newborns to lose 10 per cent of their weight in the first few days before recouping it. You know that. So they are doing better than expected.'

Will looked sceptical.

'With parents as strong and devoted as the two of you, they have every possible advantage. They've also got Clara and Kitty fussing over them and doing everything they can to support you. There is no jaundice or anaemia. One twin hasn't thrived at the expense of the other, which often happens. And Grace's milk is coming in nicely and soon she'll have enough milk for both of them. Meanwhile, the milk bank will continue to deliver supplies and the lad who brings it on his bicycle should be here any moment. So I'd best be going.'

'Just before you do, Kirsty, what about Grace? Is everything all right?'

Kirsty knew just how important her answer would be for Will to hear.

'Grace is strong as an ox. In body and soul. She's radiant. There was minimal blood loss, both the placentas were whole and intact, there's nothing she doesn't know about scrupulous antisepsis, and furthermore she has you to look after her. So, get upstairs, Will, and see what needs to be done. I'll see you tomorrow.'

Will saw her out and closed the door behind her, then climbed the stairs and went into the bedroom. Although the window was open and the curtains fluttered in a gentle draught, the air inside the room was warm and dry thanks to the little coal fire in the grate. Grace stood by the bed.

He went over to her, took her in his arms and gave her a lingering kiss. 'You're doing wonderfully,' he said, smiling.

'And so are they,' replied Grace, looking down at the babies lying side by side in their padded shoeboxes.

'Whose idea was that?'

'Clara's. And Kirsty endorsed it. Next best thing to those fancy incubators that pioneering American doctor Martin Couney uses in his premature baby exhibitions. He's been all over Europe with them, you know. They say he's a bit of a maverick, but at the same time he's saved thousands of premature babies' lives.'

'That's incredible. Goodness, you are in the know, aren't you? Read anything for us to worry about?'

'Not a single thing, my love. And just look at the pair of them. They are a perfect temperature and so cosy and cocooned lying on their sides in that cotton-wool blanket all around them.'

Kirsty had cut a little window out of the sides of each shoebox.

'They can look at each other, too.'

'And I think they do, Will. It's sweet to think of the way they kept each other company all this time in the womb.' She put her arms around Will and hugged him tight. The two of them stood there swaying gently as they gazed at their offspring. 'There's only one problem that I can see,' said Grace.

'What?' replied Will, sounding alarmed.

Grace smiled.

'We've got to decide on two baby names, now, not just one.'

9

Munich, Germany, June 1919

For some people when their entire world falls apart and there seems little reason to go on living, one irrepressible emotion drives them on. It is such a powerful force and burns so brightly within them that it becomes an all-encompassing passion. For some it is love, an addictive and romantic yearning for another person or an unconditional and protective tenderness towards a child. For others, it may be the opposite. A deeply rooted hatred that will only be satisfied by violent revenge.

Jürgen Altmann was firmly in the latter camp. Resentment and bitterness could almost have been his middle names. As he sat in a quiet corner of the roomy Hofbräuhaus beer hall in his home town of Munich, he waited for the latest employee that he had recently taken on at the factory to return with the drinks.

Heinrich Schulz was an interesting man and it seemed they had a lot in common. Both had served in the war. Both had engineering backgrounds. Both had similar ultranation-alist political views.

Schulz was not facially disfigured like Altmann but his attitudes towards the Bolsheviks, the Jews, the Soviet Bavarian Republic and the Weimar Republic in Berlin were just as strong.

Currently there were fifty or so various political parties in the region, all touting for power and authority. Something needed to change.

Schulz returned and thumped two frothy steins of ale on the sturdy oak table. 'So, can I ask? Your injury?'

'A legacy of war, Herr Schulz. A generous souvenir from the British at the Somme.'

'What happened?'

'Repelling an all-out attack on the front line,' he lied. 'There were only a few of us still standing. But I'd given the order that there would be no surrender and so we fought to the last man. I hadn't realised at the time that last man would be me.'

Altmann lied with such facility these days. His attempted rape of a young British nurse in a half-demolished stable block behind enemy lines had only been thwarted by a mortar shell hitting the building and ripping open his left cheek and jaw. His escape in the opposite direction from the advancing enemy had condemned his few remaining fellow soldiers to certain death, as well as ensuring the absence of any surviving witnesses to testify to his actions.

He had told the story so many times since then, he almost believed it himself. Hideous though the scarring on the left side of his face was, contracted into a fixed rictus snarl, anyone who knew him and had overcome the initial visual shock of it admired him even more for the bravery and sacrifice they imagined he must have made in sustaining it.

The facial nerve had been severed and he had lost all feeling over half of his face. His lower lip drooped and he continuously had to wipe dribbles of saliva from the corner of his mouth with a handkerchief. Lancinating stabs of pain could shoot through the area at any time and make him wince.

'Grenade thrown at short range, perhaps?'

'Nothing as predictable. An artillery shell. Threw me high into the air but, mercifully, the main force of it landed plumb in the middle of the advancing attackers. I lost my face. They lost their lives. Such is war.'

'But people see you as a hero. The workers at the factory. They look up to you.'

Altmann took a sip from his glass and feigned modesty.

'What about you, Herr Schulz? I hear your war record is commendable too?'

'I volunteered when the war began. I too was wounded. Three times in all. I wasn't demobilised until December last year in Rudolstadt.'

'Then we understand each other as brothers in arms, at least. I feel glad to have welcomed you to Altmann Engineering.'

Although the nature of their work had changed because investment had all but dried up, Altmann needed more hard-working and honest men like Schulz.

'I don't know how to be anything else, Herr Altmann.' Schulz had done his commercial apprenticeship at a machine factory and iron foundry in Saalfeld but after the war there was never enough work. As he'd told Altmann in his interview, he came to Munich to take up a job with the *Marinebrigade Ehrhardt*. He felt strongly they had to curb the revolutionary aspirations of the Communists.

They picked the topic back up now.

'The country is falling apart,' Schulz said passionately. 'First the Kaiser abdicates, only to be replaced by a Republican government that taxes us all to hell and causes crippling hyperinflation. Then we are humiliated by the terms of a peace treaty we should never have accepted.'

'I couldn't agree more. The naval blockade after the armistice condemned a quarter of a million of us to death by starvation and disease. Our country alone was blamed for the entirety of the war. Ridiculous.' Altmann shook his head. 'How can we be held responsible for all of the loss and damage? And 132 billion gold marks in reparations! We will never recover from this unless we fight back.'

'As many still want to do, Herr Altmann,' Schulz said, eyes flashing. 'But with an army reduced to one hundred thousand men, and no air force, no navy or U-boats, how can we? My comrades already scuttled our warships at Scapa Flow. How did we ever agree to give up so much territory to Denmark, Czechoslovakia and Belgium? Not to mention the ignominy of granting an even bigger re-established Poland?' The man's cheeks turned red with fury.

'Worse still,' said Altmann, 'how did we ever allow those bastard Frenchies to occupy our beloved Rhineland?'

Altmann took a large slug of beer from his stein and Schulz followed suit.

After a pause, the new recruit to the factory continued, 'But we have to face reality. While you and I would've fought on with many of our comrades by our side, there is no more appetite for war. Even before the armistice, the mutiny among our Imperial Navy in Kiel, the strikes in the munitions factories at home, and more recently the German revolution and other uprisings . . . there is defeatism everywhere.'

'Not everywhere, Heinrich. Not everywhere.' Altmann smiled with half his face. 'As a proud nation, most of us have never accepted the peace treaty and never will. Nothing is settled, in my view. Nothing. There is anger, discontent, hunger, poverty and fighting all around the city.'

As though to illustrate Altmann's point, a man in ragged clothes pushed open the doors to the beer hall, shaking a tin cup for change. He was immediately set upon by a burly drunken man, before the owner emerged, tea towel over his shoulder, and yelled at both of them to get out immediately.

'The people are crying out for strong leadership,' said Altmann, turning back to Schulz, 'and by God it won't be long before we get it.'

'And your factory is a good place to start?'

'We've had our problems. I sacked the idiot my father had left in charge of the place before he died. When the production line for ammunitions and tank components came to a standstill, we should've been ready to move with all the iron and steel needed for construction and drainage, for railways, architecture and transport.'

'But you have a good team of men around you now, Herr Altmann. A growing band of *Frontkämpfers* like you and I. Combat veterans who remain committed to the cause.'

'And united in spirit and purpose.' Altmann personally selected all his employees. He met them and their friends in the beer halls and taverns around town. Here. And in the Sterneckerbräu. In the Löwenbräukeller and the Bürgerbräukeller. None of them had any permanent meeting rooms, so the halls had become their focus.

'Speaking of united,' said Schulz with a grin, 'my glass seems to be empty, so you best catch up, *mein Chef.*'

On the way to the bar, Altmann passed a group of sequined and heavily made-up young women who were sitting around drinking like men, no doubt on their way to one of the new dance halls. Altmann scowled at them. They looked like they'd never worked a day in their life. This city was chaotic and divided. They had to do something about it before this great nation fell apart.

10

Chiswick, London, July 1919

'Kitty!' Clara called down the street.

Kitty sat on Thiago's front steps, threading a daisy chain and trying out her Spanish with him. She'd stuck a little closer to him since her playmate Freddie, whom she spent time with at Will and Grace's house, had died. Kitty found she could only approach this tricky subject in Spanish, but Thiago shied away from it in any language. And this had only been a couple of weeks after a child at their school, Daisy, had died of a bad infection. Something to do with the bones behind her ears.

'I have to go,' Kitty said in English, handing the boy her half-finished daisy chain. He clutched his small hand around it and nodded.

She ran back up the street to home.

Aunt Clara smiled at her, standing in her apron by the front door. 'The twins are coming today, remember?' she said with a twinkle in her eye.

Kitty's heart swelled. She loved those tiny little babies. But then she thought about Freddie again and felt sad.

'What's wrong, Kitty?' Clara asked.

'How can we keep them safe, Aunty?'

Clara frowned. 'We just do the best we can,' she said. 'Remember how poorly you were last year when you came down with the Spanish flu? But you soon bounced back, didn't you?' She opened the door and they went inside.

Kitty skipped over to her father, who sat in the lounge, staring at nothing.

'Daddy!'

Robbie snapped out of his reverie. 'Here's my big girl,' he said. 'Why don't you help your aunt with the lunch?'

'All right, Daddy.'

Robbie watched Kitty skip into the kitchen. He felt terrible that, some days, he barely had the energy to speak a word to his own, bright daughter. There was a whole theatre of light and noise in his head that he had to keep at bay. To keep it at bay, he had to stare right at it. Or at least that's what it seemed like. He had to concentrate or else it felt like it would escape — ooze out of his ears and on to the floor. He thought it should be getting better over time, but instead the theatre came upon him, unbidden, at all sorts of moments, and sometimes for long stretches at a time. He'd missed days of work, and though the dockyard said they had to cut his shifts back due to less demand for shipping now, he knew there was more to it. Like the way he sometimes had to sit down and still his heart for a moment after a loud noise. He tried to hide it, but there was nothing he could do when his legs went weak. The only other worker who'd had a cutback, too, as far as he knew, was 'Purblind Pete' — a perfectly capable copper-smith who'd had his leg blasted off at Flanders. He'd caught shrapnel in the eye, too, and wore a patch. Hence the crude nickname.

Robbie took a deep breath as he heard their visitors walk up the front path and then knock on the door. He hoisted himself up and went to let them in. There was his son, Will, a fit and upright young man, with one baby in his arms, and his wife, Grace, a young woman with a no-nonsense, no-fuss natural beauty, carrying the other.

'Did you walk all the way here carrying the twins?' Clara said from the kitchen doorway, shocked.

Will and Grace were perspiring slightly.

'Grace insisted,' said Will. 'She wants to feel strong again. Should have seen her, just weeks after the twins were born, up and about doing some kind of stretches she'd read about in a magazine. And anyway, we don't have a pram.'

'We could have come to you again,' Clara said, shaking her head.

'No,' Grace said. 'Please, as I told you, I need to get out of the house. We're delighted to be here.'

'For God's sake, at least sit right down,' Clara said.

'For God's sake,' Kitty mimicked, not used to hearing such words from her aunt. Will suppressed a laugh. Kitty hovered, waiting for her brother and his wife to sit so she could look at the babies.

Robbie cleared his throat, tried to push away the light and noise to find appropriate words.

'Work going all right, son?' He sat across from them. Clara had disappeared back in the kitchen and Kitty cooed, wedging herself between Will and Grace.

'Yes, plenty to do, and I think I've told you about Dr Forrester? He's been very kind, taking me under his wing. He's teaching me a lot and has promised to help me work out my path forward.'

Robbie smiled and it pained his cheeks. He was very proud of the boy. And his son's wife, too. So robust. But he tried not to think any more about that. He hoped they would be happy with two children. It wasn't worth the risk of more, as far as he was concerned. And two at once – what luck!

Clara reappeared. 'Lunch won't be long. We managed to find a very nice cheese for half off, didn't we, Kitty? From Gloucestershire, actually. Your parents don't have cows, do they, Grace?'

Grace smiled. 'They don't have many animals at all nowadays.' She paused. 'But of course they're very lucky, in all this.'

Will put a hand on hers. A secret message. Though they came from vastly different backgrounds, there was much they'd shared – loss, grief, the horrors of war, the draw of medicine. He knew her parents were struggling in their own way. And they were good people who'd welcomed him, encouraged him, and put any notions of class aside.

They would adapt to this new world, he thought.

'I also wanted to see you all as we have some news,' Clara said, clasping her hands in front of her apron.

They looked at her expectantly.

'Jack will finally be home soon!'

'Oh! That's terrific,' Grace said.

'Very relieving,' Will said. Typical of his big brother, he thought, not to write to him as well to tell him the news. But that was Jack all over. Why go to the trouble of writing two letters when one would do the job just as well? He wondered if his brother would be much disturbed by the awful work he'd been doing. He hoped it would be easy for Jack to work out what to do next. He was the kind of boy – man, now – who did have a way of falling into things, finding a spot for himself.

Kitty planted a too-hard kiss on Daniel's head and the baby started bawling.

Robbie felt his heart rate climb immediately. The wailing whistle of a shell going by his ear. His palms turned clammy and his chest tightened.

70

'I'm sorry,' Kitty said.

'It's all right, sweetheart,' said Grace. 'We know you love them very much.' Grace stood up. 'Clara, may I use your room?'

'Of course, dear,' Clara said.

Grace took the baby away for a feed, but then Emily started up at the same time.

'They often set each other off,' Will said apologetically.

'It's a welcome sound,' Clara said, but she did glance at Robbie, who was staring resolutely at the ground.

Grace came back and held out her other arm for the other baby.

'Do you want some help?' Will asked.

'No, no. Catch up with your family,' Grace said and took the screaming twins upstairs to Clara's room.

Kitty followed, peering around the door as Grace sat and unbuttoned her dress, attaching a twin to one breast while the other mewled and squirmed on the bed. 'There, there,' she said softly. She looked over to Kitty. 'You can come in,' she said.

Kitty felt shy, but she came in and sat on the chair across from the bed.

'I didn't realise baby food came from there,' she said. 'Can I feed them?'

'I'm afraid not, sweetheart. The milk comes from the mother, once she's had the baby.'

'What d'you mean, *had* the baby?'

'Oh . . .' Grace looked at the nine-year-old, worrying that she'd possibly already explained too much. How old was she when she learned about the birds and the bees? Younger, she thought. Watching the horses, the dogs and the deer rut. But it wasn't really up to her to explain. Then again, the girl didn't have a mother. But Clara was the closest to it, so she'd leave it to her. 'I think you should ask Aunt Clara about such things. You learn them when you're all grown up.'

'I'm a big girl,' Kitty said.

'I know,' Grace laughed. 'Big and also smart and curious. Those are good things to be.'

Kitty wriggled under the compliment.

'A little bird also tells me that you are especially good at Spanish?'

'I like all languages.'

'What's "twins" in Spanish?'

'*Los gemelos*.'

Grace echoed the sound.

'And *jumeaux* in French, *gemelli* in Italian and *Zwillinge* in German.'

'Kitty, that's incredible. How do you know all that?'

'I just do,' she said with a self-satisfied grin. 'Clara says the more languages I learn, the more words I'll know in English. And anyway, I like hearing the sound of the foreign words when I say them.'

Downstairs, Robbie was slowly getting control back over his breathing, the rate of his heart. His mind was not good, though. It felt sickened, awful. To go to pieces over the cry of a beautiful little baby? What on earth was he going to do with himself?

As the twins snoozed, the family enjoyed a sparse but delicious lunch. They spoke mostly of the future, of the children, of Jack returning, and the possibilities ahead. They were wary of opening up any wounds in speaking of the past.

Eventually, Will and Grace took the twins home, exhausted but fulfilled by the family time.

'My dad was very quiet,' Will said on the slow walk back.

'Isn't he always?' said Grace.

Will nodded, but was troubled. He wished there was something he could do.

'He's here, Will. He's being a father,' said Grace, ever practical and positive.

He nodded. Daniel burped over his shoulder. 'You're right. One thing at a time.'

11

Hammersmith Hospital, White City, London, November 1919

Mercifully, no further diphtheria cases had emerged since the sad loss of little Freddie, and the patients that Will had attended with Dr Forrester had, for the most part, all been faring well. Having watched the older man whip out three sets of tonsils in a week, he was confident he would be able to do the operation safely himself quite soon. The last procedure just yesterday had been performed on a kitchen table.

'It's not so difficult once you get the hang of it,' the doctor had said, waving the wood and ivory tonsillotome around in his hand while the young male patient drifted off to sleep under the influence of the ether. 'It's really just a tonsil guillotine. Look. At the back of his throat, you see the grossly swollen pitted tonsils covered in white bacterial slough and almost touching in the midline. I simply line up the open metal frame against the offending tonsil and close the blades, slicing off all the infected tissue.'

Will had watched in awe as the prune-sized tissue dropped into the fork-like attachment that prevented it obstructing the patient's airway.

'I'll now do the same on the other side . . . There. And then the uvula for good measure.'

The guillotine had chopped through the bell-like appendage hanging from the back of the young man's soft palate like a bacon slicer through raw meat.

'The tonsillar bed will bleed. But not for long. Swallowing will be painful for a week or so but after that he'll thank me.'

Will thoroughly enjoyed his apprenticeship sessions with Dr Forrester. They distracted him from money and career worries, making him feel of immediate and necessary use. They were also a refreshing change from his work at Queen Mary's because, although limbs and the absence of them were interesting and important – and he'd seen such strong success stories, like Calvin Darke, who was a new man after his operation and new prosthetics – he was also fascinated by the workings of the rest of the human body to which the limbs were or were not attached. And there seemed no end to his mentor's medical knowledge and experience.

A gentle and dignified man of sixty-four, Forrester was kind and patient with the sick and, unlike so many of his contemporaries, would only carry out treatments for which there was robust scientific evidence of their merit.

'You're like a modern-day Hippocrates in disguise,' Will had told Forrester one day. 'Wise and kindly, with a perfect blend of art, philosophy and science. If he was the father of medicine, Dr Forrester, you must be his son.'

'And you must be Galen, then,' Forrester had replied, 'a current-day version of the same. My very own disciple.'

Some other doctors, contrary to Hippocrates' most basic tenet 'above all do no harm', frequently misdiagnosed their patients and made them worse. Forrester and Will regularly saw patients who had fallen foul of other medical men's mistakes and were desperate for a remedy for their ailments.

There was Dr Ambrose Penfold who was renowned for fleecing his rich clients, although his only policy was to agree wholeheartedly with any diagnosis suggested by the patients themselves. He felt contradicting them would make him unpopular. So whatever they attributed their abdominal or other pains to he would simply agree with them and encourage them to continue with the same treatment. Sir Anthony Fraser would perform hazardous operations on women with urinary symptoms to 'hitch up their kidneys'. Norman Tulloch removed whole sections of bowel in attempts to cure simple constipation.

Forrester was different. He was not interested in the monetary rewards of medical practice. He spent a considerable amount of his time attending to the poorest and most needy souls who lived in abject poverty in the filthiest and most deprived slums of London.

'Listen to the patient with utmost care,' he had always told Will. 'Rufus of Ephesus taught us the importance of listening to our patients two thousand years ago and nothing has changed. Listen to their precise description of the symptoms and they will tell you the diagnosis themselves. Where is the pain? When did it start? Does it come and go or is it persistent? How long does it last? What is the nature of the pain? Is it sharp and stabbing or is it an ache or a colic? What makes it better or worse? What is the patient's occupation? What tonics are they taking?'

Time and time again, Forrester had been proved right.

There was the man with a mysterious symmetrical rash on the front of his thighs, for example, which nobody had been able to explain. Forrester had questioned him relentlessly until it transpired that that was where his trouser pockets lay against his leg and in which he carried a number of loose

'strike anywhere' Swan Vesta matches. It was a contact
dermatitis from phosphorus sesquisulfide in the heads of
the matches, he had correctly concluded. The man now stored
his matches elsewhere and his rash had cleared up with no
need of treatment.

There was also the woman who had been brought to him
in a catatonic state. Retarded in thought and motion, she had
been diagnosed as a hopeless case of presenile dementia,
deemed untreatable and consigned to an early death by three
other physicians. Forrester had read carefully her laborious
history in her files. She'd had progressive weight gain, constant
fatigue, recalcitrant bowel action, an intolerance of cold
weather, depression and aching muscles. His examination
revealed her slow pulse rate, her dry, scaly skin, her brittle
hair and nails and the lack of sensation in her hand and fingers
due to carpal tunnel syndrome. Without a single scientific
test, it took him thirty minutes to diagnose her underactive
thyroid gland and thirty days to restore her to full health with
the use of a thyroid extract harvested from a pig.

Forrester's proficiency in listening, empathy, observation,
examination and deduction was second to none and Will saw
him proving his diagnostic acumen on an almost daily basis.
In terms of medical investigation, he was like a real-life
Sherlock Holmes and Will could not have hoped for a better
teacher. It was such a shame, then, Will often thought, that
it would take him many, many years of scrimping and saving
to be able to afford to enter medical school after undertaking
an entrance exam. He was close to applying for his diploma
from the London College of Preceptors, at least, which would
mean taking night school on top of his work and apprenticeship. This was generally regarded as the equivalent of
more formal schooling elsewhere and would adequately make

up for the education he had missed during the war years. He had hesitated for a year now because of the cost, and because it would mean more time away from Grace and the children, but Grace continually encouraged him and it was one small step towards his dream. Whenever he got over-whelmed by the idea of the financial and social obstacles ahead, whenever he wavered, all it took was an image of his mother to strengthen his resolve.

Will returned from his thoughts to the matter at hand. He would need to prepare the next day's operating list and sterilise all of their operating instruments in the autoclave in advance if Dr Forrester was going to perform his medical wizardry again tomorrow.

12

Queen Mary Convalescent Auxiliary Hospital, Roehampton, London, January 1920

Grace was back at work on Saturdays, when Clara and Kitty were free to mind the twins. This particular Saturday was hectic. Grace had been tending to a spate of stump infections and inflammatory reactions brought about mostly by impatient ex-soldiers frustrated by their handicaps and trying to do too much too soon. It was a familiar scenario: previously fit, able-bodied men impetuously attempting to run before they could walk. Nevertheless, Grace had kept her usual composure and skilfully sterilised the open wounds, dressed any sore broken skin and given the necessary advice to each of her patients as to how to proceed. She had also warned them that if they did not heed her advice she would confiscate their prosthetic limbs completely. None of them believed her, however, as she was always smiling too broadly when she said it.

'She'll do it!' called Calvin Darke from behind her in the hall. He often tried to help her out, knowing the difference Will and Grace's interventions had made for his own well-being.

Will had already done his ward rounds and thankfully there was only one more case of Spanish flu that had developed in a twenty-six-year-old ex-sapper, who had been transferred to the isolation room and given a supply of oxygen. There was a forty-three-year-old gunnery sergeant who had been experiencing some undulant fevers, weight loss and night sweats and Will was suspicious that he had contracted respiratory tuberculosis. He had found another single room for him and warned the rest of the staff to take the usual extra sanitary precautions.

Will and Grace met up at the front of the hospital for their walk home together. Grace seemed a little flushed and breathless but had already changed out of her nursing gown, apron and bonnet and into her casual clothes for the short walk home.

Will took Grace's arm and the two of them strolled out of the gates and turned right down the hill towards their house, where Clara and Kitty would be dutifully attending to the babies.

Clara was devoted to the twins and they had no doubt that both she and Kitty would already have given Emily and Daniel their latest feed, winded them, talked to them in their best childlike voices and placed them in their basic wooden cot with the divider Will inserted for a little sleep.

As they turned the last corner before reaching the house, however, they saw Clara and Kitty standing outside in the road, each clutching an infant and apparently giving instructions to four men in matching blue overalls and flat caps. Their Henshaw's Thornycroft flatbed truck was parked at the kerbside, from the back of which they were struggling to offload a large wooden crate about 4 cubic yards in size. Grace and Will exchanged puzzled looks and sped up.

'I know you need lots of equipment for babies, Grace,' said Will, 'but this is ridiculous. How many terry towelling nappies, baby outfits, soft toys and dummies did you order, for heaven's sake?'

'It's nothing to do with me, Will. There must be some mistake.'

When they reached Will's aunt and sister, Clara handed Grace an envelope.

'Don't ask me,' she said indignantly, 'but I'm told this will explain everything.'

Tearing it open, Grace immediately recognised her father's headed stationery and handwriting.

'*To Grace, Will, Emily and Daniel,*' she read aloud. '*Thank you for having us for tea last Sunday. Dorothy and I are in love with our new grandson and granddaughter and we hope to do what we can to help them to thrive despite their rather precipitous introduction to the world. Obviously they are destined to show the same impatience and impetuosity as their mother.*'

'Clearly,' said Will teasingly, receiving an elbow in the ribs from Grace in return.

'*They certainly could not be in better hands; however,*' she continued, '*it struck us that you both also deserve some small reward for extending the Tustin-Pennington dynasty and I trust the contents of this crate will make life easier for all of you and facilitate any travel arrangements you need to make as a family. I would advise you to open it where I left instructions for it to be deposited at the roadside. Congratulations again, and enjoy your perambulations. Your ever-loving Arthur and Dorothy.*'

'What has your father thought up this time? A miniature version of his helter-skelter folly at the estate?' mused Will quizzically.

'What on earth can it be?' asked Clara, frowning. 'Whatever it is, it's very sturdily gift-wrapped.'

'Maybe it's some of Arthur's sheep from the farm,' giggled Kitty 'although I can't hear them bleating.'

'I should hope not,' said Will, 'or I'll be bleating about where we'd ever put them. I'd have to let them loose in the park.'

'Only one way to find out,' said Grace, taking a crowbar out of the hands of one of the Henshaw's men and giving it to Will. 'Let's get it open!'

The rough-sawn planks all bore the distinctive red Tustin-Pennington hallmark and had clearly been nailed firmly together at the family sawmill at Bishop's Cleeve. The first few took several minutes to prise apart but after that they came away from each other easily. Inside the first section they discovered a large cardboard box and within that a traditional coach-built baby carriage from the famous Silver Cross company in Skipton.

'It's a pram,' shrieked Kitty excitedly.

'And not just any old pram,' said Clara, 'I believe this is one of William Wilson's original inventions. The same Leeds engineer who supplied one for King George VI himself, no less.'

'It's fit for royalty, that's for sure,' said Grace, her instinct to examine every design feature and moving part kicking in. 'Look at it, it's beautiful. The body panels have been pressed from aluminium and all riveted together and then painted in this lovely dark blue with these fine lines in gold along the side.'

'Just like the coachwork of a horse-drawn carriage,' added Will.

'Exactly. And look! A C-spring suspension attached to the body with leather straps to give extra bounce. Extra-large spoked wheels and a rolling chassis.'

'You've lost me,' said Will.

'I don't know about any of that,' added Clara, 'not being mechanically minded like you, but I love how this hood seems to fold up and down. And it's quite big enough to fit both of your bonny babies in without a squeeze.'

'It is.'

Then Clara said, 'Kitty, where are you going?' Kitty had ducked down and crawled into the open end of the crate.

'What's in this bit?' she asked, tapping on a wooden partition within it. The grown-ups had been so excited about the pram they had completely forgotten about the larger compartment which constituted Arthur and Dorothy's other mysterious gift.

'My turn,' said Grace, picking up the crowbar and ramming it between two sturdy planks. As one sprang away, she bent down and peered inside. 'Oh, my word!' she exclaimed. 'My parents have really pulled out all the stops this time. You're not going to believe this, Will. But you'll never have an excuse for being late for work from now on. Look!'

She moved aside to let him see.

'This can't be real,' he breathed, standing up again with a huge grin on his face and eyes wide with disbelief.

'Will, put us out of our misery,' said Clara, smiling. 'What the devil is it?'

'It's something he's always wanted, Clara. And something he genuinely needs.'

'Well?'

'It's the other love of his life.'

Will, like a man possessed, removed the remaining planks. There, glinting in the afternoon sun, she stood. It was a George Brough Superior motorcycle and sidecar. It was quite unlike any two-wheeled machine he had ever seen before. It was long, sleek and shiny, with white-walled tyres on spoked wheels and equipped with a V-Twin 986cc OHV engine, AMAC carburettor and ML Magneto to provide its spark. Grace was as transfixed as Will was.

'It's a beauty,' she said, 'and unique. I'll bet you Daddy has had this made – a prototype for the latest batch of machines the Brough company will be working on. From what I've heard, these machines are going to be the market leaders.'

'But Grace, I've done nothing to deserve this,' protested Will, running a broad hand through his dark hair, his hazel eyes wide. 'It's beyond my wildest dreams. I know how generous your parents are, but I also know about their changed circumstances. How can I possibly accept this?'

'Father knows how much travelling you are doing getting from Roehampton to the hospitals where Dr Forrester works and soon also to the College of Preceptors in the evenings,' said Grace. 'He always said he would assist with your ambitions to become a qualified doctor and this is one way of helping you achieve it. It's in my interests, too, because you will be home to help out with the children in the evenings more promptly. Besides, think of the fun we can have driving this thing around town together.'

Will was lost for words.

'Oof, Jack is going to be right envious,' said Clara. But, she thought, he could get his own if he got off the couch and got a permanent job. He'd been back six months now.

'But . . . this really is the Rolls-Royce of motorcycles, is it not?' Will said. 'It must've cost a tidy sum.'

'I'm sure it did,' said Grace. 'But my parents know that you've looked after me and given them grandchildren. In which I've played a small part too, I hasten to add. Hence the sidecar.' Grace peered in at its seat. 'It looks quite comfortable.'

'It does. Comfort is important given the state of the roads around here.'

'And especially since you'll be spending a fair amount of time in it.'

'Me?' said Will.

'Yes, you. You didn't think you'd be the only one driving this gorgeous beast, did you? We will both drive this, and we will both push the pram. It's female emancipation, Will. Get used to it.'

Behind them, Kitty smiled mischievously at Clara.

13

Chiswick, London, July 1920

Will brought the Brough motorcycle to a standstill outside the tiny house at 368 Chiswick High Road and Clara gratefully extricated herself from the narrow sidecar. Had it not been raining, she would have preferred to walk home from Barnes rather than putting her life in Will's hands in his fearsome machine, which she sometimes had to do on Saturdays after minding the twins.

'Are you coming in?' she asked, straightening her dress, brushing off a few raindrops and stretching her legs. 'Jack will probably be back by now.'

'I'd better not, Aunt Clara,' Will replied. 'I'll only get into an argument with him about still not finding any permanent work and sponging off you. Besides, I'm sure Grace could do with a hand back home with the babies.'

'I'm sure she could. You're a good father to those wee ones, Will, and a devoted husband too. It's a pity you can't find Jack a wife!'

'Oh, he'll settle down one day. When he finds the right one. Just now, I think the most important thing for him is to find some gainful employment. I know it suits him but he can't keep loafing about forever.'

'It's not all his fault,' said Clara, finding yet another generous excuse for his lackadaisical attitude. 'There are precious few jobs available, with the economy in the state it's in. So many ex-servicemen are in the same position. But I know he is looking.'

'Hmm, in all the wrong places. Illicit gambling and the black market for cigarettes and nylons is hardly going to provide any job security in the long run.'

'Are you sure you wouldn't like to come in and tell him that yourself?'

'Got to fly, Aunty,' said Will, climbing back on the bike and donning his goggles. 'Feeding time at the zoo.'

'Off you go, then. And be careful on that thing.'

She watched him ride off and then took out her front door key and let herself in. Jack was sprawled out in the armchair reading the paper with a beer in his hand.

'Drinking at this time of the day, are we?' she chided, taking off her hat and shawl. Jack had been spending a fair proportion of her part-time teacher's salary on his food and drinks bill.

'I'm celebrating, actually. Finally got a decent job lined up.'

'Really? That is good news!' she said.

'I start tomorrow, Aunt Clara. And I'll be out of your hair for a good while.'

'And what will you be doing, pray?'

'I'll be joining the finest constabulary force in the world. The RIC.' Jack flashed her his cheeky grin.

'Ireland?'

'Yep. That rain-sodden Emerald Isle. I'll be a guardian of law and order. Me! Can you credit it? And the pay is tremendous — £3.10 shillings a week and allowances on top.'

Jack was more animated than Clara had seen him in months. But somehow, she could not share her oldest nephew's enthusiasm.

'But you told me you were done with the Army.'

'It's not the Army, Aunt Clara. It's policing. Just keeping the peace.'

Clara moved towards the kitchen and put the kettle on the stove. Jack followed and leaned in the doorway.

'Jack, I've no doubt the incentives are tempting,' she said, putting away air-dried dishes from the rack. 'But there is a reason for that. There is a lot of unrest out there and a lot of ill feeling about the failure to secure home rule among the Nationalists.' She paused with a dinner plate in her hand and looked at him. 'To be fair, I believe they have a genuine grievance. But the IRA are becoming increasingly rebellious and ruthless. The work you are being offered will be dangerous. I know from reading the papers that the RIC Inspector General has said as much.'

'It can't be that dangerous, Aunt Clara. All the lads being recruited fought in France. They know how to look after themselves all right. And with the old RIC already established there, a well-trained group of experienced local men, I reckon the job will be child's play.' He stretched and tapped his fingers on the top of the door frame.

'Don't you believe a word of it, you foolish boy,' she said, plates and cups clanking as she put them away. 'The RIC is overstretched and being ostracised by their own people. Why do you think Lloyd George is recruiting men from here?'

'Don't you worry, Aunt Clara,' he said, coming to take the kettle off the stove for her when it whistled and putting his beer glass in the sink. 'I'm booked on a boat from Holyhead tomorrow and I complete my training at Gormanston in

County Meath within a fortnight. If I get promoted as fast as they say is possible, I could even be an auxiliary within a few months and on seven pounds a week. Imagine that! I can send you money home to repay you for all you've done for me.' He rubbed her arm with his free hand as he poured the boiling water with his other. He began to make her tea the way she liked it, then made his own with two extra spoons of sugar.

'I don't want repaying. I'm just worried that having recently returned from one ghastly task, you'll be taking on another. You'll be jumping out of the frying pan into the fire.'

Jack knew his aunt meant well but she was constantly fussing over him and had adopted exactly the same over-protective attitude before he went to fight in France. He came back from that unscathed, didn't he? Well, only slightly scathed anyway! He had been living under her roof for far too long and couldn't take much more of it. His younger brother was not much better either. Always thinking he knew more than him. But then he had always been the apple of his aunty's eye and he the prodigal son. No, he couldn't take the mollycoddling a second longer. The sooner he was out of there, the better.

He sipped his sweet, hot tea. 'You worry too much, Aunty. You just look after Kitty and the darling doctor-to-be and his progeny and I'll go and earn my fortune with the Black and Tans.'

Clara gave Jack a long look of resignation, holding her own teacup between her hands, and knew there was nothing she could say or do that would change his mind. Whatever Jack decided to do, Jack did.

'You know me,' he said airily. 'I know what I'm doing and I'm more than capable of looking after myself.'

14

Hammersmith Hospital, White City, London, August 1920

Dr Gordon Forrester sat with Will in the cramped window-less hospital office and dunked a second Bourbon biscuit into his mug of tea. He left it there for exactly three seconds, then extricated it and watched the wet end of it slowly droop before popping it into his mouth.

Hammersmith Hospital was constructed on a pavilion-plan arrangement as a workhouse and infirmary to designs by the architects Giles, Gough and Trollope. The original building, built in 1905 on the site of a previous smallpox facility and administered by the Poor Law Guardians, had been added to and extended several times and Will rather liked its red-brick facade, with its numerous tall windows allowing plenty of daylight into the Florence Nightingale-inspired, dormitory-style wards within.

Forrester was thinking that the young man had proved again today just how far his diagnostic skills and surgical acumen had advanced. He possessed exactly the right motivation and dedication to make a fine doctor and all the character and empathy to make him a great one. He was a quick learner too. He already knew more than some of the quacks and charlatans in private practice in Wimpole and Harley Street whose only qualifications came from religious rather than medical institutions. Like that Major Dr Clifford Davison, who was notorious for his enthusiasm to whip out a woman's uterus and ovaries at the drop of a hat. At the mere suggestion from her husband that she could occasionally be moody or disagree with him, Davison would reach for the scalpel. He still seemed to cling to the medieval belief that a hysterectomy was the answer to female 'hysteria', whereas, objectively speaking, surgical removal of the husband would have been more appropriate.

Though Forrester would never contemplate allowing his apprentice to operate alone on his patients, he had no doubt they would be in safer and more capable hands than some of these quacks. Will, like all good healers, was as much aware of his limitations as his strengths and always exerted appropriate caution and care in all he did. He had done so ever since Forrester first spotted his potential, as a fourteen-year-old porter at the hospital near Chiswick.

When Will returned from the war, he had already served his medical apprenticeship in many ways. He had been thrown in at the deep end assisting all manner of emergency procedures, such as amputations, skull trephining, thoracotomies, bowel resections and learning how to treat gas gangrene, mustard gas asphyxiation and open fractures. He had also developed a keen understanding of afflictions of the mind – conditions that many of his more traditional medical colleagues felt were untreatable. Will had spoken eloquently about his experience of men with shell shock and often referred to one man in particular – a Captain Daniels, who Will was convinced had wrongly been shot by firing squad for desertion as a result of it.

Will could palpate an abdomen skilfully and identify an enlarged spleen, hernia or liver. He could detect ascites in the abdomen, free the fluid that accumulates following cirrhosis or cancer, and he could perform a thorough examination of the twelve cranial nerves to explore pathology in the brain, eye and nervous system.

Forrester had spent many days and months now in Will's company and had become something of a father to him. And he felt the time was coming when there wouldn't be a great deal more he could teach him alone. Will had to go to medical school and get the qualifications necessary to be officially recognised as the physician and surgeon he already was.

Dipping one last biscuit into his tea and then savouring it, he tried to broach the subject of Will's career in a delicate and respectful manner.

'Will, you are enjoying your night study for your diploma from the College of Preceptors?'

Will nodded. 'Of course. It may end up taking me a bit longer than some, but it's been fascinating.'

'I'm pleased to hear it. This will qualify you for an interview at the Society of Apothecaries for your medical degree and then postgraduate study at one of the top London teaching hospitals — any of which would be foolish, not to say negligent, if they refused to enrol you.'

'Dr Forrester, you have been a wonderful mentor to me. I'm so very grateful, as you know. My ambition to become a doctor burns as brightly as ever. More so, in fact, under your tutorship. But as you also know, medical schools are the province of young men from wealthy backgrounds. That was clear to me from working with all those doctors I served under in the war. You know my background. I'm a working-class lad who left school at fourteen. A motherless son of an unskilled dockhand who, much as I love him, struggles to hold down a job and is generally considered to be "not quite right in the head". I'm not what most people would describe as typical medical school material.'

'Stuff and nonsense! There is class consciousness and educational snobbery in every walk of life. But things are changing. And character, duty and dedication speak for themselves. Besides that, your references are glowing. Aim high and persevere, Will. I have faith in you and these things are not insuperable.'

'But . . . I'm not sure I have the wherewithal from my job at Queen Mary's to fund a medical education. I won't be able to afford it.'

Forrester frowned. He had been thinking about this dilemma of Will's for a while. Having devoted his own life to medicine, and not family or home, Forrester had money to spare, and he would like to help the young man out. But he knew Will had a strong sense of pride, and he wasn't sure how he would take such an offer.

'Will, you have been my right hand, my administrative organiser, my secretary, my operating assistant, my instrument steriliser and, well . . . altogether my general dogsbody. Your cheerful disposition has been a tonic. Look,' he said, picking up another biscuit, 'get through this first hoop and we will see what is possible. If you are prepared to continue to help me, I will help you. So that will suit both of us equally, will it not?'

Will frowned himself now, as though wondering if Forrester were implying what he thought he was implying. 'I don't know what to say.'

'Ah! nominal aphasia,' said Forrester, smiling. 'Well, don't say anything then. Just be . . . aphasic.'

'But . . . I . . . er . . .'

'That's dysphasia, Will. Dysphasia means difficulty in talking, as opposed to aphasia, which is the inability to talk at all. It's about time you knew the difference by now. Especially if you are going to be treating patients who've suffered strokes.'

Will grinned and nodded, before silently mouthing, 'Yes, sir.'

15

Balbriggan, Ireland, September 1920

Jack kept trying to tell himself it was just a job, as he wove through the streets of Balbriggan with the Black and Tans, setting fire to innocent people's homes and businesses. Just a job . . . They were sacking the town in revenge for the murder of an RIC district inspector and his brother. For months, Jack had been wily, mostly getting away with being background noise. Shoot a bullet at bricks occasionally or lay a weak fist and his fellow constables didn't question him. Keep quiet, keep to himself. But it was lonely. Not like him at all. He was confused about the men he was working with and the role he was playing. It was hard to connect, even in a jokey, superficial way. Today, he couldn't get away with being in the background. He had to help light up the town.

On the boat over from England in July, Jack had first encountered the rowdy bunch of half-drunk louts he worked with, all boasting about how they were going to put one over on the nationalist troublemakers and earn a pretty penny from it. Jack was no snob, coming as he did from a working-class background, and was used to mixing with the rough and ready of the toughest London suburbs. But even he was surprised at how seedy and unpleasant many of his fellow recruits seemed to be.

They had arrived at South Quay in Dublin and been taken straight to Gormanston for basic police training. He could clearly understand the distinction between the skills necessary for maintaining the peace as a police constable and the military duties of soldiers, but much to his surprise the majority of the other men failed to do so. Matters were not improved either by the uniforms with which they were supplied. A shortage of material meant they would be wearing a mixture of military-style khaki trousers and dark green RIC tunics, caps and belts. At the end of their rushed fortnight of instruction, they were still an ill-disciplined rabble. A motley crew of men, some of whom were even trusted with Lewis guns, revolvers and truncheons, as well as their whistles and handcuffs, and seemed horribly keen to try them out.

Jack, ever the optimist, reasoned that he had just been unlucky to have been thrown in with a bad bunch. There were plenty of decent, highly trained local RIC men simply striving to do their best for their country, but this lot were different. He could only hope that their unrestrained behaviour and immorality would be diluted by their widespread deployment to far-flung villages and towns around the country.

He was still waiting.

He had been dispatched first to Cork and then Tipperary, billeted in a cold, damp and unfurnished police barracks surrounded by walls topped with barbed wire, sentry boxes and makeshift sandbag barricades.

In Tipperary, he soon found out that the RIC were completely shunned by the local community and that food and other provisions were in such short supply they had to be requisitioned and transported from central depots in major towns far away. Despite the generous pay, none of the so-called constables like himself were happy with their circumstances and bickering and arguments broke out constantly. It never seemed to stop raining and the general atmosphere and morale was miserable. The environment was as hostile and unwelcoming as the company.

But Jack had made a decision and he was here now and had to stick to it. There was no way he was going to admit that Aunt Clara may have been right. If he stuck it out, he'd have money enough for himself and to help her out, too — repay her for all those beers he bought out of her meagre income.

Jack had been quite unsettled by the suspicion and hostility of the locals in Tipperary. He was gregarious and affable. A people person. He would have liked nothing more than to be able to amble down to the pub and share a drink with the villagers. None of that was possible. By now, the RIC's counter-insurgency role was far from being a job for policemen. This was a fully fledged war, and it was only the politicians back home in England who had outlawed the Dáil and augmented the British Army presence who did not want to acknowledge it. The Black and Tans were seen as the enemy. The unelected occupying army. The oppressors. Jack had felt increasingly uncomfortable and guilty about what he was doing there for months.

And now here he was setting fire to a shoemaker's — a humble profession. It didn't take long for the stench of burning leather to reach his nostrils, reminding him of smells of mortared flesh on the battlefields of France.

Across the street, he saw several constables beating two Republicans, their families screaming and pulling at their arms with no thought for their own safety. Simon, an eighteen-year-old lad, had a snarl on his face as he threw his weight into the baton again and again. He looked to be enjoying himself. Jack was sure they would not stop until the men were killed. He could not stand by.

'That's enough!' he called over the noises of the burning street.

No one heard as a window exploded in a burning shop near the beatings. Glass sprayed everywhere and Jack and all the people nearby ducked. It was just enough of a pause and distraction for the rebels to emerge from buildings with guns. And the Black and Tans dispersed, including Jack, running back to the barracks.

16

St Katherine Docks, London, December 1920

Robbie arrived at the docks on a miserly grey day, adjusted his flat cap and got straight to work. Barrels, crates and sacks had to come off a barge, and his muscles strained as he worked – rolling, carrying, shouldering items. Stacking and tying them, his fingers remembering the knots like language. It had been a bad night's sleep. Intrusive, repetitive thoughts. And a steady dripping after a downpour that he became fixated on.

The rain came again now and at first he welcomed it. It cocooned him from his workmates, made conversation and jokes more difficult. Most days, the banter was more draining to him than the physical work. The men meant well, tried to include him, but he just wanted to concentrate on getting on with it, then going home.

He lit a damp cigarette and drew in a good lungful before the rain put it out and he walked back up the gangplank for more cargo. He thought about Jack, how even his young and fit son couldn't get work and had to run off to Ireland. He knew he should be grateful he had this job. He was. He just also felt as dark and damp and heavy as the rain clouds.

He should have learned more, as a lad – become a riveter or driller, made himself invaluable. As it was, he was just a set of muscles and hands. And there were plenty of those around. Even men with missing eyes and limbs did this job, like Purblind Pegleg Pete, as the workers called him. Even women could do this job. Women had also been riveters and drillers, built the hulls of ships, when the men were all away. Robbie wondered about those women now. It was the right thing to do, to give the men who fought for their country their jobs back. But he saw how fulfilled Clara's work made her. Might some of these women now be cooking or washing clothes but wishing they were back out in the air, smoking and bantering and feeling their thighs and biceps burn?

He thought about this because of having a daughter. Kitty, now ten, seemed capable of anything, to him. And the twins, his grandchildren — a boy and a girl — would their lives be so different to one another? Perhaps not, with parents like Will and Grace, who showed such an open curiosity to life and an independence of thought. Who pursued their interests. Robbie didn't remember what it was like to have passion. He knew he had felt it. Sometime long ago.

His hands moved and stacked and tied knots. The rain came harder. The men around him groaned. 'Jesus Christ.' Fat, cold droplets trickled down their necks, into their shoes. Vision was blurred. And then, Robbie felt it in his bones. Like he was lying in a ditch again, muddy water rising, suffocating. The smell of gunfire and death amid the stench of the pool.

He looked down at his hands. What was this knot? He'd tied it thousands upon thousands of times. But it was gone, blasted from memory.

'Robbie, mate? You all right?' The voice swam to him. He was frozen, staring at his hand.

'The knot . . .'

99

The man shook his head and came over, tied it efficiently. 'Just grab some more weight, Rob,' he said, pointing at the ship. It was Pete.

Robbie couldn't feel his legs. Time spun backwards and forwards. He clutched at the knot, staring at the ship in front of him. The dark hole of its cargo bay. Like a bombed-out rock.

No, like a ship. Men swarming in and out.

He took a long, heaving, wet breath. Looked down at his feet and willed them to move. Willed his head to attach back to his body.

The rain eased a little, and that helped. He trudged forward and up, pulled down another barrel. Trudged back, past Pete. Pete looked up at him and Robbie nodded, a quiet thanks.

When he got home that day, he peeled off his wet clothes and ran a washer with boiled water over his skin, so hot it almost burned. Kitty had wanted to speak to him at the door but he'd grunted. He needed to come back to himself first. But inside the room, with the door closed, was peace. He lay down, still naked, on the bed, with the hot washer over his eyes. He seemed to recall that his mother would sponge his head like this when he was sick.

He fell fast asleep.

17

Cork, Ireland, December 1920

Jack was sitting in the barracks canteen one day, silent and miserable, with another man who'd become introverted by their duties, and with whom he had developed a morose companionship, when he overheard some of their colleagues talking about a brutal, overtly criminal act that had happened around a month ago in Gort.

Two local boys with no IRA connections were murdered by the Black and Tans for impudence. Just for talking back, Jack discovered. The Tans had dragged the boys' bodies behind one of their Crossley Tenders until they were unrecognisably mangled and then thrown them into a ditch. Jack could only imagine the grief of their families and the terrible anger and resolve to revenge their actions that would have been engendered.

After Balbriggan in September, other villages had also suffered mass reprisals. Kilkee, Trim, Tubbercurry and Granard. Dear God, Jack had thought again and again, some of these people had fought for the British Army in the trenches just a few months ago.

There had been many unnecessary and arbitrary reprisals against civilians over the past few months. Vicious gangs of men riding around in Crossley Tenders with the words

'Reprisals Galore' emblazoned on the sides, carrying out lootings, beatings and killings haphazardly. Women were not safe either. They were easy targets. Many had been punched and kicked, had their hair cut off or been sexually assaulted. Men would steal food from their larders, take animals from their farms and shoot wildfowl and other poultry which belonged to the very poorest so they could take it home and cook it for themselves. Jack became so terrified of his colleagues, he made himself smaller and smaller. He was lost.

The IRA were capable of their own brand of killing too. In July, they had attacked the RIC barracks in Rathmore, County Kerry, and killed Alexander Will, the first Black and Tan to die in the conflict. On 22 September at Rineen, they had ambushed and killed six RIC men. But they were only targeting the enemy as they saw it. They were fighting for their independence and liberty, Jack had begun to observe. The more the Black and Tans exerted their brutal authority, the more resistance grew among the Irish populace and the more support flooded in for the Republican Sinn Féin party which had already won the majority of seats in the general election two years before.

In November, Jack had heard that the Tans had abducted and murdered a Roman Catholic priest, Father Michael Griffin, in Galway. His body had been found in a bog in Barna several days later. Galway was apparently where the war was waged more fiercely than anywhere else.

On Bloody Sunday in the same month, the War of Independence had reached another terrible milestone when more than thirty people were killed or fatally wounded. Michael Collins had led an operation to assassinate a group of undercover British intelligence agents, killing or fatally wounding fifteen of them. Later that day, British forces raided a Gaelic football match in Croke Park with orders just to cordon off and search. Without warning, and for reasons unknown, police opened fire on the spectators and players, which resulted in fourteen civilians being killed and sixty others wounded. Two of the dead were children. How the hell could that have happened? Jack wondered. The events of the day were unclear and confused, but whatever the circumstances giving rise to it, even the military enquiry that followed admitted the shooting had been indiscriminate and excessive. Not only had British intelligence in Ireland been severely damaged, but support for the IRA both at home and abroad had increased massively.

The hairs on the back of Jack's neck were raised as he ate his gruel and listened to his colleagues recount the brutal beatings of the two boys. These were not the sort of men he had fought alongside in France, that was for sure. Jack no longer wanted to be associated with this officially sanctioned band of criminals, and yet, his pride kept holding out. To return would be to admit how bad it was and how much he'd already participated in. If he stuck it out, doing as little harm as he could get away with, he could leave at the end of his allotted time frame with full pay and never speak of it again.

18

Putney, London, May 1921

After the twins' second birthday, Grace again raised the subject with Will of going back to work full-time. They were lying in bed, contented after a meal, a relatively tantrum-free bath time and a sweet lovemaking session. She rolled over to face him.

'I love being with the children, Will, but I miss the work.'

Will brushed an auburn lock back from her face. He thought she looked only more beautiful as time passed, as she matured.

'You don't have to. We're getting by.'

It was true that Will's work and her Saturday shift kept them fed and heated, and that their basic necessities were covered.

'It's not about the money, you know me better than that.'

Will did. Of course, he wanted her to be happy. It would be seen as a bit unusual, something they'd have to explain to people — a woman wanting to work instead of raising her children, and for someone from Grace's background, too. None of her female relatives would have worked before. But she'd already passed that hurdle — she'd worked, gone to war, continued nursing while pregnant. To anyone who knew Grace, this wouldn't be unusual at all.

'Well, then, let's work it out. We'll have to figure out where the children will go during weekdays.'

'I have a few ideas,' said Grace, sitting up, smiling. 'Jenny and her child and the nanny are home all day together, just around the corner, for example.' Jenny was Grace's best friend, whom she had nursed alongside in the Yeomanry during the war.

Will nodded. 'That could work.'

'If Jenny goes back to nursing too, the nanny is still very good.'

Will nodded. 'And Clara and Kitty are happy to have them on Saturdays.'

The matter decided, they settled back into a comfortable silence. Will picked up a medical journal, began running his eyes over the page.

'Sorry, darling. There's one more thing I want to discuss.'

Will put the journal down. 'What is it, my love?'

Grace felt nervous. She knew Will supported her every decision – that he understood her, loved her in the truest sense of the word. But he was still a man and there were expectations in marriage. She took a breath.

'I . . . don't want to have any more children.'

Will frowned. He looked to the corner of the room.

'I'm sorry.'

But then he nodded, looked back at her. 'It felt like a bit of a shock when you said that, but I think I am . . . relieved, mostly. The danger of pregnancy . . .'

'Yes, that's one reason. I don't want to put you through that. But it's also for me. I'm so content with the twins, with our small family. I don't want to become one of those women who is pregnant every other year, has a large brood.'

'And your abdominal wound – I mean, we never know . . .'

'We don't.'

He sat up further as well, clasped her hands. 'And I suppose I shouldn't just be thinking of the danger. You are a person, not just a . . . vessel,' Will said earnestly. 'I understand if you desire to do other things in your life than bear children.'

Grace felt a whole-body warmth. She wasn't sure what she had done in life to warrant such a man. One who had the hard-working, practical attitude of the working class, and an expansive, thoughtful mind and heart. He considered people's situations from every angle – hers, his patients', the men he'd fought beside in war. She knew he spent a lot of time contemplating the children's needs, too. He was a doting and affectionate father. A lot of the time he simply sat by their crib, looking up from his papers, a contemplative expression on his face.

'So,' she said. 'What we've been doing in our lovemaking has been working so far, but I'm going to learn more.' She was referring to the fact that Will had voluntarily been withdrawing before ejaculating, when they made love. But she wanted to know if there were other ways about it. 'A new clinic has opened up on Marlborough Road, so I'll make an appointment.'

'That sounds good,' he said. 'Much of what I'm reading and learning is skewed towards mending rather than preventing. Do tell me everything.'

'I will,' she said.

Content, Grace reached out to hold Will again. She picked up his journal from the floor so he could read it while she rested in his shoulder.

The Mothers' Clinic was a small shopfront on Marlborough Road. A patterned curtain cut the front window in half, promising discreetness to the married women who were welcome inside. Grace paused before the building, tempted momentarily by the chocolate in the window of Fry's next door. It was nice to think of all the different flavours they would be able to introduce to the twins — and textures, colours, smells. She hoped they would only know peace and joy in their lives.

She pressed open the door and a woman in a nurse's cap stood from a small desk in front of another discreet curtain, to greet her.

'Hello, Mrs . . .'

'Burnett, Grace Burnett,' she said.

'Pleased to meet you, ma'am. I'm Nurse Roberts.' The stout, middle-aged woman smiled.

'I'm a nurse myself,' said Grace.

'Oh, wonderful,' said the nurse. 'And what brings you to our clinic today?'

Grace felt her hair coming loose from the braid at her neck.

'Well, my husband and I have two perfect children and . . .' She paused. Despite the fact Grace had spent so much time around bodies, medicine, it was more personal when it was to do with her own life, her own body, and her intimate relations with her husband. 'And I would like to learn more about how I can avoid further pregnancies.'

She fiddled with the pin holding her dark, wide-brimmed hat in place. Caught sight of the single black feather puffing out jauntily from its side.

'Of course,' the woman said. 'Come with me.'

She led Grace behind the curtain, where there were two desks facing one another, and a cabinet behind yet another curtain. She gestured for Grace to sit.

'I'll explain a bit more about what we do here,' the woman said, pulling in the chair across. 'Myself and the other midwives, we can educate you on these matters. The clinic's founders, Marie Stopes and Humphrey Roe, they are discovering new methods often, so Dr Stopes also runs safe trials with patients who are willing. And we have a rotation of doctors who come by and give talks and demonstrations, also.'

Grace nodded. 'That all sounds interesting. At the moment, I think I'd just like to know the basics.'

The midwife nodded. 'You may wish to procure Dr Stopes' book.' She showed her a copy of *Wise Parenthood: A Book for Married People*. 'But I'll give you an introduction.' She stood and pulled back a curtain covering a glass-fronted cabinet. Inside were various items, including a model of the female reproductive system, something that looked like a sponge and a brown rubber ball with some text stamped in white on top.

She began with the model, and as she explained how sperm entered the egg, Grace sat politely, wondering if she should remind Nurse Roberts that she was in fact a medical professional. Perhaps it was her own fault for saying 'the basics'.

The nurse explained that methods of birth control were all about either stopping the sperm from entering the cervix or destroying the sperm.

'We're already practising, uh . . .'

'Coitus interruptus?' the nurse said.

'Where he withdraws.'

The nurse nodded. 'Mostly effective, but there can be some . . . unreliability. This,' she said, picking up the brown rubber ball, 'is more effective, and it will mean you don't have to interrupt your husband's pleasure. You can take matters into your own hands, as it were.'

She handed the item to Grace, who now saw that the large, stamped word was 'Prorace'.

The nurse pointed back at the reproductive model. 'It sits just here, to block the spermatozoa from entering the cervix, and you remove it afterwards with the string.'

Grace turned the device to and fro. It was certainly something she could try.

'And what does this description mean? Prorace?'

'Oh,' the nurse said, 'that's what Dr Stopes called it, essentially because it provides a means of purification of society. I'm not too familiar myself with the intellectual terms, but you should come by when Dr Stopes is here. It's all very fascinating.'

Grace realised the run-together word was in fact 'pro-race'. She frowned.

'She cares about every woman's health, such as yourself, but she also cares about greater ills — you know, the great numbers of feeble-minded, degenerate and diseased children that are born. Our long-term work will be with the poor.'

Grace put the device down. She wasn't shocked — she'd encountered a eugenicist or two among the doctors she'd met, and she'd heard her father discussing the prevalence of these ideas in his political circles — but she was made uneasy by it. She nodded politely, and stood.

'I think I have enough information for now, thank you.'

The nurse stood too. 'Oh, are you certain? I haven't got to the sponge.'

Grace decided she would learn more elsewhere rather than supporting Marie Stopes. Yes, it was very good that this education was available to women, but it wasn't great that it supported the idea of racial 'cleansing'. She was certainly proud of her country, her heritage. But she knew the United Kingdom had many faces: rich and poor, white and brown, hare-lipped, bow-legged, cleft-palated and mentally unwell. She couldn't imagine having a life where the only people she encountered were pale, smooth-skinned, able-bodied British reproductions. How terribly, offensively boring and awful.

'I'm certain,' she said to the nurse. 'But I do appreciate your help.'

The nurse smiled. 'We're here if you need us,' she said.

Grace left the clinic and walked into Fry's. She would buy a nice piece of chocolate to share with Will and get the bad taste out of her mouth.

19

Munich, Germany, August 1921

At 10 p.m. on a dark, wet evening in Munich, a tall, heavily built man lumbered along Schillerstrasse looking for the unprepossessing building set slightly back from the main thoroughfare and to which he had become a frequent visitor. A bitter wind gusted along the road and despite the high leather collar of his greatcoat and the scarf wrapped tightly around his neck and face, it bit into his scarred cheek and triggered another stabbing episode of neuralgia. Cursing loudly, he bent his head forward, screwed up his eyes, unwrapped the scarf and vigorously massaged the area with his left hand.

A young couple in front of him who had just emerged from the entrance of a noisy, cosy-looking bar looked at him as they passed and their eyes reflexively widened in horror. Behind him, as the jag of sudden pain slowly eased off, he heard them trying to suppress their laughter.

Fuck them, he thought to himself.

Stumbling on another hundred yards, he came to the Haus der Bedingungslose Liebe, climbed the stone steps and pressed the bell. After a moment, Frau Freya Muller opened the door with a welcoming smile on her face, but it soon faded when she saw who it was. Behind her, the exotic and familiar scent of a medley of women's perfumes suspended in warm but stagnant air assailed the visitor's nostrils. It was an exciting olfactory promise of things to come.

Reluctantly ushering him in, Frau Freya Muller wondered which of her girls she would have to allocate to him today. She knew none of them would be rushing to volunteer their services, no matter what money she would be willing to pay them. Chances were, he would insist on choosing for himself anyway, and she fervently hoped Mia was already busy elsewhere with a different client as she had formally expressed a wish never to be paired with Jürgen Altmann again.

In the extravagant, plush luxury of the lounge bar upstairs, with its cushioned sofas, gilt-framed pictures and tapestries, Altmann scanned the room, spied a girl he liked the look of and dropped into the beautifully upholstered cerise-coloured chesterfield beside her. The girl was obviously a newcomer to the establishment and little more than a child. Frau Freya Muller was horrified and frantically appealed with her eyes to one or two of the older, more experienced girls to intervene. But the women quickly looked away and made their excuses to leave the room.

Altmann ordered schnapps for himself and his new companion and placed a spade-like hand roughly on her thigh. He was already drunk after an earlier session drowning his sorrows at his favourite *bierkeller*, but he begrudgingly understood it was accepted etiquette to indulge the girls in Frau Muller's harem in a pretence of having at least a modicum of respect for them.

Altmann did not like women. He scorned his mother for her disinteresting bourgeois life, devoted entirely as it was to her husband, whom he had never been able to please himself at the best of times. Ever since childhood, he had felt that his sister, Gudrun, had been his parents' favourite and he had hated her from the day she had betrayed him by telling them how he pinned bees and spiders to trees and watched them spin around like a Catherine wheel after setting fire to them. These days, she always seemed to have an excuse for avoiding him and he could not remember the last time he had been allowed to see her two children.

Clumsy and unsuccessful with women as a teenager and even as a young adult, any advances he had made towards women, both in England during his apprenticeship and in his homeland, had always seemed to end up awkwardly or in an argument. He was resigned to the fact he would never understand them, nor they him. It was easier just to come to the *Liebe* house and pay the going rate. That way, he did not even have to converse with them.

This girl was cute, though, he thought. She looked innocent and fresh. Her face was a little similar, he realised, to that British nurse he'd lost his features over during the war. This got him excited. She told him her name was Lyudmila and that she was nineteen and came from Koszalin in Poland. She had also sweetly pretended not to be disgusted by his facial disfigurement and had thought to tenderly stroke that side of his face. He could tell she did not find it easy. She winced slightly as she nervously downed her schnapps in one gulp.

He would have her, Altmann thought. Especially coming from Poland. Germany had given up so much to Poland lately; she could give him as much as he wanted to take from her in return. What he'd wanted to take from that nurse. She would also be able to distract him from his murderous thoughts about Matthias Erzberger, who he'd worked himself into a frenzy over alongside his colleague Heinrich Schulz. The men had been verbally assassinating the man all evening at the *Hofbräuhaus* to anyone who would listen. And many did. First of all, this incompetent politician had ignominiously capitulated to Marshal Ferdinand Foch and the Entente countries in that railway carriage in Compiègne back in November 1918. He had signed an armistice that was not only unnecessary but a total humiliation for Germany. Why had the Kaiser sent a politician rather than a military man, for God's sake? Sheer stupidity!

Then, as Finance Minister and Vice Chancellor to Gustav Bauer's new government, he had overseen all matters relating to that miserable Treaty of Versailles and taxed the life out of hard-working Nationalists like himself. What did this traitor do then? Altmann had asked his audience. He started with giving the federal government supreme authority to tax and spend as they liked, ignorant of the individual and unique situation in Bavaria. Next, like so many others, he had been robbed personally and commercially to pay for the indolent lower classes. Then what? *Kriegsausgaben* . . . war levies. After that, the first-ever inheritance tax, swiftly followed by the additional *Reichsnotopfer*, the emergency tax on wealth. It was never-ending. And crippling. The latest demand for the huge amounts of back tax on the profits Altmann Engineering were just beginning to turn was the last straw. This was why he had remained out tonight after Schulz had stumbled home – to console himself with more drink and with women. While he could still afford them. At the *Hofbrauhaus*, he and Schulz had been given a round of applause before they left. Now he felt he was entitled to indulge himself.

Here in the *Liebe* house, Frau Muller was usually not one to be easily flustered. She had been in her current form of occupation for years and there was nothing very much that really surprised her. Yet ever since Jürgen Altmann's arrival tonight, she had been on edge and had decided to put one of the girls on the front door in her place so she could stay upstairs in the lounge bar herself to supervise.

An hour and a half after Altmann had arrived and within thirty minutes of him taking Lyudmila to one of the rooms on the second floor, she heard staccato screams coming from above. Alarmed, as well as fearful of the effect the rumpus might have on other paying customers, she raced upstairs and hammered on the door. She was the madame and knew what was expected of the girls, but she was fond of them, she depended on their welfare and had a sisterly duty to protect them. She also had a reputation to protect and standards to maintain.

'*Was ist los?*' she yelled. '*Ist alles in Ordnung?*'

She heard a guttural baritone curse and some soft whimpering as if someone was sobbing with their head buried in a pillow.

'*Alles ist gut,*' answered Altmann from behind the door. '*Mehr als gut.*'

More than good? What does he mean? she wondered.

'*Geht es dir gut?*' she shouted to Lyudmila.

'*Nein, er hat mir weh getan,*' answered the girl quietly, clearly crying. 'He has hurt me badly.'

The door opened and Altmann barged past Freya Muller while still fastening his trouser belt.

'Money well spent,' he said, handing her a fistful of banknotes. 'But I'd say she's in the wrong job.'

Through the doorway, she could see Lyudmila naked and crumpled, half kneeling on the floor by the bedside, blood and other fluids dripping down the back of her thighs on to her heels.

'Get out,' spat Muller. 'Get out and never come back here again.'

Altmann turned and leered at her, his lopsided sneer exposing yellow, uneven teeth.

'*Kein Problem,*' he whispered. 'There are classier whores just across the street.'

20

Westminster, London, August 1921

Fitzwilliam Tustin-Pennington arrived at the office of Henry Hancock, Liberal MP for The County Borough of Worcester, in the mid-morning. He'd been a bit embarrassed, on the train, to find he had fallen asleep — the look on the face of the man across from him told him he had possibly even snored — but he was glad he was well-rested, at least. He glanced at his wristwatch — right on time. His father had secured him the interview with one of his colleagues, and Fitz was keen to get to work. Oxford had been a mixed experience. He'd read History, and excelled academically, but burgeoning friendships had stalled when he often couldn't join the other young men in their sport and recreation, because of his heart. He still liked a drink occasionally, but had to be careful not to overdo it. And he couldn't join in with the ex-soldiers, who had a language and attitude of their own. In short, he was quite certain that the other men considered him a bore.

It didn't feel much different to having grown up with faster, stronger brothers who were interested in different things. Rupert was married now and still climbing ranks in the Navy, Henry had gone into banking, and James was learning the auto trade at a new company, Bentley.

There had been one hopeful friendship in his first year at Oxford, a younger lad called Frith — 'Fitz and Frith', they'd laughed. 'Fitz and Frith and the frothy filibusters, and other tongue-twisters' would be the name of their book, Frith had joked. They'd talked long into the night about the Russians, about Napoleon, about Ancient Greece. But then Frith took to champagne and became very frothy indeed. He'd come to Fitz's room one night, not making any sense, and had leaned in and kissed Fitz right on the lips.

'What on earth are you doing?' Fitz had said. 'You've mistaken me for a woman.'

'Filly Fitz,' Frith had said, giggling. And he had left, and they didn't speak much after that, presumably out of embarrassment.

There was also a woman in one of his tutorials, Shauna, who was finally able to get her degree late last year. She was as studious as he was. They often sat together in class. But they were both too studious to really do anything together beyond that shared, supervised study. It was a pity. She was quite plain, but had these spectacular grey eyes that would occasionally shock him when she looked up, curious about something he'd said.

But life goes on, and here he was, about to be interviewed for his first position.

He cleared his throat, smoothed down his waistcoat and jacket, hoping the train hadn't crumpled him too much, and knocked on the door of the Victorian-era house.

A woman appeared.

'Yes, sir?'

'Good morning, I'm Fitzwilliam Tustin-Pennington, here for my appointment with Mr Hancock.'

'Come in, sir,' she said, stepping aside. She led him into a dark and ornate sitting room and told him the MP was just finishing up some business. She went to get Fitzwilliam some tea.

He sat there, listening to the ticking grandfather clock. Behind the door to the office, he could hear an Irish lilt – a man in conversation with Mr Hancock. It made him think of Shauna again, his grey-eyed, studious friend. She was Irish, too. When the topic of the Irish Rebellion of 1798 had come up in their classes, she was suddenly mute. But he'd thought he saw those grey eyes flash. One time, walking out from a tutorial together, he had dared ask her what she thought of what was going on in Ireland now.

She had taken a deep breath, pulled her books to her chest, and said, 'How would you feel if your beloved England had been swallowed up into the kingdom of another country for more than a hundred years? Would you not, by now, be feeling a little restless?'

He didn't know how to reply adequately, but he had wanted to hear more about her thoughts, her feelings on the matter. He was glad she felt safe enough to air them with him.

'I haven't considered it like that,' he had said. Something in him wanted to rise to the defence of the great empire, the country of his blood, and its colonising rights; but it was a mere flicker – something remembered but not deeply felt.

'Of course you haven't,' she had said with a small smile, nodding back towards the room. 'We're only taught one side of history.'

'May I walk you to your room?' he'd said.

As usual, she had declined. 'I'll see you tomorrow.'

Now, the door to the office opened and Fitzwilliam stood politely, putting down his teacup. Mr Hancock shook the Irish man's hand and the man gave Fitz a small nod on his way out.

'Ah, Mr Fitzwilliam,' Mr Hancock said. He was a stout, whiskery man, with a porous, pinkish nose and cheeks. He invited Fitz into his office, which had books and papers sprawled on every surface, many marked with tea rings and pipe ash. 'As you can see,' he said, gesturing to the mess, 'I am sorely in need of some organisation.'

'Yes, sir,' said Fitz, his palms tingling with the desire to neatly sort and pile.

'So, Oxford, eh?'

'Yes, History, sir.'

'We have very different backgrounds, m'boy. I worked in the pit as a child, then went on to represent the miners. I was Liberal, then Labour, then I crossed the floor in 1915 to rejoin the Liberals. It's about what can get done, for me, rather than wearing any particular stripe. I continue as a miners' agent, though am no longer financial secretary of the local association.' He glanced down at the corner of his desk, at a large stack of papers. 'I should get these to the new secretary sometime.'

He looked at Fitz as though waiting for him to respond, but Fitz wasn't sure if there was a question in there some-where.

'I'm very hard-working, sir,' he said. 'I'll know what to do with all your papers.'

'And can you write, too? Notes, speeches? And are you good with numbers? I may be approached for a treasury role.'

'I have strong across-the-board skills, sir.'

'And what is your political alignment?' Hancock steepled his fingers, leaned back in his creaky chair.

'Well, my father, as you know, is a Liberal MP also. I . . . feel most closely aligned to that.'

'Still a little unformed, eh? That's good. The issues should move you. The people should be properly heard. Opinions get a little rusted on over time, you'll see. But . . .' he leaned forward, 'I think your young eyes will help me.'

Fitz's wonky heart gave a little flutter. Was the position his?

Hancock stood. 'Welcome aboard, m'boy.'

Fitz stood and shook his hand enthusiastically. 'Thank you, sir.' He pointed to the pile of financial papers. 'Shall I get straight on this?'

'By all means,' Hancock said, looking pleased.

21

The Black Forest, Baden, Germany, August 1921

The Black Forest in the south-west corner of Germany is a large, forested mountain range bordered by the Rhine Valley to the west and south, where Matthias Erzberger relied for much of his political support on the Catholic working classes living there.

On the eastern side, it boasted gentle green slopes with rounded hills and broad plateaux, dense coniferous forests of tall pine and, in the higher areas, deeply incised, steeply sided ravines and carved-out valleys. It was the perfect place for a beleaguered politician like Erzberger to come and relax on a short holiday. He fully deserved a break as he had served his country diligently and tirelessly to the best of his ability throughout exceedingly challenging times.

It was a calm, delightful summer's day and he and his colleague Carl Diez were enjoying their stroll along the edge of the treeline on their way to their destination a mile and a half away. In patches, the morning sunshine sent bright shafts of light through the canopy of trees all the way down to the forest floor, and the rich earthy smell of wet grass, of petrichor, filled the still air.

Just ahead of them, another two men were approaching from the opposite direction, ambling along closely together in no particular hurry and apparently in good-humoured conversation.

Six hundred yards behind them, Jürgen Altmann sat in a car parked on the grass verge by the side of the road, nervously waiting. The engine was idling and he was ready for a quick getaway. This was the moment they had travelled all this way for.

The journey from Munich to Baden had been taxing, but the little Stoewer-Werke AG D10, although rather slow and somewhat cramped, had performed well, and the conversation between the three of them had been captivating.

Heinrich Schulz, Altmann's colleague, and the slightly younger Heinrich Tillessen, both shared Altmann's extreme ultra-right nationalist views and were determined to fulfil their assignment to the letter. They were both former Navy officers and members of the *Marinebrigade Ehrhardt*, which had been disbanded in February 1920. Soon after, both had joined its equally reactionary successor group, the Organisation Consul, led by the charismatic Hermann Ehrhardt. Its stated goal was unambiguous: the 'implementation of lynchings'. The chief of operations in the Munich headquarters was Manfred von Killinger, a former torpedo boat commander, and it was he who had set the two Heinrichs on this personal mission. Many of their ilk saw Erzberger as a traitor who had almost single-handedly overseen the economic and military demise of their country.

'He may be as round and as squat as a bullet himself, but he is not bulletproof,' Killinger had said to them, laughing, repeating a popular description of the man currently doing the rounds. 'The mission I offer you is to stalk him, track him down and neutralise him.'

The pair had seized the opportunity and agreed on the spot. Altmann, wanting to be involved, had volunteered to drive them.

Now, as Schulz and Tillessen approached Erzberger and his political colleague Carl Diez, they gave each other an imperceptible nod. Then, as they drew level, they each pulled a pistol from their coat pockets and shot the two men at point-blank range. Diez died instantly where he fell, but much to Tillessen's surprise, Erzberger staggered forward for a few yards, desperately trying to get away. Schulz walked up calmly behind him and stood menacingly over him as he collapsed. Then, for good measure, he took careful aim and fired two more shots into the stricken man's head. Tillessen holstered his weapon, looked around furtively and quickly walked back to the car. Schulz stood motionless over his victim as if frozen.

Altmann, terrified that they would be discovered and reported, jumped out of his driver's seat and raced over to Schulz to pull him away.

'Come on, man, for God's sake. Those shots would've been heard miles away.'

'No problem, Jürgen. I'm coming. It's just that sometimes I like to mix business with a little pleasure.'

Altmann looked down at the corpse and had to admit he felt a little envious that in some ways his employee – his friend, but formerly his inferior – had surpassed him in service to Germany. He needed to commit to thinking bigger.

22

Caheroyan Road, Athenry, Ireland, February 1922

Jack felt more miserable than ever. Not even during the worst times fighting the Germans in 1916 had he felt so low. He had risked his life laying tons of explosives under enemy trenches and nearly been trapped underground on more than one occasion. He had spent almost a year after the ceasefire removing unexploded ordnance and bodies from the battlefields. But he had never felt as abject and depressed as he did now. It was not like him. This was the last week he would ever serve as a Black and Tan and he could not wait to see it out before the resignation he had tended became effective. Sod the severance pay and the loss of any pension, he thought. He'd waited as long as he could, and he'd had enough. He would always survive. Anything would be better than this past year and a half.

When the alarm bell sounded and a truck full of injured men screeched to a halt outside, the men inside the barracks scrambled to bring them in before grabbing their weapons. They piled into three or four other vehicles and drove off down the road, shooting indiscriminately into offices and houses on their way towards Athenry Castle where the ambush had taken place. Jack tried to stay in the centre of the crowd on the truck, so it'd be clear he was unable to shoot safely.

They came to a halt in Caheroyan Road near the Clarin river and jumped off the lorries. They set off at a jog with rifles in hand, three abreast and four men deep, in both directions along the road. Again, Jack was able to stay mid-formation. Bewildered civilians going about their daily business looked on nervously and scuttled inside their homes. Jack's group turned a corner and found three young lads chopping firewood outside a stone thatched cottage beside two women in their twenties hanging out washing.

The sergeant, an officious man of about 14 stone but no more than 5 feet 6 inches tall, demanded to know their names and business and started forcibly pushing them around. Jack hung back, glum, gun raised. The tallest man in front of the cottage raised his axe to protect himself and the sergeant shot him in the chest. The other two, shocked and defenceless, bent down to catch him and cushion his fall and were instantly shot themselves by the constables in front of Jack, alarmed by their sudden movement. Immediately, a shot rang out from one of the downstairs windows of the house and the sergeant fell dead where he stood. As the two women ran off weeping, the Tans scattered about the bushes and started firing at will into the cottage. Jack aimed at the wall. Glass from every window shattered and sprayed as plaster exploded from the front and the relentless fusillade of bullets continued for what seemed like an age.

When it stopped, Jack and two other men were ordered into the cottage to make sure no one inside had survived. The first, a brute of a man whom Jack despised, ducked into the front room from where the shot had come, with Jack right behind him. A terrified woman stood before them with her back to the wall. A revolver dangled loosely in the hand by her side, but she showed no sign whatsoever of using it.

The constable knocked the gun from her grasp. She twisted and he grabbed her roughly by the neck from behind, trying to throttle her. She struggled and kicked but was no match for her assailant and Jack shook as her jugular veins became distended and her face turned purple.

'Leave her alone,' Jack said firmly, trying to appear calm. 'There's no need for that. She's harmless.'

But the fellow was murderous and not listening. He had been a close friend of the sadistic sergeant who had started the shooting.

Jack was unable to simply stand by and watch. He strode over to the struggling couple and wrestled to pull the man's forearm away from the woman's throat. The third man entered the room and raised a pistol. Thinking that the man was intent on using it, either on the woman or on him, Jack let go of the strangler and clutched the pistol with both his hands and pushed it away from the woman. The first man loosened his grip on the woman's neck, drawn to the other action. She slid to the floor. Jack swiftly twisted around so that the revolver, still clutched in the third man's hands, was brought between them and the strangler. His arms were locked with the third man, their wrists awkwardly entwined so it was difficult to exert any control. All the power was coming from their forearms and elbows. He stamped on the man's foot and suddenly the gun went off and the big man in front of them jolted. His eyes widened and he seemed to freeze. Then he fell back, and Jack could see a rapidly spreading apron of bright red blood gushing from the part of his tunic covering his breastbone. The man crashed to the floor and did not move. The man Jack had been wrestling had paused in shock, but now he wrenched the gun back. Jack looked into his furious eyes.

126

'What have you done?' he said.

He stepped back and raised the gun again, aiming at Jack.

A loud bang. The side of the man's forehead blew away, drenching the walls in blood and gore. Jack ducked and turned to see where the shot had come from, but at that moment two grenades, one thrown through the downstairs window and one into the hallway, exploded simultaneously and threw him to the floor.

Dazed, he did not see another man enter the cottage hallway and look around him. What this man saw was two of his comrades shot dead and another one presumably dead as well, lying across the body of a half-dead woman. Satisfied there was nothing more he could do, and wary of the constant danger around him, he retraced his footsteps and left.

Jack was still insensible when the burning torches hit the thatched roof and erupted in flames. He was unaware of the woman now struggling to extricate herself from under his prostrate body and of the blazing rafters collapsing into the room around him. He didn't hear the frantic whistles of the RIC reinforcements urgently signalling for the men outside to pull away from the cottage and join a skirmish further along the road. Nor did he hear the urgent but soft Irish voices giving each other instructions as they crept into the smoke-filled room from the other corner. And he never felt the two strong arms dragging him across the floor to the back door, picking him up and loading him on to the horse-drawn cart.

Jack knew he would be executed. The IRA were just as single-minded and merciless as the Black and Tans. His gun-happy murderous troop had killed three men and a woman that day and, for all he knew, they may have been innocent civilians. The sergeant had not given them a chance to say. His head hurt like hell, there was blood oozing from a neck wound, his hearing was muffled and his ankle was horribly broken. He was surprised they had not put him out of his misery already.

He could hear voices around him but could not quite make out all the words. Something to do with circumstances and decisions. Body disposal and personnel. As he came round a little more, he tried to sit up. Revolvers clicked and a chair scraped back across stone flooring. He was bodily lifted on to a wooden seat. His ankle was angled abnormally to one side, hugely swollen, throbbing and agonisingly painful.

The red-haired woman in front of him kicked it viciously and then stood on it. Jack yelled out involuntarily. So much for showing defiance.

'How many Tans do ye have billeted at the barracks?'

'Twenty,' he lied.

'No, we counted double that many in the latest raid.'

The woman nodded towards one of the men, who then smashed his fist into Jack's nose. He heard the cracking of bone and felt a deep, crushing pressure across his face and forehead. Blood dribbled over his upper lip.

'How many more are coming?'

'None. We're closing the more remote stations and relocating to bigger towns.' This time the truth.

'How many rifles and how much ammunition do you have there?'

So they were already planning an imminent attack on the barracks itself, Jack realised.

The redhead persisted. Question after question. Cold, controlled, emotional and businesslike. She was obviously the overlord of this little band of rebels.

When they were getting no useful information out of him, they propped his left wrist on to the edge of the table, thumb side upwards, and brought a thick wooden stave down on to the middle of his forearm. Both the radius and ulna bones broke in half and Jack stifled a scream and whimpered. He had been feeling increasingly sorry for these people recently and he had already resigned his commission because of his disgust with the RIC tactics and behaviour. At this particular moment, however, he hated every single one of them and would happily kill them if only he had the chance. It was kill or be killed here. There was no rationale, decency or fairness about any of it. It was circumstantial madness, where genuine personal political views and feelings were irrelevant. It was simply a matter of being in the wrong place at the wrong time.

Jack surprised himself, really. He was by no means a hero. He had always been one to avoid physical violence and to use his wits instead. He had always been one to seek out the pleasures in life, not the pain. Yet despite the punches to his face, his broken nose, the loss of several fingernails, his mangled arm and repeated blows to his fractured tibia and fibula, he had divulged nothing much of great importance. Truth be told, there was not very much he knew anyway. He was just a foot soldier. If there was anything he could have told them that would have ended his torture, he almost certainly would have told them straight away.

The group of rebels holding him deliberately avoided using any of their own names in front of him. He felt he would not live long enough to pass them on anyway, but it was part of their established routine practice and discipline. Jack just hoped this would be over quickly.

Unbeknown to Jack, the flame-haired woman was Kaitlin Byrne, a high-ranking member of the Cumann na mBan.

It was her own sister, Ellen, whom Jack had saved from being strangled. Nevertheless, as far as she was concerned, the man was a Black and Tan and no mercy could be shown to the likes of him. Three young boys were lying dead up the road.

'Do it downstairs in the cellar,' she instructed two of the men. 'And clean up afterwards.'

As they lifted Jack up by his armpits and dragged him away from the table, the three of them staggered slightly and accidentally barged into the sideboard against the wall, knocking a framed photograph from its middle shelf. It lay on the flagstone floor in front of Jack, and as he was already doubled over as a result of his manhandling, he looked straight down at it. The glass had broken, but a face that seemed vaguely familiar stared back at him. He felt himself being roughly pulled forward again, his foot screaming in agony beneath him. As he reached the doorway to the cellar, he turned his head towards the woman and said, 'Tadgh O'Suilleabhain! That's Tadgh O'Suilleabhain. Also known as Sham. Tell me it isn't?'

The men supporting him paused and looked back at her too.

She was momentarily speechless. She looked at the others in surprise.

'How do you know him?' she demanded, wondering what intelligence the RIC could possibly have on Tadgh.

*

Six years ago, 750 miles to the south-east, across the Irish Sea and the English channel, Tadgh O'Suilleabhain sat under the sagging canvas roof, screwing up his eyes and blinking away the acid tears streaming down his face.

'Mary mother of Jesus,' he cursed to himself. 'I'm going to go blind here and I'm not even going to see meself die.'

He coughed again. Another uncontrollable spasm that burned through his lungs and sent sharp stabs of lancinating pain to his throat.

The German poison gas attack at Loos-en-Gohelle in the Battle of Hulluch that day in April had killed hundreds of men of the 16th Irish Division and disabled thousands more.

Sham was now blindfolded and had been totally dependent on this man from the mining regiment next to him who had forced him to keep his head down where the trench parapets offered no protection from the constant stream of machine-gun bullets coming their way. Picking his route carefully, his guide and saviour had held fast to him and gradually weaved backwards and forwards avoiding the mud-filled shell craters, shredded barbed wire and lifeless bodies littering their path. Finally, carrying him on his back for the last lung-bursting furlong, he had led him to the safety of the casualty clearing station where they now were. Sham could not see but was also struggling to breathe.

'Sit forward a bit and breathe shallow, mate,' said the friendly English voice beside him. 'Hunch up your shoulders and rest your hands on your knees. It's what blokes with asthma and athletes do when they're trying to get their breath back.'

Jack Burnett was no doctor and nor did he aspire to become one, unlike his brother Will, but he'd seen what his comrades in the mines did after an explosion with all the dust and muck they inhaled. It seemed like good advice.

'Thank you, my friend,' rasped the Irishman. 'I'll give it a try.' He pursed his lips and breathed in and out of the little blowhole he created between them.

Jack's injury was trivial in comparison to this poor fellow's. A spicule of metal from an exploded grenade buried in his hamstring. It still hurt like hell though.

'I'm Jack,' he said, partly to take his mind off the discomfort but also because he felt sorry for the soldier sitting beside him.

'Tadgh. Tadgh O'Suilleabhain. People call me Sham.'

'Where are you from?'

'A little place in the west of Ireland called Athenry.' He paused to regain his breath. 'Where the fields are emerald green . . . And where the rills . . . and streams are as clear as crystal . . . and you can see the salmon in the water . . . smiling right back at you.' He had to pause to catch his breath even after just a few words.

Despite that, he was also tempted to add, 'And where our English landlords foist untold wealth upon us, drown us with free drinks and where rich nutritious food is aplenty,' but he thought better of it. He was in no mood or fit state for a fight just now. Besides, he sensed that this English lad sitting next to him was one of the good ones.

'And how are the girls in green, glamorous, fish-rich Athenry?' asked Jack with a grin.

Sham briefly visualised his lovely sister, Mary, and his sweetheart, Ellen, whom he hoped one day to marry. 'You leave our lovely colleens alone, you English chancer,' he gasped. 'They only have eyes for . . . devilishly handsome Irish heroes like myself, so they do.'

Tears streamed down his face beneath his blindfold now and Jack regarded him levelly. There could be nothing worse than severe eye pain and the threat of permanent blindness. The man was obviously in agony but seemed quite stoic and content to sit where he was, patiently waiting his turn to see the medics.

He was thin and gaunt and looked done in. A deep purple patch over his right cheek was particularly interesting to Jack. It looked like three almost identically sized heart-shaped leaves joined together at their apices.

'That's a whacking great bruise on the side of your face you've got there,' he said. 'How did you get that?'

'That? No, that's not a bruise. Thank you for asking, though. Everyone who ever meets me does.'

Jack looked more closely.

'It's a birthmark. My local village doctor calls it a port-wine stain. Though not a single drop of port wine has ever passed me lips in the whole of me feckin' life.'

Jack felt a bit awkward now and was not sure what to say next. As usual, his fallback strategy was an attempt at levity. 'Well, knowing what rogues you Irish all are, you'd better take care to keep out of trouble.'

The Irishman cocked his head up and turned towards Jack as if to be sure not to miss what was coming next.

'Because it wouldn't be too hard to pick you out of an identity parade, would it?'

Sham nodded as if he had heard the same such remark a thousand times before.

'Provided I was guilty and they were able to catch me in the first place,' shot back the reply, before a large, wheezing intake of breath.

'Well, I think it gives you character,' added Jack. 'I was thinking it looks a bit like—'

'A shamrock?'

'That's it!' Jack suddenly pulled a face and slapped his forehead with the palm of his hand. 'That's why you're called Sham?'

'You English know just about enough not to eat yourself, don't ye?'

Jack laughed and even the Irishman next to him managed a wide grin before coughing again and wincing.

These Englishmen were not so bad after all, Sham thought. Not the ones like Jack. Ordinary working men like him with no side to them and none of the avarice, pomposity and arrogance of the ones lording it over them in his home country. They weren't all the same, as his brother thought they were. His younger brother, Paedar, was very different to him. He was headstrong and dedicated to the Republican cause, but naive and impressionable at the same time.

His brother had refused to enlist in the British and Irish Army. But as far as Sham was concerned, it was only this fighting force that stood between Ireland and a common enemy threatening their very civilisation. He could not brook the idea of the Army defending everyone at home, while all they did was sit back and pass resolutions.

Sham's current priority was to survive. He was learning more every day as a soldier in the field and learning it the hard way. How to avoid being seen. How to creep up on the enemy unnoticed. How to kill quietly and efficiently. And what he was experiencing, he reasoned, could well prove useful when he finally made it home, if it turned out his brother's cause was, after all, worth fighting for.

*

Jack craned his neck towards the picture. 'But it is, isn't it?' he said. 'How is it *you* know him?'

Kaitlin was perplexed. Tadgh O'Suilleabhain was meant to be anonymous. He only ever worked undercover. How would the RIC know anything about him? She knew they had to find out. It could affect the security of each and every one of them. She came over to Jack and stood in front of him, her face inches from his own.

'How do you know this man?' she demanded again.

'I served with him in the British Army,' Jack said. 'We fought alongside each other in France against a common enemy. Tadgh was a victim of poison gas, asphyxiated and blinded. I found him and guided him back to the first-aid post for treatment. We sat together and shared stories as we waited our turn to see the medics. We talked about the beloved country of his birth.' He looked up at Kaitlin then and smiled. 'And the feminine charm and allure of the ladies back home.' He paused to let the irony sink in. 'He told me about his sweetheart that he wanted to marry when he returned. He told me about his birthmark and why he was called Sham.'

Kaitlin hesitated. Sham had indeed returned from France and married her sister. So it seemed this man had had a hand in saving both of them.

'Take him downstairs,' she ordered the men. 'But temper your instincts. Get Sham over here. We'll check his story. And if it's true, they can briefly get reacquainted.'

Kaitlin had been working for the cause of a republic, risking her life smuggling weapons, even scuttling a ship to avoid their capture and use by the English, and seizing buildings with the all-female Cumann na mBan. This man may have saved one or two Irish lives, but he was still English, one of the bastards who had ruthlessly stolen their land from them and stubbornly refused to share it or support their enslaved workforce, either financially or morally, ever since, even in times of enduring poverty and famine. She'd been making them pay again and again and it wasn't over yet. She could not afford to show weakness now.

23

Hammersmith Hospital, White City, London, February 1922

Dr Forrester had ploughed through a busy operating list and Will, despite being given the onerous task of anaesthetising the patients, had still been able to assist and learn a few more surgical techniques and tricks. Among other procedures they had performed, it was a wonder to Will how his mentor had managed to accurately locate and remove a man's kidney stone via the perineal route, and he marvelled at the results of his decision to postpone an appendicectomy on an elderly woman too ill to be operated on in the acute stage of the illness. He had waited for the fever to subside and the inflammation to resolve naturally and form an abscess. Today they had opened her abdomen and lanced it to evacuate a good quantity of pus and debris before stitching her up again. By the time the operating list was finished and they had returned to the ward, they had found her sitting up in bed with all her vital signs stable and had been able to reassure her that she should now make a full recovery. Once again, the experienced man's cautious medical policy of 'watchful waiting' had proved superior to the approach taken by so many of his surgical colleagues, which generally seemed to be, 'If in doubt, cut it out.'

Will left Dr Forrester to catch up on some administrative work and as he walked out of the arched front entrance on to Du Cane Road, he suddenly felt quite weary. Studying for his diploma at the Society of Apothecaries, coupled with his work at Queen Mary's and these extra sessions here and at the Military Orthopaedic Hospital with Dr Forrester, was catching up with him. No matter, he thought. It would all be worth it once he had passed the exams, qualifying him as a doctor and allowing him entrance to a teaching hospital where he could learn his specialisation. There was just the small matter of affording all this, but he was too tired to think of that now. Overall, he knew nobody achieved anything without making sacrifices.

Turning left again to find his motorcycle parked just outside the nurses' accommodation block, he saw a stout figure wearing baggy trousers, a dirty white shirt, waistcoat and flat cap standing there admiring it. As Will approached, the man took a last drag on his cigarette, dropped it on the ground and stubbed it out under his boot.

'You're Will Burnett, are ye not?' he said in a strong Irish accent.

'That's me,' answered Will cheerfully. 'How can I help?'

He wondered how this man knew his name. He could not recollect ever having met him before.

'And ye have a brother called Jack, do ye not?'

'Yes, I do . . . How do you know him?' Will now frowned.

'We know him in Ireland full well, Mr Burnett,' the man said rather menacingly. 'As I'm sure you know, he is serving with the Black and Tans. And he is in a spot of trouble, I'd say. The Black and Tans are not exactly flavour of the month over there with my people.'

'Your people?'

'Your brother is currently a guest of the IRA.'

Sweet Jesus, thought Will. All his fears about the dangers Jack might face in Ireland had been realised. Both he and Clara had begged him not to join the RIC, but, true to form, Jack had ignored them.

'He is being held following the murder of several of our compatriots and is seen as a legitimate candidate for, what should we call it . . .? Retribution.'

Will was silent for a moment, taking it all in.

'Retribution?'

'It's a tit-for-tat thing, Mr Burnett. The RIC execute Republicans, Republicans generously reciprocate. It's only what's written in the Good Book, after all. You'll be familiar with the verses yourself, I've no doubt. Leviticus 24:19–22: "If a man injures his neighbour just as he has done, so it should be done to him: fracture for fracture, eye for eye, tooth for tooth, just as he has injured a man, so it should be inflicted on him."'

That's all I need, Will thought, a religious fundamentalist on top of everything else. He had no sympathy for religious bigotry at the best of times.

'It's not personal. Except in some cases, maybe it is.'

Will was incensed by the threat in the man's tone and his apparent sadistic enjoyment of the whole exchange. Was he really serious? Was Jack's life in danger? And if so, why was Will being told this?

'There'll be no prospect of a rescue, by the way. None whatsoever. The RIC think he's dead already. Shot first, they think, and then mortally wounded by a grenade and burned to death in a house fire. A fire that the RIC instigated themselves, by the way.'

The man was loathsome. A patriot, no doubt, but a softly-spoken murderous one at the same time. Will was ready to kill him with his bare hands and, despite his fatigue, almost certainly could have done. But he knew he had to restrain himself. If the man was to be believed, Jack could still be alive and there must be a reason why he was being approached.

'Why are you telling me this? What do you want me to do?'

'Your brother has a broken ankle, broken nose, a fractured arm and a neck wound which has got infected.'

Will tried not to imagine what state Jack might be in at that moment, but he was worried. These were not the kind of injuries usually incurred in a military skirmish.

'How did he sustain those injuries?'

'I have no idea. And it doesn't matter. I'm just the messenger. But I'm told he needs a doctor, and thanks to British occupation and oppression in Ireland, we don't have one at hand. There's also the small matter of security. No one else must know. And I mean no one.'

'You're asking me to go and help him?'

'We are extending a bountiful invitation for you to do that very thing, yes. If you think his miserable life's worth saving, that is.'

'He's my brother. What do you think? So, let me get this right.' Will was still struggling to control his rage.' You want me to patch him up and treat him just so that you can exact your retribution? Are you mad?'

'Mad with desire for a free Irish state, perhaps. But that's a totally sane ambition, I'd say.' He smiled insincerely. 'Look, Mr Burnett. If I had my way, your brother would be dead and buried by now, but it seems serendipity has come to his rescue.'

'Serendipity?'

'The only reason he's still alive and breathing is because he saved the life of one of our men in France in 1916 and then recently rescued a woman from the hands of the Black and Tans. A woman, incidentally, who had become the wife of the man he saved. That's the reason he has been spared so far.'

Will stared at the man. It was quite unbelievable, but then not at all if you knew Jack.

'Quite a story, isn't it? It seems he's got . . . well, the luck of the Irish.'

Will couldn't disagree.

'And then again you'd probably say it sounds like he's earned it. Ecclesiastes 9:11: "Under the Sun the race is not to the swift, nor the battle to the strong, nor bread to the wise, nor riches to the intelligent, nor favour to those with knowledge, but time and chance happen to them all." Time and chance, Mr Burnett. Time and chance.'

Christ almighty! Will thought. He was getting a sermon from a man who would take another's life as soon as look at him. Yet it sounded as if Jack's life might still be spared.

'You have a week. One week and there'll be no extension of the deadline.' He passed over a slip of paper. 'Here is an address where you will be met and escorted. You tell them you're looking for a man with a jackhammer for sale. Good day to ye.'

'Wait.'

'What?'

'My wife is a nurse who specialises in the treatment of sepsis. The sterilisation of wounds. If she were to come with me . . .'

But he realised it was foolish as soon as he said it. Putting Grace in harm's way was the last thing he wanted.

'I don't have the authority to sanction that. But I'll pass it on. If you bring her with you, I can't guarantee her safety any more than I can yours.'

The Irishman took a cigarette from his pocket and lit it. 'I can guarantee you one thing, however. We're likely to treat your woman with a hell of a lot more respect than the RIC treat ours.'

He spat on the pavement, turned on his heels and walked away.

24

Putney, London, February 1922

After the ambush by the Irishman at Hammersmith Hospital, Will and Grace had been arguing long into the night and, despite the attendant danger and the logistics of an unlikely rescue for Jack, Will would not be persuaded against the journey to County Galway. And though he'd considered the idea of Grace's help, because of her specialisation, he couldn't comprehend putting her in such danger.

Perhaps he shouldn't have said anything at all and just left a note – because now that she couldn't persuade him not to go, she kept insisting she come with him.

'That's utter madness,' he said. 'He's my responsibility. I have no idea if this is a trap or if I'll become some kind of bargaining chip or hostage. But I can't just abandon him, Grace, you know I can't. You know I wouldn't be able to live with myself. But there's no point whatsoever in you taking risks as well.'

'Will! Think about it. I know Jack joined the Black and Tans. I know their reputation and how hated they are. But what possible benefit would there be in setting a trap for you?' Grace's normally calm face was pinched, brows lowered over green eyes, dark circles beneath.

'I don't know. By threatening me, they might have more leverage over him in some way. For interrogation, maybe.'

'They'll have even more leverage if you're physically there in front of him! But that doesn't make sense. If they intended to harm you, they could do that here. You. Us. Our family. Why go to all the trouble? If Jack's life is in danger, we just can't sit back and ignore it. And I won't let you go on your own.' She crossed her arms in front of her soft, winter robe.

'You've got the children to think of!'

'*We* have the children to think of! Look. If they know where you work, then they'll also know where we live, so we have to resolve this one way or another. And we have a better chance of doing that together.'

'But we can't leave Daniel and Emily.' Will touched a hand to the stubble on his face, found that it was shaking.

'Jenny and Reggie love taking care of them. And Daniel and Emily will treasure more time with little Doris. She's my very best friend and I trust her.'

Grace saw that Will did not look convinced. He was just as hopelessly devoted to the children as her and reluctant to leave them at the best of times. But Grace was adamant, and Will knew when he was beaten. He did not like the idea at all, but they had been in many precarious scrapes together before, and besides that, he knew he could do with a spare driver, mechanic and navigator. Not to mention his wife's expertise if they found Jack severely wounded.

'Will,' whispered Grace as they started to calm down. She gently stroked his hair. 'You also have to face the possibility that this may not have a happy ending. You remember how we've talked about the fact you can't save everyone? Not the sickest in hospital, nor the worst injured on the battlefield, nor people like your brother caught up in a vicious civil war.'

Will moved his head away from her hand. He was exhausted, but the pillow felt lumpy all of a sudden, the blanket too thin.

'We should try to get some sleep,' he said.

Grace sighed, but moved to her side of the bed. With the light off, their hands found each other's again under the covers.

Once they had made their excuses to their employers (no one wanted to see them at work with florid symptoms of rubella, albeit imaginary ones), and kissed the children goodbye at Jenny's, they had driven to Chiswick to say goodbye and to tap into Clara's current knowledge of the situation in Ireland. Grace wanted to talk to Fitz about what they were letting themselves in for as well, since he was always so up to date with current affairs and politics, but she didn't want to worry her little brother. They knew Clara's general knowledge was extensive and that she was an avid reader of the *Daily Mirror* and *The Times*. She read both newspapers from cover to cover most days, and they thought a more extensive background would be useful.

As Will took Kitty aside to give her a watered-down explanation of their hastily arranged trip, Clara informed Grace about the considerable risks they were facing. Her two nephews, her 'boys' as she liked to call them, had been in trouble before and almost certainly would be again. But this was different. Clara had enormous respect for Grace, for her courage, her fortitude and her intelligence, and she knew in her heart that by accompanying Will on their assignment, she would enhance its chances of success. Clara herself was terribly torn between the needs of Emily and Daniel and the more pressing ones of Jack. Totally conflicted, she had had to accept Grace's decision and was at least a little happier to know that Grace would be a calming influence on Will's occasional violent temper and lack of emotional control.

'Well, don't worry about the children,' she finally said, giving Grace a big hug. 'You know they will be fine and dandy between Jenny and Reggie and the two of us. Just come back safe. All three of you.'

25

On the road to Athenry, Ireland, February 1922

Sharing the riding on the speedy Brough, Will and Grace had stopped only once on the road to Holyhead, and slept the sleep of the dead on the ferry to Dublin. On that long 220-mile journey, they'd had plenty of time to ruminate on Clara's imparted wisdom. She had talked about the potato blight in 1846 and the Great Hunger that followed. She had spoken about Parnell's moderate Nationalist movement and how Gladstone had supported Irish Home Rule and split the Liberal party as a result. She had told them that the British parliament had passed laws during the last forty years enabling many tenant farmers to purchase their own land and lowered rents for many others. But it had not been enough, and now there was again great agrarian unrest and outright rebellion against landlord oppression and British occupation.

Clara had explained that it had not helped that the Liberals had promised Home Rule for the Irish back in 1914 only for that promise to be shelved when war broke out and then abandoned by Lloyd George thereafter.

The Easter uprising of 1916 had been so brutally suppressed that the Nationalist outcry for independence had been hugely galvanised, and the movement now seemed unstoppable.

Will had been risking his life as a stretcher-bearer on the Somme during this time and knew nothing about the Irish problem. It had simply passed him by. There and at Passchendaele, the English and Irish had been brothers in arms.

'Now, listen,' Clara had said. 'When Home Rule failed to be introduced in 1918, Sinn Féin won a majority of Irish seats in the December General Election. Its MPs refused to come to Westminster and instead they sat in the first Dáil parliament in Dublin and a declaration of independence was issued. Westminster did not recognise it. That's where we are now. In an Anglo-Irish war fought between the Crown's forces and the IRA. You'll be going into the teeth of it and that's why I'm so very worried about you.'

Will and Grace had gratefully taken all this in and assimilated it on the journey. Will knew that Jack being Jack would never have bothered to find out about any of it before he had enrolled and would have stumbled into danger, as usual, with his eyes wide shut.

Will had woken up halfway across the Irish Sea and snuggled deeper under the blanket, wrapping his arms tightly around Grace.

It had been bitterly cold when they had arrived, but at least it was dry, with little sign of rain. Stopping only to refill the petrol tank, they had left South Quay where the ferry had docked and motored west through Kinnegad, Kilbeggan, Athlone and Cappataggle. A thin frost lay in the shadow of the trees and hedgerows where the pale sun had failed to penetrate, but at least there was no surface ice over the puddles on the road and even at speed the motorbike cornered safely.

They had made the seat of the sidecar as comfortable as they could, but the medical equipment by their sides and at their feet still made it cramped and awkward. Most of the road surfaces were made up of undressed and unrolled water-bound macadam without the use of tar as a sealant, and for the last 90 miles or so, many of the roads were no more than dirt tracks and country lanes. Will was grateful now that Grace had insisted on coming with him. In truth, she was a better and more experienced driver than him and had twice had to tinker with the engine and fuel pipe to get them restarted. He would never have got this far without her. Now, aching and exhausted, they were just a few miles from Athenry. Their necks, shoulders and lower backs were stiff and painful and so, despite the apprehension about what they were getting themselves into, they were pleased to be nearing their rendezvous.

When they finally pulled up outside the address they had been given, an unprepossessing general store in Church Street, they dismounted and stretched out their weary limbs. Will spied a pair of men at each end of the street in front of and behind them. They could not have looked more conspicuous if they tried.

'It's fine, Will,' Grace whispered. 'It's to be expected. I don't think it's to threaten us. More likely it's to protect themselves. I suppose they need to know we're on our own.'

'You can say that again,' said Will, going inside.

An elderly man with a shock of thick white hair and wearing a well-worn, stained apron welcomed them from behind the counter.

'Top of the morning to yer,' he said cheerfully, 'and what can I be getting ye this fine day?'

On the wall above him, a wooden sign spelt out an old Irish saying: 'What butter and whiskey won't cure, there is no cure for.'

Will took a slip of paper from the inside pocket of his jacket and handed it to the shopkeeper. 'I'm looking for a man with a jackhammer for sale. I'm told I can find him at this address.'

The old man regarded them warily, examined the note and glanced up and down the street outside.

'See the alleyway where those two fine men along there are loafing about?' he said. Will nodded. 'Take your motorcycle, turn in there and drive down to the cottage at the end.' As Grace and Will turned to leave, he added, 'People can pay an awful lot for jackhammers these days, you know. I can only hope the price you've agreed to pay won't be too much.'

Will and Grace looked at each other, puzzled.

Grace paused, then returned to the counter and took out her purse. 'I'd like a pound of Tub-o-Gold butter and a bottle of Jameson's whisky while I'm here, please.'

The man nodded and smiled as he put the items in a bag. Then he looked at Will.

'A man's got to do what a man's got to do. Women must do what he can't.'

'Too right,' said Grace. Then she took Will by the arm and led him out of the store.

26

Tipperary, Ireland, February 1922

Will switched off the ignition and swung his legs over the saddle to dismount. Grace clambered out of the mud-splattered sidecar as the hot Brough engine quietly ticked as it cooled. The door of the cottage opened and a tall, heavily built man stepped out from under the porch into the light. Will had seen birthmarks before; strawberry birthmarks which were common in newborn babies and which invariably regressed within the first year of life, blue-grey naevi that took years longer to fade, and café-au-lait patches which — although less obvious — could sometimes be multiple and signify a condition of the nervous system called neurofibromatosis. But this man had the most extensive example of a port-wine stain he had ever seen. It seemed to wrap itself around half his face, from his ear and hairline across to the midline so that his eyelid on one side and half of his nose and lips and neck appeared daubed in purple ink.

'How was your journey?' the man asked.

'Long. Long and bumpy,' answered Will. 'Where's Jack?'

Tadgh O'Suilleabhain could sense Will's impatience and understood that this was no time for small talk.

'I'm Sham,' he said.

'I'm Will. This is Grace.'

'I'm pleased to meet you and glad you came. Follow me.'
He took them through the cottage and down into a cool, damp,
dimly lit cellar. Will knew there could be no escape from here
and wondered if coming to Ireland had been a terrible mistake.
But what he saw next encouraged him. In the far corner, Jack
sat propped up in a bed looking pale and thin, but soon
showed he had lost none of his usual swagger or bravado.

'Will! Welcome to the party. Glad the wife could make it
too. Let's all have some Bushmills and celebrate.'

Will was relieved to find him alive and pleased to hear that
his laconic sense of humour was still intact. He wasn't at
death's door just yet.

'Shut up, Jack. Be serious for a minute, would you? You're
lucky to be alive, by all accounts. How the hell are you?'

'I'm just grand, as they say in these parts. Apart from the
fever I keep getting, my broken nose, my septic neck, my useless
arm and my busted ankle. Otherwise, I couldn't be better.'

Will could immediately see the problem with his brother's
neck and nose and pulled aside his blanket to inspect the rest
of him.

'Jesus! The bastards!' He turned towards the Irishman with
balled fists.

Grace grabbed him and held him back. 'Will! Stop!'

'Leave him alone, Will,' croaked Jack, 'that man saved my
life. And put his own at risk by doing so. It's a long story, but
we're old friends. I wouldn't be alive if it weren't for him.'

Will looked at the man with the record-beating birthmark
and slowly relaxed.

Tadgh nodded towards him. It was true that when he had
returned from Flanders he had found his brother and compatriots fighting *alongside* the Germans against the British. It was a
world upside down. His brother Paedar's convictions soon

151

influenced Sham, for the very fact that his brother was a person who did not relish taking part in shoot-outs or killing. He believed so strongly in the cause that he would go in with fists, or stakes of wood fencing when the distribution of weapons was inadequate. And all of this with a young family. Sham partly got involved to protect him, but soon rose up the rebel ranks.

'Get the bags from the Brough, Will,' said Grace, gently pushing him away. 'I'll make a start while you're doing that. And compose yourself. I need you to be objective and focused. Let's patch Jack up and get him out of here.'

They worked for an hour or two on their patient, starting with the neck wound which had become infected and was suppurating. Reactive lymph glands struggling to contain the infection were visibly prominent around his carotid artery, above his clavicle behind his ear and at the back of his head. The episodic release of pus into Jack's circulation had been causing an undulating fever and sapping his strength.

While Grace kept Jack semi-conscious with chloroform, Will drained a large abscess, debrided a good amount of dead macerated flesh and removed a thick sliver of a grenade casing from the wound. Then they swapped places so that Grace could thoroughly clean everything and sterilise the open crater, which they decided was not amenable to stitching but would be best left to heal naturally from the sides and below. There was no room for error as leaving any pockets of infection in such a central location could easily lead to fatal blood poisoning.

Using another chloroform-soaked swab over Jack's mouth and broken nose, they manipulated and reset the bones of the fractured limbs and applied plaster of Paris casts on both to stabilise them. It was miraculous what this calcium sulphate, also known as gypsum, could do, thought Grace, and Jack was certainly going to need good immobilisation if he was really going to be travelling back to London on his brother's thoroughbred boneshaker parked outside.

Finally, with Jack still insensible under the influence of the sweet-smelling, colourless anaesthetic, Will inserted the two prongs of the Spencer Wells forceps into his nostrils and in one swift action relocated the nasal septum to its rightful position in the centre of his face. Jack groaned but mercifully would not remember anything about it once he came round.

Less than twenty-four hours later, Jack's fever had abated and his appetite had returned. He remained weak, but was able to dress in some old clothes Sham had lent him and although they were several sizes too large and hung off him like a marquee, he was slowly regaining his customary joie de vivre and was clearly keen to see the back of the place. While Will and Grace had caught up on some sleep upstairs, the two men chatted away, cementing their unique and peculiar friendship, and generally put the world to rights. But Sham was well aware of the danger they were all in and which was increasing with every passing minute. Jack was still a legitimate target for vengeful locals.

'If ye feel strong enough now, Jack, ye really should be going. I hate to be inhospitable and all. Maybe in another few years you could come over again when we won't have to hide you away.'

Jack toasted his friend and threw a glass of Jameson's down his throat. He coughed but hoped it would help to ease the pain in his face and neck. Will and Grace joined them and they collected up their few belongings, went upstairs and out into the front yard.

'I can't thank you enough, Sham,' Jack said, gripping the man by the shoulders. 'I owe you my life.'

'And I owe you mine, remember? More importantly, Ellen's, too. I'd say we were evens.'

'If I hadn't seen that photograph . . .'

'And if you'd left me on the battlefield in France . . .'

'What are the chances?'

'I know. Maybe there is a God after all.'

'I doubt it,' interrupted Will. 'But if there is, I'm sure he'd want us to get the hell out of here.'

'He's right,' added Sham. 'Your motorcycle might be covered in mud and dirt, but in these parts it still sticks out like a sore thumb. Turn left at the end of the lane and don't stop till you get to Dublin.'

'Now are you sure you'll be all right?' Will asked Grace. 'You could drive the bike and I can take the train in your place, if you prefer?'

'No, it's fine,' she replied. 'Sham's got us this far. I'm in safe hands.'

'All right. Take care, my love. We'll see the two of you to the station and then peel off and meet you at the Coast Lines quayside.'

Jack shook Sham firmly by the hand.

'In the next world, perhaps.'

'Who knows? And when you're feeling better, take a visit to O'Neill's Bar in Sheppard Street in London. Ask for Liam. Tell him I sent yer. He'll maybe find you a job better suited to your talents.' Sham winked.

Will kick-started the Brough into life and revved up. With Grace's help, Jack eased himself and his two plastered limbs into the sidecar.

'Thank you, sweetheart,' he said to her. 'You're the best.' Then, turning one last time to Sham, he added, 'Give my best to Ellen.'

'To be sure. She'll be forever grateful for what you did.' He walked with Grace over to the horse-drawn cart, waving at Jack. 'Now get out of here. And Godspeed.'

Not God again, thought Will, as he gingerly moved off.

Behind an upstairs window of the cottage, a curtain twitched. Kaitlin Byrne watched the motorcycle jolt along the lane towards the main road and the girl jump into the cart driven by Sham and set off. Begrudgingly, she had come to rather admire the young woman. She had conducted herself admirably, showing not a trace of fear or anxiety, and her professional nursing skills were complemented by an ability to keep the men calm and focused. They could do with more women like that in the Cumann na mBan. Nevertheless, being complicit in allowing a murderous Black and Tan to escape sat heavy on her heart. It was out of character for her. And at odds with her organisation's directive. By rights, that man should be dead. But there had been the issue of family solidarity to be considered. Ellen and Sham would never have forgiven her if she had acted differently. Maybe she was losing her grip. Maybe she was losing her taste for the struggle. She cursed silently. To disprove it, she would simply redouble her efforts to demonstrate her deadly resolve in the forthcoming months.

PART TWO

27

London Underground, April 1923

Amy Tustin-Pennington rushed down the stairs and under the 'Bakerloo Tube' sign, clutching the clue in her gold goatskin glove. As the train pulled noisily on to the platform, she pressed her hand to her matching gold turban, holding it in place as people surged forward. She hooked her elbow inside that of her short friend, Diana Nicholas. She spotted their reflections in the train window: their fashionable drop-waist dresses — hers a deep blue velvet with delicately embroidered collar, pockets, cuffs and a bar around the bottom of the skirt; Diana's a light green with blue polka dots and trimmed in white lace, like something a doll would wear.

And Diana was a little doll. Amy was grateful that she and her rather progressive mother let Amy and other girls stay in their large terrace in the centre of London. Amy was even thinking about getting a job, trying to make the move permanent, though she was sure her parents and brothers would have difficulty with the idea. Diana's mother was technically a married woman, but there was some scandal with her husband. He was off with a lover in Europe, or something. Amy wasn't sure and didn't care that much at all, but she knew her own family were proud and careful of their good name. And really, as she was almost twenty-eight, they thought she should be married by now.

'All right, push,' Amy said, elbowing with Diana through the afternoon peak-hour rush on to the train.

'How are we supposed to find the next clue with all these people in the way?' Diana despaired. The tiny twenty-year-old was swamped by men in dark suits and hats.

'Well, we're on the right carriage. Maybe it *is* one of these men,' she said, glancing up into the eyes of a blue-eyed young man beside her. He looked flustered and tipped his hat politely. Another man looming over Diana, older and fustier, asked them if he could be of service. Diana glanced at Amy, who was holding back a giggle. She shrugged.

'Ah, well, sir,' Diana said, 'we're on a treasure hunt, see?' She held up the previous clue, which had been baked into a loaf of bread and still had crumbs on it. It said the name of the station, the train time and the carriage. Already today they'd ridden buses, bicycles and walked several blocks. Amy was glad for both the fashion for small-heeled shoes and the flask of gin tucked into her dress pocket, but mainly the sense of fun and adventure spurred them forward. And gathering stories they'd be able to talk and laugh about later with the group.

'I see,' he said. 'This seems to be a riddle: *An open-and-shut case or are you falling between two stools.*' He stroked his chin. 'Hm, yes, well, this could mean the doors, or it could mean the gaps between the seats.'

'Let's check there,' Diana said. But they couldn't move until the next stop. When the doors opened and people got off, the man followed them over to the seats lining one side of the train. Other passengers made 'tsking' and 'Well, I never' noises, unimpressed by the folly.

Amy saw Diana then hesitate, as the seats all had people in them. But if they hesitated, they might be beaten. The other team were probably right behind, with their own, also possibly crumb-laden, clue – or they may be on the same train, in a different carriage. The treasure hunts usually led different people in slightly different, but aligned, directions.

Amy took the initiative and dove forward, saying 'Excuse me' and plunging her hand between the cushions. One woman swatted her with a rolled-up newspaper. Diana laughed. The man looked on, amused, peeking at Amy's behind as she bent over.

'Got it!' She pulled out an envelope as gold as her turban. 'This calls for a celebration.' She took out her flask and offered it to the man, who looked tempted, but he shook his head.

'I'm abstaining,' he said.

'Well, goodbye then,' Amy said, grabbing Diana again and leaping off the train at the next stop.

At the end of the day, when they finally stumbled, exhausted, into their friend Eleanor's garden, they found they weren't the first to get back at all. They may have indeed been the last. Eleanor, the inventor of the game and planter of clues, sipped champagne and narrowed her eyes at Amy.

'Darling, you look frightful,' she said.

'Oh dear,' Amy said, hands going to her face.

'Here,' Diana said, running a finger under each of Amy's eyes, where the make-up had pooled.

Eleanor had the place to herself, her father on assignment in India and her mother looking after an ailing relative. She had the maids running this way and that with morsels of food and trayfuls of champagne and cocktails, and lighting outdoor lamps.

Amy sat on a blanket on the lawn, watching her friends. The sun was beginning to go down. She thought about the quiet of home, the succession of marriage proposals she'd rejected, the many possible lives. She was most happy among these people, as bright and bubbly as the champagne they drank like water. Life was *fun*. Nothing else mattered but that.

Across the lawn, she saw a new figure in the group. New, but familiar. He was a film star, she was sure of it. American. Dark, slicked-back hair, large brown eyes, sharp cheekbones. Slim but fit. He saw her looking, as he continued his conversation. Their eyes remained on each other.

No, she wouldn't want to be anywhere else.

28

Chiswick, London, June 1923

Robbie took off his flat cap before opening the door, like a man about to knock and deliver news of a death. It felt as grave as that — losing his job. In this economic climate. And with Jack living with them, Kitty — a growing thirteen-year-old — and his sister, who was becoming a little too thin. It felt terrible that she would be the only one supporting them, for the moment.

They'd been too kind to him at the docks, anyway. Slowly moved him to a paper-shuffling job, away from the noise. And he did all right for a while, grateful for the change. But then sitting in a chair all day — his muscles ached worse than ever, his head ached, and he started to lose and misplace important invoices, files. A girl would come in once a week and basically tidy up all the work he was supposed to have done. She let him get away with it for a long time. But then her husband got sick, couldn't work himself. Presumably she asked for more hours. And the only hours they had to give were Robbie's.

He pushed open the door. No one was home. Clara teaching, Kitty at school, Jack God knows where — hopefully finding permanent work himself, but likely also gadding about. It had taken Jack a while to fully recover from the injuries he sustained in Ireland, but he'd hobble out on his healing ankle day and night and Robbie suspected he'd be close to burning through the money he brought home. He'd done only odd jobs and short contracts since returning. Both of Robbie's sons were alien to him at times, but in very different ways. Will had a similar porousness to Robbie, yes, but he pushed past it — only let it spill over in moments. He was smart, driven. His brother had called him 'Brainbox' as a kid. Jack, on the other hand, was able to calmly embrace whatever was unfolding before him, and if knocked down, stand up and take some more. And then make a joke about it. He was tough, and he enjoyed life like no one else Robbie knew. Well, Evie had been a bit like that. Jack's cheeky smile reminded Robbie of his beloved, departed wife. It almost made it a little hard to have his son around, though he knew it was terrible to think that way, especially after all these years and all this time apart.

He sat silently at the old, scratched dining table. He should really get out his tools and buff it up, give it a new polish. Do something useful.

Even that thought made him tired.

He sat there staring at the wall until Clara and Kitty walked in. He noticed the wrinkles on his dear sister's face more and more these days. He hardly looked in the mirror himself, preferring to see himself ageing through her visage. As she said, 'Home early, Rob?' the lines intensified between her brows.

'I've been let go, Clara,' he said. He tried to hold his voice steady.

He saw her shoulders drop, her worry, before she caught herself. 'Oh . . . never mind. We'll get by.'

'I can get a job!' Kitty exclaimed.

'You'll do no such thing,' Robbie said firmly. 'You're a child.'

'Only just,' she said, twirling back and forth with the endless energy of youth.

'Your dad's right, Kitty,' Clara said. 'You stay in school a couple more years and learn as much as you can.'

'*Si*,' Kitty said. 'You'll get a new job, won't you, Daddy?'

Robbie and Clara shared a look.

'Of course.'

Clara said, 'Kitty, can you go and read or play before dinner? I want to talk to your dad.'

Kitty nodded reluctantly, then skipped off.

'I'm so sorry, Clara,' Robbie said.

'Nonsense.' She rubbed his shoulder. 'I've got work, and Jack will get something soon.'

Robbie's emotions moved from a dizzying, sinking feeling to a smoothed-over numbness. He stared forward again. He was as flat and featureless as the kitchen wall.

Clara continued rubbing his back. She tried not to despair. She and Kitty had got by before, without the men. Yes, expenses were higher now. But they'd make it work. Jack would probably move out once he secured a permanent position, but that was all right. He was a grown man.

Long ago, she had picked up forms for the war pension, but as Robbie had not claimed on discharge, she knew it would be a lengthy process, including a medical assessment arranged by the Pension Issue Office. She knew that Robbie would not want to go through such an examination. But if they got desperate, she would gently ask her brother if he would.

She also felt terrible because the finances weren't the only thing on her mind. The thought of Robbie, wraithlike, floating up and down the halls of the empty house all day worried her. Sitting and smoking and staring at walls. Without distraction, all the memories and looping thoughts might flood in. She didn't know how to help. She thought she should ask Will, as a medical professional, but then — it was his father. She didn't want to worry him. He was working and studying and being a father himself. She would have to figure this out on her own.

Jack sat at a table at The Diamond, sipping Irish whisky, watching women on the dance floor and waiting for the band to start up again. After devoting so much of his young life to destruction and death, to fighting, Jack had an overspill of desire for living large – for loving and laughing and drinking until dawn. He had to catch up properly on being young. Entering some of these London clubs was like leaving the land's surface to dive underwater – into a deep, dark, velvety jazz hum, an underwater palace full of exotic creatures only found in such environments. And the later in the night – or rather, earlier in the morning – the stranger and more otherworldly the environment and clientele. Jack found it all fascinating. Dreamy. He never knew there were so many varieties of human being. And alcohol. And other substances. By day, many of these people must look completely different. Certainly the men who wore eyeliner and sometimes even pearls. The young girls who dressed in silky slips that showed their nipples. The people of all different colours, from different classes, who mixed here, equal in the act of letting go.

These clubs were the result of the 1921 Licensing Act, where revellers were allowed to keep drinking as long as they had something to eat. Jack looked down now at the half-hearted plate of pickles and cold meats in front of him. He probably should eat it, as there wasn't much at home. He sipped his champagne and rubbed the scar on his neck with the wrist that still had slight angulation after his arm being broken. He was aware of the dwindling coins in his pocket.

Mrs Taylor, the proprietress, walked past his table, past the vine-circled columns in front of the dance floor — on her way out somewhere all wrapped up in her furs. Possibly to her other club down the street, the one that was all geometric lines and gold suns. He lifted his hand, but she was too fast. He would try to pull her aside on her way back, if he wasn't too intoxicated. Some people he'd met last night had told him her legendary story — once a humble cook and washerwoman to a London family, a position she took up after the death of her middle-class husband, she received an unexpected inheritance and put it all into her club, which was so successful she opened another. She planned to pay for her daughters' education. The police frequently harassed her clubs, ensuring adherence to strict codes. She'd twice been arrested so far, once spending six months in Holloway while her daughter took over the running of the clubs. Jack had seen this daughter too — a gamine woman who always wore trousers.

He would like to talk to Mrs Taylor, because she made him realise someone from his background could have a place in all this. Make some money, live in this night-time underwater world all the time, and perhaps become as successful as her.

Breaking through the sound of piano rolls and saxophone came a voice: 'Are you Jack Burnett?' In front of Jack was a slim, pretty woman in black and pink lace, carrying an over-sized pink feather.

'Why, yes,' he said, standing. 'I'm sorry, I don't believe we've met?'

'No, but it was only a matter of time. I'm Grace's sister, Amy.' She smiled. She indicated to a shorter, younger woman behind her. 'And this is my Diana.'

Very odd use of the word 'my', Jack thought. He wouldn't mind that Diana being his, though. She had a shy, sweet look, but she barely glanced at him, in thrall to her friend, seemingly waiting for her next instruction.

'I recognised you from photographs.' Amy sat down without invitation, and Diana followed suit. 'We'll just stay a moment,' she said. She ran the feather across her lips. 'You look better in person.'

Intrigued, and a little confused, he asked, 'Do you go out often to Wardour Street?'

'Oh, yes, all the time, and this joint the most — it's the classiest,' she said. 'I hear you're just back? You've a lot to catch up on.' He noted she was speaking rather fast, now twitching the feather, and her eyes were glassy.

He tilted his head at her. 'I know we've just met, but are you quite drunk, sweetheart?'

'Oh, positively ossified, baby. A little gowed-up, too. Would you care for some?'

He wasn't familiar with all the party slang yet, but he was pretty sure she was asking him if he wanted drugs. Why not? he thought. Wouldn't be the first time.

He nodded and she took a long chain from around her neck that had a little vial on the end of it. She sipped her champagne and peered around, keeping a lookout, as he unscrewed the cap to find a perfect little spoon inside. He scooped up the powder and expertly held his other nostril closed as he inhaled. The effect was instant — euphoric. The rhythm of the music entered his blood, and the faces of the two women were so full of life and beauty.

Diana was peering at him shyly from under a sculpted brow.

'Dance!' Amy declared, wrenching her companions up. It was not a question. Jack again thought Why not? And let himself be led.

29

Chiswick, London, June 1923

Jack woke with the light streaming in the window, having no idea what time it was. The house was quiet. His dad had erected a modesty screen between Jack's army-style cot and his bed but had given Jack the best spot by the window. It did mean, though, that Jack had to creep by his father when he came in late at night. He often glanced over and saw the gleam of his open eyes in the dark, no matter what time, and Robbie would sometimes grunt 'evening' before rolling over to settle in another position.

Jack stretched out the stiffness of old injuries, scratched his bristly cheek. The sun was a bit too bright and his head throbbed. His stomach growled.

He walked downstairs to find his father in the old worn-out armchair he spent hours in, staring at the wall. His lips were moving.

'Morning,' Jack said.

His father's head snapped towards him, eyes coming into focus. 'Oh, hello, Jack.'

'Having a good time with your friends there?'

Robbie frowned.

Jack couldn't help but make light. He wanted his dad to snap out of it. Jack had seen more war than him, pulled dead bodies out of the ground, lost people, been held hostage. Surely his dad wouldn't stay like this forever?

'Is there anything to eat?'

Robbie blinked. Jack thought he looked thinner than ever since he'd lost his job. It wasn't a sacrifice, him not eating, he just didn't seem to have much interest in food.

But Jack couldn't have his dear sister Kitty looking like that. He had to secure permanent work.

And he wasn't sure how much longer he could stand living here, either. He longed for his own flat, somewhere near the clubs. He'd work and then party on, inviting people back. One day he'd take a pretty wife and come home to a full English. Then she'd go out and shop and let him sleep.

He rustled through the kitchen, found a couple of potatoes to cut up and fry. He'd share them with his dad. He hoped Clara didn't have plans for the potatoes for dinner.

He put the kettle on the stove and scooped three generous spoonfuls of black tea into a teapot. One each and one for the pot. He wished there was a bit of rum around to spruce it up. He slid a tin out of his pocket, extracted one of the pre-rolled cigarettes and placed it between his lips. He'd light up before pouring the hot water into the teapot, and then enjoy the mix of scents.

In the living room, Robbie was starting to come back to himself. He could smell the potatoes frying, hear Jack humming as he worked. He pushed himself up out of the chair, his bones creaking, and went into the kitchen to sit at the little dining table.

'You want some, Dad?' Jack grinned.

'If there's enough,' he said.

Jack plated up and poured him a cup of strong, black tea.

Robbie glanced at his son's face — he looked tired, and a bit rough, but sunny as usual. He was looking a little older than his years, but so did every man who'd been to war.

Jack sat across from Robbie, pinched out his cigarette and stuck it behind his ear, then began eating with gusto.

Jack's plate was clean by the time Robbie had eaten just a couple of slivers of potato.

'You can have some of mine,' he said to his son.

'Share it with your friends,' Jack said haughtily, not sick of his own joke.

Robbie had more energy now. 'I did not bring you up to be cruel,' he said firmly.

For a moment, Jack's face returned to that of a chastised child. Then he leaned back, retrieved and lit his cigarette. 'It's just a joke, Dad.' Jack stood up and put his plate in the sink. 'I'm having a shave and then I'm going out,' he said.

Robbie was relieved he'd have the house to himself again.

Mrs Josephine Taylor entered her club from the stairs behind the bar. She'd slept well. She wore earmuffs and had had all the cracks in her bedroom blocked off so it was harder for the noise to get through. There was always a murmur, still, and she liked it. It was a happier sound than the crying and clanking of Holloway.

The bar, tables and dance floor were quiet and spotless, the staff having cleaned before leaving for the night. The sweet smell of liquor remained, and a permeation of smoke. Sun came through the windows high up in the walls near the ceiling on one side, highlighting the faux-classical mosaics. The club was like a Grecian bathhouse at this time of the day, dappled light on the vines and columns. Adding to the effect was the trickling of water from the powder rooms.

Wait a minute. She swept her layers of scarves back and powered to the bathrooms, her footsteps echoing in the large empty space.

She opened the door and passed the row of sinks, each with their own oval mirror, and saw, in front of the stalls, a great pool of suspicious-looking water on the ground.

Her staff weren't due for a few hours. She'd have to run down to Shaftesbury Avenue, look for a plumber.

The pool was growing and spreading by the second. Then there was a knock on the front door of the club.

What now?

Josephine gathered her fabrics about herself again and went to the front door. She touched a hand to her head – no hat, but surely they would understand. This was practically early in the morning for her. At least she had her eyes drawn.

Through the window in the heavy door, she saw a handsome young lad, sandy blond hair, a scar on his neck and flattened nose that somehow only added to his allure, and slightly rumpled clothes. He flashed her a smile. She opened the door.

'Mrs Taylor? I'm so glad I caught you.'

Josephine realised that, whoever he was, his timing was actually perfect.

'You need to help me right now,' she cut in. She opened the door and waved him through.

'Oh . . . of course. That is why I'm here.'

Again, he grinned at her. His eyes were hazel, large, more green than blue.

'There's a disaster in the powder room and none of my staff are here yet.'

As she hustled him towards the spot, Jack looked around. How different it was in the daytime, he thought. Still beautiful and otherworldly.

But . . . stinky, once he got in here.

He'd smelled worse.

'Can you help?' she said.

He traipsed into the puddle to take a look at the offending toilet. 'You'd better show me where the mains are first,' he said.

'Oh, yes of course,' she replied.

'And then, if I fix it,' he said, 'I would like you to give me a job.'

She looked back at him. Her hand went to her lips in consideration, her jewellery tinkling.

'Who are you?'

'Jack Burnett's my name.'

'And what's your experience?'

His lips curled. She noticed they were quite plump, a little too sensuous for a man's. She could put him behind the bar. That roguish look – the customers would eat him up.

'I've poured a drink in my time,' he said vaguely.

The water continued to pool, reaching the pointed tips of Josephine's boots.

'Christ . . . all right, just make this stop.'

'Yes, ma'am,' he said happily.

As she led him to the mains, she said, 'I'll take you through the rules, but there's one main thing.'

'Yes?' he said.

'The police raid us regularly. You probably know the reasons. But if you're working here, you have to uphold a level of decency. You are *working*, not carousing. You can do whatever you like when you finish your shift, but when you're

on duty, you maintain a certain level of sobriety and professionalism, you understand?'

He nodded. 'Of course. I wouldn't do anything to jeopardise
your business.'

'Good,' she said. He closed off the mains. She watched his
lean body working and thought, I don't believe him for a
second. Nonetheless, she was old enough to know she was
willing to be charmed. To a degree. She'd just have to keep an
eye on him.

He went back to the powder room and she waited in the
bar, thinking about what she would eat at the café up the
road once this was done. He came back and asked her where
the mop was. So he had initiative, at least, she thought.

'Can you start tonight?' she asked, as he wrung the mop
in the lane out back afterwards.

'Absolutely,' he said.

Jack practically skipped home. He couldn't wait to tell
Kitty. She'd probably tell him how to greet the customers in
a range of different languages, which would be fun. And
soon, hopefully, he'd be able to rent a place of his own.

30

Saint Bartholomew's Hospital, Smithfield, London, October 1923

Berkeley George Andrew Moynihan, 1st Baronet, was a noted abdominal surgeon based in Leeds who, within a few short years, had made an extraordinary medical name for himself. He had attained the rank of Major General in the British Army by the end of the Great War, had been Chairman of the Council of Consultants from 1916 and was now serving as President of the Royal College of Surgeons.

So it was something of a surprise to Grace when he had insisted on having her as his first-choice scrub nurse for a week of operating lists he had organised during one of his trips down to London, even though she was often called upon due to her record for infection control and antisepsis. His fearsome reputation preceded him and it had once been said by a notable rival that he was 'not handicapped by possessing any trace of modesty'. Grace prepared for the first day of surgery with a fair degree of trepidation.

Moynihan was something of a pioneer in sterile techniques, having been the first to perform a successful blood transfusion in 1906 and making a point of changing out of his ordinary clothes into clean white garments before entering any operating theatre. He was the first doctor to wear rubber gloves for surgery and adhere rigorously to his ritual of thorough handwashing. Grace also knew it was Moynihan who had introduced the use of green towels in 1912, rather than the traditional white, in order to reduce fatigue of the eyes.

Jealous colleagues initially ridiculed him for these innovations but soon came round to them as his results spoke for themselves. He was not a man who suffered fools gladly and, unfortunately, in medical circles there were quite a lot of them around.

This, however, is what Grace liked about him. He was confident without being arrogant and was willing to push the boundaries of what was possible. Neither did he share the pervasive prejudice against women in medicine which she had always found a handicap. As they now performed a particularly long operation to remove a chronically inflamed gallbladder, Moynihan became very persuasive.

'You must forget the bigots so stuck in their ways, Grace,' he said as he wrestled with the patient's intestines and separated the adhesions from the liver. 'Look at Elizabeth Garrett Anderson and what she's achieved.'

Anderson was one of Grace's idols.

'Physician and suffragist. The first woman to qualify in Britain as a physician-surgeon. Co-founder of the first hospital staffed by women, the first dean of any British medical school and the first female mayor in the country.'

'I've never had the pleasure of meeting her, but I certainly know of her. She is quite remarkable. But I should let you in on a little secret.'

'Really? What's that?' he said, looking up from his bloody instruments.

'She wasn't actually the first woman to qualify. I believe that accolade should go to Dr James Barry who was born and raised as female but presented herself as a man from the age of twenty and lived her adult life as a man just so she could pursue her career as a doctor.'

'Bloody hell! There's dedication for you. You learn something every day,' said Moynihan while carefully tying off the patient's thick and fibrotic bile duct. 'I can assure you, Grace, my own gender is not in doubt.'

'That is patently apparent, sir.'

'Would you pass me the Spencer Wills forceps, please? And a swab? Thank you.'

Grace peered into the gaping abdominal cavity. 'With all of the adhesions and scar tissue this chronic inflammation has produced, I must say you are making a tricky operation look relatively straightforward.'

'The perfect surgeon, Grace, must have the heart of a lion and the hands of a lady. As opposed to the claws of a lion and the heart of a sheep like so many of my colleagues seem to have.'

She grinned behind her mask and the surgeon was delighted to see it in her eyes.

'Infinite gentleness, scrupulous care, light handling and purposeful, effective, quiet movements which are no more than a caress are all that is necessary if an operation is to be the work of an artist and not merely of a hewer of flesh.'

She dabbed the bed of the gallbladder with another swab to mop up a small seep of blood.

'Now, you are particularly interested in microbes and infection control, are you not? You're interested in pathology?'

'Yes, sir.'

'Do you know of Maude Abbott?'

'A little. A Canadian woman doctor and a renowned expert in congenital heart disease. My younger brother suffers from that.'

'Does he indeed? Well, I don't believe it will be long before we are operating on the heart and making headway into that area of surgery as well. Abbott had to fight like hell to overcome prejudice against women too. But she did, and how stupid did she make them look afterwards.'

He bluntly dissected the gallbladder away from the liver and cut through its root, placing it in the kidney dish that Grace held out for him. Then he looked up at her over his mask and straightened up.

'The point I'm making is that you should follow in her footsteps.'

Grace was quiet for a moment. How does a nurse qualify as a doctor? A nurse with four-year-old twins and a husband who was working and studying so hard himself?

'I'll wager you won't find it too difficult,' Moynihan continued. 'Garrett Anderson was a nurse initially herself, like you. She studied anatomy and physiology in the evenings and had private tuition in *materia medica* with her hospital's apothecary. You can do that as well. You can visit the dissecting room and attend chemistry lectures.'

'I still don't think the medical school will accept me. . . Even my husband still has an uphill battle.'

'So go through the side door like he is doing. As Garrett Anderson did. Under their own charter, the Society of Apothecaries cannot legally exclude you just because you're a woman. And you are a woman, are you not?'

'I can assure you, sir, my gender is not in doubt.'

Moynihan laughed out loud behind his mask and continued stitching.

With such distinguished encouragement, Grace felt emboldened. Will had finally almost finished his diploma. They'd saved as hard as they could – enough money that hopefully would cover the first stages of his higher degree, and they'd try to work out the rest as they went. She knew Dr Forrester had hinted to Will that he could help out, but she knew Will was reluctant to accept. But standing there with Moynihan, she tried to remove her thoughts from her husband and ask herself what it was *she* wanted. There was nothing more thrilling than the idea of becoming a doctor herself.

31

St George's Hospital, Tooting, London, February 1924

Major Doctor Clifford Davison was revelling in his newly appointed role as chief of surgery and provost of the college at the London teaching hospital where he worked. Being a close old school friend of the head of the hospital and recommended by the Army top brass to the dean of the medical faculty, his appointment to the role had proved something of a formality.

And despite the Army pushing him on quite quickly after the war, the Major clung to his title like a limpet glued to a rock. He flaunted it on his headed stationery and on the brass plate outside his private practice in Mayfair as if it was the Victoria Cross itself.

Clifford Davison, however, had always taken care to studiously avoid being anywhere near the front line during his time in France and had delegated any difficult decisions ever asked of him to his subordinates. That way, if anything backfired, he would never have to carry the can. Nobody really knew how he had managed to elevate himself so rapidly from the role of assistant surgeon in the Territorial Army to Major in the British Army, but the general assumption was that his training at Sandhurst and the desperate shortage of personnel in 1915 had helped him avoid significant scrutiny.

The lasting impression he had left on his immediate subordinates in fact was as a strict and ruthless disciplinarian who delighted in his role presiding over court-martial charges brought against his fellow soldiers. He saw himself as upholder of the honour of the regiment, its moral backbone and ramrod enforcer. Unlike others given the unenviable task of imposing discipline on exhausted, despairing, shell-shocked men, he had passed the death sentence on a greater number of men and commuted less of them than anybody else in a similar position. It was a record of which he still boasted at regimental dinners. In 1916, in the quiet confines of his HQ in Querrieu, he was often secretly referred to as Dr Death.

He sat now at the head of a wide, semicircular baize table in the conference room just off the hospital library with three of his medical colleagues.

He found it tedious to have to waste his precious time sitting on a selection panel for aspiring medical school applicants, but since it was part of his role as provost, he had reluctantly agreed to do it. There was an assistant surgeon from his own department and a fellow of the Medical Psychological Association to his right and a consultant physician to his left. Quite why the powers that be had considered them necessary at all eluded him. Decisions by committee were never straightforward or speedy, in his experience, and besides that, the only worthy judge of potential and character was his own. He rather resented the presence of his colleagues and as they discussed ad nauseam the relative merits or limitations of the last candidate, he stared disinterestedly out the bay window on the second floor of St George's, watching the omnibuses and horse-drawn carriages as they circled and wheeled around Hyde Park Corner.

They had already interviewed four would-be applicants hoping to enter their medical school and only one – who had not had the privilege of having been to a top-drawer public school nor having a parent who was also a doctor or vicar – had failed to win their approval. The colleagues assisting Dr Davison were generally more interested in personality, presentation and achievements rather than social background, heritage and prerogative, but Davison was a forceful character who was intolerant of contradiction, and as head of the surgical department, they knew he was probably best appeased rather than crossed.

'The next fellow,' he announced as he turned the pages of the handwritten application, 'has fulfilled the necessary entry criteria to be considered, although I see no record of any traditional education after the age of fourteen.'

Dr Paul Rowlands, the physician, looked at his own copy.

'Nevertheless, he's achieved the standard required off his own back and has been working for the last five years as a surgeon's apprentice at Queen Mary's Auxiliary Hospital in Roehampton.'

'That institution has an impressive and growing reputation,' added the surgeon. 'And their advances in the field of amputation, prosthetic limbs and rehabilitation have been nothing short of miraculous.'

'Before that,' said Peter Collinson, the psychiatrist, 'I see he was a stretcher-bearer on the Western Front. He joined up at the age of fifteen and lasted the course. He must've witnessed many terrible things.'

'And comes with a number of glowing references to boot,' said Harvey Peterson, the assistant surgeon.

'A Dr Lamerton, a lieutenant surgeon in the RAMC, a Mr Aubrey Conway-Smythe and a Dr Forrester at the Hammersmith.'

'Can't say I've heard of any of them,' cut in Davison, somewhat piqued by being upstaged by such a junior man's military credentials. 'They were probably just grateful to have someone do their spadework for them. And what's taken him so long to complete his qualification?'

Peter Collinson lifted his head and raised an eyebrow. 'Financial and time constraints, I'd suppose.'

'Well, the proof is in the pudding,' continued Davison, who was chairing the meeting. 'So let's take a look at the greenhorn, shall we? What's his name again?'

'Burnett,' said the assistant surgeon. 'William Burnett.'

This was the moment Will had been waiting for all his life. Ever since the promise he had made to himself after feeling so utterly helpless as he watched his mother die of sepsis. Ever since his teenage apprenticeship working as a hospital porter in Hammersmith. Ever since the experiences he had endured during two brutal years in the trenches and working as a surgeon's assistant in the casualty clearing stations of France.

All that was left now was this interview and three years studying for his MRCS, his Membership of the Royal College of Surgeons degree. And paying for it, something he and Grace were still working out.

He arrived well before the appointed time so as not to risk being late, but despite Grace's constant reassurance, he was still a bundle of nerves. This was, undeniably, a pivotal moment in his life.

When he first entered the room, he nervously scanned the faces of the men quickly and then looked down, gathering himself. He took a deep breath, and raised his head again, only to peer directly into the eyes of a man he hated. The man he held solely responsible for the unnecessary and unwarranted execution some years ago of his friend and mentor, Captain Jacob Daniels.

Davison. Major Clifford Davison.

Six years previously, in the sheltered seclusion of his comfortable headquarters many miles behind the front line, Davison had presided over Captain Daniels' undefended court martial and summarily ordered his death by firing squad.

Will had sought the Major out, surreptitiously engineering an unscheduled audience with him and begging him to reconsider his verdict. Daniels was a decorated war hero who had fought in many different theatres of war, a great and fearless leader of men, who had been blown up by a German shell, buried alive, concussed and nearly suffocated. Disoriented, unseeing and incoherent, he had wandered off, only to be arrested for desertion by officers ignorant of the circumstances. These days, they called it shell shock. In 1916, the term had been banned by the Army as if the condition did not exist. Will had explained all that, yet the Major, who was medically trained, had shown no interest whatsoever in listening. Will had been unceremoniously bundled out of the room, only to discover — devastatingly — that the captain had already been executed.

As Will glared at the Major now, he realised his loathing had not diminished in the slightest.

How many nights had he lain in bed reliving that day? When his efforts to save the life of the man who had saved his own life, and many others besides, had come too late? The captain whose men would have followed him anywhere. The exemplary soldier who had been twice decorated for his bravery. The caring man who had, in the cloying mud of no man's land, seen young Will's courage but also his natural reluctance in taking lives. He had redeployed Will as a stretcher-bearer rather than keeping him as an infantryman and Will had risen to the task.

Davison was an arrogant prig. Supported by his obsequious and unctuous subordinates too spineless to challenge him, he had failed to recognise or consider the captain's shell shock, refused to take into account his exemplary war record and ignored the accepted protocol of providing the accused with legal representation. In Will's mind, he had single-handedly killed an innocent man. It was nothing short of murder.

Will looked at the carefully groomed moustache beneath the stubby nose on the red veiny face of the Major. His lips were moving, but Will could not make out the words.

Does he recognise me at all? This monster whom Will himself could never forget? Would he remember a young lad dressed as an orderly bursting into his room in a town hall in France requisitioned as an Army headquarters so long ago? It seemed unlikely. To such a self-important man, it would have been an insignificant and instantly forgettable moment. A moment of fleeting irritation gone in the blink of an eye.

For Will, however, it had been a defining turning point in his life. The point at which he realised the extent of man's inhumanity to man. How ignorance can prevail over common sense. How absolute power can corrupt. How those people often considered insignificant should speak up. Even though, when they try, their voices may fall on deaf ears.

Will had not heard the Major's question, but the man on his right was already asking another.

'Why have you chosen surgery as your preferred career path?'

The voice seemed to come from somewhere far away, to the side, above or somewhere behind him.

'What medical advances impressed you most during the prosecution of the war?'

'Tell us about the new above-knee prosthesis they're using at Queen Mary's.'

Davison. That bastard. Sitting there in judgement of him again.

The four men behind the table were looking at one another with puzzled expressions. Why was the candidate not responding?

The Major, beginning to lose patience, persisted.

'What was the single most important lesson you learned from serving in the Great War? How to treat the victims of Spanish flu? How to deal with penetrating wounds?'

'No, sir,' said Will in a loud, clear voice, looking around the table at his interviewers.

The men waited, brows furrowed.

'Not treating flu. Nor physical injuries, nor mutilation of bodies or faces,' he said. 'Nor watching helplessly as men gasped and coughed and died of asphyxiation from the effects of poison gas. These live in my memory, of course. Every day. But what I struggle with most is the dreadful effect of warfare on a man's mind. What it does to the souls of men. How it can turn courageous men into trembling shadows of themselves, incapable of rational thoughts or action.'

Will stared the Major straight in the eye.

'And how other men in positions of authority, protected by their rank and privilege yet with no experience of what it is like to face death at every turn, can sit in judgement on them and punish them, even as they wrestle manfully with their agony and torment.'

Something in the Major's demeanour was changing. A frown had formed on his forehead and he sat further forward in his chair. His shoulders had tightened and he had clenched his fists. It appeared some distant memory was being dragged from the remote past inside his head.

'You, of all people, Major Davison, should know that.'

The Major, still uncertain as to the young man's meaning, sat up straighter, folded his arms across his chest and raised his chin. He was suspicious of what was coming next but confident that no aspiring undergraduate would dare to challenge him personally and jeopardise their chance of selection for medical school. Something was stirring in his mind. He thought he vaguely remembered this upstart's face now and something about him was making him feel intensely uncomfortable. Yet he still could not quite put his finger on it. He was about to speak, when Will continued.

'I have no idea if you remember when we last met. You had just sent a war hero suffering from severe shell shock to death by firing squad.'

'Now, wait a minute . . .'

'He was my friend,' said Will, his voice getting louder. 'And you? You were the sole judge, jury and executioner and, as it was discovered later, the man who ignored commands from above to commute or at least delay the execution until the decision could be reviewed.'

'How dare you!' roared Davison, jumping to his feet. 'I won't tolerate some oik from the working classes coming in here and ambushing me with ridiculous accusations . . .'

Will pressed on. 'I wonder if your colleagues here know how many men in a temporary state of mental incapacity you sent to their deaths, Major?'

Davison's face was livid with rage and apoplectic with fury.

But Will was out of control too. At 6 feet 4, 14 stone and athletically built, his physical energy was immense. This was a rare and violent outburst of unresolved emotion the usually calm young man could never have contained. Any thought of the context in which it was happening was absent. The now disastrous nature of the interview was nothing compared to his need to take this man to task.

'Who the hell do you think you are? You must be out of your mind,' Davison spat, loose cheeks wobbling. 'You did not know the circumstances then and you don't know them now. You're nothing but an impertinent, ignorant little meddler. Get out of here. I will not tolerate such insubordination.'

Will continued glaring at the Major.

'Don't worry, Major,' he said. 'I'm on my way. But I'm not your subordinate any more. I'm no longer part of your Army. As for being out of my mind, we all know what your prescription for that is.'

'Get out, or I'll throw you out.'

Were it not for the heavy mahogany desk in front of him, Davison looked like he would have hurled himself at Will. His colleagues were struck dumb. They had never seen anything like it. The two on either side were physically restraining him.

'You'd better go, lad,' said the psychiatrist, suddenly at Will's side and quietly taking him by the elbow, opening the door and ushering him through it as the yelling and cursing continued behind him.

'Thank you,' replied Will, disoriented. 'Thank you for listening.'

He grabbed the handle and shakily closed the door behind him.

The glittering medical career he had dreamed of for so long was in ruins even before it had begun.

32

Putney/Barnes, London, December 1924

'Will?' Grace came into the living room to find Will in the armchair he was beginning to wear a groove in just like his father had done at Clara's.

Will looked up at his wife, standing there in her favourite evening dress that had been repaired and restitched over and over again. On a surgeon's wage, he could have bought her a new favourite dress. But that wasn't the most important thing, he knew. He could also be saving lives.

'The guests are starting to arrive.'

He attempted a smile and got up from the chair. Grace had insisted they host Christmas for once, thinking the company would help get Will out of his funk. But there hadn't been much giving him joy this year, and he didn't know how to turn it around. He gave all he had to Grace and the children, and his patients, but he felt somewhat embarrassed that Dr Forrester still spent time nurturing him when he had failed him so greatly. And the rage he felt all the time, just knowing Davison was out there, not just working but in a leading, influential role. Making decisions every day regarding the health and well-being of others.

Clara came through the door and Will took both her hands in his. 'Happy Christmas,' he said to her.

'Happy Christmas, Will.'

And then he pulled her into a hug and she felt frail and small. 'How are your pains?' he asked.

'Now, no doctoring today,' she said. 'From either one of you.' She pointed sternly at Grace.

Kitty came in after her.

Emily and Daniel raced in and wrapped their arms around their aunt and great-aunt.

Soon Jack arrived, and Amy and Fitz, and Jenny and Reggie and their daughter, Doris. They'd see the rest of the Tustin-Penningtons on Boxing Day. It was a squeeze to fit their family and friends in the front room, but it was cosy with the smell of roasting turkey, sherry and laughter.

Will helped Grace to ferry out trays of drinks and titbits of food before the main meal.

He paused in the doorway to take a sip of his own beer and saw that Amy was already a little drunk, spilling from her glass as she spoke to Fitzwilliam, who seemed slightly breathless and red in the cheeks. Jack still had an almost imperceptible limp from his previously broken ankle. Clara, talking to Jenny, was rotating her wrist as though to shake the stiffness from it. His dear children played with toy trains on the floor – so small. His father was missing, home alone in the cold because of his dark thoughts.

All of them so vulnerable.

Grace's hand was on his shoulder. She had been so patient with him this year, he thought.

'I hope the Christmas spirit will find you?' she said. He looked into her sparkling eyes. His beautiful wife, on her way to becoming a doctor herself.

He took a deep breath.

'You know I love you,' he said.

'I do,' Grace said, smiling. 'And we all love you.'

He nodded. He tried to become comfortable, for this moment, with his limits.

There came a knock on the door. Will frowned.

'Are we expecting anyone else?'

'No,' Grace said.

Will went to the door and opened it. Outside, his father stood in the snow without a coat, his buttons askew and wearing one glove. 'Have I found the right house?'

'My God, Father, come inside. You'll freeze!'

Robbie shuffled in, wiping his nose with his sleeve.

Clara, hearing Robbie's voice, leapt up and came through to the door. 'Robbie!'

'I thought I should come after all,' he said. 'Bit of a ghost of Christmas past, as it were.'

Grace was rushing over with one of Will's coats. They placed it over his shoulders and it swam on his thin frame. 'Come and sit down,' she said.

Everyone in the front room was quiet, watching the dishevelled man be placed on a chair. 'Merry Christmas,' he said to the floor, unable to face the eye contact.

Young Daniel came over and took his cold, ungloved hand in his own. 'Are you all right, Pop?'

Robbie now just grunted and nodded. Grace placed hot milk in front of him and insisted he drink. Clara was busy turning down the wireless, knowing Robbie wasn't good with too much sound.

When they'd got over the shock, Will and Grace looked at each other. Will felt a fresh surge of love and gratefulness. He smiled at his wife and she smiled back, relieved to see the change in him. Will thought his father's presence was a kind of odd, last-minute Christmas miracle. He looked around and realised that everyone in this room needed him and Grace in some way. And it didn't matter what job they were doing, they would always figure out how to be there for them as best they could. And that would have to be what held him for now.

Emily was pushing through legs and arms to get to her grandfather as well. She stopped to look at her parents. 'Mummy, Daddy, we need a new house!'

'I didn't want to say anything,' said Jack, 'but it is a tad squashy.'

'Oh dear,' said Will, bending down to his daughter. 'We'll see what we can do about that.'

33

Hammersmith Hospital, White City, London, February 1925

Gordon Forrester looked at his watch again. He was a patient man and didn't usually appear hurried, except in emergencies, and Will wondered what appointment he was obviously determined to keep.

They were nearing the doctor's office now, but Will wanted to get home to his family and made ready his excuses.

'I'll be off then, Dr Forrester,' he said. 'Don't worry about tea and biscuits today. I've got the motorbike outside and I mustn't keep you.'

The older doctor smiled. 'Hold on, Will, there is someone I'd like you to meet. And Sister Jane should have tea all ready for us. Come in.'

As they entered the room with a laden tea tray on a table in the centre, a man rose from his seat and held out his hand. Forrester shook it, but Will hesitated as he could not quite believe who it was. Peter Collinson had been the psychiatrist on the selection panel at St George's Hospital for his disastrous interview one year ago.

Well, well, thought Will. Just as he was finally moving on and resolved to being a general doctor and surgeon's assistant and they had come to give him a right royal ticking off. It had probably been wishful thinking that he could have got away with putting four doctors to all the time and trouble of interviewing him for a place at their medical school and then verbally assaulting the chairman of the panel without expecting any repercussions at any point. But now they obviously wanted their retribution and to deliberately embarrass him in front of Dr Forrester. It occurred to him that maybe Davison had taken this time to work them around to taking legal action against him. Now he understood why Dr Forrester had taken such pains not to be late. But why had he not warned him about this reprimand?

'Dr Burnett,' the man started, retaking his seat and gesturing to Will to sit down. 'I wonder if you remember me? I'm Dr Collinson. I was on the selection panel—'

'Yes. Yes, of course. How could I forget?' Will said defensively, recalling vividly how the psychiatrist had physically escorted him out the door. 'I'm sorry I caused such a fuss. Really. I . . . It was all wrong! It should've been a private matter between Major—'

'Please don't apologise. Not at all. I'm not here to rake over the past or cry over spilt milk.'

'The only one crying, sir, is me. For ruining my chances of ever obtaining a place at such a fine teaching hospital.'

'Just hear him out, Will. Just hear him out,' Forrester said calmly behind him.

'I'm a psychiatrist, young man, a specialist in the workings of the human mind. An interpreter of moods, spirits, thoughts and emotions. At that interview, I was struck by three things. Firstly, by your impressive work ethic. Secondly, by your exceptional curriculum vitae, experience and references. And lastly, and for me more importantly, the intensity of your passion regarding those terrible events you had witnessed and about which you held such conviction.'

'I must confess that on occasions I can be guilty of outbursts of anger, but normally I am—'

'A quiet, calm, thoughtful and rational person. A gentle giant, I would say.' It was Forrester interrupting again from behind him, peering over his glasses. Will turned back to the psychiatrist.

'Precisely. I would rather people express genuine heartfelt emotion towards people and their circumstances than show none at all,' Collinson said. 'The world is full of intelligent but heartless, unemotional people who are either evil, sick, psychopathic or all three.'

'So . . . I'm not in trouble?' said Will quietly. 'My interview can be forgotten?'

'Well, to be utterly frank, I'm not sure it can forgotten entirely.'

'I see.' Will's shoulders slumped and he looked down at the floor.

Behind him, Forrester winked at the psychiatrist and pursed his lips as he struggled not to laugh, his jowls shaking lightly.

'You see, Major Davison has stepped aside from his role on the selection panel this year and my colleagues and I unanimously felt you had been badly served. Indeed, I personally was most interested in the mental traumas and the sequelae of war which you so eloquently described.'

Will lifted his face.

'St George's Hospital would like to offer you an uncon-ditional place at our medical school.'

'What?' said Will, standing up in disbelief. 'Is this true?'

'I'm delighted to say it is.'

'So . . . so I'll be given another interview?'

'It's an unconditional offer, Dr Burnett. There will be no need for an interview.'

'Dr Forrester,' Will smiled. 'You knew about this.'

'I did. My little secret. They wanted to tell you themselves. Congratulations. You thoroughly deserve it.'

Will turned again to Dr Collinson. The psychiatrist stood and held out his hand, which Will shook vigorously.

'Personally, I'd be honoured if you wanted to join me in my own department exploring the machinations within the mysterious labyrinths of the human mind in both sickness and health. But I rather suspect your main interest remains in surgery?'

Will considered his answer. 'In truth, I'd like to combine them both.'

'A wise answer indeed. Especially as prefrontal leucotomy is now being mooted for certain psychiatric cases.'

'And . . . and Major Davison?'

'We'll keep him out of your way. And you his. He's still there, for the time being, and I cannot elaborate on that . . . but your future is secure. We'll be delighted if you accept.'

'Thank you, sir. I would of course have no hesitation whatsoever in accepting your kind offer on the spot if I could. But I hesitate because . . .' Will and Grace had since put their savings towards other necessities, including the initial costs of Grace's own diploma study and recently moving house — to a three-bedroom Victorian town house in Wandsworth with a little garden out the back.

'I've told you, Will,' jumped in Dr Forrester. 'I am more than happy to cover your medical fee expenses myself.'

'Oh,' said Dr Collinson, 'there'll be no need for that. I quite forgot to tell you. The grades you achieved in the preceptors and apothecaries examinations were outstanding.

Consequently, we are pleased to be able to offer you a scholarship. As long as you can put food in your mouth and clothes on your back you can look forward to becoming a Bachelor of Medicine and a Bachelor of Surgery at St George's Hospital in a few years' time.'

Will was speechless with surprise and joy and could hardly believe his ears.

'I know what you're thinking,' said Forrester, his eyes crinkling with joy. 'You're thinking you must be going mad.'

'I can assure you, you're not,' said Dr Collinson quickly. 'And I, of all people, should know!'

34

Wandsworth, London, February 1925

Grace had been over the moon to hear about Will's scholarship for St George's and they had pushed the boat out and made their way to Jack's part of London to share a fashionable brandy Alexander or two to celebrate. Though they were home well before the clubs really got going.

Will's celebratory mood was tempered by a visit the previous day to Clara and Robbie's. His father, this time, was almost catatonic. When Will spoke, his father had squinted at him, as though from a great distance, before looking away again. He wondered if he would come out of it again, if they'd ever be able to talk somewhat normally with him, or if Christmas had been the last time.

'That's his way this week,' Clara had whispered. She'd led Will into the kitchen by his elbow.

'Clara, how much longer can you do this?' Will had said.

'Please,' Clara had replied. 'He's my brother. I can handle it.'

Will had shaken his head. 'I wish I could do more.'

'He's safe,' she'd said. 'And I'm safe and well. You have the children to think of.'

Now, Daniel and Emily were fast asleep. They had their own rooms in the new family home in Wandsworth. Emily's was filled with hanging fabric butterflies and fairies, and a rock quartz collection on a bookshelf. Daniel's bookshelf had a range of picture books which he could already read himself. He asked his mum and dad lots of questions about why the characters did this and that: Why did they go that way? Why did they leave the ugly duckling behind? Will and Grace did their best to encourage the twins' burgeoning interests, no matter what they were.

Will and Grace were in their own bedroom, which looked down on their little yard and the lane out the back. Grace had never understood the rationale of dressing for bed. Donning voluminous nightgowns and being encumbered by reams of lace and cotton only made her feel hot and claustrophobic. Ever since she had been old enough to defy her fussy mother's insistence on the practicalities of nightwear, she had slept in the nude. Free, unrestrained and as nature intended.

Will, who was previously in the habit himself of wearing pyjamas all his life, had been more than willing to discard them and adopt Grace's liberating night-time philosophy as soon as they were married.

The two of them now lay there in bed together, skin to skin. Will lay on his left side, propped up on his elbow, idly twisting locks of Grace's auburn hair through the fingers of his left hand. With his other hand, he moved the diaphragm of a stethoscope further to the middle of Grace's left breast. He stared into her large green eyes and his palm was cupped over the endpiece of the device with his fingers fanned out over the sides of it, almost imperceptibly touching her nipple. The earpieces were in his ears and he could hear the normal lub-dup, lub-dup sounds of her heartbeat, but his mind was elsewhere.

'Beautiful,' he whispered quietly.

'Is it normal?'

'Perfect.'

'What does it sound like?'

'I don't know. I'm talking about your breasts.'

'Oh, Will!' she said, giggling. 'You're terrible. And taking advantage!'

'Want me to stop?'

'No. Take advantage.'

'Anything else you'd like examining while my instrument is accessible?'

Grace now looked into Will's eyes and smiled contentedly. 'Everything. All of me. But take your time, would you? Palpate and probe slowly and methodically. Should you find anything of interest and worthy of further exploration, feel free to linger. I wouldn't want you to miss anything. Anything at all.'

Will tried to let his troubling thoughts about Clara and his father fall away, and about running into Major Davison, to be present with his wife and in the joy of finally moving into the final steps to achieving his long-desired career.

35

Southall, London, May 1926

Fitzwilliam woke early in the bedroom of his flat in Bear Court, Southall. He often woke early, these days. Sometimes it was due to a sudden rapid heartbeat. At other times, he came out of a dream of a swelling desire he couldn't quite name in waking life. He rolled over and peered at his wife, on her own single bed, separated by bedside tables in between. She was still asleep this morning. She often woke early too, and he'd go downstairs and boil a pot of tea for them and they would sit in companionable silence and watch the sun rise.

He hadn't been able to believe it when he'd run into his grey-eyed friend from Oxford, Shauna, working in the House of Commons Library when he'd been doing some research for Mr Hancock for a bill that was being put forward. This time, unlike in their university days, she had accepted his offer of a walk. After that, he'd come by once a week, and every time they'd return to the library, it became a little harder to let her go. They enjoyed each other's company immensely. And he realised that this was the only prerequisite, for him, in a life companion. But he had wondered what it was that she wanted.

One day, he had asked her to lunch, and worked up the courage to have a more personal conversation, instead of their usual far-ranging historical, political, literary and social discourse.

'Shauna, my dear,' he'd said, his knees trembling a little. 'You know I am very fond of you.'

Her grey eyes had sparkled. 'I am fond of you too, Fitzy. No other man enjoys talking with me the way you do.'

'I suppose I wondered . . .' he'd said. 'What I mean to say is . . . If you were interested in more than talking with me,' he'd blushed, 'I would like to discuss that. You see, my heart precludes me from some . . . exertions, and I would want to know your expectations, your desires. I wouldn't want to waste your time.' The last sentences had come all in a rush.

Her face had remained calm, reserved. She had put down her teacup and taken up his hand. 'Fitzy, my heart, though it does not possess the same kind of physical defect as yours — one that can be diagnosed by a doctor — nonetheless doesn't seem to work quite the way of other women.' She had paused, looked into his eyes. 'It's something I've accepted. Perhaps, if we would both be comfortable with a companionship that, to others, seems perfectly conventional, but to us is . . .'

'Is determined by its own rules?' he'd finished.

She'd nodded.

He had thought, then, that perhaps he had seen this in her — seen their suitability — from those very first days in Oxford.

They could try, he had thought — they could try to do everything any other couple would, they could each meet their individual limits, but then they could accept whatever shape they fell into if some aspects didn't work. For his career, it would certainly be better for him to not be a bachelor, and for her, it made financial sense. She could keep working, too. That would make her happy.

Their marriage hadn't been perfect, he thought now as he put on the tea in the dawn light. There was loneliness sometimes in their house, each of them only able to fulfil some aspects of a loving life together. And her distancing of him sometimes felt cruel, like when she was in thrall of a new friend, and he was relegated to something akin to a piece of furniture. Perhaps he was envious of her, he thought. She seemed more able than him to reach out for what she wanted. But he had his work to keep him busy, and his parents and siblings and their families.

It had been five days since the General Strike had started on 3 May, and Mr Hancock had given Fitz the task of getting the feel for the word on the street in the capital.

Fitz had watched Mr Hancock speak for the miners through waves of inevitable change, including huge net losses in the industry last year, restructuring and unemployment increases. In the export fields, like Northumberland, Durham and South Wales, 90 per cent of miners had been laid off. An increase in export prices due to the returning of the gold standard to its 1914 parity had had an impact, and miners' unions had had enough.

The prime minister, Stanley Baldwin, refused to provide any subsidies to mine owners. In March last year, he had said that the government would not 'attempt to control the industries of this country'.

Fitz's natural diplomacy rankled at the hard line of both the PM and the unions. But what he'd learned from history was that change rarely happened unless the push was total. Through his work with Mr Hancock, especially visiting the mines themselves, he'd also learned about the true conditions and the great toll of the work. Men covered in soot who squinted at the sun as they emerged, like moles. Thin and wiry men, who showed up every day and did their part to keep the lights on.

The miners had rejected a deal of longer hours, lower wages and locally negotiated agreements in April, and on 1 May were locked out of the pits.

Now the General Strike had begun, which went well beyond the miners. Day by day, more workers were joining. England was on hold.

Fitz finished his tea, poured one out for Shauna and went back to the bedroom. He sat the cup and saucer as quietly as possible beside her bed, then began to get ready for the day. He tried to ignore the tightness in his chest.

Fitzwilliam boarded a bus on a quiet street heading south-east. He was glad he'd remembered to pack a sandwich as many stores were also closed in solidarity. A man in a nice suit was driving the bus. Fitz sat behind him.

'Volunteer?' he asked.

'Someone has to get people to their work and families,' the man grunted.

Many of the essential jobs were now peopled by these middle-class volunteers.

'You don't agree with the strike?' Fitz said.

The man took a corner a bit too narrow, almost clipped a light pole. 'Oops. No, I don't. I think they're selfish. The miners, the dock workers, they're an essential part of keeping this country running. They should be proud of that and get on with their work.'

Fitzwilliam thought this was a slightly short-sighted view, but from having read the papers, he knew it was common.

'I wonder, though, if their very essentialness does make it justified that they should be paid accordingly?' he challenged.

'Whose side are you on?' the man said grumpily. 'My parson arrived at the docks by ship at 4 a.m. this morning, same time as the guards escorting a bunch of lorries, to do the stevedores' work and get supplies into town. People are starving.'

'This morning?' The strikers weren't going to be happy about that.

'Yes, he shouldn't be having to do that. It's not his job. But people are saying there's only two days' worth of flour and bread left for the whole of London.'

'You're right,' said Fitz. 'It's not his job.' He wasn't here to argue, just to get a feel for what was unfolding on the ground.

As they moved through the city, the streets became busier. There were noisy picket lines. He saw a cluster of workers with placards angrily moving towards a building that boldly advertised 'We need volunteers for essential services', no doubt ready to call 'scabs' and spit on the people who were undermining their efforts.

Fitz shifted in the hard bus seat. Fluid pooled in his ankles today. He needed to go and see the doctor again soon. It was so hard to do his job with this condition.

As they passed important buildings, Fitz saw that they were manned by groups of what he knew to be special constables, wealthy-looking young men who appeared as though they'd just come from Oxford or stepped off the polo field.

'Thinking of going up north tomorrow,' the driver said. 'There's a real shortage up there. In London, there are plenty of volunteers.'

'Good for you,' Fitz said blankly.

And then they turned a corner and the driver said, 'Shit.'

The street was full of parading strikers, and as soon as they spotted the bus, which had come to a standstill, they encircled it, yelling and even pushing the bus. Fitz tried not to worry — it was a display of displeasure and disappointment, surely there would be no real violence. He turned to look at the other passengers. A couple of them looked scared – a small boy and his mother in particular. 'We're just trying to go to the bank,' she called out to the noisy crowd who wouldn't hear her. Other passengers sat with their arms crossed, defiant.

And then, outside, a police and military presence. Uniformed bodies started peeling the workers away from the side of the bus, yelling and waving batons as a threat. Now Fitz saw the violence. One young policeman barely gave a woman time to get up off the ground where she fell, catching her hard in the calf with his baton.

Once the crowd had dispersed, the bus driver shakily opened the door to let one of the military men on.

'Everyone all right in here?' the man asked.

People nodded. 'Thank you,' said the mother, clutching her son to her.

Fitz felt torn, and a little ashamed. 'I'll get off here,' he said, standing.

'Are you sure?' the driver said.

'Indeed,' he replied, and the soldier stepped aside to let him off.

The uniforms walked beside the bus until it was through the most crowded part of the street, and then it drove off. Fitz began walking in the direction of the docks. He hoped he didn't look too out of place, too blue blood. But he could see, everywhere, that it wasn't just an either/or. There were all kinds of gawkers on the street, including children and dogs wagging their tails.

He followed a group of strikers. Their faces were brave and determined beneath their flat caps. The atmosphere did have a tinge of hope, and even joviality, among the frustration. Fitz considered that a sense of solidarity, and cooperation, brought joy to people. He paused to exchange a penny for a copy of the morning edition of the *British Worker* from a man at the sidelines. This would tell him what the propaganda in the *British Gazette* would not. He folded it into his jacket pocket.

The crowd slowed as they came closer. The armoured cars and the police with fixed bayonets were intimidating. Fitz's heart did one of its dances. He wondered if he should get out from the crowd. If he fainted, he'd be crushed. He hesitated.

'You look worried, mate,' said a man next to him. Fitz turned to find him offering a smoke.

Fitz put up his hand. Cigarettes only made his chest tighter. 'Thank you, but no. I'm not worried, just unwell.'

'Hungry? Me too.'

'No,' he said. He pulled out his sandwich, a little squashed now, and offered half to the man.

The man took it. Fitz watched him take the cigarette from his lips and then lift up the triangle with the other hand and bite down on the crust. 'Cheers,' he said through a mouthful. He was young, maybe twenty, had a light smattering of freckles across his nose. Worked in the sun. Probably a docker. Fitz realised he was watching him eat for a little too long. The man's face changed. 'You all right?' he said. More curious than angry.

Fitz had lost all the questions he wanted to ask. His heart was jumping about now. 'I'm afraid I really must go.'

The man looked disappointed.

'Good luck,' Fitz said, and put his head down and moved through the crowd.

He had to brave a bus again to get home, unable to rely on his shaky legs. He was glad he'd got out and got a feel for the atmosphere, but he was uneasy, too. The government didn't seem to want to budge, and the workers were passionate. He didn't know if he had what it took to be a politician, if he couldn't find the way in between. Mr Hancock had been kind to him – often worrying he was holding him back, since he'd been with him a few years now. He'd increased the pay appropriately, but it was the same position. But Fitz enjoyed his job immensely. He'd realised over time that he was good at being on this side of the desk – immersed in research and policy and information – not out there on a lectern or calling out from the floor. His father still hoped his ambitions were greater, he knew, and Fitz generally avoided the topic.

You had to be bullish, he thought. You had to be certain. You had to make decisions and defend them. The problem, for him, was that he always saw both sides.

When he finally arrived home and opened the door, Shauna came straight out from the living room.

'You didn't get me up,' she said. She looked upset.

'I was working,' he said, a little baffled.

'I told you last night, I would have liked to go down. History in the making.'

He remembered now that she had expressed that. 'Oh, Shauna, I'm sorry.'

She shook her head. 'Never mind,' she said unconvincingly. She went back to what she was doing.

Maybe he'd deliberately forgotten. She often was interested and wanted to be involved in what he was doing. But he wasn't really welcome at her own soirees and adventures. They were women-only. He didn't resent it, he just wanted to have some adventures of his own.

A few days later, Fitzwilliam and Shauna listened to the BBC as the prime minister addressed the nation, saying that he was a 'man of peace'. He said there was a difference between a strike against a company and against a government.

'He's mismanaging this terribly,' said Shauna over the top of her newspaper. 'Even the clergy don't agree with him, think there should be compromise.'

'Yes, he has a lot of opposition.' Fitz had kept thinking about the worker he'd met briefly at the protest. His freckled face had warped into a symbol of the movement in his mind.

On 12 May, the Trades Union Congress rolled over and agreed to end the dispute with the government, though pockets of striking continued all throughout the country. Rumbles went on, but the threat of starvation meant some workers drifted back. Moscow offered miners money to remain on strike, but this 'red gold' was not accepted.

Fitz wondered if the man he'd shared his sandwich with had had to go back to work under the exact same conditions as before. Every morning, he cut his bread and wondered if the flour had come off the docks, hauled in sacks by the sun-damaged young worker.

In July, he was distracted by another cause.

*

Grace put on her hat and coat and stood by the door, waiting for Will to be ready and for Clara and Kitty to arrive. Daniel and Emily were playing on the lane behind the house, Daniel with his wooden popgun that shot a cork on a string, and Emily with her pair of velvet dolls — a boy and a girl pair, which she made twins like her and Daniel. Clara was going to mind them while their parents went to the march. Grace had considered taking the twins, now seven years old, introducing them early to the idea of equal rights, and for standing up for what matters, but she was too worried about losing them in the crowd. Emily in particular had a way of running off if she saw something shiny or interesting. They'd already had a few scares with her when shopping or at a museum. And Daniel had a way of asking very loud questions about strangers that could be difficult to navigate – Grace and Will encouraged his curiosity but also wanted him to understand how to be respectful. It was a balance that was hard to strike in a larger crowd, where he might enthusiastically point out everyone's wrinkles, limps and smelly clothes.

They would meet Fitzwilliam and Shauna there, coming in separately from Southall. It would be a bit of an adventure to Hyde Park Corner. A big day out. She'd packed sandwiches, a flagon of tea, and her placard was standing ready by the door.

'You're eager,' Will said, emerging from the back of the house.

Grace smiled. 'Did you know Mrs Pankhurst will be there?'

'That's terrific,' Will said.

'She's already worked so long and hard, and she's still fighting for the next generation. For our daughter.'

'And for you.' He took her hands in his. 'You can't even vote yet.'

'That's right. At twenty-seven!' She shook her head.

'Well, it'll be an energising day,' Will said.

She so appreciated him accompanying her. They still both often worked on Saturdays, but this was important.

She heard Kitty before she saw her. She whooped as she came up the path. Grace opened the door, and Kitty leapt into her arms. She'd always been a physically affectionate child, with everyone. But she wasn't a child any more. She was a tall and slim sixteen-year-old, with blue eyes, naturally rosy cheeks, and a dainty chin. The current fashion of a straight up-and-down line skimmed her figure perfectly. But Kitty herself barely seemed to notice. She had the energy and demeanour of a child, still — curious, sometimes quite loud, with an unrestrained laugh that made strangers' eyes bulge.

Kitty ran past Grace to envelop her brother. Will was always delighted to see his little sister — she brightened up the world with her joy and vivaciousness.

'Are you ready to stand beside us, big brother?'

'Of course,' said Will.

'Where are *la niña y el niño*?' she asked.

'In the lane,' Will said.

'I'll say hello.' She disappeared out the back.

Clara greeted Will and Grace and came into the house. Clara loved to spend time with the children. Since Kitty had grown, and she'd never had children of her own, she relished being the twins' great-aunt. She was never one for marching or any public displays of politics, and she was a little too worn out these days to have many exertions outside of work. Her knees and hips often ached, disturbing her sleep, and sometimes her thumbs and wrists were so stiff she had to get Kitty to open bottles and jars for her. Though she wasn't one to complain. She just had to save her energy for those three days per week. But watching the children was fine. In their own neighbourhood, they knew the parameters. If they were outside, she only had to check on them. If it was raining and they were inside, they still often occupied themselves with books and drawing and toys and their own secret language with each other. But she also would read to them or share memories about family members. Daniel especially loved to hear about Jack's adventures, though she sanitised them appropriately. Robbie was harder. Sometimes they asked about Pop, or 'funny old Pop', as they called him, and she tried to talk about their grandfather in a way that was kind and would foster tolerance and acceptance of difference. The truth was, he was now entirely a shadow of his old self.

Grace and Will said goodbye to the children and gathered Kitty and they set off for the bus, Grace holding her placard by her side.

People glanced at them on the bus. A man even sneered at the upside-down placard which stated, very simply, 'Give all women the right to vote.'

They met Fitzwilliam and Shauna at Marble Arch, ready to walk to Hyde Park Corner.

Once they arrived, Grace said to Kitty, 'Look, that's Ada Moore.' The woman was very old, but stood tall, next to a woman with pure white hair. 'Oh, and that's Mrs Despard.'

'Important women?' Kitty asked.

Shauna said, 'Oh, yes, original suffragettes.'

'They've been campaigning for our rights for a long time,' Grace said. She had shivers running up and down her arms. At home, she had felt sad about the fact these women had had to fight for so long. But being here, she saw that they were buoyed up by the crowd around them. That they could play a role to inspire, to pass the baton. *If we can do it, you can too.*

'Mrs Despard has been imprisoned four times for the cause,' Shauna said. Grace watched her sister-in-law. Her usual reserve had dropped away somewhat. Her features seemed lighter, more relaxed. And then she broke into a smile as she spotted a group of women. 'Excuse me,' she said.

Grace and Kitty watched, fascinated, as Shauna took these women into her arms, laughing.

'Her friends,' Fitzwilliam said behind them. 'She goes to many meetings, is very involved.'

Grace wanted to express how surprised she was, that she'd never seen her sister-in-law show overt emotion, but she knew it would be rude.

They began marching, and Shauna stayed with the other women.

'Fitzy,' said Grace, holding her placard aloft.

'Yes, sister?'

'Does Mr Hancock know you're here?'

He cleared his throat. 'Not entirely.'

Will joined in. 'He doesn't support equal rights?'

'Like many politicians, he has interests in certain rights, like workers' rights, but then he can also be quite a conservative man. He's often grumbling about the youth, and often he means young women — he thinks they should be grateful to keep to their role of childbearing and wifely duties.'

'What does he think of Shauna?' Grace asked, looking back to see Shauna hooked arm-in-arm with another woman, marching proudly.

'Well, she's very good to me, you know. She always makes conversation that's right for the situation.'

'Sometimes she doesn't say much at all,' said Kitty.

'Unlike you, Kit-Kat,' Will said. Kitty playfully smacked him on the arm.

Grace realised they were in fact being rude. 'Sorry, Fitz, we just get curious.'

'I know,' he said. 'You always have been.'

Crowds had built up at the sides as they marched. Most people looked happy, and clapped and waved, but there were some women and men with their arms crossed, glaring. The police stood in groups here and there.

'Do you think this will work?' Kitty said. 'It's so exciting!'

'It is exciting, to speak peacefully as a group, to ask for change,' Will said. Grace smiled at him.

'I hope it will work, Kitty,' Grace said.

Kitty watched the old women walking proudly near the front. Mrs Pankhurst, Mrs Moore and Mrs Despard. She wondered about the fights of the future. Once women had equal voting rights with men, what then? She knew there were still many things men could do that women could not. But were there some things that were more natural to men, and natural to women? That was a message she had received over the years. She thought about the women in her life. Had their sex held them back? If they didn't let it, they were still chastised for it, weren't they?

Not only chastised, punished. Mrs Pankhurst, she'd seen, wore a badge depicting a prison grille. What must it have been like to suffer behind bars?

Kitty realised she possessed a desire she hadn't previously understood, something she'd been keeping close. The desire was to see the world. To speak to people in other lands, in their own languages. To learn about other cultures, to see how others lived, to taste and smell the air, the water, the food, in a place she didn't know. In a place that was foreign to her.

She marched now with new vigour. To her, this now wasn't just about the vote. It was to live a life that was entirely her own.

36

Bishop's Cleeve, Gloucestershire, August 1926

Arthur was in his study looking out at the old oak tree when Dorothy entered.

'I've just heard from Amy on the telephone,' she said. They'd had a telephone installed in the house this year – the same year of the first transatlantic call from the British Post Office to Bell Laboratories in New York. Arthur had realised they should keep up with the times, and it would make being in touch with the children – who could use the telephone in post offices – much easier. Will and Grace also had access to one at the hospital.

'And what does our bright young thing want today?'

'Oh, Arthur.' Dorothy looked worried and tired. 'She wants to bring a party of her friends here for the weekend. They arrive tonight.'

'Dear God, we have to play smiling host to her friends?'

Dorothy gave him a crumpled look.

They had hosted Amy's friends when she was younger, but she'd been in London for so long now, barely even showing up at Christmas, that they thought they'd got out of hosting whatever passed for upper-class soirees these days. They knew the times had changed a lot – they read the papers and spoke with their children – but Amy had really embraced the lifestyle of a new generation, one that seemed alien to Arthur and Dorothy. She was thirty years old and had not shown any interest in getting married. She had turned down plenty of potential suitors, and she also seemed to change jobs week to week. At one point she was a model, at another she worked in a department store, then she was a photographer's assistant, and Arthur and Dorothy were sure she'd done some other more unsavoury jobs also. She was always cheerful when she spoke to them, wrote to them or showed up – not in a need-ing-to-please way, more in an 'everybody needs to relax' way. And a lot of the time she seemed to be at least a little drunk.

Dorothy would lie awake at night, and when her thoughts were troubled, they first turned to Charlie, her forever-young son who had died in the war, and then they turned to Fitz, worrying about his heart condition and whether he was pushing himself too much, and then they settled on Amy. And she thought about Amy for a long time. How much she'd loved that little girl and how much she still seemed to *be* that little girl, but not in the right way.

Dorothy felt terrible for thinking so badly of her daughter. She felt ashamed. But she just didn't understand. Where did Amy think she would end up? Did she think she could support herself in ten years, twenty? If she wasn't going to marry, she ought to get some kind of qualification. She could be a teacher, for example. She needed some stability, because Arthur and Dorothy weren't sure if the family home would be there in later years for her to fall back on. And what was she going to do here anyway? It wouldn't go to Henry or James. Henry was now married and embedded in the London banking world and James was soon to go to America to work at Ford in a junior management position, attracted by their new model and forty-hour work week. Rightfully, it should go to their eldest son, Rupert. And he and his wife and children wouldn't want Amy banging about the place, getting drunk and inviting a ragtag band of friends over. It was, frankly, embarrassing.

Standing there with Arthur in the study, Dorothy said, 'Let's try not to judge. Maybe they'll bring a little life to the tired old house.'

Arthur nodded. 'Anything has to be better than that last hunting party.'

'Well, they have different customs in Sweden.'

Arthur could see she was trying. He could see it every day. And he could see how very tired she was.

He took a deep breath.

He was tired, too. Profoundly so. In fact, he'd been finding it harder and harder to get up in the morning. He'd been getting headaches, too. And digestive issues. He'd presumed it was just general ageing, but perhaps he ought to see the doctor.

'We'd better get ready for them.'

Since they'd been able to rent out a wing to the hunting parties and for other getaways and celebrations, they had their cook back on four days in the week, and some maid staff too. Dorothy went to brief them for the arrival.

At three-thirty, Amy and her friends sped up the driveway and spilled out of a convertible motor car. Arthur and Dorothy could hear them coming all the way up the drive, their laughing ringing out even above the revving of the car and crunch of tyres on gravel.

Amy rushed up to her parents and pressed her face either side of theirs, in the French fashion. 'Hello, Mummy, hello, Daddy.' She wore a salmon-pink dress with a long loose tie and see-through sleeves that ballooned and then nipped in at her wrists with fine lace detail. On her head was a matching cloche hat. Her eyelids were painted dark and her brows were drawn in fine arches.

Her friends waited by the car to be introduced.

'Come, come,' Amy said to them. 'This is Alf.' She pointed out a young man in jodhpurs and a cardigan, as though he'd just stepped off a horse. 'And Bebe.' A white-haired young woman with a long face like Virginia Woolf, in candy cane stripes. 'You've met Diana.' The pretty young woman nodded. 'And this is Edgar.' And here was a young man in soft pastel colours and wearing make-up like a woman. 'And finally, Clarke.' Amy fawned and draped her arm over this dark-featured, handsome young man in a suit. 'Do you recognise him?'

'Should we, darling?' Dorothy said, overwhelmed.

'Oh, no, Mrs Tustin-Pennington,' the man said in a mid-Atlantic accent.

'Yes, they should,' Amy countered. 'He's in the pictures,' she said to her parents. 'But I suppose you never go.'

'We have much to look after here, I'm afraid,' said Arthur. 'I'm sure your acting is very good.'

Clarke waved them away.

'Well, do come in,' Dorothy said. As they followed her, she asked how they had all fitted in the car. They all laughed as at some private joke. 'Well, isn't it a little dangerous?' asked Dorothy.

'Oh, Mother, you mustn't worry so much.' Amy patted her mother's shoulder.

Dorothy leaned in to whisper to Amy. 'I do wish you'd introduce their *full* names to us, dear. You know we're not used to addressing strangers on a Christian-name basis.'

'Oh, they'd prefer it, Mother. Such formalities are stuffy.'

Dorothy tsked, upset. She would have to ask each of the

young people herself. Why had their daughter abandoned
every lesson in politeness and propriety they'd ever taught
her? Or had they just never sunk in in the first place?

'Tea in the sitting room,' Dorothy said, spreading her arm to
the couches and inviting each of them to pass her. The men
removed their hats as they went, giving her a little bow. She
found it difficult to look into the eyes of the boy wearing
eyeshadow and blusher. 'The maid will attend you,' Dorothy said.

'You won't join us?' asked Clarke.

'You must,' Diana said.

Arthur and Dorothy knew they were simply being polite.
'For dinner,' Arthur said.

As they left the room, Amy called out again.

'Yes, dear?'

'Can the maid bring us champagne with the tea and treats?'

Dorothy glanced at Arthur. He frowned but nodded lightly.

'Yes, darling. But we'll be having wine at dinner . . .'

Amy gave a great sigh. '*Mother*, it will be fine.'

Arthur went out to supervise some gardening while Dorothy
attempted to rest and read in her bedroom. Even all the way
up here, she could hear the revelry – her daughter's voice
seemingly the loudest. She should probably have told Florence
to limit how much champagne to give them, though that
would be putting the maid in an awkward position. She was
not looking forward to dinner.

Around seven, they all piled into the dining room. Dorothy sat
across from her daughter. She watched as Amy forked pheasant
into her mouth and the skin around her jaw looked loose and
translucent. Amy had a sheen on her chest, and Dorothy could
also see the dark hairs on her upper lip and cheeks that were
showing through her make-up. But her daughter was having an

exquisite time, it seemed. Laughing and talking nonsense with her friends. Speaking through mouthfuls of food.

What are the mornings after like? Dorothy wondered. Surely she doesn't feel good then.

The guests talked about motor cars, fashion, London clubs, and a whole host of people Arthur and Dorothy had never heard of. They spoke of people, often with derision, in a tight and sarcastic tone.

Arthur, sitting at the other end of the table, nearer the strange young men, felt himself getting angry. All those youth wasted on war. All these youth wasted on frivolity and gossip. He knew in some ways it was a reaction to war, a reaction to what could have happened to all of them. A dismissal of worry and responsibility. But he couldn't stand it.

They'd drained another bottle of champagne during the main course.

'Sherry for dessert, Daddy. Maybe some cognac?' Amy said. It was always 'Daddy' rather than 'Father' when she was asking for something.

Arthur looked at her half-lidded, heavily painted eyes. Her head wobbled on her neck. He didn't want to embarrass her in front of her friends, but this was his daughter. Such a high consumption of alcohol was unhealthy and unnatural.

'I'll get it,' he said.

He went to the storage and decanted half a bottle of cognac. Then he added water. He did the same for the sherry. He had to slow them down somehow, and they were so sozzled they surely wouldn't notice.

When he got back, Dorothy said, 'I'll have some of that.' He was surprised, but saw the resignation in her eyes. She couldn't bear this company without being a little drunk herself.

He poured a round, and everyone raised their glasses.

'To our fine hosts, the Tustin-Penningtons,' slurred Clarke.

The man in the jodhpurs put his arm around the man with the make-up. They hooked the arm that held their glasses through one another's and raised the glasses to their lips, their faces close. Dorothy looked away. She would put them in the bedrooms furthest apart from one another.

After dinner, Arthur invited the men for cigars, but Amy pooh-poohed her father, saying that women liked cigars too. 'Let's just have them here,' she said.

'Perhaps we'll just leave you to it,' he said. The guests hollered their protestations, but Arthur and Dorothy continued to excuse themselves, leaving the liquefied young people to their debauchery.

On the way past the entrance to the cellar and store, Arthur squeezed Dorothy's arm. 'Perhaps I'll just lock this.'

'Should we really?' Dorothy said. 'It's not very hospitable.'

'Truthfully, Dorothy, I think we've been hospitable enough.'

She nodded, and then waited while he turned the key in the lock and put it in his pocket. They retired upstairs.

Dorothy would have no control over who slept in whose room. All night, she tossed and turned to the sounds of voices and music and laughter and doors opening and closing.

In the morning, Arthur found the outdoor entrance to the cellar and store had been jimmied open with something — a tool, perhaps. They'd even got into some of the good wines. He stared at the gaps on the shelves for a long time. He thought about storming upstairs and waking Amy and her strange and awful friends. But then he thought about Dorothy, finally snoozing peacefully.

He closed and fixed the cellar door as best he could.

*

221

Amy woke at noon, her head pounding, and looked over at Diana sprawled beside her, spittle at the corners of her mouth. She groped around on the bedside table for her flask. Two drops of gin, just to take the edge off.

She laid her head back on the pillow.

Clarke had been in one of his moods last night. Distant, cold. It was so strange to her — how he was like two different people. When they were alone, he was attentive, sensual. In front of others, he treated her like a friend or sister. If she tried to show affection, he gave her only a pressured little smile. It had been like this for years, since he first started visiting London in the summer. When he wasn't here, she tried to put him out of her mind. She had fun with Diana and the others. She went to every party on offer. But she had been wondering — *was* she getting just a tad too old for this? The hangovers lasted longer, her jobs shorter, and fewer invites were showing up. She and Diana still lived with Diana's mother, who partied with them when she felt like it. She fed them and cleaned up after them, and Amy had often wondered why her own parents weren't so accepting.

But if she was going to marry anyone, it could only be Clarke. She'd go to America, of course. Why not? Maybe she could get into the pictures, too.

He'd be better today. Surely. Maybe he'd had some bad news, or just drank too much too early. She would have a bath, wear his favourite dress. They could go for a drive, just the two of them. He loved the way she drove.

He'd been off this whole trip, though, hadn't he? She tried not to think about it — about whether he was perhaps thinking of another woman back home.

37

Green Man pub, Belgravia, London, March 1927

'What would you rather have?' asked Tom Sunderland, one of Will's fellow medical students at St George's. 'Chronic myeloid or lymphatic leukaemia?'

The small group of medics were discussing the relative outcomes of the two conditions and came to the conclusion that, although neither was particularly welcome, the lymphatic variety was preferable. The group had all been attending the prestigious monthly grand lecture in the Colville Auditorium at St George's. Now they were sitting around a table sticky with stale beer in the Green Man public house in Kinnerton Street. Each had a pint of pale ale in their hand, except for Grace and her friend Bonnie who were drinking gin.

What would you rather have? was a game they played after a lecture or a ward round with any of the consultants. Dr Frank Cunliffe had introduced it to them early on in their training.

'As a ten-year-old child, what would you rather have, diabetes or polio?' he had asked.

The question had taken them by surprise, but it had certainly made them think. The mysterious and unexplained random onset of diabetes in children, leading as it did to intense thirst, loss of weight and exhaustion, was as yet incurable. It was exceptional for people to live with it for more than a year or two. Banting and Best's discovery of insulin in 1921 had certainly been revolutionary and their experiments on patients had ably demonstrated that it worked. Yet the pharmaceutical company Eli Lilly could still not produce enough of it or make it sufficiently affordable to treat everybody affected. As for polio, that illness could also kill people through respiratory and nervous system paralysis or leave them physically handicapped for life, but many people still made a full recovery after a relatively short acute febrile illness. So most of the group had decided they would rather opt for polio.

There were no end of other comparisons to be made. Rickets or congenital dislocation of the hip? Cholera or typhoid? Measles or malaria? Rubella or relapsing fever? The debate was both interesting and enlightening and as an entertaining form of exam revision, it served its purpose well.

Grace was a welcome and particularly vocal member of the group, despite still being at the diploma level, as she was experienced and knowledgeable about microbiology and infectious disease.

'Polio!' she exclaimed, when the comparison came up again now. 'Good God! It seems incredible that any of us would actually prefer polio over anything else. It's such a terrible disease.'

'Do we have any idea what causes polio yet?' asked Brian. 'And why are we seeing so much more of it today when other diseases like typhoid and cholera have been decreasing in prevalence as a result of better hygiene?'

'Nobody really knows,' said Grace. 'But we're definitely seeing more epidemics. In 1916, an outbreak in America affected twenty-seven thousand and killed two thousand people in New York alone. They closed cinemas and banned public gatherings. They kept children away from parks and playgrounds. Thousands fled the city as if a modern plague had arrived.'

'I suppose it had,' said Tom.

'We are seeing increasingly significant outbreaks every summer now,' continued Grace. 'I've personally attended many cases. It's heartbreaking. People develop a raging fever, crushing headache, unbearable aching and stiffness in their muscles and utter exhaustion. Many experience only temporary weakness, but the worst affected develop permanent paralysis of their limbs within forty-eight hours.'

The men could not help but be impressed with the depth of Grace's knowledge. Unusual, some thought, in one so feminine and attractive. Will just basked in the reflected glory of being her husband.

'How many people remain paralysed?' asked Gordon.

'Thousands. Everywhere you look you will see people with withered legs or arms getting about on crutches or limping awkwardly along the street.'

'Like that bloke,' Gordon said, indicating a man on the street whose shirt was rolled up over his shortened arm.

'Well,' Will said, 'that could be a war injury.'

Grace nodded. 'Going by his age.'

'You two certainly have seen a lot,' Bonnie acknowledged. The group of mostly slightly younger men and women murmured in agreement.

'But with polio,' Grace continued, 'if the illness reaches the brain and spinal cord, one in two hundred will die from it.'

'Can't anything be done to prevent paralysis? To stop spasticity in the muscles and prevent contractures?' said Gordon.

'Splints help. Casts to support the limbs to keep the muscles from shortening. People can remain in plaster body casts for months sometimes, but the trouble with that is atrophy of any remaining healthy muscles. You can't win. These people face decades of agonising rehabilitation to regain whatever function they can.'

'But why are we seeing more of it?' asked Brian again.

'If only we knew. I have a theory, but I can't prove it.'

'What's that?' asked Will, intrigued. They occasionally 'talked shop' at home, but he had not heard Grace mention this before.

'Well, look. Think of the pattern of this infection. Newborn babies who are breastfed by mothers who have previously recovered from polio don't seem to be affected. I think something in the breast milk protects them. Maybe during this time when the infants are exposed to whatever it is that causes it, they react in a way that gives them immunity for life.'

'And we're seeing more polio because . . .?'

'Because of better sanitation. Improved hygiene has reduced risks of other infections, but apparently it has increased the risk of polio. So suppose whatever it is that triggers the disease isn't there so much in a baby's early life when the benefit of breast milk is still present but is there later . . . When any protection from the breast milk has been lost . . .'

The group all looked at each other, trying to take this in.

'So you're saying we should scrap hygiene and sanitation?' said Bonnie.

'No, I'm not saying that. I don't know. It's just an idea.'

'It's worth exploring,' said Gordon. 'And it sounds like you're the person to do it, Mrs Burnett. So, anyway, where were we?'

'What would you rather have? Scarlet fever or erysipelas?'

And so it went on.

Will enjoyed this circumstantial circle of friends because although they came from different backgrounds, most of them privileged and aristocratic, they were not like some of the other students who did not seem to care about the welfare of patients and were only interested in a medical career as a means of becoming rich.

'So what would you rather have?' asked Grace. 'A society that penalises the poor, the sick and the disabled and prevents them from having children on the basis it would improve the hereditable quality of the nation? Or a society where strength is measured by the moral and ethical way it treats its weakest citizens and works towards greater fairness and equality?'

She had listened intently along with everyone else that afternoon to the lecture given by R. A. Fisher and Julian Huxley of the Eugenics Society and had been horrified by the ideas they had been propounding. Ideas that, ever since the Eugenics Education Society had been founded in 1907, had been gaining in popularity.

'I don't think that is the only choice they were suggesting,' said Tom. 'What they were saying, I think, is that eugenics has its advantages. Benefits in terms of more responsible parenthood, care and protection of the feeble-minded, and help for paupers, those with venereal disease and women rendered incapable by alcohol.'

'Come off it, Tom,' said Will, conscious of his background and personal experience. 'Their idea of care and protection is locking up the most impoverished in our society in work-houses, the forced sterilisation of the feeble-minded, whatever that means,' (he was thinking now of his poor father Robbie) 'and the artificial insemination of women with the sperm of men deemed mentally superior in an attempt to better the race.'

'That's just Huxley's extreme view,' chipped in Gordon. 'What did he call it? Eutelegenics. It's just an idea.'

'It's a monstrous one,' said Grace. 'It's not the fault of the poor that they're destitute. If there are no jobs to be had, they don't have the opportunity to work. It's not the fault of the infirm if they're not physically perfect. According to the eugenicists, my sister, Amy, would be considered "genetically gifted", but despite that has had her problems in the past. My brother, Fitz, was born with a heart defect, yet he is currently working in our parliament and devoting his life to the welfare of this country. Are you saying you want to deprive the likes of him from a useful and fulfilling life? Or premature babies like my own twins who would once have been written off and left to die but whose outcomes continue to get better and better with every medical advance? Daniel and Emily are now perfectly healthy, normal children.'

'Who claims to be superior anyway?' asked Will. 'The top-brass military who sent millions of working-class men to their deaths in France in 1916? The aristocratic and middle-class scientists and clergy who propose limiting the number of children born to poorer parents and taxing the rich less than everyone else in order to incentivise fertility and encourage the birth rate in wealthier circles? It's a disgusting and highly immoral policy.'

Grace grabbed Will's hand under the table and squeezed it.

'"Quality not quantity",' Fisher said, didn't he?' said Gordon. '"Survival of the fittest".'

'Well, I wouldn't want too many little Leonard Darwins or Earls of Limerick running around telling us all how many children we should or shouldn't have,' said Will. 'And as for that so-called "man of the church" Reverend William Inge, the Dean of St Paul's Cathedral, thank God he's taken an oath of celibacy. I wouldn't want any of his perfect offspring spouting their supercilious piety to all and sundry.'

'Oh, come on, Will!' said Tom. 'We're only being provocative.' He raised his glass of beer.

'I hope so. Otherwise why are we studying medicine?' said Will. 'What's the point if we don't want to help people less fortunate than ourselves or who have fallen on hard times or been unlucky enough to be born with a hereditary condition?'

'Take it easy, Will. It's only chit-chat,' said Gordon, trying to lighten the mood. 'Tell me, Tom, who would you rather have? The blonde serving drinks in the snug or the brunette pulling pints in the saloon bar?'

'I'd rather have them both, given the chance,' he answered, which made everyone laugh out loud.

'We attribute far too much to heredity anyway, I think,' said Brian, being serious again. 'Nurture, in my opinion, is much more important than nature.'

'Good point,' said Tom. 'We can all pull ourselves up from our position in society if we only put our minds to it.'

After a thoughtful pause, Will cleared his throat and thumped his empty beer glass down on the table. 'Right,' he said. 'I know what you ladies are having, but what would you lads rather have? Another pint of this rather watery pale ale or a decent pint of heavy with a whisky chaser to put some hairs on your chests?'

38

Soho, London, July 1927

Jack was relieved to step out of the cold wind into the warmth of The Diamond. Mrs Taylor was leaning on the bar, smoking. She nodded when he came in and poured him a cup of tea from her pot and handed it to him without him asking. He smiled at her. He had found a home, here. He was now the weekend manager of The Diamond. He booked the bands, did the stock orders and signed off on the roster that Josephine's daughter put together. He spoke to the cleaners and maintenance people. He made sure the tills balanced and took care of safety issues on the floor. It was a lot of responsibility, but he always thought back to being inside that tunnel in Flanders, hearing the scratching noises of the enemy underground, and his confidence and joy soared. *That* was responsibility – life and death. This was a piece of cake.

The regulars knew him by name, now, and he indulged the VIPs – roping them off at the best table and bringing the finest champagne. Pausing with them to take in a spectacular trumpet solo.

Josephine now looked Jack up and down. 'You're looking a bit thin, Jack.'

'All this running around,' he said.

She narrowed her eyes at him. She thought he was mostly on the ball, and as she'd predicted, the customers did love him, but he was also unpredictable. She'd been tolerating his reliance on putting stuff up his nose to stay awake all night – it wasn't unusual – but she knew from experience that it could go too far and he'd be useless. She'd had a previous employee, a young woman, whose moods had begun to change – from grumpy to anxious and paranoid. She had started to experience nosebleeds. Eventually, she had developed strange delusions about angels and devils living in the faux frescoes on the walls.

Jack had had to take time off six months ago. They didn't discuss the reason, but she'd seen the rash coming up under his collar, the sores on his tongue. She was glad to get him away from the club until *that* had cleared up. She hoped he hadn't passed it on to any poor young woman. He did seem to have a different lover every fortnight. And all ages, and from all backgrounds, too. He certainly wasn't picky.

Jack started to turn on lights and set up, and he greeted the staff as they entered. His left eye throbbed in short bursts, so painful he sometimes gasped and clutched it before he could stop himself. He took some aspirin and continued setting up. A glass of whisky would also help take care of it.

Soon the club was in full swing and Jack raced around, performing various duties. There was a clutch of loud Americans tonight, escaping Prohibition and segregation. The women had on short, shimmery, flapping dresses and they revelled in the black bottom and shimmy dances. Men joined in but also stood in their suits and smoked and watched these sparkling figures bopping and kicking and shaking their skirts and limbs. Shimmy dances were banned in many clubs, but not The Diamond.

Jack paused to admire a woman's slim and muscular legs moving in time with the beat of the drum but was struck again by that intense pain behind his eye. The music covered his audible cry, but he also dropped a trayful of champagne glasses and it smashed dramatically to the floor. His main barman raced immediately over with the broom.

'Good man,' Jack said, patting him on the shoulder and walking away quickly in embarrassment. It wasn't like him to drop anything.

Behind the bar, he took a few deep breaths. The pain was spreading through his head. He pulled down a bottle of Scotch and poured out a glass, neat. He threw it back. That only added a little dizziness to the pain.

Come on, Jack, you've been through worse pain than this.

He went back out on to the floor.

And just then, the doors slammed open and four cops walked in, bringing a blast of freezing air with them. Jack saw Josephine disappear upstairs. He walked towards them.

'What can I do for you this evening, gentlemen?' He glanced at the tables out of the corner of his eye, hoping there was no obvious drug paraphernalia, or any women who looked overtly like working girls — though it was hard to tell in here.

'This is a raid,' one of the policemen said.

'Brilliant,' Jack said sarcastically. 'Like you didn't scare enough customers away last week.'

'Just doing our job.'

Jack wanted to say more, but he knew how handcuff-happy these police were, so he gestured for them to go ahead and take a look around.

The band stopped and lowered their instruments as the police moved through the club. They picked up glasses and sniffed their contents, they questioned people, and at one table they paused and beckoned Jack over. This table was filled with Amy and her friends, regulars at The Diamond. Amy gave Jack a mischievous look, but he wasn't in the mood. The policeman pointed to a plate sitting on the table. A cold, forlorn sausage curved around a piece of stale brown bread.

'All guests are supposed to eat with their alcohol. I don't see much here.'

'We've had several plates already,' Amy said.

'We'll need to see the receipts.'

'They were on the house,' Jack said, and, by way of explanation, 'Her sister is married to my brother.'

'That's not enough for us,' the policeman said. 'For all we know, this could be a prop.'

'Have a taste,' Jack said to the policeman. The cop grimaced. Jack then nodded and raised his eyebrows at Amy, hoping she might pick up the sausage and eat it so they'd move on. But when he thought about it, he had no idea when it had been delivered to the table. Could have been at the start of the night. And everyone in the club knew the food was pretty much just for show, so he couldn't guarantee it was a good sausage in the first place. It shone a little in the soft light − slimy.

Amy looked bored; she moved her eyes to the dance floor. Jack's head throbbed.

And then Diana came to the rescue, picking up the sausage and shoving it in her mouth. She bit down and chewed, with a sour smile, and chewed and chewed as they all quietly watched, until it was all gone.

Jack was going to have to give her some whisky to wash her mouth out.

'Well, then,' the policeman said. 'I want to see more food out before we go, Mr Burnett.'

'Of course,' Jack said. He moved them on, in case Diana had to rush to the powder room.

At the table, Amy watched Jack walking away. She was filled with mirth and wanted to fill the now quiet, murmuring club with her laughter. Poor Diana! She was slurping up champagne like her life depended on it. Amy couldn't wait until the police left so they could dance again. She wanted to shake and shimmy all her trouble and heartbreak away. This time, it seemed her movie-star boyfriend had returned to America for good. A cheap gossip rag had a double-page spread of him and his new co-star, who was also, apparently, his fiancée. That was the first she knew of it.

Amy watched Jack again. And then saw something awful.

Jack almost looked like he was going into a shimmy, but then he collapsed to the ground, still writhing and shaking, his head horrifically knocking on the hard floor. She leapt up and ran to him.

'Move!' she said to the police. 'Jack?' His eyes were rolled back in his head. 'Can someone run to a telephone?' she yelled.

'We'll take him to the hospital,' one of the policemen said. She eyed them warily, but then accepted. Their motor car would get him there quicker than anything else.

'I'll come,' she said.

Will and Grace awoke near dawn to the sound of pounding on their door. Will wrapped himself up and went down. They opened the door to find Amy, in a big fur coat and thin stockings, make-up running.

'Oh, Will, it's terrible,' she said immediately. He bundled her in out of the cold.

'Shh, Amy, you'll wake the children.'

But she burst out crying and wailing, trying to speak through it, and he walked with her to the kitchen.

'I'll put the kettle on,' Will said. Grace had told Will that Amy's relationship had gone south, but her showing up at their house upset like this was unusual. He filled the kettle at the sink and sat it on the stove.

'It's Jack!' she managed to get out.

'What?' His head snapped back towards her. 'What's happened to Jack?'

Grace arrived at the doorway, and seeing her sister's distress, rushed towards her.

'He got taken to the hospital. He fainted, had a fit or something. And in the police car . . .'

'The police car?'

'They were raiding the club, but they took him to the hospital. In the car, he vomited and vomited. It was such a mess.' She opened her coat and the waft of sick came off her. 'And his eyes . . . the pupils were all big and strange.'

'Which hospital?' Will said, leaving the tea and going to the door for his coat.

'Hammersmith.'

'Good,' said Will. Dr Forrester was on tonight.

The twins appeared, rubbing their eyes. 'What's happening, Daddy?' Daniel asked.

'Nothing to worry about, son. Just have to go check on your uncle.'

Emily ran to her Aunt Amy's side. 'Are you crying, Aunty?' She started to cry in sympathy without waiting for a response and buried her face in the fur coat.

'Oh darling,' Grace said, bending down.

'I'll be back,' Will said, putting on his coat and hat. 'It'll be all right, Amy. Thank you for coming straight here.'

He left and Grace led Amy to the bathroom. 'Want to stay with her, Emily?' she asked. The eight-year-old nodded. 'You're such a caring girl.'

Grace went back to the kitchen and found the brandy, to pour a snifter for the shock. Daniel followed her around the house, wanting to be useful too.

'Will Uncle Jack be all right, Mama?' he said, taking her hand as she carried the brandy in the other.

It was always such a difficult decision, whether to tell children the whole truth, which might help prepare them for bad news, or whether to protect them for as long as possible from feeling fear and sadness. She decided to try to find some middle ground, as she and Will often did.

'Sounds like he's quite ill, darling, but he's in hospital with the doctors, so he's in the best of hands.' She smiled reassuringly at him.

Perhaps she was also trying to convince herself. She didn't know how Will would cope if his brother were mortally ill.

Will found Dr Forrester in Jack's room at the hospital. Jack looked wretched on the bed – pale and dehydrated. His eyes were closed and his hand clutched his stomach.

'Is he awake?' Will said.

Jack groaned.

'His pulse is low and he's passed barely any urine. We're trying to get some fluids into him.'

'What is it?' Will said.

'Looks to be syphilitic. Your brother managed to tell me that he'd been treated for the sores around six months ago. Topically, and then with neosalvarsan and mercury. One night in the arms of Venus leads to a lifetime in the embrace of Mercury, as they say . . .'

Oh, Jack, Will thought.

'All symptoms cleared up with that treatment,' continued Dr Forrester.

'But it's progressed,' Will said. Syphilis could lay dormant in the body, and then affect the organs, the brain. 'So, more neosalvarsan?' Will suggested.

'Well, I wonder,' Dr Forrester said, 'if, instead, we try to induce fever paroxysms. I've had some success from this, following the work of Wagner-Jauregg.'

'The Austrian physicist,' Will remembered. 'That's right, you showed me that patient you treated with Salmonella typhi.'

Jack moaned again.

'Yes, well, the fever in that case was a bit too hard to control. I went in that direction because of what was at hand. But malaria will be easier, as we also have ready treatment.'

'Quinine.'

'Correct.'

'It's what Wagner-Jauregg recommends?' Will said.

'He does.'

Will looked at his pitiful brother. If they didn't act quickly, this could get very serious indeed. Will had encountered patients who had neurosyphilis, affecting their memory, emotions, muscles and motion, often giving them a whole different personality.

Will nodded.

First, Jack was injected with blood containing the parasite. He soon experienced fever paroxysms, as expected, lasting about six hours. Once his core temperature returned to normal, quinine was injected over several cycles and over a couple of days. Will came and went from Jack's room, around work and study at St George's. Sometimes Clara would be by Jack's bedside too. So far, they'd managed to keep it from Kitty. It was what Jack wanted.

One day, Will came by to find Jack getting up from the bed.

'Jack, you still need to rest,' Will said.

Jack looked caught out. He huffed and sat back in the bed. A sandy beard to match his hair was growing across his broad jaw. 'I'm fine, Will. Just a bit achy now. Can you get me something for the pain?'

Jack's face was drawn; he scratched at his arm. He seemed twitchy, restless.

'Glad to see you have some energy,' Will said.

'Just a pill or something,' Jack said.

'I'm not sure that's a good idea.'

'I knew you'd say that,' Jack replied, frowning. 'That's why I was going to find the nurse.'

'I'm just trying to keep you well, Jack. Your lifestyle—'

'Is my own, thank you.' He crossed his arms.

Will sighed. There was no getting through to him. 'All right, I'll be back later.' He went to leave.

'Will?' Jack called.

He looked back.

'How's Dad?'

'The same,' Will said. 'Not speaking much. Not moving much.' He knew Jack generally avoided visiting their father and was surprised he even asked.

Jack nodded. 'Can you send in the beautiful nurse, the one with the legs?'

Will smirked. 'Maybe if she's not busy.'

'Thanks, brother.' Jack leaned back, arms behind his head, suddenly relaxed.

39

Soho, London, August 1927

A fortnight after his discharge from Hammersmith Hospital, Jack felt like a new man. Thanks to Clara's excellent home cooking, he had gained back the weight he had lost, and despite the aches and pains he always felt in his shoulder, hip and arm, he had even been encouraging Kitty and the twins to join him for long walks along Strand-on-the-Green or Kew Gardens and Richmond Park.

After a further two weeks, he felt confident enough to return to work and pitched up one Friday afternoon at The Diamond.

It was closed. Boarded up and deserted.

'What the hell's gone on here?' he demanded of the newspaper boy selling the *Times* on the street outside.

'Police shut it down,' he said. 'Someone died in there.'

Jack was stunned. It was a fairly insalubrious establishment all right, with sex, drugs and prostitution, but he had never expected anybody to actually die there. Not on the premises, anyway. How bloody thoughtless. He went round to the side alley and rang the bell for the top floor.

Josephine Taylor opened the door a few seconds later in her dressing gown. She looked like she had not slept for days.

'Jack!'

'Mrs Taylor, are you allright? What's happened?'

She did not know what to say at first. She wanted to physically punch Jack in the face for not being there when the crisis occurred, but she also knew he had been rushed to hospital after collapsing at the club and had been very ill himself. She also felt slightly guilty that she had failed to visit him. She felt anger, pity, remorse and despair all at once.

'You'd better come in.'

Upstairs, she sat in the once rather chic lounge of her flat and told Jack about the fateful night one of her customers had overdosed on cocaine and suffered a heart attack. It hadn't helped the legal action being taken by the police against The Diamond that the woman in question was a high-class prostitute who used the club to meet her clients. Nor that the heroin she had taken earlier in the evening had sedated her sufficiently to require a significantly higher dose of cocaine to get her high. Her heart hadn't been able to take it and she had clutched her chest, fallen headlong across the gambling table, spilling alcohol, powder and resin in all directions, and lain there, face up, covered in her own puke, with hugely dilated pupils reflecting the spinning lights in the ceiling above the dance floor. 'The whole thing was a nightmare.'

This time it was Jack who was almost lost for words.

'I'm sorry, Mrs Taylor. Really, I am. It wasn't your fault.'

'Maybe not, Jack, but I'm beginning to think I've had enough of London nightlife. I've got some savings put aside. Just enough for a little place in the country for a quiet life. It was fine while it lasted, but what with all this, it's become too much of a headache.'

'I'll tell you what, though, Josephine. You provided one hell of a service while it lasted! You certainly gave people what they wanted.'

'Except for the poor girl who died, I suppose.'

Jack grinned back at her. 'Well, if there's anything I can do for you in the future, you know where to find me.'

'Thank you, Jack. But how are you? You haven't told me.'

'I'm fine, Josephine. Just fine.'

'Fine? F.I.N.E? Do you mean fucked up, insecure, neurotic and emotional, like the rest of us?'

'Exactly that,' said Jack, getting to his feet. 'But I'm better than I was and only using the drugs my brother prescribes for me. You just take care of yourself. It's been a blast.'

'Goodbye, Jack.'

'Goodbye, Josephine.' He took her hand, kissed it and let himself out.

Jack walked the couple of blocks back to his tiny flat. Clara had insisted she stay with him after being in hospital. When he went into the flat, the air seemed stale. He looked around at the spartan furniture and lack of decorations. It was as neat and uniform as an army tent. And from his recovery time, he was already behind on the rent.

And then Jack thought of his sister. Kitty was now seventeen and surely there would come a time when she wanted to move out from Clara's, get married, have a life of her own. Who would Clara have to rely on? She wasn't getting any younger or more spritely, and he could already tell it was quite a strain for her to keep up her work and look out for his poor old dad, too, who really should be in a facility.

Jack fired up the stove for a pot of tea. It was unbecoming for him to be the one who would look after an older female relative. It made more sense for Kitty. He wouldn't even know what to do, he thought. He'd have a cup of tea and then head straight back out to look for another job. This time he'd go to Sheppard Street and look for the man Sham had told him about all that time ago. Sham had said the man might find Jack a job 'suited to his talents'. Well, he was curious to see just what those were.

40

Wandsworth, London, February 1928

When Will entered the house, more buoyant than he had ever remembered being, he found the children playing alone in the lounge.

'Daddy!' they called, but didn't let up with their game.

'Hello, where's your mother?' he smiled down at them.

'She went to lie down,' said Emily, a slight puzzlement to her voice.

Will frowned. It certainly was unusual for Grace to rest before bedtime. He went up the stairs and gently pressed the door open. She did seem to be asleep, and he watched her for a moment — her calm and beautiful face. He wrestled with whether to wake her up. No, his news could wait.

He went downstairs and found a loaf of bread and some eggs and got started on some dinner. The children soon joined him in the kitchen.

'Why is Mummy sleeping?' Daniel said, twisting his body this way and that.

'She must be tired,' Will said, slicing the bread.

'But why?'

'Don't you sometimes get very sleepy?' Will said. 'Even while it's still light?'

Daniel considered and nodded. Emily let out a yawn.

'Did you visit Uncle Jack?'

'Not yet,' said Will. 'I thought you might like to come with me, see the demolition site?' Jack had started working in the building industry. 'But I don't have a day off for a while now.'

Daniel and Emily both looked disappointed. 'How long?'

He put the pan on the stove and lit the gas.

'Well, I'm not certain. I can help a lot more people now.' He wondered if it was unfair to Grace to tell the children first. But he decided she wouldn't mind. 'I officially qualified as a surgeon today.' He grinned.

The children looked unimpressed.

'That's good, I suppose, Father, but Uncle Jack gets to work outside and blow up buildings and bits of rock, doesn't he?' Emily this time.

Will sighed, checked on the eggs in the pan.

'Are you teasing your father?' came a sleepy voice from the bottom of the stairs. Will and Grace locked eyes and he could see how happy and proud of him she was. How deeply she knew what it meant to him to have got to this point in his life – a dream that had seemed impossible fulfilled after countless hours, dedication and much hard work.

The children started giggling.

Will shook the spatula in mock reprimand as Grace came over to embrace him. He saw something slip in her face, something that was wrong, and he questioned her with his eyes.

'Later,' she said.

After they'd eaten a gourmet meal of fried eggs on toast, Will and Grace settled the cheeky children to bed and relaxed on their lounge with a cup of tea.

'I'm so proud of you, Will,' Grace said. 'First a doctor and now a surgeon.'

'Well, you're not far off being a doctor yourself,' he said. 'But what's wrong, my darling?'

Grace sighed and set down her cup, a lock of auburn hair falling in front of her furrowed brow. 'I'm not sure it's anything to worry about yet, but it just seemed to overwhelm me on top of everything else. My father, he doesn't seem to be well.'

Will's heart became heavy. There was never much distance between joy and trouble. 'Has his own physician made a diagnosis?'

'Not yet.'

'Allright, well, I know he's had a trustworthy doctor for years, but if you need me or Dr Forrester to step in at any time . . .'

'He wouldn't want you to do that, Will. Nor me.'

'I understand.'

He looked into her eyes. They'd had enough moments like this that nothing more really needed to be said. They steeled themselves, and each other, with a squeeze of the hand.

'We'll get through this,' Will said.

41

St George's Hospital, Tooting, London, November 1928

Clifford Davison was livid as he let the two men once again into his office. How dare these two interfering nobodies challenge him about his clinical work? And why had the dean himself not had the decency to come and see him to put the matter straight? He was the provost and head of the surgical department, after all.

He had become increasingly irritated by a number of people questioning his authority lately and he was determined to put an end to it. He was a major in the British Army, for God's sake, and a consultant surgeon at the very top of his profession. He would not tolerate his reputation being impugned.

'I'm afraid the enquiry into the loss of Mr Collins three days after his surgery has not quite been concluded, Major Dr Davison,' the first of the silly little jobsworths said. 'There are one or two points that still need to be clarified.'

'What points?' Davison snapped impatiently. This ridiculous and unnecessary investigation would still not bloody well go away. What was the point of it? It wasn't like they could bring the man back to life.

The second of the two men, a neatly dressed, bespectacled and rather serious-looking gentleman, then spoke up. 'Well, the main one being the actual identity of the surgeon who carried out the procedure.'

'That's obvious from the operative records, you cretin. Collins was my patient, but a simple appendicectomy did not warrant my expertise, so I instructed my junior house surgeon to perform it. Read the notes.'

'Er, we did, sir . . . Major. But there seems to be some discrepancy.'

Davison stood glaring at them from behind his desk. 'What discrepancy?'

'Dr Fenwick, your house surgeon, denies carrying out the operation.' The second man again.

'Well, he's lying, isn't he? To cover his tracks. Frightened of the consequences and frightened of me, I should think.'

'That would appear unlikely.'

'Why? He wouldn't be the first surgical assistant to be in awe of his auspicious superior. Who would want to own up to a careless perforation of the bowel after the removal of a perfectly normal appendix in an operation which clearly wasn't indicated in the first place? He signed the surgical notes, didn't he? Surely that's proof enough. Check the notes.'

'We have. Several times. And had them scrutinised. So, you'll be pleased to hear that we've left no stone unturned.'

Davison looked from one man to the other.

'The notes are handwritten in the traditional way.'

'Of course.'

'And signed by Fenwick.'

'Well, there you are,' Davison said with an insincere broad smile. 'Good day to you, sir.'

He turned and went to open the door.

'But Dr Fenwick was nowhere near the hospital that day.'

Slowly, Davison turned back. 'I beg your pardon?'

'Dr Fenwick was sitting his conjoint examination in Queen's Square that day. Along with forty other doctors. He couldn't have performed that operation.'

'Or written the post-operative notes and signed them,' added his sidekick.

Davison was momentarily speechless and thinking furiously.

'Well, somebody did. What are you saying?'

'The notes have been forged, Major. It seems someone wants to avoid the blame.'

'If Fenwick didn't do that operation, then who did?'

'The other two duty surgeons are accounted for. One in Outpatients. One in another operating theatre on a thoracic case.'

'The theatre roster and the nursing staff identify you as the surgeon.'

Davison was silent, but his mind was in turmoil. He felt trapped. He huffed beneath his moustache.

'Then there's been a mistake!' he bellowed. 'And a very grave one. I will not be accused of . . . I will not be bullied and harangued by people who know nothing about surgery and the difficulties of . . . of the risks and consequences . . .'

'We had the writing analysed, Doctor. By a Mr Gordon Webb, an expert forensic graphologist, one who is retained by the Metropolitan Police at Scotland Yard for his professional expertise.'

Davison's face turned deep red. Beads of sweat sprang up on his forehead. He could feel his heart thumping under his ribs and the rapid pulsation of blood behind his ears. The bastards were ganging up on him, he thought. This was just the last in a steady stream of recent insinuations. A cabal of jealous so-called colleagues envious of his reputation and standing. It was a peculiarity of his profession. He took a deep breath and tried to compose himself. He had blustered his way out of more serious allegations than this in the past, that was for certain, and he was sure he could do so again.

'Well, I expect he'll be able to tell you who the real author was then.'

'The writing is yours, Dr Davison,' said the man in the glasses. 'And you forged Dr Fenwick's signature yourself.'

'Nonsense.'

'You changed the medical records two days after the operation was performed and attempted to blame your junior when you realised the patient was dying as a result of your mistake.'

'That is preposterous!' spat Davison, but he was rapidly running out of responses.

'Making a genuine clinical error is one thing, Doctor. And according to my investigations, this would not be your first. But fraudulently altering the medical records and blaming a third party is not only illegal but constitutes a serious civil offence.'

'You'll regret these unfounded charges, you snivelling little shit! I'll see to it personally that you're removed from your job for incompetence. What's your name again? Who is your superior?'

'My name is Walters. Ernest Walters. Here's my card. I'm a barrister by profession and that's the address of our firm in Lincoln's Inn Fields. This is my assistant, Jenkins.' The print on the lawyer's business card was bold enough, but Davison could barely read it. His vision swam and he struggled to focus. 'I'm instructed to tell you that your work here is suspended pending this enquiry. If I were you, I would seek some legal representation of your own, Doctor.'

And then, clearly relishing his work, and with a hint of a smile on his face, he added, 'Good day to you, sir.'

Davison closed the office door behind the men and leaned against it for support. How the hell had this come to pass? If only the bloody man had not died. Anyone could make a mistake. Medicine was not an exact science. Accidents happened. Why hadn't his junior been there to help out? How would these young tyros get the experience they needed if they were never there? In his day, it was different. They were on call day and night, around the clock. But he would find a way out. He always did.

The hospital would not want to admit any error. It would be bad for their status and reputation. They could hush it up. Find an extenuating circumstance. People died all the time. Yes, that's it. He would talk his way out of it. Obfuscate. Blame the patient's sepsis. Blame his own tiredness and exhaustion. Blame the hospital itself for putting too much pressure on him and rendering him unfit to work safely. They would not want that. Not at all.

He would do a deal. The dean was a man he had known for some time as a friend. Albeit, that friendship had cooled somewhat in recent months. He might be too cowardly to confront him with these accusations himself and send a lawyer to do his dirty work, but he wouldn't want a scandal impugning the glorious reputation of St George's Hospital. This was not the Army and things could not be swept under the carpet as easily as it might be during wartime. But it was still the medical profession, and it was almost as capable of closing ranks as any other profession.

Yes, he would do a deal. Find a way out. Save his skin. What matter if the hospital decided to forego his services and cut off their nose to spite their face? He still had his private practice in Mayfair to fall back on. And that was doing nicely, thank you very much — earning him a pretty penny. Why should he worry? Yet the more he thought about the two men who had ambushed him in his office and their impertinent interrogation, the angrier he became.

The more he ruminated on the recent attitude towards him of his fellow surgeons, those useless snake-oil salesmen who called themselves physicians and those madcap dream-analyst disciples of Sigmund Freud, the more bitter and resentful he felt.

He loathed the lot of them, with their petty jealousies, their newfangled ideas and their holier-than-thou ethical perspectives.

Suddenly he needed to get out of there. If they did not want him to honour the surgical outpatient's clinic with his presence, so be it. Some other fool could do it. Besides, they had even had the gall to suspend him. Those cowards.

He needed a drink. Badly. And the member's new smoking room, with its wide ornate bar, at the Army and Navy Club in Pall Mall, where he was a regular visitor, was just the place.

42

The Great Hall, Worshipful Society of Apothecaries, London, November 1928

Grace was loving her medical training, particularly her time spent in the dissecting room and any patient-centred demonstrations and ward rounds. Much to her surprise, she found she was completely at ease. She had seen so much trauma and disease first-hand on the battlefields of France, and as a nurse and assistant in operations, that she already had a sound basis of understanding. There was not a single aspect of the various branches of medicine in which she was not completely absorbed, but her overwhelming interest, stemming as it did from her current expertise on infection control and asepsis, was pathology.

It was incredible, she thought, that before the turn of the century many doctors still believed that diseases were caused by some sort of chemical poison or noxious elements in the air, known as miasmata. It seemed instinctive to her that microorganisms were responsible, and she had so far devoted her nursing career to eradicating them. Thankfully, Louis Pasteur and Robert Koch, his younger German contemporary, had proven once and for all the germ theory of disease and had revolutionised the understanding and practice of modern medicine.

What do you need to prove that a microbe is responsible for any given disease? Koch had postulated. That the specific organism is always present in every case of the disease. That it can be cultured. That inoculating experimental animals with that culture would always reproduce the disease. And, finally, that the organism can again be recovered from the inoculated animal and grown in pure culture. This man's model postulates had been accepted and followed by the medical fraternity ever since and now everyone knew which particular germs caused tuberculosis, cholera, typhoid, pneumonia, leprosy and so many other diseases. The challenge now was to find effective treatments and vaccines, just like the one Pasteur had developed to protect people against rabies.

They would be sorely needed. Would her own children come through childhood unscathed by a serious illness? In her profession, it was difficult not to think about such things. She often thought of their former neighbour's boy, Freddie. The terrible grief his parents carried in their eyes thereafter.

It was different with her father becoming ill – more expected, when you grew old. At least, that was what you told yourself to cope. She hoped she'd be able to go and see him soon.

Grace had witnessed the last few hours of one patient suffering from rabies and it had been a most distressing experience. The poor man had been bitten on the hand by a stray dog three weeks previously and after a period of intense tingling in his arm had presented himself to the hospital with a fever. Then, after a day or two of retching and vomiting, he began thrashing about violently, became super-excitable and confused. He snarled and would become aggressive whenever anybody offered him water, or for that matter even if he caught a glimpse of it. He had subsequently suffered seizures, lost consciousness and died.

A rabies vaccine was now available as a preventative measure, Grace knew, but it could not protect people once a dog bite had already occurred.

There were many tragic cases like this and, as Grace learned, many different microbes responsible for them, yet it was a stimulating and exciting time to be studying medicine as advances were being made so quickly. Just as Will was so focused on surgery, Grace was engrossed in the prevention and treatment of contagious disease. Sometimes she wondered what it would be like if they could work together. Will doing the cutting and sewing and Grace ensuring the absence of infection. Whenever she was studying hard and he was at St George's or at work with Dr Forrester or elsewhere, they had little opportunity to spend much time together, and she missed him. She also missed the twins, but she knew that, between Clara, Kitty and their time with Jenny and Reg's child, Doris, and the nanny, their days were filled with care and their education lacked for nothing. It made the bond between mother and children ever stronger when they were together.

Nonetheless, her heart raced again for a moment. If one of them did get ill, would she regret the time she gave to her career?

Just then, the tutor's voice at the front of the auditorium interrupted her reverie and he had moved on to talking about the success of the BCG vaccination for tuberculosis that had been created in 1927. It was already making a huge difference. Tuberculosis had been a major scourge of mankind since time immemorial. Finally, he concluded his lecture.

After a quick bite of lunch with Jenny who had an afternoon off from her own nursing duties, they settled down at the back of a larger hall to hear a talk from a man called Alexander Fleming, who was a pathology researcher based at

St Mary's Hospital. He was quite short, at around 5 feet and 6 inches in height, had light hair and a small, flattened nose, but even from a distance, the two women could see that he had noticeably large, strikingly blue eyes.

Unfortunately, a more unprepossessing man would be hard to find. His delivery was so slow, quiet and monotonous that however exciting his subject might have been to him, most of the audience were quickly switching off and falling asleep within a few short minutes.

'I do hope he doesn't ramble on for too long,' said Jenny. 'We could've gone shopping instead.'

'We still can after this,' answered Grace. 'But unfortunately, since several of my tutors are here in front of us, I think we should wait.'

So they did. The gist of the lecture was that in July that year Fleming had returned from his holiday to find a petri dish in which he had been growing a culture of staphylococcal bacteria that had somehow become contaminated by a blue-green mould. That in itself was nothing unusual, as moulds commonly found their way into everything. What was interesting, the quiet Scot went on to say, was that no bacteria seemed to be present just adjacent to the mould, only dead transparent cells. He surmised that something in the mould had killed off the bacteria.

This grabbed Grace's attention for a moment as she realised the possible therapeutic implications. But Fleming's subsequent departure into lysozymes, the liquid enzymes produced by microbes which were not capable of replicating themselves and which he had been studying intently for years, sent her off to sleep again.

'Not very novel,' she heard one of her professors sitting in front of her say. 'Not very impressive. Not even worth recording. Just another lysozyme experiment but with a mould this time.'

'I'm not sure he knows what he thinks his so-called discovery really means,' said Jenny.

'But even if he does, he isn't putting it over very well,' agreed Grace. 'And I can't see it has any immediate relevance to our patients.'

'Well, it sounds like he's finally coming to the end now,' said Jenny with obvious relief. 'Hopefully there won't be many questions.'

The room was full of researchers, doctors, nurses and pathologists, all with a particular interest in microbiology, and it was usual for a dozen or so questions to be put to the speaker after each talk. Such was the uninspiring subject and delivery, however, that on this occasion there were none.

43

Army and Navy Club, Pall Mall, London, November 1928

Norman Sykes swished the tea towel around the last of the washed-up whisky tumblers and placed it on the drainer to dry. He had been the bartender at the Rag ever since his discharge from the Army on medical grounds and was grateful for his job because paid work of any kind was in increasingly short supply. He also enjoyed the company of his fellow servicemen and the esoteric bond they shared by way of their common experiences.

Tonight, however, his mood was not so cheerful. Major Davison was the one officer who was less than affable and had never been one to converse much with the lower ranks. As a mere ex-private, Norman had always been made to feel rather inferior and inadequate in his presence. On more than one occasion, the Major had made a public joke about his slow service, his shaking hands and his clumsiness. But it was not his fault. Norman was frustrated by his handicap more than anyone. But as the neurosurgeon who had treated the head injury he had sustained at Ypres had told him, the tremor and the 'motor retardation', as he'd called it, was a small price to pay considering the original damage, and he was lucky to be alive.

As he glanced over at the table by the far window overlooking St James's Square, Norman saw the man in question greedily knocking back yet another glass from the bottle of his favourite Scotch whisky. He had brought it over to him an hour or two beforehand. And just as he had been ordered, he put the cost of it on to the Major's growing and unsettled bar tab.

The Major was alone now, the last of his rowdy group of companions having departed some time ago.

'Sykes!' he had yelled at him earlier. 'Bring me your finest single malt, ice and six glasses. And shake a leg, would you?' he'd added, laughing and holding his hands out in front of his pals in an exaggerated mock tremor. 'Some of us are gasping.'

When Sykes had brought the drinks over, the Major had dismissed him curtly. 'Leave the bottle on the table, old man! And don't pour, you'll only spill it.'

That was hours ago. Now Davison poured the last few drops of the Vintage Star Blend Fine Old Highland Whisky from the bottle into his personally engraved crystal tumbler and downed it. A while ago, three of his fellow members had shared a dram or two from the same bottle and had expressly made a point of commenting on its provenance and quality. But the Major himself had consumed three quarters of it. They had listened patiently to his increasingly aggressive protestations about his version of the lamentable treatment he had received at the hands of his hospital colleagues and whenever they had had a chance to speak had diplomatically proffered their sympathies.

The few friends Davison did still socialise with tended to share his views that ordinary civilians rarely understood the experience that uniquely characterised the military man.

None had ever become accustomed to their authority being challenged. However, as the evening had progressed and Davison had become increasingly morose, slurred in speech and clumsy, his rude and hectoring treatment of Norman Sykes, the bartender, had begun to embarrass them. One by one, those companions around the table had taken their leave.

Now, at 11.15 p.m., Davison, the last man swaying, stood up, steadied himself on the back of his chair, ordered Sykes to add the latest bill to his tab and left the room. He entered the Great Hall, oblivious to the ornamental detail, the military and naval symbols and the defensive armour adorning its walls, and descended the steps under the centre of the three open arches on to George Street.

It was dark outside, with heavy clouds obscuring a waning gibbous moon. A strong blustery wind hit him in the face. He pulled up his collar and tightened the scarf around his neck. Pausing briefly to remember where he had left his car, he turned up the slope towards St James's Square and found it parked on the other side, opposite Charles II Street.

The 1922 Bullnose Morris Cowley type MC 119 tourer was his pride and joy. Kindly left to him in the will of a sixty-four-year-old spinster who had unfortunately died from an undiagnosed chronic illness while under his care, it was his most precious possession. The 1922 roadster with its dicky seat at the rear was so popular now that it had become one of the bestselling cars in Britain. Davison had personalised his own vehicle, however, obtaining a licence plate with his own initials and having its bodywork resprayed in military olive green.

He fumbled to get the key into the barrel lock of the driver's door but finally opened it, jumped in and gunned the four-cylinder Hotchkiss engine into life. He selected the first of the three forward gears, revved up and jumped off the clutch. The wheels spun on the loose gravel road, and he accelerated away. Turning right into Pall Mall and up St James's Street, he eased back into the leather-covered driver's seat and glanced along Jermyn Street towards his favourite retail outlets, popular with British royalty and the London gentry. He bought his unique Meerschaum and Briar pipes from Dunhill's or Astley's at number 109 and his shirts and tweed suits from Turnbull & Asser. He also spent many a happy evening in the various men's clubs in Duke Street and the Bunch of Grapes public house further along.

He was also partial to a smoke after an evening of drinking and the thought of that aromatic Captain Black tobacco in its green and black tin in the glove compartment was too much to resist.

He leaned over and extricated it, together with his trusty Windshield pipe, which he had purchased not so long ago from Alfred Dunhill. The latter was a brilliant innovation from the famous tobacconist. He had designed it in 1904 to combat the difficulties faced by smokers while driving. It was ugly but it worked, and Davison was much more interested in function than aesthetics. Since it was a particularly blustery night, the Windshield pipe was perfect.

He much admired that man, Dunhill. Whenever he had sold a pipe to an officer serving in France during the Great War, he had sent one or two more with it to be distributed among his fellow soldiers, to be paid for only on their return. And it had made his fortune. By the end of the conflict, his pipes were known internationally and sold widely in America, Canada, Belgium and France, as well as at home.

Turning left now into Piccadilly and passing the Ritz Hotel, Davison was steering with his right hand and trying to unscrew the tobacco tin lid and fill his pipe with the other.

Looking up through the horizontally split windscreen, he saw the familiar outline of St George's Hospital at Hyde Park Corner in front of him. He thought bitterly again about the trouble that was brewing there. The whisky was not helping, and he could hardly control the rage building inside him. He had got the lid off the tin now, but it was skidding across the passenger seat and he was losing most of the tobacco on the floor. Cursing, he put the tin between his legs and put both hands back on the wheel to skirt around Wellington Arch at the top of Constitution Hill. Once into South Carriage Drive on the south-west side of the park, he opened the throttle and pushed the car's speed up to its maximum of 55 mph. With nothing but a straight road in front of him, he took his left hand off the wheel again and resumed the job of filling the bowl of his pipe. He felt tired now, and a smoke would revive him.

The task was fiddly, but he had nearly completed it as he approached the sharp right-hand turn into Exhibition Road to cross the Serpentine. Two more thrusts with his index finger would tamp the tobacco down firmly enough, ready to be ignited by the lighter in his pocket. It would not be a problem, even driving along. His 1923 Dunhill Unique lighter, mounted as it was on a Colman's Mustard tin, was a one-hand operation with a single wheel action and was guaranteed to light first time. The road was dark, with leaves blowing in fluttering clouds across the carriageway. Davison's reactions were sluggish from drink, his thoughts elsewhere, and what concentration he had was focused on lighting the pipe. Finally, he managed it and took a deep, long, satisfying suck on the stem.

Suddenly the car was already at the junction and the speedometer was still hovering at 50 mph. Swearing, he grabbed the wheel, braked hard and swung the car into the turn.

The back of the car slid on the loose surface and he struggled to control the spin. He overcompensated and the rear wheel swung back out to the other side, taking the front of the car off to the nearside and on to the pedestrian walkway nearest to the Albert Memorial. The whole manoeuvre was over in seconds and a blur to Davison, but at some point through the screeching of the tyres, he thought he'd heard a dull thud and felt a slight jolt of the car.

He brought the Morris to a halt, killed the engine and stepped on to the street. Puzzled, but still pulling on his pipe, he made his way around to the front of the car and looked to see if there was any damage. Still struggling to focus his vision, he could not immediately see anything obvious. He scratched his head and went to the back of the car. He was aware that he needed to empty his bladder, but that could wait. Twenty yards behind him, there was an amorphous shape in the road. He headed over to take a look. When he got there, he could hardly believe his eyes. It was a woman, probably in her thirties, grievously injured and barely conscious. Blood trickled from her mouth and her breaths came in shallow gasps. Her right hand reached up to the man standing over her, her forehead creased into a frown and her eyes searching his face imploringly. But she could not speak.

Christ Almighty! Davison thought. I must have collided with this woman. But what was the fool doing there on her own at this time of night in the first place? And in the dark? What idiocy allowed her to bring this upon herself?

His doctorly instincts kicked in. She was not moving or showing signs of attempting to move. He felt her pulse.

Rapid. Thready. He looked at her chest and noticed the paradoxical in-pulling of the thoracic cage on inspiration. She had broken ribs. He prodded her abdomen and she moaned. Possibly a ruptured spleen or liver.

He glanced over his shoulder at the road ahead and to the left and right. There was nobody. The woman was dying and there was nothing to be done. This was the last thing he needed. Especially now, with everything else going on. He let go of her wrist, straightened up and averted his eyes from her pleading expression. She was not long for this world and there was no point hanging around to witness her leaving it.

He had to get away while the going was good. He was in enough trouble already. He climbed awkwardly back into his beloved Bullnose Morris and drove away into the night. In twenty minutes, he would be at his home in Little Venice. He would park the car in the drive opposite the canal, get to bed and sleep it off. It was a pity about the woman, whoever she was, but it was an accident. It could happen to anyone. There was no saving her and there was nothing to be gained by complicating his life by allowing himself to be associated with it.

A shambling figure emerged from behind the bushes and watched Davison's car disappear into the darkness. At the same time, nearby, a crowd emerged from the Albert Hall. The man had witnessed the whole episode and was shocked and distressed by it. Yet he had not been able to get there quick enough to announce himself. He knelt down awkwardly beside the stricken woman and took her hand. She looked at him briefly, but she was blinking rapidly, and her eyes were rolling back inside her head. He talked

to her quietly, softly, reassuring her, knowing it was hopeless, but nonetheless being there with her, not letting her
slip away alone, crumpled up in a public street in the dark.
He vaguely heard a woman's voice calling from the crowd
in the distance.

He stayed focused and present with the dying woman.

Soon, he heard the arrival of a vehicle and what sounded
like a motorcycle, then footfall running towards him.

'Stand back,' said a strident voice, pushing him roughly
aside. It was a policeman with three of his colleagues.

The bystander acquiesced and moved aside, happy to let
the professionals take over. Two of the officers leaned over
the victim and went through their procedures. The witness
crossed his fingers and silently prayed. After a few minutes,
the policemen rose as one and bowed their heads. She was
gone.

The fourth policeman, standing in the background, came
over to the man and prodded him in the chest with his
forefinger.

'What did you do to her?'

'I beg your pardon?' came the astonished reply.

'I said what did you do to her?'

'I didn't touch her. I saw she'd been hit by a car, and I
came over to see if I could help.'

From the policeman's view, the man looked uncertain
and scared. Dishevelled and unshaven, poorly dressed and
unwashed. He had guilt written all over him. And the
policeman's instincts were seldom wrong.

'I don't see any car.'

'It drove off. Before I got here. Before you arrived.'

The policeman squinted down the dark road. 'What's your
name?'

'Calvin. Calvin Darke. Private. Lancashire Rifles.'

What the hell is he talking about? thought the officer. He is a strange one indeed.

'You'll be coming with us. I'm arresting you for the murder of this woman.'

And before he could react, Calvin Darke looked down to see that the officer was attempting to cuff him.

'That's a prosthetic,' he said, indicating to his right arm. The officer paused, then roughly grabbed him around his left bicep and led him towards the police car.

44

St George's Hospital, Tooting, London, November 1928

Will sat quietly in the doctors' office enjoying a well-earned cup of tea, having just discharged the last of his long queue of patients that morning. It was part of his remit as a junior surgeon at St George's to look after any emergencies requiring medical care during his shift, with hospital services being generally provided through workman's compensation plans, railway companies and other municipalities.

Although tiring, Will enjoyed the work because he never knew what sort of patient he was going to see next, nor what kind of pathology they might present with. Today he had seen the usual gamut of minor injuries and infections: a man with obvious tuberculosis, another whose foot had been trodden on by a horse and an elderly lady who had fallen from a moving tram. He came across sick or injured people from all walks of life and he realised that the variety and range of the cases he saw all served to broaden his general medical experience and education. He was learning all the time.

The knock on the door made him look up. Miss Celia Watkins, the department's rather portly matron, stood there filling the door frame.

PART TWO

'There is an Inspector Jarvis from the Metropolitan Police to see you, Doctor,' she said. 'I'll show him in.'

Will shook the policeman's hand and gestured to the chair opposite him. 'Pleased to meet you, Inspector. How can I help?'

The visitor made himself comfortable and took out his notebook. Will imagined he would be making routine enquiries into one of the many cases of drunkenness or affray that frequently kept him busy. Helping the police with their enquiries was part of Will's job.

'I'm wondering if you know a gentleman by the name of Calvin Darke? He claims to be one of your patients.'

'I do, yes. And he is. Has been for a long time. What's happened? Is he all right?'

'Yes. Yes, he's fine. Well, he is no worse off than I imagine he usually is, put it that way.'

'Life has not been entirely kind to him, Inspector. Is he in some kind of trouble?'

'I'm afraid he is. He is currently under arrest and languishing in one of Her Majesty's cells for the suspected and unprovoked murder of a young woman in Hyde Park.'

Will was shocked. Murder? He had not expected that. 'I can hardly believe the man I know as Calvin Darke would be capable of such a thing.'

'And why is that?'

'Because Calvin Darke is a gentle soul who, despite his misfortune, has shown a great strength of spirit, and when attending here for recurrent problems with his health is patient and never aggressive. After a rough start, he's understanding about the limitations of what we can offer him and is invariably courteous and grateful for all of his nursing care.'

267

'It sounds like you'd be happy to give him a favourable character reference, then. How long have you known him?'

'On and off for almost ten years. He was a patient of ours at Queen Mary's Auxiliary Hospital, where we have revised treatment a couple of times, and he's been a regular attendee at St George's since I've been here.'

'What kind of care does he require?'

Will paused.

'I realise, Doctor, that you are bound by medical confidentiality, but . . . if I am to help him at all . . . perhaps . . .'

'It's no secret that he's an amputee: an arm and a leg. You will have noticed his gait and restricted movement.'

'Indeed.'

'He continues to be on quite large doses of pain relief on a daily basis.'

'I see,' said Jarvis, looking pensive. 'And what might he have been doing on his own in Hyde Park late in the evening on a wild blustery night, do you think?'

'What he does most nights, Inspector. He sleeps rough.'

Jarvis was making notes and waiting for more.

'Calvin was not only physically maimed in the war, he was mentally scarred as well. After the shell at Ypres that injured him, he remained mute for several weeks afterwards, a condition not helped by him having to come to terms with a severe disability and incessant pain. Like so many others, he suffered headaches, dizzy spells and nightmares. Vivid dreams where he relived the explosions and the noise. Seeing in his mind's eye his friends and comrades being shot to pieces or vaporised in an instant. He suffers from what is known as shell shock. And the tragedy is, he probably always will.'

Will swallowed. He felt passionately defensive of the men who had suffered in this way. Like Captain Daniels. Like his father.

'Is he deranged? Could a man such as this, a man not right in the head, be driven by such anger, terror and grief that he might want to take it out on others? To lash out and kill indiscriminately?'

'I'd say the opposite,' said Will emphatically. 'His experiences have made him terrified of any confrontation or violence. Even loud noise. He runs from it. That's why men like him are of no future use to the Army and are pensioned off. I've seen him curled up and cowering from fear in this very department after a nurse simply dropped a metal steriliser off a trolley.'

Jarvis nodded.

'It's not that he's not right in the head. Not at all. His intelligence, his behaviour towards others, his sense of morality, his ability to distinguish right from wrong, that hasn't changed.'

'But jobless and living rough? Outdoors? Among the bushes and foliage of a public park? How desperate. What does that do to a man's sanity?'

'Calvin has a job, Inspector. He sells newspapers in the morning on the corner of Beauchamp Place. He isn't penniless and doesn't need to steal. Nor would he, I believe. The man is perfectly sane.'

'But if he can afford a place to live, why on earth—'

'Because he can't tolerate being shut in. To him, being enclosed within four walls and under a ceiling became insufferable. It engenders panic and the intense desire to run and get out. It's an acquired claustrophobia caused by his previous ordeals. Even here, when he needs treatment or medicines, it's as much as we can do to persuade him to stay.'

Will also thought briefly of his brother, Jack, who lived in a small, controllable environment and who could never seem to commit to a relationship.

'So, in your opinion, Doctor, our suspect is an unlikely killer?'

'I learned many things during the war, Inspector. And one of them was that some men are content to kill. For them, it's all very clear. In a war situation, there is an enemy and it's your duty to fight. It is self-defence. It's a matter of kill or be killed. They do it once, twice, even multiple times, and they never think about it.' Will glanced out the window, the memories flooding back. 'Sometimes it's face-to-face, intimate, hand-to-hand combat; at other times, the killing is remote — firing artillery shells at random targets or detonating huge explosives in mines under enemy trenches. Some even delight in it. Enjoy it.' He pressed his lips together to control the emotion. Took a deep breath. 'I've seen men laughing as they repeatedly shoot or stab the enemy with their bayonet. For others, killing never comes easily. It didn't come easy to me. I never killed. I don't know if I ever could. But that doesn't make someone a coward. I had to be persuaded of that. Some men kill but relive the moment over and over again, fraught with guilt and self-loathing. We're all different, I suppose, but it's a mercy that born killers are a rare breed.'

'And Calvin Darke?'

'I don't know if he ever killed anyone in action. He may not know either. Who knows where the bullets you fire end up or if they kill? It's all so random. But he's a gentle and kind soul, Inspector. As I say, I can't believe you've got the right man.'

'Is he reliable?' The inspector tapped his pencil against his chin.

'I should say so. Why do you ask?'

'One or two things he's said.' He gesticulated with the pencil. 'Claims a car struck the victim and then drove off. Some man got out first and examined the victim as if he

PART TWO

knew what he was doing. Taking the pulse. Looking at the eyes. Checking the breathing.'

'Is it possible?'

'We think it might be. He said he got to the victim as soon as he could after witnessing all this, but he had taken his artificial leg off to lie down and sleep and was struggling to reattach it quickly enough.'

'That would take several minutes, for sure.'

Miss Watkins appeared at the door with a pot of coffee just as the sound of some commotion echoed along the corridor.

'It's all right, Doctor, I'll deal with it,' she said, turning to leave.

'Thank you,' said Will, standing to take the tray and place it down on a coffee table. 'You are very kind.' He turned again towards Jarvis, who looked down at his notebook and continued.

'We also found one or two items of interest at the crime scene which might corroborate his story. I must admit that initially I was a little too hasty in jumping to conclusions about him without sufficient evidence.'

'And do you have evidence?' Will said, pouring two coffees. 'I'd like to help Calvin if I can.' He pushed one coffee to Jarvis's side of the table, sugar and milk in view, then sat again.

'Well, the single most telling piece of evidence comes from Darke himself. He is something of a tricky witness as far as we are concerned. He is reluctant to talk much and seems to be distrustful of authority. Perhaps his treatment by the Army after the war and his meagre pension has a bearing on that.'

'I imagine so, Inspector. The evidence?'

Jarvis sipped his coffee, smiled his thanks. 'Darke doesn't know the make or model of the car in question, but he claims he took note of its registration plate.'

'That was very forward-thinking of him. But in those traumatic circumstances who on earth would—'

'There was a reason he remembered it.'

Will was intrigued.

'The number plate was CD35.'

'And what's so memorable about that?'

'It's his own initials and his age. It struck him as strangely coincidental at the time and he couldn't forget it.'

'Oh yes.' Will sipped thoughtfully. 'So you can trace the car?'

'We have. The Motor Car Act of 1903 made the registration of alphanumeric plates on all vehicles mandatory. The car is a Bullnose Morris Cowley.'

Will frowned.

'And this one is owned by a Major Dr Clifford Davison, who I believe is a surgeon at this very hospital.'

Will put down his cup, now rattling in its saucer. The coincidence was indeed extraordinary. An accident just around the corner from there. His patient in the dock. His long-standing personal nemesis possibly responsible.

'*Was* a surgeon here,' Will almost whispered as his thoughts whirred furiously.

'What do you mean?'

'He was suspended from duty on disciplinary grounds just three days ago.'

'Was he indeed?' Jarvis scribbled another note in his little book. 'What can you tell me about the Major, Dr Burnett?'

When the policeman looked up at his interviewee, Will was smiling.

'How long have you got?'

45

Chiswick, London, December 1928

It was a Friday evening and Will and Grace were both looking forward to a rare weekend off duty together. As Grace came through the front door of Clara's and gathered Emily and Daniel in her arms, smiling at Clara, Will handed her a large white envelope. It bore the Worshipful Society of Apothecaries' stamp in the top right-hand corner.

'Your exam results, I imagine,' he said.

'Oh my goodness,' she said, giving each of the children a sweetie she had bought from the corner shop on the way. She could still vividly remember the questions she had answered two weeks previously.

1. Examination paper in Surgery: Describe the male urethra. Discuss the pathology of carcinoma of the large bowel. Describe the diagnosis and treatment of strangulated umbilical hernia.

2. Examination paper in Forensic Medicine, Hygiene and Insanity: Describe the manifestations of lead poisoning and the mental disorders resulting from the chronic abuse of alcohol.

She could recall every question in Medicine, Obstetrics and Pathology as well, as she had gone over every answer she had written in her head several times since.

But she was so nervous about opening the envelope that Will had to do it for her. She looked at him expectantly as his serious, handsome face scanned the paper enclosed.

'Congratulations, Dr Burnett,' he said eventually, hazel eyes twinkling, 'you've been awarded your Licence in Medicine and Surgery certificate and it seems you came equal top in your class of twenty. Not bad for a woman who used to do all her nursing on horseback.'

'So now she's a doctor too and equal to you, Daddy,' said Daniel proudly.

'I wouldn't say that,' said Clara, smiling broadly herself. 'She's always been much more accomplished than your father.'

'Well, thank you, Aunt Clara,' said Will, feigning hurt.

'My pleasure, Will. My pleasure.'

'In all seriousness, though,' Grace said, 'I'm not yet a specialist like Will. I still need to do my lab training and further exams for the pathology qualification.'

'Slow down for a moment,' said Clara. 'This alone is spectacular. Let's all have a celebratory drink. I think there's some of Jack's gin hiding in the kitchen dresser.'

As Clara went to leave the room, she clasped her hip and let out a gasp.

'Aunt Clara, are your pains getting worse?' Will asked with concern.

She shook her head, but he could see the wince on her face.

'I forgot my Aspro is all,' Clara said. 'But the gin will do the trick.'

She left and Will and Grace looked at each other. Clara had finally received a diagnosis recently, of osteoarthritis, but she continually refused any help, saying that the aspirin was doing its job.

Grace held her hand out for Will's and said reassuringly, 'I'm sure there'll be more treatments available soon.'

'You're right,' Will smiled. He was keen to update Grace on the news from the hospital, too, that Davison was close to being arrested, but now was not the time.

Clara returned with the gin and some teacups.

'Is Pop here, Aunt Clara?' asked Daniel as she poured.

'Yes, but he's not having a good day, Daniel—'

'I'll cheer him up,' the young boy interrupted, bounding up the creaky old stairs. Emily stayed put.

'I worry about Daniel seeing him like that,' Clara said. 'Should we stop him?'

Grace shook her head. 'He's a strong boy.'

Clara poured the gins and some water for Emily.

'To Dr Grace Burnett,' said Will, and they clinked teacups.

'To Mum.' Emily made a pouting, mock-adult face when she sipped her 'gin'.

46

The Old Bailey, London, February 1929

The Central Criminal Court of England and Wales is commonly referred to as the Old Bailey as it sits on the road of the same name, which follows the path of the ancient outer city wall, or 'bailey', that originally encircled the City of London.

The trial of Major Dr Clifford Davison had attracted a great deal of public and press attention and Will had arrived early in order to ensure a seat.

Outside, he looked up at the imposing Edwardian baroque architecture of the building in which he fervently hoped that the despicable man he had hated for so long would finally get his comeuppance. Pomeroy's imposing statue of Justice sat at the very top of the building – her arms outstretched with a traditional pan balance in her left hand and a slim sword in the right. She stood there, bold and resolute, in stark contrast to the bright sky above, perched on a golden globe.

As he entered the domed Grand Hall adorned with paintings by Gerald Moira and William Blake Richmond, Will came across another of Pomeroy's sculptures – this time representing justice, mercy, temperance and charity.

How very fitting for the occasion, Will thought. If only Davison had shown mercy to poor Captain Daniels before having him unjustly executed. If only his charity had extended to those patients who could not afford his grossly inflated private fees. If only temperance had prevented him drink-driving and killing an innocent woman.

Well, Lady Justice, Will said to himself, I am glad to notice that, contrary to what I had thought, you are not actually blindfolded as the ancient Roman Justitia was. Because I want you to see very clearly just how guilty this bastard being tried here today really is.

He joined the gathering throng of people streaming into the courtroom and found a place in the fourth row, next to a pale and gaunt lady. After a brief conversation, it turned out she had been one of Davison's patients whose procedure had not gone at all well.

Moments later, Lord Chief Justice Munroe swept into the room and bid everybody be seated. He issued a few initial words of greeting and then, without further ado, swiftly began proceedings.

'Our duty today is to hear the case against Major Dr Clifford Davison, who is charged with the offence of manslaughter. The grand jury has assessed the relevant indictments and decided, rather unusually I must say, that there is sufficient evidence to try this case before a trial jury.'

He gave some formal instructions to the jury and then invited the counsel for the Crown Prosecution to make his introductory remarks.

'Ladies and gentlemen of the jury,' Gerald Penton QC began. 'It is my duty to demonstrate that at 11.30 p.m. on the night of the eighteenth of November this past year, the accused, Major Dr Clifford Davison, did drive his car reck-lessly at speed and under the pernicious influence of drink so that, losing control as he turned a sharp corner, he did

277

strike and run over an innocent bystander, causing her substantial internal injuries from which she tragically died. Mrs Tennant, the innocent victim, was a healthy thirty-two-year-old mother of three and had just finished her evening's work as a waitress at the Albert Hall, a stone's throw from where she met her death. The Brunswick Hour Orchestra had been playing through their famous repertoire that night, including those songs you will be familiar with, such as, "Ah, Sweet Mystery of Life" and "I'll See You in My Dreams".

'I wonder if this poor woman, who has left behind three young children and a disabled husband who relied on her modest income, can now "see you", members of the jury, in her dreams? I wonder if that mystery, not of her life but of her death, can be resolved, and the perpetrator punished appropriately?

'Mrs Tennant had left on foot, as she always did, and started her walk home to Bayswater on the other side of Hyde Park. It was the route she always took and she was familiar with it. We will hear that she was struck from behind so would have had no visual warning of any impact. We will also hear that the tracks made by her body being dragged along the road demonstrate clearly that she was undoubtedly on the pavement and not on the road itself. Her hearing was perfect, of that we can be assured, since she had a keen interest in music and was something of an accomplished violinist herself. So, whatever it was that collided with her was moving so fast she had no time to hear it. She had no time to leap from its headlong rush.

'I intend to prove to you that we cannot only be sure of the car which hit her but of the identity of the man who was driving it. I will show that he had been drinking heavily prior to the collision, that he initially stopped at the scene, stepped out of his car to inspect the damage to it — his cherished prized possession — and that only afterwards, almost as an afterthought, went over to the broken body of his victim to look at her.

'Worse is to come. The accused is a doctor, the head of his department no less, yet despite his so-called medical expertise, instead of helping her or summoning assistance, he abandoned her where she lay and hastily drove off to save his own skin. Ladies and gentlemen, Mrs Gloria Tennant was still alive when the defendant cowardly left her for dead, knowing full well from his cursory inspection of her that she was unlikely to live long enough to ever bear witness against him. The accused should be found guilty and a just and proportionate sentence passed upon him.'

As Gerald Penton QC sat back down, the jurors exchanged shocked glances at one another and the courtroom erupted in a loud hubbub, which was only silenced when the counsel for the defence stood up and Lord Chief Justice Munroe rapped repeatedly with his gavel.

Theodore Cotterell QC strode dramatically towards the bench and paused. He turned slowly and meandered over to the jury. He was a skilled barrister of great repute and, despite being the most expensive in London, was forever in great demand, especially among the rich and famous. He rarely lost a case.

'Ladies and gentlemen,' he began, 'the gentleman who stands accused of this unexplained road accident is a man of outstanding character and reputation. He not only served his country dutifully and heroically throughout the Great War, but such was his diligence and high standing that he rose to the rank of major, having been promoted with impressive, almost unprecedented speed. Clearly he was considered reliable, trustworthy and proficient by that most disciplined of organisations, the British Army. He is also a doctor, a consultant surgeon whose sole ambition and raison d'être in his career is to save life, not take it. Are we really to believe that a man as honourable, brave and selfless as he could behave in a way previously described by the prosecution or possibly be responsible for some mysterious yet tragic event without sound and irrefutable evidence? Of course not. And thankfully for him, the evidence is patently lacking. The case brought against him is built on a tissue of coincidence and supposition.

'That the death of Mrs Tennant is a tragedy is obvious. Any death is a tragedy. Yes, sadly, deaths on England's roads today are increasingly frequent. With well over one million drivers on the road, accidents and collisions are becoming all too common. Last year in Britain, 6138 people were killed this way. Regrettably, the thoroughfares of our capital are something of a free-for-all, with few established rules and police hard-pressed to interpret and enforce them. I have personally been campaigning for some kind of "Highway Code", but, alas, one does not yet exist. Yet clearly this road accident, if that is indeed what it was, for that is yet to be proven, was not run-of-the-mill. If the events which the prosecution describe really did happen, it would have been reckless, and, as we know, it was fatal.'

'I hope, and I'm sure you all hope, ladies and gentlemen of the jury, that any driver responsible for this heinous crime will in due course be caught and punished. So, as quickly and efficiently as I can, I will endeavour to prove beyond all doubt that Major Davison is innocent and should be allowed to go back to saving the lives of his patients as soon as possible. But every second wasted here haranguing a man totally without blame allows the real culprit to divert attention elsewhere and escape justice. I trust you will bear this in mind. The prosecution needs to prove that the accused is guilty of the crime he is charged with beyond all reasonable doubt. I intend to prove that the only thing beyond any doubt is his innocence. Thank you.'

Will waited with bated breath as Clifford Davison, the man he hated, took the stand.

Attired in his customary three-piece tweed suit, he sat ramrod straight, with his chin jutting out, his moustache elegantly trimmed and the air of a man who felt rather inconvenienced to be there at all. He swore on the Bible to tell the truth and nothing but the truth and did it in such a loud and commanding manner as if to suggest that the entire exercise for him was completely unnecessary.

The judge then read out the charges and asked the Major how he would plead.

'Not guilty, your honour.'

Gerald Penton QC approached the witness stand.

'Would you be good enough to state your full name please.'

'Major Dr Clifford Davison.'

'Thank you, sir. Although you are not in fact a major any longer, are you?'

'That is indeed my title.'

'Although you no longer serve or indeed have any role in the British Army?'

'It remains my title. I believe my service to this country fully justifies it.'

'Yet it is unusual, is it not, for someone of your previous rank to have been dismissed so perfunctorily?'

'Objection, your honour,' said Cotterell. 'The defendant's title is not in question and is neither here nor there. We know who the doctor is.'

'Objection sustained. Please proceed.'

'May I call you Doctor, perhaps?'

'You can call me Charlie Chaplin if you wish, but please get on with it.'

A ripple of laughter spread across the room.

Will could scarcely believe Davison was making light of the proceedings, but again, nothing about this man really surprised him. From his discussions with Penton, he knew what was coming next.

'But even then, you are not actually practising as a doctor at the present time?'

'I am a licensed practising surgeon based at St George's Hospital and have been Provost and Head of Surgery there for the last five years.'

'Until three months ago,' countered Penton.

A pause. Davison glared at the prosecutor malevolently. This was an unwarranted presumption from a professional man, as far as he was concerned.

'Objection, your honour,' said Cotterell, standing up again. 'The prosecution is clearly attempting to belittle my client's credentials and unfairly impugn his good reputation.'

'Sustained. Would you please proceed with your cross-examination and confine your remarks to the relevant issue,' said the judge.

'Your honour, I'm merely trying to clarify the defendant's current status, bearing in mind—'

'The objection is sustained. I would ask you to move on.'

'Very well. What car do you drive, Doctor?'

'A Morris Cowley.'

'A very covetable vehicle indeed. And what particular model would that be?'

'A 1922 Bullnose, type MC 119 tourer.'

'Ah, the tourer,' Penton nodded. 'How very luxurious. With a top speed of, what, 40 miles per hour?'

'You don't know your cars. My car is capable of a top speed of 55 miles per hour.'

'Goodness, that *is* fast. How exhilarating it must be to be able to travel at such a rate. And how long does it take a car travelling at 55 miles per hour to stop in an emergency?'

'I have no idea.'

'No? Maybe that sort of information would be useful. As a matter of safety, I mean. Perhaps we might see it noted one day in my esteemed colleague's proposed Highway Code.'

Penton smiled at Cotterell benignly and continued.

'Do you smoke a pipe?'

'Objection, your honour,' said Cotterell. 'My client's personal habits are a matter for him. Next he will be asked how many times he brushes his teeth or what shoe polish he uses to shine his shoes.'

Will clenched his teeth, desperate for Penton to be able to follow his thread.

'If it pleases the court, I will demonstrate the relevance of this question in due course. It may have a strong bearing on the available evidence.'

'Proceed,' said the judge.

'I enjoy a pipe in rare moments of relaxation,' Davison admitted.

'And who do you buy them from?'

Davison pondered the point of this question. He recalled he had not been able to locate one of his pipes or lighter ever since the night of the accident.

'Far and wide. I have purchased them in France and had them bought for me. I've also taken my custom to many a tobacconist in London. You may be surprised to hear there is in fact more than just one of them.'

Again, some audible laughter could be heard around the room.

'Could I have exhibit A, please?' asked Penton.

A clerk duly handed the item to the barrister on a tray.

'Is this one of your pipes?'

'I don't see how it could be. Unless you have burgled my property overnight.' Davison was enjoying himself.

'Nevertheless, would you be good enough to take a look?'

The defendant glanced at it briefly.

'No. I don't recognise this as one of my pipes.'

'It is what is known as a Windshield pipe, ladies and gentlemen. The ingenious invention of Alfred Dunhill, who designed it in 1904 expressly so that gentleman could happily smoke their pipes while driving. Unfortunately, the uniquely raised leading edge of its bowl, although serving its intended purpose, was generally considered rather ugly and very few sales were ever made.'

'Objection, your honour. This court can surely have no interest in the design or history of gentlemen's smoking materials.'

Penton cleared his throat. 'I'll get to the point. Have you ever bought a pipe from Alfred Dunhill of Jermyn Street, Doctor?'

'I may have done. I really couldn't be sure.' He glared at Penton.

'But the store itself is sure, Doctor. The records show you bought such a pipe two years ago. This pipe bears the characteristic white spot unique to Alfred Dunhill.'

'Quite possibly.' Davison crossed his arms across his tweed vest.

'And that you brought it back there as recently as four months ago to have the stem replaced. Exhibit A shows a pipe with a very new-looking stem.'

'Your honour,' interrupted Cotterell. 'The provenance type and quality of the kind of pipe smoked by my client is all very interesting but hardly of relevance to this case.'

'Except, your honour, that this very pipe was recovered from the scene of the tragedy that very same night by Sergeant Rowley of the Metropolitan Police. Together with a lighter bearing the inscription, "To my darling husband, Clifford, from your loving wife, Francis".'

'Objection, your honour. This is all circumstantial. It doesn't directly connect Dr Davison with the alleged crime scene whatsoever.'

'Overruled. Let's see where this is going.' The judge leaned forward.

'I presume your wife, Francis, would testify under oath that she gave it to you, Doctor?'

'If the items are mine, I'll be glad to have them returned. I have no idea how they fell into the hands of the police, but I have told them that I drive the same route home each and every day. Hundreds of other cars do the same. These things could easily have fallen out of my car without me knowing. My grandson could've been playing with them and simply been clumsy and dropped them.'

'Of course. At precisely the location of the incident. Quite a coincidence.'

Penton scanned the faces of the jurors and let the implication linger for a few seconds.

'Doctor, did you know the victim Mrs Tennant at all?'
'No.'
'Not personally? Not as a patient, perhaps?'

'No.'

'Not in any capacity whatsoever?'

'No.' He stroked his moustache.

'You had never seen her before in your life, nor had you ever had any contact with her?'

'No.'

'Mr Penton, you have established that now and our clerk has duly noted it, so would you please move on.'

'Certainly, your honour. Doctor, did you drive home at 11.30 that night, lose control of your vehicle and strike a pedestrian when your attention was diverted elsewhere?'

'No.'

'Did you stop the car, inspect the front of it, then walk back to find a dying woman lying in the road?'

'Absolutely not.'

'Did you bend over her, look at her pupils, take her pulse and check her breathing?'

'No. I wasn't there.' Davison's arms were still crossed.

'Having established how seriously injured she was, did you realise that you had probably caused a fatal injury while driving under the influence of drink and decide that the consequences to your upstanding reputation would be catastrophic, so you decided to cut and run?'

Davison reddened and looked furious.

'Even suggesting such a thing is an outrage. I've told you, I wasn't there.'

'If you weren't there, where were you?'

'I was at home.'

'All day?'

'I had been at work at the hospital and then later I went to my club – the Army and Navy Club in St James's.'

'Did anyone see you there?'

'Of course. I was enjoying the company of several of my fellow servicemen.'

'What time did you leave?'

'I can't be certain. Around nine o'clock, I should think.'

'Nine o'clock. And you went straight home?'

'Indeed.'

'And your wife would corroborate the time of your arrival?'

'My wife tends to retire earlier, around seven o'clock these days. She suffers from neurasthenia. So I dined alone.'

'So you have no alibi, as such?'

'You have my word. My word is my bond.'

Penton kept rapidly firing off questions. 'How much did you have to drink?'

'That's difficult to say. I'm not much of a drinker. I've seen too many cirrhotic livers and patients with yellow jaundice as a result. Including several who are members of your own profession.'

There was another murmur of amusement in the room, but this time more muted as the deliberate slur on the behaviour of the legal profession was not lost on them.

'But roughly?'

'Oh . . . one whisky, perhaps . . . or two at the most. With water and ice of course.'

'Do you know a gentleman by the name of Norman Sykes?'

'He is the bartender at the Rag.'

'The Rag?'

'The Army and Navy Club.'

'Oh, I'm sorry. I'm not privileged with familiarity with that nickname. Yes, the Rag. The thing is, Sykes will testify that you were there until 11.15 p.m.'

Davison paused, but he had been well rehearsed.

287

'Then he is mistaken. You may not know it, but the poor man is handicapped. Pensioned out of the Army because of it. The Club took pity on him and out of charity gave him a menial job behind the bar. He is a decent fellow and conscientious enough but is slow, rather clumsy and prone to making mistakes.'

'That's interesting. Because I don't know if you will be aware, Doctor, but during the war, he worked in reconnaissance. Where accuracy and attention to detail are a vital prerequisite.'

'I didn't know.' Davison shook his head. 'What a shame then that all of that was taken away from him. The head injuries would have affected him significantly.'

'His memory, he admits, is not what it was. Which is why he writes everything down. Everything. Table bookings. Membership numbers. Times of arrival. And of departure. His notes clearly say you left at 11.15.'

'They're wrong.'

'They also say you ordered a bottle of vintage whisky and ordered him to leave it on the table. They say that your three companions had a dram each before leaving, but by the time you left, there was an empty bottle on the table.'

'As I say, they're wrong.'

'Yet the bill was put on your tab, Doctor, as you expressly asked, and you signed it before you left. At 11.15.'

'Objection, your honour,' jumped in Cotterell. 'The defendant has already told us what time he left.'

'Sustained. The prosecution will move on,' the judge said.

Penton steepled his fingers and nodded. 'You'd had a tiresome day that day, had you not, Dr Davison?'

'A surgeon's day is always challenging.'

'And especially that particular day.'

Davison's head snapped up. 'What do you mean?'

'You were suspended from duty by the hospital that very day, were you not?'

'Objection, your honour. The doctor's clinical work and the administrative affairs of his workplace have no bearing whatsoever on this case,' said Cotterell. 'His medical and military record is completely untarnished. This is another blatant attempt to malign Dr Davison and prejudice the jury unnecessarily.'

'Your honour, I'm merely trying to establish that whatever the current circumstances at the hospital, the act of being suspended would have caused great distress to someone as grand as a provost and head of department. To the extent perhaps that it may have been a powerful catalyst for someone to be tempted to drown his sorrows in drink.'

'Objection. This is pure supposition and conjecture.'

'Sustained. You will confine yourself to the facts, Mr Penton.'

The seeds of doubt in the jurors' minds had now been sown however, and Will, who was relishing seeing Davison squirm, could see the suspicion in their faces. He was such an arrogant swine, Will thought. He could still sit there, calm and aloof, bereft of remorse, trying to bluff his way out of trouble. Will could not wait for the guilty verdict and to hear the sentence. Nothing would be too severe.

'I had two small glasses of whisky all night,' he heard Davison say.

'Before you drove home through Hyde Park around nine o'clock, you say.'

'You seem to have grasped it now.'

The sarcasm was an error. It was clear to everyone he was still trying to belittle the lawyer, and it backfired. Theodore Cotterell winced.

'Oh, forgive me if I appear a little slow here. I think the penny has finally dropped. You couldn't have been the driver of the car that collided with Mrs Tennant and you had never met her before the night of her death.'

'Sometimes the bullet just gets stuck in the breach.'

No laughter this time.

'Would it surprise you then to hear, Doctor, that there is in fact a witness to the events that night?'

Suddenly, Davison looked less sure of himself. So did Cotterell. They knew about Darke, but because he had been an initial suspect and because of his personal situation, they'd been confident he would not be called to the stand. Perhaps it was a bluff. After a pause, he said 'Well then, I trust the testimony will absolve me. I wasn't there.'

'But our witness says you were. He saw what happened: a car exactly fitting your vehicle's description, and a man jumping out and examining the victim's body just like a doctor would — his words, as you will hear in due course — before quickly driving off. When our witness reached the poor woman, she was still alive. Her eyes were darting from side to side, her pulse thready and rapid and her breathing coming in shallow desperate gasps.'

The jurors were on the edge of their seats now, transfixed. You could hear a pin drop in the courtroom.

'Moments later, the police arrived and took over. But it was too late. Mrs Tennant died at the scene.'

'That man was caught at the scene of the crime with nobody else within a million miles and in his diminished circumstances with every reason to accost a young woman walking home alone at night!' Spittle flew from Davison's lips as he spoke.

'It would certainly be convenient for you if he *was* responsible. But he was not. All the evidence points to the perpetrator
being someone else. And that person is you.'

Davison was looking increasingly angry. And trapped. He
continually looked over for guidance from his brief, but it
was not forthcoming. He'd been told by Cotterell to remain
calm, to answer the questions honestly and not lose his
temper. He was innocent after all, was he not?

'When Calvin Darke, our witness, saw you drive off—'

'Objection, your honour, the defendant has already told
the court he was not there.'

'Let me rephrase the question. When Calvin Darke saw
the driver accelerate away, he couldn't help noticing the
registration plate of the car. Number plates are unique, as
I'm sure you all know. And he remembers it distinctly for
a very good reason. You see, the letters are his own initials
and the numbers his own age. His initials are CD and he
is thirty-five years old. What is the registration of your car,
Dr Davison?'

Davison looked frantically over to his QC and tried to
suppress a twitch around his left eye.

'I, er, I think it may be something similar.'

'Very similar. Identical in fact. The number plate of your
car is CD35. We checked with the national register. This is
your car. You are the registered owner. We have established
that your wife does not hold a driving licence herself. So
you must have been the driver.'

'I don't deny that that is the registration plate of my car.
But the witness is mistaken. I imagine lots of number plates
look similar from a distance and in the dark. A "C" can look
like an "L". A "D" can resemble an "O". A three an eight
and so on. I've often seen plates which resemble my own.

Besides, people see what they want to see. Their own initials on the car they envy. I'm sure your witness would love to own my car. I can see how this looks. But it's nonsense.'

Gerald Penton walked slowly over and stood in front of the jurors.

'So many coincidences, aren't there? And so many contradictory statements. So many apparent mistakes made by others. If there still remains any remote doubt in your mind as to the defendant's guilt, I believe it will be dispelled by the end of these proceedings. That will be all for now, Dr Davison. You may stand down.'

If Will thought the result of the case was all but sealed, he was wrong.

The defence counsel's cross-examination was just as slick and raised further doubts and questions that were difficult to answer. He depicted Davison as something of an unsung hero, rubbished the evidence so far provided and implied that both Norman Sykes and the so-called witness were at best mentally unwell and at worst blatant liars. Yet the verdict Will wanted so desperately depended on proving guilt beyond all reasonable doubt.

47

St Paul's Churchyard, London, February 1929

At lunchtime, Will walked off his adrenaline, worried about the trial outcome but also distracted by thoughts of his current patients. He raged all over again at Davison for the time this trial was making him take away from his work — from the people he was hoping to save. Like little Stevie Smith.

Little Stevie Smith had been a sorry sight when Will had first encountered him in Manchester last month. At eight years old, he was just 3 feet and 6 inches tall, with severely bowed legs, prominent ribs at the front of his chest and a spine bent both forwards and sideways. He had peered at Will with interest from beneath his prominent forehead as he told him about the pain in his limbs and his trouble sleeping.

Will had seen enough of this Victorian disease in the course of his travels and he knew that only surgery would be able to correct this little chap's skeletal deformity.

Engaging with this boy in many ways reminded Will of Freddie, his old neighbours' son back in Barnes, who had tragically died from diphtheria. This young lad too never seemed to stop talking and had a wonderful sense of humour, mercifully unaffected by any intellectual impairment, which rickets could sometimes engender.

"'Ere, doctor,' he had said to Will. 'I may not be able to walk properly, but with legs like these I can ride a horse like a good'n'.'

The limb-fitting centre at Queen Mary's in Roehampton had established a number of regional centres throughout the country, many of which surgeons like Will would occasionally visit to perform operations. These centres were now treating civilians and children, as well as injured servicemen. From 1922, Will frequently saw men from the London and South Western Railway who had lost limbs as a result of accidents at work, and soon the hospital was able to welcome miners, policemen, school-aged children and even infants with congenital deformities.

The Ministry of Pensions, however, would only pay for soldiers, naval rankings and able seamen, and clearly there was no way this unfortunate child's family could ever afford to pay for private treatment.

It was for this reason that Will now devoted a day and a half a week to his small private practice in Wandsworth. Being the son of a working-class stevedore who'd had to struggle against the prejudices in the medical profession, he loathed the idea of private practice and only maintained this limited interest in one in order to fund his charitable work. He had resolved to carry out the operative correction of Stevie's limbs and to pay for the hospital facilities' staff and equipment out of his own pocket.

In Manchester, Will had taken a stroll over to the Stanley Hospital, made famous largely by Sir Robert Jones, to visit the museum and library. Robert Jones was a Welsh orthopaedic surgeon who had been instrumental in establishing the modern specialty of orthopaedic surgery. He had been specialist super-intendent during the construction of the Manchester Ship

Canal and responsible for the twenty thousand workers carrying out dangerous work during that seven-year project. He set up a string of first-aid posts in sections along the entire length of the thirty-six-mile canal and staffed hospitals with doctors specially trained in fracture management. It was the first comprehensive accident service in the world. He oversaw the entire project and treated some three thousand cases and performed three hundred operations himself.

He also believed very strongly in the value of radiography. He used it as an essential aid to accurate diagnosis, an invaluable adjunct to any surgeon's skill and expertise. It was something Will had taken on board himself many years ago.

When Will had looked at little Stevie Smith's X-rays, they confirmed the soft bones, the poor mineralisation of the weight-bearing parts of the skeleton and the flared cupping of the bones, which resembled sticks of cooked rhubarb that had been banged down on a hard surface. Previous treatments for rickets might have included cautery, splinting and even suspending patients from pulleys using gravity in an attempt to straighten them out, but success was extremely limited.

Will knew that only surgery would offer Stevie a reasonable chance of living a normal life and together with some sunlight, fresh air and nutritional supplementation, he had the potential to do well. But that surgery was now stalled by this trial.

Will entered a post office to use the telephone as he desperately wanted to hear Grace's voice, which always put him at ease. But the nurse on the other end said she was in surgery so couldn't come to the phone.

'Of course. It's not urgent,' he said, and hung up, morose.

His guts churned as he walked back towards the courthouse. It would surely soon be time he was called to the stand.

48

The Old Bailey, London, February 1929

Will, now on the stand, looked out at the sea of faces, champing at the bit to tell the jury everything. Davison stared back at him intently, his face a picture of sheer contempt.

'How long have you known the defendant, Dr Burnett?' asked Penton.

'I first came across him in 1916 during the war in France. Then he interviewed me for a place at medical school in 1924 and he was Head of Department at St George's Hospital where I have worked, among other hospitals, for the past five years.'

'What was your first recollection of him?'

Will clutched his hands together in his lap. 'He had sentenced a brave man to death by firing squad and I was appealing to him—'

'Objection!' yelled Cotterell. 'The defendant's military activities as a senior high-ranking officer have no bearing whatsoever on this case.'

'The defence has made much of the defendant's honourable character and distinguished reputation,' countered Penton quickly, 'I'm merely trying to suggest that we may not be able to take that for granted.'

'You may proceed. But let's see where this is going,' advised the judge.

'What made you challenge the Major's verdict in that court martial? How were you involved?'

Penton was hoping Will's description of his intervention all those years ago would impress the jury and call into question the Major's wisdom and compassion.

'I knew the man accused of desertion to be suffering from shell shock. He was mute, traumatised and totally unable to defend himself. He was a brave man, twice decorated and a great leader of men. Despite the Major's verdict, this sentence was never commuted as the standard orders from above had officially recommended and so a good man's life was unnecessarily ended.'

'You don't believe the doctor gave him a fair trial?' Penton paced back and forth.

'I know he didn't. He wouldn't listen. He had no interest.'

'Objection,' said Cotterell. 'This witness was a young boy at the time and not involved in the trial whatsoever. His biased opinion is irrelevant. The Major's job was onerous and difficult, and he is not on trial for his unenviable role at a time when the world was at war.'

'Sustained. The witness's remarks will be expunged from the record and members of the jury will ignore them. Please restrict your remarks purely to how you know the defendant and in what capacity. We are not interested in your personal opinions of him.'

Will felt disappointed to be so stymied. The despicable way he needlessly ended a courageous man's life and ignored orders to commute his death sentence said everything about Davison's character.

'He also interviewed you for entry into medical school.'

'He did.'

'And was your interview successful?'

'No.'

'Why was that?'

'We argued. About what had gone before. He didn't immediately recognise me, but I reminded him about our previous meeting.'

'With what result?'

'He didn't like it. Not at all.' Will glanced at Davison's cold, rigid face. 'He bellowed at me and had me thrown out. Again.'

'So your selection was unsuccessful.'

'It was. And I admit I was out of order. Perhaps it wasn't the right time to rake up the past. But I felt so aggrieved at what had been done—'

'Objection.'

'Sustained.'

'Very well,' said Penton. 'The jury will be pleased, I'm sure, to know that you are now a qualified doctor and surgeon who works across London's finest hospitals and also in a limited private practice capacity, which you carry out purely to fund your voluntary and charitable work. What then is your opinion of Dr Davison's clinical work?'

'Your honour!'

'Again, if you would permit me,' Penton clasped his hands as if in prayer, 'I will get to the point.'

'The sooner the better,' the judge grumbled. 'Well?'

'Dr Davison's role as Head of Department is mostly in name only. He is rarely present at the hospital, spending the majority of his time at his private clinic in Mayfair.'

'Objection.'

'My last question, then. What is the general view among your medical colleagues of this doctor's clinical expertise in relationships with patients?'

Will pondered this for several seconds.

'It isn't my role to evaluate other doctors' work. But Dr Davison has a reputation for undertaking surgical procedures that are often considered to be unconventional and experimental.'

'With good results?'

Will rubbed his hand on his neck. 'Hardly . . . My mentor and colleague Dr Forrester has had to correct the results of several of his untried methods and at least four of his patients have lodged a complaint against him. Including Mrs Smithson, who I have had the pleasure of sitting next to in row four.'

All heads in the room turned towards Mrs Smithson and found her nodding.

'Objection. I really must insist this attempted character assassination is terminated forthwith.'

'Objection sustained.'

Giving Will a look of tacit congratulation, Gerald Penton QC sat back down.

Theodore Cotterell QC walked slowly to the stand and stared at Will for what seemed like an age.

'I want to take you back to 1916,' he began.' Under what circumstances did you challenge the Major about this court martial you mention?'

'I went to see him at the Army headquarters in Querrieu.'

'With an appointment?'

'Well, no, it wasn't really possible.'

'So you just, what . . . barged in, did you?' He gesticulated this violence with his hands.

'I had no choice. It was so urgent and I—'

'And you told the Major you were an orderly, whereas in fact you were a stretcher-bearer.'

'I told the adjutant outside that just to get in the room.'

Cotterell tsked and shook his head dramatically. 'You lied.'

'I did what I felt I had to do.'

'You lied. Let's turn to your interview at St George's Hospital. You took that opportunity to attack the Major when he was merely using his expertise to select the best doctors for the future, didn't you?'

'I admit I wanted to challenge him about what he had done.' Will's hands now shook in his lap. 'A man I admired died in such terrible circumstances.'

'It was unfair, unprovoked and inappropriate. This obviously raises questions about how important a medical career really was to you. Yet you come here and criticise the Major's own comportment and character. A man vastly more experienced than yourself. I think,' continued Cotterell, turning towards the jurors, 'this is what is known as the arrogance of youth.'

Now it was Will's turn to look towards his counsel for support.

'Those patients you say Dr Davison has harmed. They were all very sick to begin with, presumably?'

'No. Not at all. One lady had an operation to "hitch up the kidneys". Another a length of bowel removed for constipation. These are not recognised indications for major surgery. They were all very ill, however, by the time they had been discharged from his care.'

'Do all of your own patients fully recover, Dr Burnett?'

Will blinked. 'It depends on the underlying diagnosis. Some suffer from conditions—'

'Do all of them fully recover, Doctor? Yes or no. It's not a difficult question.'

'Of course not. No doctor can work miracles.'

'No indeed. Did you actually see any of these patients pre-operatively? Did you take a history from them? Examine or investigate any of these people you say were harmed by Dr Davison prior to seeing them later?'

'No, sir.'

'No. No doctor is infallible. No doctor can work miracles. And Dr Davison is not arrogant enough to claim so. But he is brave enough to take on difficult cases that no one else is willing to tackle. Without medical pioneers, we would not have inoculations and modern medicines. We would not have antiseptics and artificial eyes and limbs.' He turned towards the jury. 'How else can medical knowledge progress without men like Major Davison?'

Now he turned back to Will.

'You don't like Major Davison, do you, Dr Burnett?'

'It's not a matter of me not liking him, it's more—'

'You feel aggrieved that as your superior in both military and medical life he's had to discipline you on more than one occasion. You've borne a grudge against him for years. You've admitted to lying and using inappropriate occasions to attack him and you have a sense of personal grievance.' He held a hand to his heart, head tilted. 'And I put it to the jury that because of this, and at your own admission, your testimony is unreliable and prejudiced and is therefore inadmissible.'

Will was stunned. The QC had made him look foolish.

'All I wanted to say was that—'

'That will be all,' said Cotterell abruptly. 'We have heard all you wanted to say. You may step down.'

By the end of the first session, Will's conviction that Davison would inevitably be found guilty had been severely shaken.

He was angry for allowing himself to be so easily manipulated by the defence counsel and dismayed that other key witnesses had fared little better. Cotterell was a shrewd operator.

Unfortunately, Will had to leave the court halfway through the afternoon session to fulfil a promise to Dr Forrester to assist in a thyroid operation to remove a massive goitre from the neck of a woman whose breathing had been severely restricted by its growth and then attend a ward round at the Children's Hospital in Horseferry Road in Brentford. He did so reluctantly, fearing that the strength of the case the prosecution had built against Davison had been overestimated. There was only one more witness for the prosecution to be called and no doubt the Major himself would have a number of powerful allies to help his cause.

Will finally returned home at six o'clock that evening as Grace was busy putting the twins to bed. He gave her a kiss, read the children a few pages from *Uncle Titus and His Visit to the Country* by Johanna Spyri and then slumped into his favourite armchair in the sitting room. Grace thought her husband looked exhausted.

'So tell me. How did it go?' she asked.

Will said nothing to start with.

'Did the malevolent Major get his marching orders?'

'Not exactly. Not at all, in fact.'

'How so? I thought you said it was an open-and-shut case.'

'I thought it was. But now I don't know if justice will ever be served. I didn't do our case any favours. What I wanted to say didn't come across at all well. The defence made me look such an idiot.'

'I can't believe that,' said Grace, coming over to sit on the armrest next to him and giving him a restorative glass of rum. 'I'll bet all the jurors loved you. Here. To keep your strength up.'

'Just before I had to leave, it got worse. They called the bartender at the Major's club to the stand. Made out that he was an imbecile. Implied a head injury he'd had rendered him error-prone and unreliable. They even claimed his records and timekeeping were inadmissible on the basis that he'd once tried to pretend he was at the club longer than he actually had been in order to fraudulently earn a little over-time money.'

'What about the other members he'd been drinking with?'

'All closed ranks. Couldn't remember exactly when they left the club, but some left early in the evening to visit the theatre and others stayed on longer with the Major. Nobody incriminated themselves with exact timings, however, so it didn't help.'

'There's a surprise.'

'Then they called Darke.'

'Your key witness. I remember him.'

Will nodded. 'He is not an easy man to interview, but Penton made a good job of coaxing out of him exactly what he saw. The car. The man. Clear descriptions of them. The number plate. The way the woman had been examined as if by a doctor.'

'So it effectively incriminated Davison?'

'You'd think so. But Cotterell was on his mettle. He questioned the reliability of Darke as well. A man living rough. From hand to mouth and unable to hold down a regular job. He brought up his disability and his mental health. Insinuated he'd invented the registration plate of the car, having seen it parked at the hospital on numerous previous occasions. He also pointed out the constant pain the man was in and the mind-altering effects of the morphine he was taking on a regular basis. The mere mention of the word morphine was enough to convince the jury he was just an attention-seeking addict who'd had another hallucination. Especially when he blurted out that he'd never liked the Major anyway after he'd once been unsympathetically treated by him at St George's. That really didn't help.'

'Oh, Will, I don't know what to say.' She rubbed his shoulder. 'Maybe I should have let you kill the Major as you wanted to do back in Querrieu all those years ago.'

He sipped his drink bitterly. 'I'd have gladly done so.'

'And you would've been shot, and we would never have married and had Emily and Daniel. So don't talk like that.'

He looked into her eyes and softened. 'I'm sorry. The man obviously has friends in high places, Grace. It's just that I thought justice would prevail.'

'Maybe it will.' She touched his hand lightly.

'Well, I'll try to sleep tonight thinking of Lady Justice with that sword of truth in her right hand. Hopefully with that blindfold off she will see the wretched man for who is.'

'Come on up to bed then, my darling,' she said, running her fingers through his hair. She had her own worries, too — her unwell father, her sister's escalating drinking and erratic behaviour. They could both use an early night and try to start tomorrow with a clear head. 'It's early, but I can think of a lovely way to get you off to sleep. And you'll need your strength to hear the verdict tomorrow morning.'

49

The Old Bailey, London, February 1929

As usual, whenever it seemed imperative for Will to finish his ward round on time, something would crop up to delay him. This time it had been a young woman who had experienced dehiscence of an abdominal wound. Will had had to quickly return her to the operating theatre to restitch it.

When he finally arrived, breathless and flustered, at the Old Bailey, he had missed the verdict. Several large groups of people had gathered on the steps outside in the road and were gossiping excitedly among numerous members of the press.

The first thing Will saw was an obvious cohort of Army personnel in uniform, looking very pleased with themselves. Will's spirits sank. It looked like the old boy's network, together with its rank and privilege, had come through again. A different group of civilians were huddled together, consoling and hugging each other.

What the hell had transpired? Not seeing anyone he recognised, he ran up the steps three at a time and straight into the Grand Hall. On the far side, he saw Gerald Penton looking quite solemn. Why did he appear so deflated? So serious and dispirited? He had obviously lost the case. Will could hardly believe it. He raced over to him.

'I'm sorry I got held up.'

'Ah, Will. No matter. Your presence wouldn't have affected the outcome even if you'd been here on time.'

Will felt broken. It had all been for nothing.

'So, what happened?'

'Much to everyone's surprise, the jury only deliberated for a mere twenty minutes. It's difficult to believe, but they returned a unanimous verdict. Apparently, they were not in any doubt.'

'Can we appeal?'

Penton looked puzzled. 'Why would we? He was found guilty, Will!'

'Guilty?' cried Will so loud that everyone remaining in the hall turned to look at him.

'Guilty as hell, I'd say,' said Penton, laughing now. 'I couldn't resist keeping you in suspense, knowing how much you loathed the man. Firstly, he was found guilty of reckless driving and being drunk in charge of a mechanically propelled vehicle in a public place. Luckily for us, the Criminal Justice Act of 1925 made that an official offence. For this he has been disqualified from holding a driving licence for a minimum period of six months and fined the maximum penalty of fifty pounds.'

'Fifty pounds? But he killed a woman.'

'He did. And then callously left her to die helpless and alone. And for that he has been imprisoned for a minimum period of fifteen years.'

'Fifteen years!' cried Will again, grabbing the lawyer by his shoulders and hugging him. 'That's wonderful. I've been wishing Newgate was still next door and the gallows still operative, but I'll settle for that. I'm delighted.'

'You and I both. And of course all the relatives of Mrs Tennant, whom you no doubt saw milling about outside as well.'

'That's who they were. But at first I saw a lot of military people who looked happy.'

'They were! Well, almost. It seems Major Davison must have made quite a few enemies over the years during his Army career. You certainly weren't the only one. At the end, he had precious few allies here at all. Even his wife left the court before he was taken down. And she didn't weep for him either.'

'But . . . but how did you turn things around so well? When I left yesterday, Cotterell had embarrassed me and ridiculed your two other main witnesses. What did you do?'

'Not me. Inspector Jarvis. He was peerless. His professionalism was outstanding, his calm, authoritative delivery unparalleled and his evidence incontrovertible.'

'What on earth did he produce to convince the jury? When I left, they were clearly wavering and, if anything, siding with Davison.'

Penton, having gathered up his belongings, then began walking from the hall.

'What didn't he produce?' he said. 'It turns out that he had followed up on Calvin Darke's eyewitness account and gone to inspect Davison's car. When he got there, he found it was up for sale. His prized possession being sold off, just like that. He didn't say he wanted to buy it, just take a look at it. That meant no one could accuse him of entrapment of any kind. What he found was crucial. The registration plate CD35, for example. The defence argued it could easily be mistaken on a dark blustery night for similar lettering. But 0D35 and 0035 do not exist, nor is there a CD85. The tyre marks at Exhibition Road were consistent with the axle width of the Morris Cowley.'

'Was that enough?'

'It was just the start. The headlamp glass on one side was shattered and matched pieces found at the crime scene. A small brooch belonging to Mrs Tennant was found lodged in a vent below the windscreen. Strands of her hair were wedged in the radiator grille. Jarvis had dried blood from the same place analysed by a specialist laboratory at Scotland Yard. You will know, Will, that Landsteiner, the pathologist, and his students had famously described human ABO blood groups at the turn of the century. What you probably won't know is that the very first conviction for murder based on the analysis of bloodstains occurred in Germany in 1901. The antibodies Scotland Yard used showed that the blood from Jarvis's collected sample was blood group AB. So was the blood taken from Mrs Tennant' s body. Only 2 per cent of the British population are blood group AB. Plus, a spring coil in a suspension bar beneath the vehicle exactly matched the deep impression left on the victim's shoulder at post-mortem.'

'My God. How did Davison react?' Will paused, looking back up to the front of the hall, wanting to picture it.

'He continually denied it. He kept saying that there was some terrible error. Said he'd never been there at the time and, as everybody heard, that he had never seen the woman before in his life. And that, young William, was exactly what I had wanted him to say. Because it was his biggest mistake of all.'

'How so?'

'Because his right thumbprint was all over the poor woman's watch face and strap. Darke had testified that the figure had taken her pulse from her left side — the side on which she wore her watch. More than twelve features of the thumbprint were an exact match with Davison's prints. Fingerprint evidence is still in its relative infancy, but using the precedent of a famous case in February 1905, when Alfred and Albert Stratton were found guilty of bludgeoning seventy-one-year-old Thomas Farrow to death based on their fingerprints alone, I was able to convince the judge and jury of its validity.'

Will was struggling to take all this in.

'So he had incriminated himself. He had already denied he'd ever seen the woman before in his life. It was irrefutable evidence that he had been there and touched his victim that one and only possible occasion.'

'And the jury had no further doubts?'

'None whatsoever. He's got fifteen years now to cultivate some remorse and humility. You got the result you wanted and which he deserved, Will. Davison looked apoplectic. He was not a happy man.'

'And he'll be even less happy now,' added Will with a grin.

Penton raised an eyebrow.

'I've come straight from the hospital, and he's also just been struck off the medical register.'

Will allowed lightness to fill his chest. His muscles relaxed for the first time in a while. And then he saw Calvin Darke filing out from the side of the courtroom, slowly but steadily on his cane.

'Excuse me,' Will said to Penton. 'Mr Darke!' he called.

Calvin Darke stopped and smiled when he saw who it was. They shook hands.

'I'm sorry you had to go through this,' said Will.

Calvin nodded. 'Justice has been done for that poor woman now, that's all that matters.'

'It is a huge relief. And are you well?'

'Never better,' said Calvin. And indeed he looked well, Will thought. His face was well rounded and had colour. He

309

did not wince in pain as he walked. 'I know the borders of myself,' he continued.

'I'm glad you've found that,' said Will. 'Come again to me soon for a check-up?'

'Will do,' said Calvin. 'Cheerio, doctor.' He walked away and Will stood there in the courthouse, and the relief trickled slightly from him when he thought of Captain Daniels. Fifteen years – it could not be enough for all the lives the Major had taken. But it would have to do.

He could ponder this more on the train, though. He had to get up to Manchester to operate on little Stevie Smith. The boy had waited long enough. Will had just enough time to stop off at home and tell Grace and the children the good news.

Will arrived in Manchester the following morning, having taken the sleeper. He went straight to the hospital, where he would meet Stevie and his mother. While Will relished this additional scope of his work at St Mary's other outposts, it also confronted him with the striking health inequalities between rich and poor, which only seemed to be growing wider. Everywhere he looked in these smoke-filled industrial communities, he was struck by the awful prevalence of preventable, curable, non-infectious disease among the most socio-economically deprived.

Rickets had been observed for centuries, but the underlying cause was only now becoming clearer. Attributed previously to a side effect of tuberculosis or congenital syphilis, it was Edward Mellanby in 1919 who first suggested it was the result of a deficiency of an unknown food factor. The fourth vitamin, or antirachitic factor, as he had described it. But even when cod-liver oil, which was rich in vitamin D, had been recommended in the years that followed, few people had access to, or the wherewithal to afford, such supplements. Consequently, rickets was still commonplace and treatments remained barbaric.

Will had stumbled upon Stevie Smith by chance, and he would be one of the lucky ones. Will would carry out an expert operation today and, at his age, little Stevie, with the supplements that Will would provide for him, would continue to grow and reach a near-normal adult height. Tens of thousands of other children would never be so lucky.

PART THREE

50

Chiswick, London, October 1929

Clara sat at the small dining-room table, reading the paper, with her hip padded by a cushion, while Kitty got ready for Grace's visit. Her niece had rather reluctantly set aside the French translation she was making of Sir Frederick Treves' *The Elephant Man and Other Reminiscences*. Will had left the book lying around, as he did often with medical tomes. Kitty liked to use them to practise. '*Il y avait encore plus d'homme que de bête,*' she had written. 'There was still more of the man than the beast.'

Clara looked down at the worrying headlines in *The Times*. She'd followed the news in September when the London stock market crashed after the arrest of the financier Clarence Hatry for fraud. Since then, the US stock market had fluctuated, and two days ago the Dow Jones lost 13 per cent of its value, and then another 12 per cent yesterday. According to the news story, it was unprecedented, and a major panic was ensuing.

Clara put the paper down and looked at the empty seat across from her. She wished Robbie were here to talk to, but the Robbie she grew up with had ceased to exist. Guilt roiled in her gut. She'd finally given in to Will a year ago and let him be taken to the Maudsley, a psychiatric hospital in south

London. It was after a few times he'd disappeared for several days. She had realised she could no longer guarantee his safety. She was working herself up to visit him again. She didn't like seeing him in such an environment, but she tried to trust he was getting the treatment he needed. Will and Kitty visited regularly, and Will said they seemed forward-thinking in their methods. Jack hadn't even visited once.

If only they had money. Will said there'd been a wonderful hospital in Devon just after the war, where the men were encouraged to get outdoors and work, and to talk about and write down their experiences. It had a high success rate of recovery.

Clara looked at the paper again, but then put it down. She had to return to hopeful thoughts. She had a part-time job that she loved, and soon Kitty would too. Teachers were always needed. Even if this crash resulted in a downturn. She tried not to think about the pain she was often in and how long she could stand it.

Kitty came downstairs and gave a little spin. 'Look all right?' she said.

'Beautiful!' Clara said.

'I added bows,' Kitty said, indicating to her sleeves and around her hem. She'd spruced up a well-worn day dress with new decorations.

'Exquisite,' said Clara. She meant it. Kitty knew what colours went well together and she was so vivacious she could probably make even an old sack look good. It wasn't just her slim shape and good bones, it was the way she carried herself: confident and bright.

Kitty poured herself some tea off the stove and sat across from Clara, tapping her foot impatiently. Grace was coming by to take her for a Saturday stroll. The twins were at home with Will. They did this occasionally, and Kitty loved how Grace treated her like an equal. Shared what she knew about being a woman in the world. They were good friends.

Kitty hadn't revealed all her plans to Grace, though. She still kept them close. In two years, she'd be twenty-one, old enough to vote — since in 1928 they had finally lowered the age — and independent; she'd have been teaching and gained experience; and she would have saved just enough money for a train or boat fare. She didn't know where she would go first, but as a teacher with many languages, she was sure she could gain employment abroad.

She tried not to think about how that would mean Clara would be on her own.

Kitty ran to the door when she heard the knock.

'Grace!' She wrapped her arms around her. And there, behind her sister-in-law, was Grace's sister, Amy, shimmering and glamorous under her open coat in a champagne-coloured dress with pleated skirt, and the softest looking hat with barely a brim. The hat capped the wisps of blonde hair framing her rouged cheeks. She had dainty pointed shoes and a boxy gold purse.

'Hello, darling,' Amy said. 'I'm coming along.'

Kitty hugged her, even though they'd only met a couple of times.

Grace, hovering on the steps, felt a little nervous. Amy had shown up unexpectedly two days ago and had been camping in their living room, sleeping heavily most of the day and smelling strongly of alcohol. Grace had made efforts to speak with her, trying to be compassionate to whatever drama was occurring, but she wanted her to go back to Diana's because she didn't want her drinking so much around the children. But Amy was her family. And perhaps she could get through to her and help her see what a state she'd ended up in. This morning, she'd thought that getting her out of the house might at least help her to talk. And maybe she'd feel useful, showing Kitty the make-up counters where she sometimes worked, sharing her tips on fashion and other interests that Grace didn't have as much knowledge of. Interests that Kitty, as a young woman, might be leaning towards.

Kitty immediately hooked her arm in Amy's and they said goodbye to Clara and trundled off towards the tube.

Walking along the Strand, the three women peered up at billboards atop billboards, for sales, shows, alcohol brands, films, tailors and hatmakers. The street was noisy with motor cars and pedestrians walking every which way.

The catastrophe of the stock market wasn't overly evident on the street. But behind closed doors, business owners and their employees wondered about the potential fallout. It still felt like they were recovering from the war, and the disastrous decision to introduce the gold standard in 1925, which stalled recovery further. Workers' wages had been lowered, and stayed lowered. Now what would happen? Grace and Will were back on a diminished income while Grace undertook the science and laboratory components of her further training, nursing only on Saturdays and some evenings where possible. Luckily, her parents had at least been able to help a little with the higher degree costs.

On the street, Kitty pressed her face up against the window of a department store. She saw women in chairs at little counters and mirrors, with other women painting their faces. She went to ask Amy if she'd worked at this make-up counter, as Grace had told her that was one of the jobs Amy did, but Amy had already wandered further down the street and was standing in front of a restaurant — Simpson's. She pushed on the door before Grace or Kitty could protest.

They followed her in and Kitty gasped as they arrived at the reception desk. Behind it was an elegant room with wood-panelled walls and a roof the champagne colour of Amy's dress. Chandeliers hung above the tables, casting yellow light.

Grace said, 'Sister, I don't think this is in our range.'

Amy ignored her and smiled at the arriving maître d'hôtel.

'A spot of lunch,' Amy said to him. Kitty noticed that every time there was something to lean on, Amy leaned. When there was nothing to lean on, she held one hand on a cocked hip, as though leaning against a wall.

The man looked at the three of them, and said, 'I'm afraid we're booked up today, madam.'

Several tables, however, were bare.

'Let's go,' Grace said quietly. But her sister did not take her eyes off the maître d'. Her painted lips were pulled into a smile.

'Don't you remember me, darling?' she said confidently, throwing her purse over one shoulder. 'I used to come here all the time with Clarke Ivello.'

The man adjusted his tie. 'We are booked out,' he said, enunciating clearly and lifting his eyebrows with finality.

'Well,' Amy said, 'you can shove a chandelier up your arse.' She spun and walked towards the door.

'Amy,' Grace said, pulling Kitty to follow her. But she couldn't help a laugh bubbling up as well.

Kitty was shocked and delighted.

Outside, Amy lit up a cigarette. 'I need a drink,' she said. Kitty thought she looked quite tired now. Her lines were showing through her powder, like the fine cracks that ran through the walls of their house.

Grace said, 'Well, I *am* hungry. We'll find somewhere else.'

As they walked along, Kitty considered the two sisters. They were like the sun and the moon — *el sol y la luna* — opposing but complementary. *Mais des pôles opposés.* Grace she admired for her passion and commitment, which she showed as fully in her medical life as she did with the children. And she also shared a spirit of adventure with Kitty, and a lack of fear and worry. But Kitty admired Amy, too. She defied every rule that seemed to have been set down by society for her. She lived for sensation, for fun, for joking around. Kitty had heard people talking about her and knew that words like 'untoward' and also 'lost' were applied, but Kitty wasn't sure about such labels. She thought that every person carried different desires, and it was brave of them to live fully in those without indulging anybody with an explanation or an apology.

Her brother Jack was a bit like that, too. Kitty barely saw him these days because he worked all day and hit the clubs in the evening, carrying the dust of demolition sites on to the dance floor.

'Let's try that one,' Kitty said, pointing out an even fancier-looking establishment.

'That's too much, Kitty,' said Grace, laughing.

But Amy was off, swaying her hips while crossing the road, making cars slam on their brakes. One man leaned out and whistled to her, and she blew him a kiss.

Grace shook her head, but Kitty could see she was smiling.

'Come on, ladies,' Amy beckoned.

51

Bishop's Cleeve, Gloucestershire, November 1929

Grace rode the motorbike up the driveway of the estate, Amy's head lolling on her neck in the sidecar. She felt horrible about what she had planned, but she didn't know what else to do. The house was now to have two people confined to their rooms, their sickbeds, and Grace and her mother would look after them as best they could.

'Where are we?' Amy slurred, not moving, as Grace parked.

'We're home,' Grace said.

Amy looked up and shielded her eyes from the sun breaking through the trees that surrounded the driveway. They were in need of paring back. Grace could see branches scratching at the upper windows.

'Come on,' she said, and helped haul her sister up and inside.

'Are we having a country basket?' Amy said, not making any sense.

'Something like that.'

Dorothy greeted them at the door, handkerchief held to her mouth. Grace could see that her mother had lost weight. She looked drawn and pale, a worn dress skimming her frame.

Grace's heart ached. Not only was her beloved father bedbound, her sister was a mess, and she would miss the children and Will while she was away. She'd also had to ask for some time off her training and work.

But it was necessary.

'Let's get her upstairs,' Dorothy said. Dorothy despaired at the sight of her younger daughter carrying the older – Amy looking like a rag doll with hair of straw.

The two women got Amy upstairs, and Grace heard her father grunt as he changed position in bed as they passed his door. They laid Amy on the bed in her old room, and she made small sounds of recognition. There was already water by the bed, and some dry food that would keep.

Then they exited, and Grace's stomach churned as she turned the key in the lock.

Will had given her some pills to give Amy at intervals. 'She'll need sedation,' he'd said, explaining that she would get horrific cramps and would experience a range of dark and terrifying emotions. 'She will scream at you, say many things she doesn't mean.'

For now, she was quiet, and Grace asked her mother if her father was up for a visit.

'Of course, dear.' She still clutched the handkerchief close to her face, like a comfort blanket.

Grace entered her dad's room. The curtains were half-closed, so the light was dim.

'He likes it like that,' Dorothy said, seeing Grace glance at them.

'Grace!' said the shrunken figure under the blankets. Grace sat on the chair beside the bed and took his hand. Her father's wrinkles were now deep grooves. He took shaky, shallow breaths. She felt tears rising in her throat and tried to swallow them down. She remembered how, as a child, he was always distressed by her crying. He'd immediately imitate bird sounds to distract her and make her smile. Sometimes he'd flap his elbows like wings.

Dorothy hovered by the door.

'Save your strength, Daddy,' Grace said. 'I'll read to you.'

He nodded, smiling, his own eyes misted.

She picked up a book from the bedside table: a volume of Sherlock Holmes, sitting among all his favourites.

A few hours later, Grace and Dorothy were having tea when Amy awoke. They heard her call out, and then bang on the door. Dorothy put her hand over Grace's.

'I feel so cruel.'

'It would be crueller not to do it,' Grace said. 'She could poison herself.'

Dorothy was feeling torn. She frowned. All her life, when her children called for her, she went to them. She couldn't help but wonder if Charlie had called for her in those final moments. They say that men often die with the word 'mother' on their lips. She felt utterly ill and couldn't finish her tea. She knew every family had its share of heartbreak and loss, but she'd never been able to be resilient the way some women were. She didn't know how to teach herself to be. Without Arthur . . . She couldn't comprehend it.

Grace walked up the stairs and approached the door to Amy's room.

'Grace? What's going on?'

'You're drying out,' Grace said firmly. 'You've become a danger to yourself and others.'

'Oh, pish, posh, sister. Don't be awful.'

'You don't remember what happened with the children yesterday?'

Amy went quiet.

'You wanted to play a game with them, and you pulled them out into the street, gripping their hands so they couldn't get away. And even when Emily screamed that there was a lorry coming, your reflexes were so slow . . .'

'What?' Amy seemed genuinely shocked.

'They saved your life, Amy. And you almost killed them.'

'I'm sure he would've stopped,' she said defensively.

Grace sighed. 'I'll come back in a few hours with dinner.'

'I'm thirsty, Grace,' Amy said in a small voice, like a child's.

'That's too bad.'

They didn't let Amy out for a week.

Dorothy pleaded with Grace. She couldn't stand hearing her daughter crying, shaking behind the door. Grace told her mother to look after their father and that she would take care of Amy. She gave her the sedatives for the shakes but weaned her off them too by the end of the week. She wanted her sister to be present, really present, to see what was happening to their father. Grace lay awake and wondered sometimes if she were cruel. But then she remembered the screams of her children, and played back over some of what Amy had let slip in conversation — in the moments around being superficial and witty and 'fun' — that she was unhappy, and afraid, and that she didn't know what to do next. Surely, being sober would give her a chance to think that through properly. And her liver truly wouldn't cope if she kept this up.

But Grace had worked long enough as a nurse to know that this also possibly wasn't the end of anything, just a new beginning. She might need psychiatric help once the fog had cleared and there was nothing in between her and her sober thoughts. It might all be too much. And she had to prepare herself for the fact Amy might have a lifelong habit, a crutch.

The liquor was all double-locked up the day they let Amy out. Now she could roam the big, dry house. Grace haunted her, making sure she didn't run out the door. At night, they still locked her in.

Amy cried and cried some more. Dorothy held her daughter and cried with her. Grace read louder to Arthur to cover it.

One day, Amy appeared at the door to her father's room. Grace got up to leave, so they could spend time alone together.

'Hello, precious,' Arthur said.

Amy twisted like a little girl.

She sat by his bed, and leaned forward to rest her head on his heart.

52

Royal Tunbridge Wells, Kent, March 1930

Grace and Jenny finally went riding together over a couple of incredible, crisp spring days. They'd been wanting to do so for a long time, and always missed each other's spare moments. Grace, in particular, was so busy with work, study, children and family duties that she barely had a moment to herself. She felt guilty even now, as her father lay gravely ill at Bishop's Cleeve. The doctors were so indefinite on the time frame, and she'd been by his bed lately so often. She hoped it was all right to get away just for a little while.

Grace loved spending time in Jenny's company. Not only was she her best friend, but they had experienced the extremes of happiness and heartache together in times of both war and peace. With so much in common, and living in close proximity, the families had frequently been able to babysit for one another and help out in any crisis to ensure they could always still pursue their careers and ambitions.

Grace was getting closer to being able to take the examination to become a qualified microbiologist and Jenny was content with her prestigious role of Matron at the Royal Free Hospital in Gray's Inn Road, having chosen to spend any of her spare time eventing with her beautifully trained horses which she kept at her parents' stud in Royal Tunbridge Wells.

They had spent most of yesterday out in the paddock, jumping and parading the animals around the circuit, making them dance and sidestep, half-pass at trot, canter, pirouette and piaffe. Grace had been a marvellous rider while serving in the FANY during the war and although she was now a little rusty, she was still able to impress Jenny with her skill, balance and rhythm. As for Jenny, she was sublime.

'Actually,' Jenny had told her, 'the reason I've been disappearing up there so much is because we're training for the 1932 Summer Olympics.'

'Los Angeles?'

Jenny nodded.

'How incredible.'

'Though the Depression may get in the way of several countries' participation. I hope not. Anyway, as you know, I bring Doris back home with me and Reg stays in London to work and, I must say, I rather like getting to have these two lives.'

'I understand,' Grace said. Though, for her, both the country life and city life currently seemed full of pressures and stresses. Her father's illness, worrying about her siblings, ensuring her children were happy and healthy and well-educated, her challenging studies, and on work days, the endless stream of people in need. For once, though, she was not as worried about Will. He'd been calmer since Davison had been put in jail, but he'd also been very busy working in surgery in various hospitals and one and a half days at his small private practice.

Today Grace and Jenny took a gentle path, meandering through and around the village. Seed pods and flowers crunched beneath the horses' hooves as they entered a grove. Grace was starting to get a bit nervous about the lecture she had to give that afternoon, but there were bigger concerns overriding it.

'Are you all right, Grace?' Jenny asked. Thin, lichened branches arced above them.

Grace felt like she hadn't been asked that in a while. She and Will had been getting on with things, supporting each other, but through action, not so much through words.

'I'm very sad about my father. I know it's the way of things – we get old, we get sick and die – and I know, from my work, it's the better outcome—'

'Oh, Grace, he's your *father*. You don't have to rationalise it. Of course you're sad.'

'He's a wonderful man.'

Jenny smiled with sympathy. 'Sounds like he's a great father and grandfather.'

Grace returned the smile, clutched the reins as they came out of the grove on to a soft, yellow-green field. A candle burned in the window of a farmhouse nearby, despite the sunshine.

'And how is your fascinating work?' Jenny asked.

Grace was grateful for the change of topic. 'Well, that relates to what I mean about the way of things. The diseases we now have vaccines for – they took many people before their time. Whooping cough, diphtheria, tetanus, tuberculosis . . . You'll hear more about all that later.'

'Yes, having just the one child, I'm so grateful for these advances. If anything had happened to her . . .'

Grace knew Jenny and Reg had hoped for more children. It had always been quite an awkward topic between them, since Grace had chosen not to try for more.

'It's true that, even in our children's lifetimes, the dangers to their health have lessened,' Grace said. 'But we can't forget that that is also because we are privileged. It is certainly not the case for all children, in this country or elsewhere.'

'Yes,' Jenny said. 'That's a very good point.'

And then Grace began to think of all the dangers that still existed, too. Like bacterial infections. Even a toothache, a scratch on the ear, a common cold that developed into a throat infection – these could all turn deadly. Medicine had come so far, but it still had a long way to go. She kept this thought to herself, not wanting Jenny to imagine her precious daughter – or even her husband or herself – in peril. She'd hear enough at the lecture this afternoon.

They took a small hill and then rode between a hedge and the road towards a beautiful stone church. The town was quiet. Grace wondered if there were people here affected badly by the economic crisis, or whether in the tiniest villages like this, they all gathered around each other – sharing the vegetables they grew, praying as a community – like ancient times. But then they also relied on old, established families like hers for employment, fair rental rates and amenities. England was changing rapidly. The whole world was.

Later that afternoon, they travelled up to London by train, recalling the day they had first met on another train on the way to France back in 1914 and the fun they'd had putting a bunch of drunken, rowdy soldiers firmly in their place when they had tried to goad and proposition them.

'I can't help feeling nervous,' said Grace. 'I'll be speaking in front of so many of our peers.'

'Don't be ridiculous. You could do it in your sleep. You've already established quite a name for yourself, and the work you are doing is pioneering.'

'Well, it might be, but there'll still be quite a few men in the audience who clearly resent the increasing presence of women in the medical profession.'

'And since when has that bothered you? It'll only make you more determined!'

Grace had been invited to speak at the Royal Society of Medicine on the current and future role of vaccination in the enhancement of public health. Though she hadn't graduated yet, she'd worked on several papers with fellow students and her professors and had begun publishing in the area. But she was well aware of a proportion of dissenting voices and it was quite possible the meeting could be interrupted by disgruntled members of the Anti-Vaccination League who had been making their feelings known ever since smallpox vaccination for infants up to three months old had been made compulsory by the Vaccination Act of 1853.

'Don't worry about them,' said Jenny. 'They're ignorant fools who only protest because they've never seen a case. If they did witness the devastation it can cause and the horrible way it kills 10 per cent of adults and 70 per cent of children who catch it, I'll bet they'd be fighting people off to be first in the queue for a jab.'

'Maybe,' said Grace quietly. 'I'll just be happy if the majority of the audience is on my side.'

'They'd better be,' Jenny reassured her, 'or they'll have me to deal with.'

They sat in the lecture theatre of the Royal Society of Medicine waiting for an address about the management of rheumatic fever by Professor Clarence Burridge of the University of Cambridge to finish. Grace felt rather grateful that the talk had been both far too long and extremely turgid.

She could sense the audience's boredom and impatience and hoped she would be able to wake them up and lift the mood.

She was introduced in glowing terms by the chairman of the meeting, Mr James Moffat, and made her way up to the lectern.

'Ladies and gentlemen,' she began, 'as you will all be aware, the leading cause of death in all age groups today is infection. Half of all children born will perish before their fifth birthday as a result of measles, polio, smallpox, diphtheria and a host of other infectious diseases. Their mothers may die from puerperal fever. Our soldiers in the Boer War succumbed in their hundreds to the ravages of cholera and typhoid, which still decimate whole populations in our towns and cities. A far greater number of our troops lost their lives in the Great War to infection rather than to the injuries themselves.' She paused for effect, tucking an auburn strand behind her ear. 'Even now, with better sanitation and hygiene, the spectres of smallpox, scarlet fever, whooping cough and tetanus haunt us. Tuberculosis, the illness that has killed more human beings in the history of mankind and whose presence centuries ago is evidenced in the preserved corpses of the ancient pharaohs, remains unchecked and deadly.'

She projected a large picture of a solemn-looking gentleman on to the presentation screen.

'Some of you will recognise this splendidly dressed fellow. He is the English physician, Edward Jenner. He is generally considered to be the first doctor to successfully inoculate patients against smallpox at the end of the eighteenth century. As we will discover in a moment, he wasn't.'

She pulled the wooden slide holder in and out of the lantern slide projector for the second image, which showed a small teenage child covered from head to toe in opaque pustules and clearly near to death.

'What he knew was that smallpox was a highly infectious disease that was endemic around the world. He had witnessed the raging fever and the red rash, which spread across the body like this,' she pointed, 'forming hideous blisters and pustules. In those who survived, he had seen the pustules turn to scabs, which in turn fell off, leaving deeply pock-marked skin. And, of course, he wanted to make a difference. To do something about it.'

Jenny looked at the faces around the room and all but two seemed riveted. A couple in one of the middle rows were writing notes, whispering to each other and shaking their heads. She looked back at Grace in her smart and demure dark grey wool skirt-suit, with its low-slung waist, collared white shirt and tie.

'He worked in Gloucestershire in a farming community,' Grace continued. 'And he noticed that milkmaids who were renowned for their smooth and clear complexions were usually immune to smallpox and its scarring pockmarks. Why? Because milking cows brought them into contact with cows' udders and cowpox. Cowpox is a mild disease of cattle which merely leaves one or two small pustules on the skin of the milkers. But afterwards they very rarely suffer from smallpox. So the locals began to inoculate themselves with fluid from cowpox pustules in order to avoid smallpox, which they knew was so much more deadly.

'Jenner observed this and decided to test it out scientific-ally. In 1796, he asked Sarah Nelmes, a milkmaid, if he could scrape some liquid from a cowpox pustule she had. He then injected it into the arm of a young boy called James Phipps. I have no idea what incentive the good doctor offered the lad, but I wouldn't be at all surprised if money or sweeties had been involved.'

A round of polite laughter spread through the auditorium. Jenny caught the eye of a dark-haired woman next to her and they smiled at each other.

'What happened to James? He developed a scab at the injection site, some soreness and a mild fever for a day. Six weeks later, Jenner inoculated the boy with smallpox matter and he subsequently saw no sign whatsoever of the disease. The boy had been rendered immune and it was a triumph.'

'Or an unethical experiment on an unsuspecting minor,' shouted one of the two people in the middle row. All other faces turned to look at them and several tut-tutted quietly. The woman sitting next to Jenny shook her head.

'A triumph which has been reproduced thousands of times since and saved countless thousands of lives. Jenner called the technique "vaccination", from the Latin word vacca, meaning cow.'

'He should have been disqualified from medical practice,' yelled one dissenter, 'for daring to try out an untried new procedure on innocent children.'

'Shush,' came cries from the others.

'You're welcome to ask your questions later in the normal way,' said the chairman calmly. 'In the meantime, please follow protocol.'

'Jenner, in fact, wasn't trying out a procedure that was new at all,' continued Grace, unperturbed, 'he was confirming the validity of a method that had been used as long ago as one thousand years. A method recorded and documented in China.'

This was new to the audience, who turned to one another with raised eyebrows. Jenny's seatmate simply nodded along.

'Inoculation was also practised in Asia and parts of Africa, reaching Europe and America by way of word of mouth among travellers in the 1700s. In around 1720, an American churchman called Cotton Mather learned about inoculation from his enslaved worker Onesimus, who had himself undergone the procedure as a child in his homeland in Africa. Mather then campaigned for widespread inoculation against smallpox during an outbreak of the disease in Boston.'

'All these men are just dangerously interfering with nature,' started up the louder of the two protesters. 'They're playing God and they have no right.'

'Nature gives us the diseases, sir,' answered Grace calmly before the chairman could intervene again. 'Nature left unchecked could kill all of us. Mother Nature can be sweet and life-giving, but she can also be cruel and ruthless. The Spanish flu was natural and within two years it killed 75 million people on our little planet. May I ask you, sir, did you yourself know anyone who died from it in 1918? Were you personally touched by it in any way?'

'Well, er, yes,' said the man, standing and worrying his hat in his hands. 'As a matter of fact, I lost my sister and an uncle to it.'

'I'm sorry to hear that. It claimed them and more than two hundred and twenty thousand other people in our country. And it was natural. It was as natural as appendicitis or pneumonia or sepsis. Isn't it our role as doctors to combat the darker side of nature and save life?'

'Only God can decide who lives and dies!' The other protester this time.

'Piffle!' yelled Jenny from her seat. 'Why do we perform appendicectomies, then? Or drain abscesses? Are you seriously suggesting we should do nothing? Sit back and let nature take its course? If that's what you think, you have no right to be here. Your brand of philosophy just takes us back to the Middle Ages. You should be ashamed of yourselves.'

PART THREE

'That's right,' said the woman next to her, also gesturing to the crowd. Her accent was German. 'The modern Church's view is that God creates doctors expressly in order to carry out their good work. They aren't defying God, they are simply one of his instruments.'

'These men are heretics!' insisted a dissenter, to the fury of the crowd.

Grace raised her hand and asked for quiet. Everyone settled back and sat down.

'But it's not just the men. As we will see.'

She projected another slide on to the screen, this time of an elegant woman dressed in a full-length gathered gown and dripping in expensive jewellery.

'This,' continued Grace, 'is Lady Mary Wortley Montagu. She was the wife of the British ambassador to Turkey from 1716 to 1718. She was an aristocrat, writer and poet. She was so engaging and enchanting, in fact, it is said that Alexander Pope himself fell madly in love with her. A love that sadly for him remained steadfastly unrequited.'

Laughter again rippled around the room. Jenny beamed up at Grace.

'Her own brother died from smallpox in 1713 and although she herself recovered from it, it left her with noticeable pockmarks on her face. In Istanbul, she witnessed the locals "engrafting" – taking live smallpox virus from a mild smallpox blister and introducing it into a scratch made on the skin of a previously uninfected person. They called it "variolation" and the recipient would develop a much milder, survivable case of smallpox compared to the much more virulent one they otherwise might have contracted.'

'Did she have enough courage of her conviction to inoculate herself?' asked the same nuisance.

'She didn't need to. Having already suffered the disease, she was immune. And that's what she wanted for everyone else. Don't you see? She advocated vaccination to protect the world.'

'By doing it to anyone but herself.'

Grace shook her head.

'She went one step further. In order to protect her five-year-old son, she persuaded the surgeon at the British Embassy there to carry out his inoculation. So, since there is nothing stronger than a mother's love, I would certainly say that meant she had the courage of her convictions, yes. The boy became the first English person ever to undergo the procedure and Lady Montagu wrote letters home about it. Word soon got round.'

The next slide showed various members of the Russian and European royal families, who had availed themselves of the vaccination.

'Funnily enough,' Grace continued, looking pointedly at the two dissenters, 'the medical establishment initially agreed with your unenlightened views. They saw it as nothing more than a folk remedy and suspected its safety.'

'Quite right,' said one under his breath.

'Then, in 1721, a smallpox epidemic struck England. Thousands died a terrible death. So Lady Mary inoculated her daughter. People took notice. She persuaded the Princess of Wales to test it out. Seven prisoners awaiting execution at Newgate Prison were even offered variolation in return for a pardon . . . as guinea pigs . . . All survived and all were released.'

The dissenters were silent now, had sat back down and were looking at the floor.

'Inoculation, however, was not always completely safe,' said Grace.

The dissenters' heads snapped up.

'Sometimes recipients developed a real case of smallpox. Some of them infected others. But it was rare. It saved thousands more lives than it took.'

The dissenters looked ready to pounce, but Grace beat them to it.

'But then Jenner made the whole procedure significantly safer. By using his cowpox vaccine, instead of the smallpox vaccine, which, with the help of James Phipps and a few sweeties, provided the same level of protection.

'Ladies and gentlemen, we already have effective vaccinations against cholera, thanks to Jaime Ferrán in 1885, and typhoid, which was first used in 1909. We have vaccinations against rabies and tuberculosis. But I predict that in years to come we will be able to prevent many more dreadful diseases instead of desperately and often unsuccessfully trying to treat them once they have already wreaked havoc. Vaccination will save millions of lives around the world. People like your sister, sir,' she said, looking directly at one of her inquisitors, 'and your uncle. And this, I believe, will come from the advancement of science rather than blind trust in God.'

The audience rose to its feet as one, clapping enthusiastically for several minutes. As the crowd dispersed, Jenny pushed her way to the front, the dark-haired woman who'd been sitting beside her following behind. She was disconcerted to see Grace being confronted by the two troublemakers. But she need not have worried. They were all smiles now, shaking her hand and apparently apologising.

'We may be prepared to reconsider the principles involved,' they said quietly. 'But thank you for allowing us to frame our reservations.'

They left the room without further disruption under the beady eyes of the watchful chairman.

'You were marvellous,' said Jenny, grinning. 'You had the audience in the palm of your hand.'

'Bugger that,' said Grace. 'The only thing I want in the palm of my hand right now is a large gin and tonic!'

Grace then acknowledged the tall woman waiting patiently beside Jenny.

'Pardon me,' the woman said, 'I wanted to congratulate you on such a fascinating lecture. In my education I have not yet heard about this Mary Wortley.'

'You are German?' Grace said.

'Yes, my name is Lieselotte.' She held out her hand. Grace shook it and then introduced Jenny.

'And you are studying medicine?'

'Yes, back in Germany, but I am on exchange here for one year.'

'Well, you must join us for a drink!' Jenny said, smiling enthusiastically.

'Indeed,' said Grace. 'We can compare notes about how women in medicine – and vaccines – are treated in your part of the world.'

53

Bishop's Cleeve, Gloucestershire, April 1930

It was shocking to see how fast Arthur had deteriorated. He lay in bed, a shadow of his former self, his cheeks hollowed out from such rapid weight loss, the whites of his eyes bright yellow in colour and the bones jutting out of the parchment-thin, jaundiced skin over his body. He had stopped eating a few days before, being unable to swallow solids, and could now only manage a small sip of water at a time. All of the family gathered downstairs in the house and each who visited his bedside in turn knew he only had days or hours to live. His cancer had devastated them all. He had always been such a strong and physically powerful man, resilient in mind as well as body.

Amy remembered visits to Bishop's Cleeve at what must have been the start of his decline, where he had seemed tired and not his usual self, but she had been intoxicated by her wild lifestyle and rather amused by the parental disapproval of her behaviour.

How dreadful she felt about that now. Yet another doomed relationship had recently foundered and now here was Daddy — her kind, precious, beloved daddy, her rock, her saviour and the only man in her life who had ever given her unconditional love — on his deathbed. She could not bear to lose him.

Dorothy was totally distraught and quite helpless. Grace and the brothers were in pieces, too, but it was Amy who seemed to be suffering most, tortured by guilt over her own selfish behaviour and her negligence regarding her parents' needs. The awful situation seemed to be forcing her to reappraise her life and her future in ways that she thought Arthur, for once, might be proud.

A few weeks previously, his shortness of breath and the change in bowel habit, the loss of appetite and weight and the abdominal discomfort had become worse and Dorothy had finally persuaded Arthur to pay another visit to his doctor's surgery over in Cheltenham. The doctor had immediately recognised the obvious anaemia and early jaundice and estimated correctly that Arthur's previous chronic pancreatitis may have progressed to carcinoma of the pancreas.

The surgeon he had urgently referred him to had agreed. 'Classic case, I'm afraid,' he had said when the two doctors had met. 'Pale, frothy, foul-smelling motions. "A flash in the pan," I call them. But without a functional pancreas, he can't digest any fat in his bowel and that's the result.'

He had operated on Arthur the following day, but it was hopeless. The cancer had spread throughout his abdomen, and his liver was riddled with the creamy-white knuckles of metastatic tumours that blocked the bile ducts, causing the jaundice. He had sewn his patient up again and delivered the sad news that same evening.

From his bed in the upstairs room at Bishop's Cleeve, Arthur could look out of the tall sash windows and see the great coastal redwood which Grace had climbed to the very top at age seven all those years ago. He could appreciate the beauty of the formal gardens in the foreground and the shafts of sunlight playing across the neatly mowed lawns beyond. He could see the faces of his children at his bedside and the photograph of his beloved son Charles, the only one who could not be there physically, but whom he would be joining in a better place very soon.

With his family at his bedside, he spoke slowly, the words slurred as a result of the morphine and laudanum administered for pain relief. At the same time, beautiful hallucinatory images of the life he had enjoyed drifted in and out of his conscious-ness and made him euphoric. There was Charles in his biplane performing aerobatic barrel rolls and loop-the-loops over the avenue of trees at the top of the hill. Here were the children screaming with delight as they hurtled down the slide around the helter-skelter. Here was the blacksmith on the battlefield of Stormberg holding up his bloodied, amputated leg in defiance and triumph. It didn't hurt at all. There was no fear any more, only gratitude and contentment.

He had had a good life. He hoped that in a small way he had made a difference to the world, and he asked them all to look after his dear wife, Dorothy. He knew he could rest assured that the estate was in good hands with Henry, his second son — the banker — and his wife, and he had made a point of telling them how immensely proud he was of all of them. Then, as the sun dropped behind the folly on the hilltop, the helter-skelter he had insisted on being built so many years ago and in which the children had had so much fun, he smiled at them and slowly closed his eyes for the very last time.

54

Chiswick, London, June 1931

Clara was planning a party. Kitty was almost twenty-one, and she wanted to make it special for her. They had never got around to properly celebrating her graduation, either, as Kitty had gone straight into work at a local high school, teaching French. She'd invite Will, Grace and the children, though she knew Grace was still experiencing terrible grief over her father. She'd invite Jack, if she could get on to him. And she'd invite Kitty's friends — she'd secretly asked Thiago for their names and addresses.

And then there was Robbie. He'd been doing well lately, and surely he would want to attend his daughter's twenty-first, but Clara wasn't sure about disturbing his routine. Could it cause some back-pedalling?

There was only one way to find out.

Clara arrived at the red-brick building of the Maudsley Hospital. She walked through the classical-style columns flanking the front entrance. It was slow-going as she now used a cane. Her heart raced and she almost turned around and walked back out. She'd become so set in her routines, she realised. Cooking at home, going to work and buying groceries. Taking her Aspro. Avoiding the Maudsley. She'd created a kind of safety zone, and when she stayed within it, she didn't have to think about the world outside or the future that lay ahead. In fact, she'd been thinking even more about the past. Perhaps seeing Kitty coming into her womanhood had inspired it. Remembering her dear, departed husband, Harold, and being with him at that same age. Those spring-time walks through Hyde Park. The dreams they had together.

A nurse showed Clara into the large common room, where people played chess and cards, spoke and laughed. Some just lay around or stared into space or out the windows. Clara tried not to focus on any one face too long. She feared to see pain and suffering. She thought of all the children she'd taught over the years. Might some of them end up like this?

And then there was her brother. The fifty-one-year-old man, hair streaked with grey, sat in an armchair like his favourite one at home and peering out the window. He looked relatively serene. The nurse whispered to her that he was quite sedated today, having had a bit of a relapse the day before.

'Oh,' Clara said, her heart dropping to her stomach.

She experienced a surprising twinge of frustration. She, too, had lost her spouse. And, no, she hadn't gone to war on top of that, but she'd held herself together all these years, for Robbie and his children. For her niece and nephews. And in recent years, through her constant arthritic pain. She'd never remarried. She'd never had her own children. She'd worked all her life.

The feeling passed quickly when her brother looked at her, and compassion swept in. She loved him, and she understood that he was broken.

Until recently, though, she had to admit she'd been hoping it wasn't irreparable.

'Clara,' he drawled, reaching for her hands.

She took a seat next to him. 'Robbie.' She smiled and held his hands. 'Not a bad view,' she said.

He smiled wryly. 'You can people-watch, at least.' He spoke as though he had cotton wool in his mouth.

'I'm . . . sorry I've taken so long to come again,' Clara said.

Robbie frowned. 'To tell you the truth, sis, I don't know how long it's been. Time's a funny thing to me these days.'

'Well, Kitty is almost twenty-one,' she said, hoping it wouldn't shock him.

'She is? My big girl.' His face stretched. 'Twenty-one years, hey?' His eyes then unfocused. Now she knew he was thinking about how it had been the same amount of time since Evie died.

'I'm sorry, Robbie.'

'Well, you must get her something for me. She does come and see her old dad from time to time. Though I often wish she wouldn't.'

'She loves you.'

He sighed. 'She'll remember me like this.'

'She's strong.'

'Oh, I know that. Very robust.' He let go of Clara's hands and scratched at his chin. He was both greying and grizzly. Clara never spent much time looking in the mirror, but she knew she was a bit grizzly these days too.

'I'm planning a party for her. Would you like to come?'

Robbie looked at Clara. Would he like to come? He thought about that. He celebrated his daughter, his children, in his thoughts, in his own way. Being around people at a party, being expected to talk and laugh and sing and contribute – he wasn't sure he'd be up for that ever again.

'I don't think I can, Clara.' He put his head down, ashamed.

There was a certain freedom in being locked up here. He knew other patients didn't feel the same. He heard their awful cries and screams. But for him, it was safe. To be in a place where, if he slipped into the past, there was always someone there with a needle, or there was a room to go to where he could be alone until it passed. He wasn't inflicting himself on his family any more. And he wouldn't.

Clara took his hand again. 'Well, Robbie, shall I get her a gift from you?'

'Oh yes,' he said. 'What does she like these days?'

They talked about Kitty, and then more broadly, and Robbie caught her up on his daily schedule in the Maudsley and told her about his doctor and nurses – about his world. He didn't ask much about home, but he did ask her about herself – how she was.

'I'm doing fine,' Clara said. She smiled to reassure him.

'What about your bones?'

'Will says there are promising new treatments being trialled with X-rays, but I'm managing just fine without all that for the moment.'

'I'm glad,' he said.

After a pleasant hour of chatting and staring out the window, Clara said she must be getting on with the party preparations and she left her brother. He turned back to the window and let himself drift. She was glad she came.

Kitty arrived home from work on the day of her birthday to find ribbons and bows along the front fence. How festive! she thought. As she opened the front door, she thought the house seemed unusually quiet. Normally, Clara was cooking by now – making the sound of footsteps, chopping, sizzling, boiling and the clanging of pots and pans.

'Surprise!'

Kitty's heart leapt into her throat. 'Christ!' she said, then clapped her hand over her mouth, seeing the children. They giggled.

'Happy birthday,' said Clara and came forward to kiss her cheek. The smiling faces around her were her beloved family and friends. There was an enormous cake on the table, waiting.

'I'm not dressed for a party!' Kitty said.

'We'll give you five,' Clara said. 'But the twins won't wait one minute longer for that cake,' she laughed.

'It's chocolate!' Kitty heard Daniel say as she raced up the stairs.

They were all sitting or leaning around the table drinking tea when she got back. She rushed forward and wrapped Clara in her arms, careful of her fragility. 'Oh, Aunt Clara, this means the world.' She felt a little sick with guilt, behind the frills of her party dress. What was Clara going to do when she was gone?

She is not decrepit, she told herself. Maybe she would move in with Will and Grace? But Kitty felt, really, as the closest thing to a daughter Clara had, that she should perhaps be responsible for looking after her.

Either way, she would probably break her aunt's heart a little when she left.

Among this group, only Thiago knew of her plans. And, anyway, she had to save a lot more money first.

She should enjoy this moment. Here it was — twenty-one, her life her own. They all sang 'Happy Birthday' and she cut the cake, carving off extra-large slices for Emily and Daniel.

She closed her eyes as she bit down on the rich chocolate and creamy icing. Clara had outdone herself.

'I wish Old Pop was here,' said Daniel through a mouthful of cake.

Kitty looked at the dark-haired twelve-year-old, who was lagging a little in development compared to his sister, who was now taller than him. He was empathetic just like his dad, and curious like his mum. Emily was staring out the window, watching a bird — secrets in her eyes, just like Kitty herself.

'I wish he were too,' said Kitty. 'You know what? We can go together to take him some cake later.'

Daniel nodded enthusiastically, but Emily scrunched up her face. She loved her grandfather but was uncomfortable around the other patients, whereas Daniel was fascinated by the people, their symptoms and conditions.

Will said, 'Emily, you can stay and keep Clara company while we go.'

'I'd love that,' said Clara.

They were all quiet as they enjoyed the last bites of their slices of cake.

Jack lit a cigarette as he left the warm little house he'd grown up in. He couldn't believe his little sister was twenty-one. He shook his head. He thought of the places on the walls where cracks were beginning to show, the tap that didn't stop dripping in the kitchen, and the way Clara had winced as she carried the cake.

He thought of his sister's face, smiling and mischievous and curious. Just like him. He could not imagine her staying there with Clara in the crumbling house.

Jack worked long hours in construction and demolition, but no longer as a grunt — as someone who told others what to blow up. He still got his hands dirty if necessary. He wound down at night at a classy establishment — full table service, a generally respectful clientele. He didn't see many of the crew he used to hang around with. Including Amy, since she'd gone on the wagon.

As he walked to the tube, alone, the laughter and warmth reverberating, the birthday cake sitting in his stomach, he had to admit he felt a little lonely. Maybe it wouldn't hurt to move back in, keep Clara company and save some money. It would give Kitty the option to make use of her languages.

He could just do it for a little while, until he met the right girl to settle down with or found a new adventure for himself.

55

Kingsley Hall, Bromley-by-Bow, London, August 1931

It had been an eventful year so far for Fitzwilliam, working as an assistant secretary in the Ministry of Foreign Affairs. In August, he had gained new colleagues in Under-Secretary Anthony Eden, and Secretary Rufus Isaacs, 1st Marquess of Reading.

On 24 August, Ramsay MacDonald's Labour government had conceded to form a National Government. Four Labour, four Conservatives and two Liberals. The new Cabinet was formed after MacDonald's proposals for cuts in public expenditure were rejected, to restore confidence in the government following the economic slump and in the lead-up to the Budget in September.

Fitz worked out of the Foreign Office building, with views to St James's Park. He loved to look out on the park, though regretted how little time he had to take a stroll in it over lunch.

He also travelled a lot. More often than not lately, he found he had to answer questions that related to trade, the suspension of reparation payments from Germany, what was happening in India and the schisms within the Cabinet itself. Answers depended, of course, on whom he was talking to – a foreign dignitary, the head of a trade organisation, his equivalent in Commonwealth nations.

It was now the end of August and Fitz was due in the East End to look in on the accommodations Mr Gandhi had chosen ahead of his visit to London for the second Round Table Conference. Normally, foreign dignitaries stayed in the West End, and Fitz would settle them in and join them for drinks. Mr Gandhi's visit was to be an entirely different affair.

Some politicians, such as Mr Churchill, had very strong feelings about Gandhi's 'campaign of civil disobedience' in India, dismissing what they saw as his poseur status – wearing the loincloth and pretending to be for the people, while taking power and attention for himself. Churchill, on the whole, was outspoken on opposing the granting of dominion status to India.

Children played in the street as Fitz exited the car and looked up at the brick building built in 1927 known as Kingsley Hall. It was the second building known as Kingsley Hall, and the first still existed. During the General Strike in 1926, the first had become a shelter for those out of work and increased demand meant that Doris and Muriel Lester sought funds and donations for the new building.

Muriel met Fitz at the door downstairs. She was an unassuming woman, with a healthy, freckled visage, sans make-up, a loose floral dress and her long hair parted in the middle and in two buns either side of her head.

'It's a pleasure to meet you, Miss Lester,' Fitzwilliam said.

'I'm delighted to show you around, Mr Tustin-Pennington,' she said, smiling. Her accent was upper crust, with strongly rounded vowels, but she carried no other airs. 'Come,' she said, and he followed her up the stairs inside.

'How long have you been doing your work with the poor?' he asked as they climbed.

'Well, our father, Henry Lester, had very humble beginnings, like his father before him, and while Doris and I grew up in comfort, our father never let us believe that was the only way to live. The first charitable building we had was the cottage my father bought and named after our mother, Rachel. Nursery children could holiday there. Then Doris and I established a nursery school on Bruce Road . . .'

They arrived on to an open roof, the sun streaming down on a series of modest daybeds. Muriel sat on one and gestured for Fitz to do the same.

'We established a system where wealthier clients could sponsor mothers in need. And then it expanded into activities for older people as well. Everything, for us, is about whole-person development — the spirit, body and mind together. And all classes, races and religions.'

The blankets and rugs on the roof were woven, colourful. It was cosy, Fitz thought. He felt strangely at home.

'We got Eagling Road in 1915, after our father died. People could come there together for worship, study, fun and friendship. And then there's the Children's House, opened in 1923. And now here . . .'

'It is quite . . . peaceful,' Fitz said.

'It's simple. It's a place where people can work out their own salvation. And I knew Gandhi would feel more at home here than in other parts of London. With a mixed crowd just like his.'

'And he'll be sleeping . . .?'

She stood. 'Right over here.' She led Fitz to a small room off the roof. 'Or outside if the weather permits.'

'That may be a bit cold in his, uh, state of dress.'

'Ah yes, I know some people think it an affectation, the loincloth,' Miss Lester said. 'But he believes in approaching the poor with the mind of the poor. It's genuine.'

Fitz nodded, hoping he hadn't caused offence.

'There was a factory girl in here until last week,' she said, indicating to the bed. 'She's gone to Birmingham.'

Fitz nodded. The spartan room awakened some strange longing within him. He was thirty-one, now. Settled in his career. No children on the horizon. This way of living seemed adventurous, honest. But then, many had no choice about it. His romanticism, he knew, was distinctly middle class. After one night on the roof, he'd probably long for his claw-footed bath, his expensive single malts.

'We have artists and doctors of law, teachers and navvies — all sorts — living together like one big family.'

Her face was so warm. Could she tell there was some-thing different about him? Something that polite society shunned?

He cleared his throat. 'You're doing necessary work, Miss Lester.'

'Well, so much unemployment in recent years.' She shook her head. 'I'm pleased there's some way we can help.'

'I shall report back that our dignitary is in good hands,' he said. He touched the brim of his hat, not wanting to take up any more of her time.

'Come any time, Mr Tustin-Pennington,' she said, in her calm, friendly manner.

On the tube on the way back to the office, Fitz tried to concentrate on Virginia Woolf's new novel *The Waves*. He kept getting lost trying to navigate the conversations in the novel.

It felt another failing, but he was possibly just a bit too practical for Woolf. Perhaps if he lived in a spartan room by an open roof, the ideas would expand within him.

But that, he thought, is someone else's life.

56

Manchester, October 1931

Amy walked into the hall and sat on one of the fold-out wooden chairs halfway to the front. She wanted to be close enough to get to see him, but far enough back to be able to observe others and gauge how she should react. She didn't normally come to political speeches or rallies. But having spent the past year rattling around that big house with Henry's family and her rapidly shrinking mother, she needed some stimulation.

She'd heard Oswald Mosley was handsome. And charismatic. He was giving talks about the party he'd formed, the New Party, after he left Labour. Amy knew some people were cranky about that, blaming him for Labour's defeat. But, for the most part, she hadn't been following the what or why. Maybe she'd see some action. The black-uniformed guards surrounding the stage seemed to anticipate it.

The other reason to come was that apparently sometimes Lady Cynthia spoke at her husband's events. Amy would love to see what she was wearing.

Amy waited amid the excitable murmurings of the middle-class crowd. She yawned. She'd somehow managed to stay sober all this time, mainly because she'd remained cut off from her friends in London, away from temptation. But life was hideously boring. She was too old for any gentleman visitors to drop by and show interest. She'd been whiling away her days reading film and fashion magazines, following her mother around the garden, eating far too much and learning cross-stitch. Henry and his family mostly kept to themselves in the former guest wing of the house. She looked forward to visits from family she was closer to, especially Emily and Daniel, and prepared for them days ahead. She put together treasure hunts, challenges and creative activities like painting, sculpting and drawing with fun materials. Dress-up was her favourite activity, and sometimes she and the children even wrote little plays together and acted them out for Will, Grace and Dorothy.

One day after one of these visits, her mother had said to her, 'You would have made a wonderful mother.' And Amy didn't talk to her afterwards for two days. Because it was not too late, was it? She hated that even her mother saw her only as a spinster, a dried-out and dried-up hag that no one would want.

She had carried a baby, once. It had been Clarke's. But it had chosen to leave her body before anybody really knew about it. They worked out at the hospital she'd probably been about seven weeks along. But the days and nights and weeks were always blurred together, then. They could have told her anything and she wouldn't have felt much.

Mosley took the stage to polite applause from the now-full audience. Amy's view was regularly interrupted by the smoke clouds of the man in front. The woman beside her clasped her hands together in her lap.

He could not disguise that he was aristocratic — the cut of his suit and waistcoat, neatness of moustache, his handsome broad chest. When he opened his mouth to speak, his teeth gleamed white.

Yes, Amy thought, handsome indeed.

He had two rosettes in his lapel, one black and amber, and one amber. His blackshirts also wore rosettes.

He spoke without a microphone, beginning by making some wry references about his reputation before losing his smile and getting serious, leaning towards the audience as they too leaned in towards him. He expounded passionately on everything that was wrong with England and the 'old men' of politics who had let the flag slide into dust.

He got louder and shook his hand with one finger extended at the audience, his chest moving in and out with great gusts of fervour, as he spoke about the ex-servicemen and how ill-treated they had been by politicians. About how a new generation must transform parliament from a 'talk-shop' to a 'workshop'.

'Politicians know how to talk, but not how to act.'

He talked about the vast machine of industry and the devaluing of skill. How illiterate 'Orientals' would do the job in less time for a bowl of rice. That England's market must be protected from these dangers, and at the same time export trade could be improved.

'If you want our order and there's another man who wants it — take down your wall by this much.'

Amy didn't really follow. What did he mean by a wall? Did he mean England should keep to itself? So all the jobs would go to English people and they'd be paid properly, and they'd all use English products and eat English food? But trade when appropriate . . .? Something like that. It sounded good in theory, to her. But she wasn't sure how it worked currently. And what about a Chinese person who already lived here? Would they not be allowed to have a job?

He said, in relation to unemployment, that England had all the resources and they must be mobilised.

Mosely said that he was confident that if his party got footing, his ideas would sweep England.

The way he said it was convincing and exciting. Amy felt a shiver go through her. Perhaps the very fact that his thinking was different was what made it right for England. There was also something very controlled about it all. About what was good and what wasn't. Though she supposed all political parties drew hard lines like that. And despite her free-floating life, and being drawn always to play and fun and chaos, she found the structured ideas very compelling.

When he finished, the audience rose to their feet, applauding and cheering. Amy clapped, too, and then began to glance around the room for any men on their own.

57

Barcelona, Spain, November 1931

Kitty's months in Spain so far had been incredible. Beyond her wildest dreams of adventure, connection and expanding the knowledge of her mind and heart. She lived in a modest apartment in a decadent-looking art nouveau building in Barcelona with another British woman who worked at the same English-language school, Jean.

She wrote home regularly and she missed her family, but she had no regrets at all about going abroad. This desire had been beating in her blood for so long. Clara had been quieter than she'd expected when she had told her – and Kitty wasn't sure if it was from shock or more an acceptance of what she'd thought had been inevitable. In the months leading up, Kitty hadn't been able to help dropping hints about her desire to go somewhere. And Jack moving in had made it possible.

Her father was hardest to say goodbye to, and she had to swallow a lump every time she thought of him, because what could happen with him was unpredictable, and she didn't know how present he'd be in mind or body when she got back.

Will and Jack had both displayed their different versions of brotherly concern. Jack offhand, but fond, and Will listing all the dangers and holding her for too long. Poor Daniel and Emily were very upset, and she had to reassure them copiously that she would write, and return.

Kitty and Jean's building supervisor, Blanca, had taken them both under her wing and often invited the two young women to her apartment for wine and food and open and passionate discussions about the city, about Spain in general, about politics and about men. Kitty began to pick up on unfamiliar words Blanca sometimes slipped in, especially when she was getting worked up, and she soon learned they were Catalan. She instantly wanted to learn the dialect and Blanca was delighted.

One evening, Jean had gone up to bed and Kitty was practising her Catalan with Blanca. Blanca seemed very distracted this evening. She said that the group she was a part of were very worried about their future and were preparing to fight for their rights.

Kitty didn't quite understand what was happening in the country, but the grounding Blanca had been giving her made her see many echoes in Europe – the rise of fascist ideologies which oppressed a great many people. Even in the newspapers from home, she read of the clashes between Sir Oswald Mosley's mob and protestors. But here, it seemed more present – like arrests that were made over organised action over the huge discrepancy between wages and rent increases.

Blanca said they'd been preparing for an uprising against the government, that the small strikes and clashes that Kitty had witnessed in Barcelona were all leading up to this. That it would involve the miners in regional Spain but have reverberations all throughout the country.

'If you want to help the workers make a difference, my child,' Blanca said, 'you can help teach reading and writing.'

Kitty nodded, listening.

'Literacy is a tool to empower the workers and help them participate in the meetings and actions for their own emancipation.'

Kitty understood. Before coming to Spain, she hadn't known much about the differences within the left side of politics: Labour, socialism, communism. As far as she knew, Blanca was aligned more with something called anarchism. Kitty was learning fast in this country, and if she could help make a difference to the lives of those oppressed by the government, then she would.

In fact, this idea gave her a feeling of fullness and satisfaction like she'd never experienced before. Teaching back home, especially getting through to reluctant students and inspiring in them a love of languages, had sometimes come close to this feeling. But life back home was also complicated by the heavy weight of her father's condition — something over which she'd never felt she had any control or influence.

She'd probably thought of herself as a pacifist, and many of the women she'd marched alongside in London were. After the war — and after they'd all seen the effects of the war on the men in their lives, if the men had come home at all — they only wanted peace and understanding. To find common ground so citizens would never be put through such conflict again.

But, in Spain, Kitty was beginning to see things differently. That perhaps there were some causes worth agitating for, revolting for, maybe even taking up arms. She was becoming swept up in the enthusiasm and ideas around her, not just from Blanca, but in cafés and in the school and on the street. People wanted change. They wanted to be well and safe, not poor, diminished, forgotten, discriminated against and afraid.

'Of course I will help,' Kitty said to Blanca.

Blanca thanked her and got up to pour another drink.

'*Sant Hilari, Sant Hilari, fill de puta qui no se l'acabi!*' Blanca toasted – a vulgar toast that made Kitty laugh.

'*Salut!*' replied Kitty.

Blanca advised Kitty and Jean to stay home a couple of days later as the streets of Barcelona filled with strikers, anarchists and followers of Lluís Companys, who was proclaiming the Catalan State. All day, they leaned out their window, feeling strange to be apart from the action but afraid to get in the way. It seemed chaotic and loud, and with multiple interests being represented, they thought they should wait it out. Kitty was glad she'd secured a way to help for the next little while.

Martial law was declared at 9 p.m. General Batet moved against the militia headquarters and the trade union, and both surrendered. The Generalitat and city hall fought on until 6 a.m. and then Companys surrendered, too.

The rebellion, they later learned, had resulted in forty-six deaths.

Jean was appalled, and wanted to leave Spain. Kitty told her she was sure things would calm down for a while. Kitty herself was feeling a strong pull towards the excitement of revolution, but she wasn't sure it was right.

'Please stay, Jean,' she said. 'Blanca knows what's happening – she'll keep us safe. She did this time, didn't she?'

Jean sighed and lay across their small sofa. 'All right, Kitty. But we must remain together outside.'

Kitty pursed her lips. She was going to start teaching the workers soon. She couldn't promise.

'We'll do our best,' she said.

PART FOUR

58

Wandsworth, London, July 1936

'Will, I'm leaving you,' said Grace with a deadpan expression one evening after work.

Daniel and Emily, now seventeen, looked up from their books in horror.

'Me too, funnily enough,' chirped Kitty, who was tutoring the twins. 'I was just waiting for the right time to tell you.'

Will stood from his armchair by the hearth. He could tell by their faces that neither of them meant for good, but it had jolted him nonetheless. 'Well, if you're all buggering off, perhaps you'd be good enough to tell me to where and when?' Will answered, playing along. 'But the sooner the better, in my opinion.'

'Charming!' laughed Kitty.

'And will anyone be surprised?' added Grace. 'The thing is, my darling, I've just been offered a wonderful opportunity to attend the annual international conference on bacteriology in Berlin. My head of department's wife has rheumatic fever and has taken a turn for the worse, so he feels he should really stay with her. And he's offered me his invitation.'

'Mum, that's terrific,' said Emily. 'Will you be able to see your pen pal, Lieselotte?' After the young German woman had attended Grace's lecture six years ago, they had remained in touch, sharing their medical journeys in different landscapes.

'Yes, she's also attending,' said Grace. 'It'll be wonderful to see her, and I hope she won't mind acting as a guide and translator — the papers will be in a mix of languages.'

'So that's not where you're going, Kitty?'

Daniel interrupted, 'The Berlin Olympics are taking place at the same time. Will you be able to attend that too?'

'I do hope so,' said Grace. 'I've always wanted to see the Games in person.'

'Isn't Fitzy also going to be there?' asked Will. 'In some political capacity or other?' Despite his wife's strength and independence, he did prefer to know she'd have people to rely on.

'He is. And we're hoping to meet up and watch some of the athletics together. And Jenny is coaching the equestrian team!'

'All right,' said Will. 'I'm glad you've got it all planned out. As usual, I seem to be the last to know anything.'

Grace gave him a sympathetic look. Sometimes they were each so busy with their work that their shared conversations were only to organise the house and discuss the children. Will held her eyes. No matter the time that had passed and the changes in their life together, they did still have that deep love, that spark.

'While you're swanning off on your "conference",' Kitty said sarcastically, 'I'll be heading back down to Barcelona.'

'Wait a minute,' said Will, taking the conversation seriously for the first time. 'You speak Spanish fluently already. You spent a year there. I'm sure it hasn't escaped your notice, but there's a civil war that is just about to break out and, from what I've heard, it's already a very unstable and violent situation.'

'I'm aware of that, dear brother, but that's the reason I'm going. The Fascists are fighting to overthrow the democrat-ically elected Republican government and re-establish the supremacy of the rich and powerful, the monarchy, the landed gentry, the Church and the military so they can crush everyone else. If no one does anything, the whole of Europe will soon be embroiled in another war instigated by a group of far-right nationalist fanatics happy to wipe out anyone who gets in their way.'

Will looked at Grace, who looked equally alarmed. They glanced at their children, aware that when they were their age they were already off at war. But they didn't want them getting any ideas.

'Let's discuss this in the kitchen,' Grace said, clearly reading Will's mind.

'I didn't know you felt so strongly,' Will said once they got in there. 'Have you been speaking to Fitzy by any chance about the political situation there?'

'Of course I have. And if anyone's got genuine sympathies for the Communist cause, it's him. I often meet up with him in Westminster when he's not busy lobbying and we both think it's terrible that our government is determined to sit back and do nothing while Spain self-destructs.'

Grace was closest to her brother and knew that what Kitty was saying was true. He could also be quite persuasive about his political views and clearly this had influenced Kitty. Since Kitty had first come back from Spain, she'd often gravitated towards Fitz at family gatherings to have these kinds of polit-ical discussions.

'You haven't mentioned this before,' said Grace. 'It's a bit of a surprise, that's all.'

'Only because I knew my brothers would try to talk me out of it.'

'I will talk you out of it and you're not going,' said Will firmly. 'It's a noble thought, I'll grant you, but it's too dangerous. Clara won't allow it either.'

'Well, you're wrong there. She knows me and how determined I am and she, for one, realises it's hopeless to try to stop me. I'm twenty-six, for goodness' sake, and can make up my own mind without my big brother breathing down my neck all the time. I've spoken to her at length about it and she's finally given me her blessing. On one proviso.'

'Which is?' asked Grace.

'I go with the Red Cross. The Spanish Red Cross are already stretched to the limit looking after soldiers and civilians for Republicans and rebels alike. They don't take sides. They will be supporting people of all nationalities and have appealed for translators. With home-grown volunteers joining those from France, Mexico and the Soviet Union in a struggle against Spanish, Italian, Portuguese and German rebels and Falangists, they're going to need them.'

'Kitty,' said Will imploringly, 'I admire your passion and your political instincts. You know I do. But it's a war. Grace and I have lived through one and we were lucky to survive. And it's because I love you, little sister, that I won't let you go.'

'You can't stop me.'

'I can.' Will stood up and looked as if he wanted to put her over his knee and spank her. For a few seconds, you could hear a pin drop.

'Will,' said Grace softly. 'You remind me of what my mother said to me before I left for war myself with the FANY. If Kitty is this determined, you have to let her go.'

'Thank you, Grace,' said Kitty quietly.

Will shook his head but sat back down.

'I won't be putting myself at risk like you both did,' she said. 'I'll be nowhere near the front line or where the fighting is. I'm simply going as a translator and will be safe in the protective embrace of the Red Cross. Besides which, the Red Cross won't be taking sides. It's just there to help the victims of either cause, whether they're civilians, soldiers, prisoners or detainees. I don't want to be part of a world that just sits back and does nothing. We may not be able to save everyone, but we can still save some. We can make a difference.'

Will was quiet. His sister put forward a powerful argument, and without the support of Clara and Grace, he realised he would have to relent.

'So you really are both leaving me,' he eventually said.

'But not for long,' said Grace.

'And only for a very worthy cause,' added Kitty cheerfully.

Will scowled.

'And,' Grace said, 'there is one thing I would love you to do while I'm away and meeting up with Fitzy in Berlin.'

'What's that?'

'Just recently I sensed his heart condition has become a little more troublesome. He's been a bit more breathless and tired lately.' Will could see the worry set in the fine lines around Grace's green eyes. 'I wondered if you could find out if there is anyone or anything that could help him. Investigate further. Research new types of diagnosis or treatment. I know we have, over the years, but Fitz seems to just ignore the issue now, hoping it will go away. He pushes on even when he should rest. If there's anything . . . I'd appreciate it.'

'OK. Sure,' he said resignedly. 'It's not like I've got anything else to do.'

In the living room, Emily and Daniel were quiet, eavesdropping and giving each other looks when their parents became stern, not a tone they'd heard very much.

'I wonder why they felt they had to talk about that away from us,' Daniel whispered once it seemed like the conversation was winding down.

Emily shrugged. She turned back to her book on new inventions. She was fascinated by the way humans created environments and modes of transport that imitated nature. The city was an anthill, an aeroplane a bird.

'I hope Aunt Kitty doesn't experience anything too scary or dangerous over there,' Daniel said.

Emily put her book down. 'She will be all right, Danny.'

'I just think about . . . what it does to people, you know, sis?'

Emily looked at her brother, his face earnest and thoughtful.

'Some people,' she said, knowing he meant their grandfather. 'I think Aunt Kitty is resilient.'

He nodded thoughtfully. 'Yes, you're probably right.' And then he snatched the book out of her hands.

'Hey!'

'What is this, anyway? The Richter scale . . . measures earthquakes. Boring.' He laughed.

Emily tried to snatch the book back. 'It is the furthest thing from boring, Danny, you silly twat.'

'Don't let Mum hear you say that,' he laughed.

Too late, Grace was back in the doorway. Her hands were on her hips, but she couldn't hide the hint of bemusement on her face. 'You two, go and do something useful. Clean the kitchen, do some weeding, help me pack — anything but laze around like this.'

Daniel and Emily both pretended then to fall asleep. Often their minds worked so differently, but sometimes they synced right up. The three of them laughed.

Later that evening, Grace was lying in bed, waiting while Will brushed his teeth. She was debating whether or not to share the other big thing that was happening to her. She knew it would make him worry and mean that he might try everything to prevent her from going to Berlin. But this conference was important to her.

They had been so careful for years, but since nothing had happened, she knew they'd become a bit more lax lately. As she lay there, she remembered the conversation they'd had a long time ago, after she'd visited the Marie Stopes clinic but had been disheartened by their alignment with eugenicist views. Grace had done more research and told Will that 'the timing is everything'.

She'd explained at the time that, in 1905, Theodoor Hendrik van de Velde, a Dutch gynaecologist, showed that women only ovulate once in every menstrual cycle. Fifteen years later, Kyusaku Ogino, a Japanese gynaecologist, and Hermann Knaus, an Austrian, independently demonstrated that ovulation happens about fourteen days before the next menstrual period.

'Go on,' he'd said.

'Ogino developed a formula to help infertile women time their lovemaking to help them get pregnant.'

'But that's the opposite of what we want.'

'Yes. I know.' However, she had continued to tell him, a few years later, John Smulders, a Roman Catholic physician in the Netherlands, used the same discovery to create a method to *avoid* pregnancy. He called it the rhythm method. 'And that, my darling,' she'd said, 'is why you sometimes think I love you and sometimes I don't.'

Over the years, they'd developed a shorthand: 'Do you love me tonight?' Will would ask cheekily. And Grace would answer, 'Completely' or 'Partly, darling,' with a smirk, and that determined how their lovemaking would go. Often, unless either of them had been away for family or work reasons for a while, Will was completely in tune with the rhythm and could say, 'I'll love you partly tonight.' The understanding between them had always been special, but at this level — Will's acknowledgement of her body's natural cycles — it was even more intimate.

Which was why Grace decided that she could not keep this secret from him now. They shared everything. And she just hoped that he would still be OK with her going away.

Will slid into bed beside her. She took in his handsome face, his combed dark hair, his mint and soap smell.

'What is it, my love?' he asked immediately.

'I think I might be pregnant, Will.'

His eyes and mouth widened. 'But . . .'

'I know. We're so careful. But nature has its ways.' She smiled softly.

'It's too dangerous,' he frowned, sitting upright. 'Your wound, but also your age.'

She nodded. 'Many women carry and deliver healthy babies at thirty-eight, and beyond. You know that.'

He stared into her eyes — worried, loving. Waiting for her to tell him more about how she felt about it.

'My career is going so well, Will. The timing is not good. But I don't think I could . . .'

'Oh, no, that would also be risky.' He held her hands in his.

'We just have to see what happens,' she said.

He nodded.

'And I am still going to Berlin.'

Will sighed. His grip of her hands tightened. 'I knew you'd say that.' He shook his head. 'It's going to be a long couple of weeks. Promise you'll call as much as you can?'

Grace nodded. 'I'll have Fitz around, and Jenny, too. And Lieselotte, who knows everything about medicine. I won't be in any danger,' she said.

59

Hammersmith Hospital, White City, London, July 1936

Will worked less often with Dr Forrester these days, even though the eighty-one-year-old doctor was still as active as ever, refusing to give up his life's work, his cause. Will had a heavy roster of his own and every day he still used the lessons taught to him by his mentor. When he saw him across a corridor, it was like seeing a family member. Always a warm smile and a wave.

Dr Forrester was really starting to show his age, though, Will thought. In the past couple of years, Will had seen him shrink down, and he was moving much slower. When Will visited him in his office, he no longer dunked biscuits into his tea and when he stood from his chair, he always had to clutch the desk until dizziness passed. Many times, Will had insisted he should lie down and let the younger doctor check him over. But Forrester always waved him off.

'It's old age. It's normal,' he'd say. 'Bit of a shock, but we knew it'd catch up with me eventually.'

Will would shake his head, and warn, 'I'm keeping an eye on you.'

Grace had left this morning and as Will entered the hospital, he had the urge to talk to Forrester, as his old mentor, as a friend. He was worried about Grace, and Fitz, and Kitty, not to mention his dad and Clara — though Clara's radiographic treatment seemed to have done wonders — and he needed to steel himself so he could be brave and strong for the children.

He knocked on Forrester's door.

'Come in,' said the old man in a weak voice.

Will opened the door and found Forrester shrunken in his chair, sweating and breathing shallowly, dabbing at his forehead under his receding hairline with a handkerchief.

'My boy,' Forrester said.

'Doctor, you look terribly unwell.' Will raced over to place a hand on his forehead. Clammy.

'A flu, perhaps,' the doctor said.

'Then you must get home to bed.'

The doctor looked frustrated. 'I've barely been sick a day in my life.' He went to stand and then plonked back down, dizzy.

Will was panicked. What had he missed? Had he been so distracted lately by everything happening with his family? How could he let down the person who had helped him become who he was in the world?

He concentrated and remembered the lessons the man in front of him had taught him long ago. *Listen to the patient with utmost care — they will tell you the diagnosis themselves.*

He pulled up a chair across from him, and listened. 'Dr Forrester, tell me what you are feeling.'

Forrester groaned. 'Thirsty, very thirsty. Some cramps, headaches.'

'I wonder . . . You've been losing weight for some time, yes?'

'I don't eat as much now I'm older.'

'Hmm,' Will said. 'Maybe it's just that, but what about the thirst? Is that new?'

Forrester looked down into his empty cup. 'No, actually. I have noticed I've been taking more fluids for a while.'

Will nodded. He came back over to Forrester and asked if he could look into his mouth.

Forrester looked put out and embarrassed.

'Would you rather I call up Dr Stephenson?'

Forrester's eyes shone with mirth. He was reluctant, but proud nonetheless. He slowly opened his mouth. As Will suspected, there was a little scarring on his gums.

'Do you have any pigmentation changes on your skin?'

Forrester frowned. 'Not sure. I don't tend to look at myself. I see my father in the mirror and think, how did that happen?' He chortled, then had to clear his dry throat.

'All right, let me get you some water,' Will said. He left the room to use the tap and thought about the possibilities. Again, he knew he shouldn't intervene without being sure. His old friend wouldn't like it, but Will was going to have to admit him to the hospital for further tests.

His heart beat hard in his chest as he handed the water over to Forrester. He looked so frail. Will knew he was old, but he'd never considered a world without him. He would do everything he could to find out what was wrong.

60

Oranienburg, Berlin, August 1936

Lieselotte Fischl was giggling behind the wheel as she spun the car around the tight right-hand bend. The two women might have only met a few brief times many years ago when Lieselotte was in London, but through their letters they had already become the best of friends. It seemed as if they had known each other for years. Next week, they had tickets for the eleventh Olympiad in Berlin and they had just spent a wonderful late evening at Lieselotte's parents' house in Oranienburg and were now on their way back to the Beelitz-Heilstätten TB Sanatorium where they had been attending the German Society of Bacteriology annual conference and staying in rooms in the nurses' residence.

It was a warm August evening, and although it was dark, the road was dry and the carriageway ahead of them deserted. Lieselotte was driving her father's magnificent 1933 Mercedes-Benz W21 200 Kurz convertible rather too fast for safety. They were each intoxicated by the thrill of it.

Grace, who certainly knew a thoroughbred car when she saw one, adored its two-tone burgundy red and black finish and its tan leather interior, but most of all she loved its shape and impressive speed and manoeuvrability. It was a superlative machine. Luckily, she was feeling no nausea yet from the pregnancy, which she'd had confirmed before leaving, so she could enjoy every bend in the road.

As the car accelerated into the straight, the beam from the three giant front headlamps swept across the grassy bank to the left and momentarily torchlit some kind of commotion. Was it a brawl or fight of some kind? As they drew nearer, it became clear that two heavily built uniformed policemen were savagely beating an unarmed and defenceless civilian with their batons.

Lieselotte slowed the car and touched Grace's forearm. 'What the hell is this?' she said.

'Whatever it is, it's brutal,' answered Grace.

The attackers relentlessly rained blows down on the victim.

Lieselotte's instincts kicked in and she did not hesitate. She pulled the car over to the kerbside and stopped. She wound down the window and said in German, 'What's going on?'

The two policemen looked up, angry. They had not expected to be interrupted as they went about their business. Not by a couple of women in elegant evening dresses anyway.

'Never mind! We've got it under control, so on your way, ladies,' said the taller one of the two.

'That man is defenceless. And hurt. Leave him be now. What's he done anyway?' Lieselotte was not going to be fobbed off.

'Like he said. It's under control,' said the portlier one. He motioned to the 8-foot-high barbed wire fence behind him and added, 'We work here and this trouble-maker is trespassing.'

'Trespassing? What, *outside* the perimeter fence?'

The tall one, smiling now at his friend, strolled over to the car, leaned in, grinning, and stared long and lasciviously at Lieselotte's cleavage. He figured that two young women travelling alone could be frightened away. He was wrong.

Lieselotte herself was not easily intimidated, but before she could react, Grace had opened the passenger door, marched around the front of the car and was walking towards the dishevelled figure slumped on the ground at the other policeman's feet.

'Grace!' shouted Lieselotte. 'Wait!'

She swung her door open hard against the man's groin, winding him, then pushed past him.

Much to the consternation of the two thugs, she ran over and joined Grace by the fence. The two men looked at each other uncertainly and the broader one took half a step to the side to block Grace's further passage. Unperturbed, Grace sidestepped him. It was not the first time she had been threatened by aggressive men, and certainly not the first time she had seen nasty injuries. She knelt down next to the beaten man and examined him. His clavicle and nose were clearly broken, blood poured down his face from a head wound, and waxy yellow subcutaneous fat protruded from a vicious, gaping laceration across his left cheek. There were fresh, livid bruises all across his neck, jaw and arms.

'Dear God, are you trying to beat this man to death?' she said, looking up, but aware they might not speak English.

The taller of the two men, who had followed Lieselotte from the car, took a pace forward and was just reaching down to pull Grace back up when Lieselotte pushed his arm away.

'Leave her alone. This man needs help.'

'This man is trouble. You don't understand.'

'What I do understand is that he's hurt and needs medical attention.'

The two men looked at each other.

'He can get medical attention here. Look!' He gestured past the wire fence to a monstrous and forbidding concrete building block surrounded by military-style barracks and watchtowers. Lieselotte could just make out the words 'ARBEIT MACHT FREI' etched into the lintel above the giant archway at its entrance. 'WORK MAKES YOU FREE.'

This was Sachsenhausen, Lieselotte realised. The recently constructed 'camp' for so-called political activists and dissidents that her father, Rolf, had told her about. '"Dissidents" meaning anyone who happens to disagree with the ideology of the National Socialists,' he had said. The camp where at least six thousand men and women had already been taken, but from which none had re-emerged. A sudden shiver of alarm ran through her, and Grace sensed it.

'Help me get him into the car,' she said to her friend.

'*Nein*! This man stays here!' snapped the stouter man menacingly. He stepped forward and raised his baton like a cosh. Grace looked at Lieselotte with a raised eyebrow.

'I don't want my English journalist friend to get the wrong idea at this important time,' said Lieselotte suddenly. 'You know how things can sometimes be inaccurately reported in the newspapers.'

The policeman looked stunned.

He immediately stepped back and dropped his baton arm. How many times had he had it drummed into him that for the duration of the XI Olympiad no acts of discrimination or violence must be allowed to be witnessed by foreign visitors?

Grace wasn't exactly sure what Lieselotte had threatened, but she tried to look serious and back her up.

'You consort with him at your own risk,' the policeman said grudgingly. 'The man is a menace. So on your own head be it.'

The second man now stood directly in front of her, his face just inches from hers. His breath stank of stale cigarettes.

'Don't say you haven't been warned.' His meaning was not lost on Lieselotte.

'This filthy parasite will slit your throat as soon as look at you,' said his sidekick. Then he gestured to his friend and the two men ambled off, taking in the sleek lines of the Mercedes enviously as they left.

The women each took an elbow and helped the wounded man into the back seat of the car. Grace removed the shawl from her shoulders, wiped the blood from his eyes and nose as best she could and tied it firmly around the wound on the man's head. Jumping into the front quickly themselves, Lieselotte gunned the engine and roared off down the avenue, looking frequently into the rear-view mirror as she did so.

'Will they follow us?' Grace asked.

'No need. They clocked the registration plate. They'll soon find out who we are.'

'I'm sorry,' rasped a voice from the back. 'They said I was trouble. And I've brought you a heap of it.'

'Nonsense,' said Lieselotte, eyeing the man's bruised and bloodied face in the mirror. 'Any decent person would do the same.' She translated for Grace.

Not any more, he thought. The few decent people still around were increasingly invisible or silent and would not have dared.

'*Adank, got zol dir beider bentchen,*' he whispered.

Lieselotte glanced at their passenger in her rear-view mirror.

'*Zei gezunt,*' she replied softly.

Grace looked across enquiringly.

'He said, "Thank you and God bless you both." I told him he is welcome. In Yiddish.'

The stab of fear that Grace had noticed earlier in her friend of course made sense. Grace thought back on all their letters and she did remember Lieselotte talking about her faith and certain family traditions here and there, and she realised she had failed to be more curious. Her own family was religious in only the most ordinary way: church at Christmas and Easter, and an encouragement to pray before bed. So that might be a reason why she never delved much into other people's religious identities.

'Lothar,' the man said, now in English. 'My name is Lothar Stein. And I think you two may have just saved my life.'

61

British Embassy, Wilhelmstrasse, Berlin, August 1936

Fitzwilliam Tustin-Pennington refolded the note from Grace and slid it into the inside pocket of his jacket. What on earth was so urgent that she needed to talk to him today? he wondered.

It was only two days ago that she had been eating and drinking with him in the bars and taverns of the capital until the early hours.

He could recollect the twinkling stars on the ceiling of the Bar Atlantis in Behrenstrasse and just about remember the sounds of *die verrückt Jazzmanner* and the Weintraub Syncopators in the Alt-Berliner Wirtshaus, but after that everything was a blur. He still felt a little nauseous thinking about it, more from all the food than drink as Grace had been worried about him drinking too much because of his health.

Fitz was now on the balcony of the Palais Strousberg in which the British Embassy was situated. As he looked to the right, he could hear marches, wake-up calls and the song *'Freut euch des Lebens'* ('Rejoice in Life') emanating from Pariser Platz around the corner. 'The Great Awakening' ritual was the ruling Nazi party's chosen way of honouring the International Olympic Committee in their midst.

'Sorry I took so long,' said the man who had pushed through the throng inside and now stood beside Fitz again. 'Bit of a scrum at the bar, I'm afraid.'

Fitz took the glass of champagne from his hand and sipped it. He was quite breathless today — had probably been going a bit too hard — but he tried not to let it show. 'Mmm! Krug. Grande Cuvée, if I'm not mistaken,' he said, smiling.

'I'm impressed. Pity wine-testing isn't an Olympic sport. You'd win gold.'

Fitz laughed ruefully. With the hole in his heart, he knew it was the only kind of medal to which he could realistically aspire. Though taking too much wine was not so good for his symptoms either.

'From a champagne house in France founded by a German.'

'Really?'

'Joseph Krug. A humble accountant turned expert viticulturalist.'

'An excellent career move, I'd say.'

Fitz had warmed to Hugo Lowenthal immediately. He was the cultural attaché at the Embassy, so not particularly high in the pecking order and not restricted by the usual stifling formality to which most officials were subject. He was an interesting man.

'Are you a fan of military marches?' Hugo asked.

'Not particularly. I'd have preferred something inspirational rather than indulgent.'

'Wait until you hear Richard Strauss's specially commissioned "Olympic Hymn" in that case. Apparently, Joseph Goebbels, their esteemed propaganda minister, didn't like the original lyrics, "Peace shall be the battle cry".'

Fitz regarded Hugo expectantly.

'He changed them to "Honour shall be the battle cry". I wonder why?'

Fitz sensed that the cultural attaché had more to say on the subject. Perhaps, he thought, with three glasses of champagne already inside him, he might be persuaded to offer it up. After all, wasn't that why Fitz had been sent here? To eavesdrop and report back?

He still could not quite believe that he had been sent on this mission at all. Ostensibly an administrator with the British Olympic delegation, he was actually there in his capacity as assistant secretary to Foreign Secretary Anthony Eden. Eden had become increasingly concerned about growing criticism of his support for Baldwin in his policy of appeasement of Nazi Germany, as well as his non-interference in the Spanish Civil War. The uproar caused by the German reoccupation of the Rhineland and Churchill's increasingly vociferous condemnation of the Cabinet's continual concessions to a defiant and belligerent European neighbour had prompted him to garner more information.

Unprepossessing, physically disabled Fitzwilliam, while diligent, discreet and intelligent to a fault, would never be suspected of being one of his spies.

'Fitz!' the Foreign Secretary had cried one morning. 'To what degree are you interested in sport?'

'I enjoy sport very much, sir,' he had replied. 'Although because of my dodgy ticker purely as a spectator.'

'Splendid. So how would you like to go and spectate for me at the Berlin Olympics? As my eyes and ears, as it were?'

'Well, I think I'd like that very much, sir. Although . . .'

'Officially you'll be part of the British Olympic delega-tion. As such, you will attend the official ceremony, join in the formalities, and meet and greet as many of your fascist hosts as is humanly possible. Preferably without attracting suspicion.'

Fitz was both flattered and surprised to be asked. He'd always enjoyed being 'behind the scenes' in politics, and taking on a secret reconnaissance role was as behind the scenes as you could get. He didn't tell his boss, though, that he'd been warned more and more by doctors about doing too much travelling with his heart defect.

'I want to get a feel for what the Nazi regime are really up to. I want to know what they're planning. In sport. Domestically. And in foreign policy. Think you can do that?'

'I'll try my best, sir,' Fitz had heard himself saying. With four brothers and a sister who had served in the war, he had always longed for an opportunity to show them what he could do, in his own way. He hoped Shauna would be proud of him too. They'd had a strange conversation recently when he'd had to become firmer than he normally was and insist her lover did not stay in the house so often. If anyone found out, the damage that it could do to his political reputation . . . But their marriage on the whole still worked, as a great friendship and a domestic partnership. He couldn't imagine living with anyone else.

'Good,' Eden had said. 'Go and see Margaret, my secretary, who'll make the arrangements. And, Fitzwilliam?'

'Sir?'

'Wish our team the best of luck from me.' Then, winking at Fitz, he'd added, 'Without giving the game away, if you see what I mean.'

Since then, Fitz had done plenty of listening. And watching. Somehow, he did not think Eden would relish what he would have to report.

Hugo was staring down at the crowds below. The contrast between his sad, expressionless face and the excitement of the masses was stark.

'You think German aggression is likely?' Fitz asked.

'Fitz, dear boy, I believe war is inevitable.'

Fitz raised an eyebrow. It was a trait he had copied from his sister. But then he lowered it, nervous it might appear flirtatious. He was always second-guessing himself like this around men.

'Just consider the facts,' Hugo went on, serious. 'The reoccupation of the Rhineland. Totally unopposed. The brutal oppression and persecution of Jewish people and other minorities. It's been escalating relentlessly since the Nazis came to power three years ago.' He looked over his shoulder to see if he was being overheard. He was not. 'We've seen over three hundred anti-Semitic edicts enacted and the Nuremberg Laws stripping half a million people of German citizenship. As a Jew myself, if I wasn't working here in the British Embassy, I'd be forbidden from holding any office in the civil service. As a doctor, as a judge, even as a lowly administrator. My nephews and nieces would be effectively barred from schools or universities.'

He looked over his shoulder again.

'The blonde girl with the blue eyes in the silver dress I introduced you to earlier?'

'Christel?'

'Yes. We're — how shall we say? — together.'

'Lucky man,' said Fitz, glancing back inside at the coruscating beauty surrounded by men. He may have meant, *Lucky woman*. He pushed that thought away.

'Except we'd never be allowed to marry if we stayed here. And she being a German of pure blood, I'd be committing a crime for even sleeping with her.'

'Worth the risk though, I imagine,' grinned Fitz, attempting to lighten the mood, but then instantly regretting the faux pas. He pushed his glasses up on his nose.

Hugo gave a tight smile. 'What do you think? Last week, Fitz, soldiers were marching through the street down there openly singing anti-Jewish slogans and smashing up Jewish shopfronts. People are going missing, and people are scared.'

Fitz swallowed. This was deadly serious. He felt his heart palpitating again. He should stand out of the sun. 'Are you scared yourself?'

'For myself, no. I have diplomatic immunity. They wouldn't touch me. Too sensational. But for German Jews, yes. Every day, we have hundreds of applications to emigrate. They see what's coming.'

'Can you help?'

'To an extent. Other countries express sympathy but do little to assist in practical terms. Their immigration quotas are paltry.'

'I don't suppose the worldwide depression brought about by the war has helped either.'

'True enough. But many countries deliberately turn a blind eye. Jews are not welcome there either. Maybe you can raise awareness of this on your return?'

'It's terrible, but I don't think I'm really in a position to—'

'You're a good man, Fitzwilliam, but you're a terrible liar. You know bugger all about sport and you've shown no interest in anything other than politics for the last week. Olympic delegation official, my arse.'

'Well, I . . .'

'Don't worry. Your secret's safe with me. But the situation here is dire and getting worse by the day.'

'Persecution and discrimination is awful in any society, Hugo. And yes, I will report back. But your prediction of another war? That's quite another matter.' He put a hand to his chest, cleared his throat.

'It's as inevitable as Germany winning twice as many gold medals at these games as their nearest rivals. I'd bet on it.'

Fitz turned and looked Hugo in the eye.

'Hugo. This is the British Embassy for God's sake. You work here. I'm just an observer. Why the hell do you need me to send the message?'

'Because anti-Jewish and fascist ideology is not solely the province of German officialdom. It runs in rich seams through other foreign embassies and governments too. Oswald Mosley, for example. I think he'd feel very at home here.'

He glanced back over his shoulder a third time.

'And I'm not the Führer in this establishment either.'

62

Lustgarten, Berlin, August 1936

Jürgen Altmann was enjoying himself in the Lustgarten.

He stood at the edge of the park and for the first time in years felt things were finally going his way. Thirty thousand boys and girls of the Hitler Youth had arrived at the rally and all of those under his direct supervision had saluted him with their customary deference.

Those he had indoctrinated and trained to perform the *Mutprobe* were especially fond of him. This bravery test could involve several different types of physical challenge and Altmann had devised an interesting array of them. The ones who plucked up the courage to dive from great heights into deep water or climb vertical rock faces earned his greatest respect. It also entitled them to carry the iconic Hitler Youth dagger, a tangible symbol of Nazi pride and honour.

The grotesque keloid scarring on the left side of his face that over the years had contracted and pulled the outer corners of his eye and mouth towards one another merely seemed to add to his allure and stature in the eyes of the youth. It was a wound, they knew, sustained fighting for his country during the last war. The fact he never spoke about the details engendered further admiration and respect. He was too humble to boast, they assumed.

The whole event had gone like clockwork. First, Goebbels had addressed the crowd. Then, as he had finished, an athlete carrying the Olympic torch had run through the ranks of the Hitler Youth and ignited the Olympic flame in its massive cauldron. Even the torch itself had been especially crafted by Krupp, the German steel company currently churning out thousands of Nazi weapons. What a stroke of genius that had been, thought Altmann. A German innovation, of course. Never before had anyone thought of a relay of more than three thousand athletes running thousands of miles over twelve days from Olympia, Greece, to the host stadium, and in this instance via Sofia, Vienna and Prague. Never before had anyone brought antiquity like this to the present day. It had captured the imagination of the world and likely no one would ever forget it.

Hitler's open-topped Mercedes had led his cavalcade along the seven-mile stretch of the Via Triumphalis to the stadium — the route decked dramatically with swastika banners as forty thousand stormtroopers guarded the procession in full Army uniform.

The procession now over, Altmann looked to his right at the Brandenburg Gate and the glorious Quadriga that stood atop it. A chariot pulled by four magnificent galloping horses. A Roman goddess at the reins and holding aloft a pole bearing a Prussian eagle and an iron cross decorated with a laurel wreath.

At the edge of the park, he saw a small group — the woman, Christel, he recognised. That must be the British cultural attaché with her. Altmann shuddered. A Jewish man working so high up at the Embassy. How were the British not ashamed? At least he would have his uses. Beside him, a small man who looked out of breath. Altmann walked a bit closer. His face seemed quite familiar.

He saw the woman give him a warning glance and he walked far to the right of them. Silly woman. As if he would endanger their important work.

He looked up at the sculpture again as he walked. It contrasted starkly with the overcast sky and looked bolder and more combative than ever. Originally an emblem of peace, it was now universally regarded as a potent symbol of victory following the Prussian defeat of Napoleon in 1814. Another victory over France could not come soon enough, Altmann thought. The German chariot would ride roughshod all over it.

He put the breathless man's face out of his mind.

63

Charlottenburg, south-west Berlin, August 1936

Christel lay on her side in the giant king-size bed. She was in a wonderful twilight zone between a semi-erotic dream and wakefulness and was not inclined to leave it. The soft, quilted duvet felt light against her skin and the lavender-scented pillow lay gossamer-smooth against her face.

The early-morning sun sent shafts of light across the room and tiny bright images danced on the architraves, walls and dressing table where they hit their target.

The window of the apartment was partly open and a warm August breeze occasionally stirred the edges of the closed curtains, making them quietly flap and tinkle.

Her eyes still closed, she stretched as she stirred and gently arched her spine, easing her perfectly shaped buttocks backwards. Behind her, she suddenly became aware of another warm body shifting closer towards her and she thrilled at the almost imperceptible touch of the strong thighs against the back of her legs and the urgent pressure above them.

The hand which had slid around her side was now on her breast. The soft fingertip gently stroked the dark brown skin of her areola and then squeezed and coaxed the nipple as it became upright and firm.

Christel's lips parted in a smile as she felt the sensation transport wave-like secretory messages to other parts of her body. The effect of these hands on her skin was almost magical.

Christel turned slowly on to her back. She stretched her arms above her head now and her toned flat stomach invited attention. The hand still cupping her breast glided downwards over her velvety skin, stroking in long horizontal sweeps further and further downward.

She turned to Ilse then, running the fingers of her right hand through her long dark hair and the other pulling her shoulder towards her. She sought out Ilse's generous full lips and they kissed tenderly and softly at first, then harder, each kiss more imploring and passionate.

She hardly felt the fingers as they slid inside her, but she could feel what effect they were having as that spectral motion of their tips glided up and down against her beckoning treasure, and then, at either side of it, beginning to overwhelm her.

Christel found herself involuntarily arching the small of her back. Ilse eased further inwards and upwards against the special place. And as Christel responded, she expertly and lovingly performed the two actions together. One moment the movement was rapid firm and insistent; the next, just as waves were promising to crash and break, it fell back to becoming slow and languid, lazy and soft. Ilse's deep brown eyes were hugely dilated now, her own growing excitement coursing through her every sinew. She could feel the upward thrust of Christel's pelvis and the liquid swelling of the tissue beneath her fingers. Christel was lost to Ilse's touch. She was dissolving.

Once again, Christel felt a subtle change in direction and pressure. And she became aware of a different sensation. A primeval seiche which was gathering speed and strength. It was beautiful, all-encompassing and unstoppable. Her legs quivered and her throat became tight. She gasped in short rapid breaths and her whole body spasmed and shook as wave after wave of powerful contractions brought her to ecstasy.

Later, at noon, Christel was dressing while Ilse reclined in bed watching her.

'Will you be seeing Hugo later?' asked Ilse eventually.

'I'm seeing him tonight.' Then, seeing the hurt in her eyes, she quickly added, 'But you shouldn't worry about him, Ilse. Really, you shouldn't. You are the love of my life and always will be.'

Ilse looked at her uncertainly as Christel sat on the edge of the bed and kissed her. Sex with Hugo would be expected on his part that evening, she knew, but it was something she would just have to go along with. It was not love. She liked him, and the sex was certainly not a chore. But it was different. Not as meaningful, deep and emotional as it was with Ilse. Not nearly as satisfying. It was more primitive. More corporeal, wanton. Ilse had always known about Hugo, and Christel fervently hoped that she had fully convinced her that she had less fondness for him than she actually had.

The truth was that with Ilse it was making love. With Hugo it was just raw sex.

And with Altmann . . . Well, she tried to avoid it as much as possible.

She loved Ilse more than she loved herself and knew she could not contemplate life without her. She would do nothing to jeopardise what they had, but nevertheless had taken the risk of being a little economical with the truth.

'Hugo means nothing to me, Ilse, you know that. But he is a means to an end and I'll see it through.' She would never tell Ilse about Altmann as well. Not if she wanted to keep them both safe.

Ilse needed more.

'Will you sleep with him?'

Christel bent down and kissed her on the cheek.

'Only if not sleeping with him would arouse suspicion. Sleeping with Hugo cannot compare to sleeping with you, Ilse. I love you. And besides,' she added, tenderly running her fingers over Ilse's lips, 'you know that my motives for anything I do with Hugo are totally different.'

She smiled, turned and sashayed from the room.

64

Beelitz-Heilstätten TB Sanatorium, Berlin, August 1936

Grace and Liese had chosen seats in the middle of the hall near the aisle for extra legroom. The medical presentations could often drag on a little, so it was a relief to be able to stretch their legs from time to time, and get away, if necessary, with minimum disturbance to others. Sometimes the doctors rather liked the sound of their own voices.

They would not be doing that during the next submission, however, because Liese's father, Professor Rolf Fischl, was due to deliver it himself.

The prof was famous for his intriguing presentation titles. This one was called, 'The Phage and the Bacterium: a microbiological allegory for David and Goliath'.

The auditorium was packed, such was his reputation for education and entertainment in equal measure, and his talk was eagerly anticipated by experts and academics from around the world.

The hubbub faded and the host of the conference stepped up to the podium to introduce Professor Fischl.

Grace listened to his talk, spellbound.

What a privilege it had been to visit the historic laboratories at Berlin University and the birthplace of such famous physicians and medical pioneers as Robert Koch and Paul Ehrlich. Koch, the first to postulate the germ theory of disease, had grown specific pathogens in pure laboratory cultures and isolated the causative agents of tuberculosis, anthrax and cholera. Meanwhile, his friend Ehrlich had found a cure for syphilis and invented techniques to distinguish between different types of blood cells and stain bacteria to make them visible.

To Grace's mind, their work equalled the earlier work of Louis Pasteur and Edward Jenner, who had developed the earliest vaccines to protect against viral infections like smallpox, something she often lectured on. It was not known at the time that viruses as such actually existed. Soon, however, when experiments using Chamberland filters with pores tiny enough to retain all bacteria were used, it became evident that something in the filtrate that was not bacterial remained infectious to living organisms. That something came to be known as a virus.

By now, many viruses had been discovered and named. Yet it was only ten years ago that it had been realised that they were tiny particles and not fluids or toxins. Thanks to Wendell Meredith Stanley's invention of the electron microscope in 1931, their tiny but complex structures could now be clearly visualised. First, the cause of foot-and-mouth disease in animals was discovered, and soon after, the yellow fever virus in humans.

Despite this, however, there were still many horrendous and lethal infections taking a terrible toll on human life, where the causative agents remained elusive and unidentified. Further still from their grasp were effective treatments.

Grace was passionate about her work in microbiology, pathology and wound management and was convinced that in her lifetime significant advances would be made that would preserve thousands, if not millions, of human lives and prevent terrible suffering. She wanted desperately to be a part of it and that was why she had almost bitten off her boss's hand to accept this invitation to the conference on bacteriophages.

She briefly thought about the tiny but complex structure that had taken residence in her abdomen, so incredibly different to a virus. Life and possibility.

She turned her mind back to the work. No matter what happened, she would not waste this opportunity. Maybe these particular viruses that could infect and replicate inside bacteria held the key to the holy grail of infectious chemotherapy.

After thirty fascinating minutes, Professor Fischl had concluded and was receiving a rapturous and prolonged standing ovation from the delegates. He was shaking hands with his host, who was complimenting him on such a fine speech.

Everyone began to leave their seats to break for coffee.

The great oak doors at the back of the hall swung wide open. A dozen brown-shirted *Sturmabteilung* military troopers marched in and lined the back of the room. Two of them strode straight up to the professor and were insisting he followed them outside. Liese was puzzled and anxious, but there were far too many people in the way to allow her to immediately intervene or investigate.

He was being bundled out of the room quite unceremoniously. She could see him indignantly trying to remove the stormtroopers' grip from his arm as he was led from the auditorium. Liese began pushing past other people to go to his aid. Grace could see a few curious faces turn towards the fracas, perhaps imagining it was some kind of security detachment squirrelling the star of the show away from the masses, others not convinced. Then she saw something else. The SA men at the back of the hall were now moving forward against the flow of traffic, craning their necks in search of some other target.

'Liese,' said Grace urgently. 'Is this something to do with what happened the other night?'

Liese looked thunderstruck.

'I thought there might be repercussions. But not so soon.'

'They are not holding back with your father, Liese. There is nothing you can do.'

'But I have to try, Grace. I have to.'

'There are ways and means. Revealing yourself here might only make the situation worse.'

The Brownshirts were getting nearer. Peering along every row of seats and examining every face. Grace grabbed her friend's arm and pulled her into the aisle.

'Come with me!'

They ran towards the stage at the front of the hall and darted through a door to the right. It led to a corridor towards an emergency exit, but much to their alarm, it was locked when they reached it. They heard shouts approaching from behind them in the hall. They froze. They were trapped. Then Grace turned back towards them.

'Grace. What the hell?'

'Quick,' she replied.

'The door to your left.'

'DAMENTOILETTE' said the sign on the door. They threw themselves inside. They could hear someone rattling the emergency doors at the end of the corridor to confirm they were locked. No escape there. They could also make out the sound of doors further along the corridor being opened and closed.

Grace pulled Liese into a cubicle and locked the door. Liese seemed paralysed with fear.

'Liese, why would they want to hunt you down like this? We were just doing our civic duty the other night. Not committing a crime.'

'You don't understand, Grace. My family has committed a different kind of crime in their eyes.'

Grace stared back at her.

'We . . . we don't conform to their idea of pure blood.'

'But . . . but your family is Roman Catholic, Liese. The crucifix in your mother's hall . . . The rosary beads hanging from the rear-view mirror of the Mercedes?'

'Grace, we are. I have been brought up as a Roman Catholic. Baptised in that faith as a child.'

'But?'

'But my grandmother was Jewish.'

Grace just blinked.

'In the eyes of the Nazi party, that makes us Jewish, too. And embarrassing their militia the other night has stirred up a hornets' nest.'

The banging and crashing in the corridor outside was getting closer. Grace stood on the toilet seat and pushed open the square window above the sill. It gave on to the pavement outside.

'Up here!' she said. 'A sylph like you can easily squeeze through that. Come on, I'll give you a push.'

It was only 30 centimetres on each side, but going arms and head first and turning diagonally to ease her hips through, Liese slid through like a butterfly emerging from a chrysalis and dropped to the ground on to her outstretched arms. She looked back at Grace's face at the window, blew her a kiss, then turned and ran. Grace barely had time to descend and sit down on the toilet seat before a fist was banging on the cubicle door.

'Occupied,' she shouted. 'Sorry.'

'Open the door,' cursed the man.

'One moment.'

Grace waited just long enough to pretend she was rearranging her dress and flushed the toilet. She slid open the lock and the stormtrooper burst in.

'What on earth is so urgent?' she asked indignantly.

But he was not looking at her. He was staring at the wide-open window behind her.

65

Olympiastadion, Berlin, August 1936

'Tell me more,' said Fitz.

Grace had filled him in on the incident outside Sachsenhausen, but she had only just finished describing Rolf's arrest and Liese's escape from the stormtroopers at the medical conference at the sanatorium.

They sat in the seats that Liese had originally been given by her father, but she could obviously not dare reveal herself in the Olympic stadium and Grace had not heard from her since her flight from the conference.

The excited throng pressed around them, and they had to almost shout in each other's ears to make themselves heard.

Fitz was looking forward very much to seeing the great Jesse Owens run in the 4 x 100 metres final in the next few minutes but was totally distracted by what his sister was telling him. He was also increasingly out of breath and slightly dizzy from it, so was glad they were sitting down.

'You seem quite friendly with Hugo, the cultural attaché at the Embassy,' she said. 'Is there anything he could do to help? I'm so worried for Liese and her family. In a way, I think I made the problem worse by getting involved the other night. Bringing more attention to the family like that.'

'What you did was a decent thing, Grace. In anybody's eyes. But you put yourself at risk, which is just like you, by the way — a bit foolhardy, perhaps, but with the best of intentions. As always.'

'What do the authorities want with them? Rolf is internationally renowned and respected. One of Germany's finest doctors. Liese is an award-winning and hugely qualified expert in her own right. Why are they feeling so threatened?'

'For one simple reason. Their scientific standing and success is a threat to the Nazis. An academic. A professor. These things actually make it worse.'

Grace unconsciously ran a hand across her belly and squinted into the sun. She had begun to feel nauseous but didn't know if that was just from the worry. 'Can Hugo help?'

'I don't know. He made it clear that his superiors at the Embassy harbour their own prejudices. Some of them sympathetic to those of the National Socialist party. Hugo is also Jewish himself. It's tricky.'

'But in special circumstances?' she said. 'If Rolf and Liese were allowed to emigrate and granted residency in England, they would be an enormous benefit to our scientific community.'

'Of course. I don't doubt it. But the Nazis have clamped down on emigration. They are identifying applicants and arresting them. Taking away passports and rounding people up.'

'My God,' said Grace. 'Poor Liese. Her poor parents. Poor Lothar.'

'I'll talk to Hugo again. His girlfriend, Christel, works on the emigration side at the Embassy too. Maybe they can put their heads together on this somehow. I'll try.'

Grace smiled briefly and gave her brother a peck on the cheek.

'Thank you, Fitzy. I know you'll do what you can.'

Fitz would move heaven and earth if necessary. But he would have to proceed cautiously in the current political climate and avoid embarrassing Hugo in his own precarious position. Furthermore, he would have to be careful not to reveal his own clandestine role as amateur spy.

Then Grace put her hand on Fitz's arm. 'And, Fitzy, you know I'm worried about you, too. Your shortness of breath seems more . . . prominent.'

'Oh, don't be, sister. Same old, same old. Now who's going to win this race?' he said, changing the subject.

'My money is on Jesse Owens,' she said, allowing him to move away from the topic he found vulnerable. 'Although the Italian team are tipped for gold as well. You can never rule out the German team either. Certainly not at these Games. They've already amassed almost twice as many medals as any other country.'

'They have. One way or another.'

Grace looked at Fitz with a raised eyebrow. 'How can they?'

'Well, let's just say that if there's an advantage, they will find it.'

'Advantage?'

'I was talking to Alec Scott the other day. You remember Alec? The dear boy just got himself a bronze medal for the British equestrian eventing team.'

'Yes, my friend Jenny speaks highly of him.'

'Well, he told me that there were good reasons why the German equestrian team were so easily able to dominate the medal board this year.'

'How?'

'In the cross-country, for example, there was one partic-ular fence where about half of all the riders fell off their horses. It was the fourth fence. It was a 3-foot post and rail, dropping into a pond. Alec said the landing was much deeper than anyone could've anticipated and the footing underneath didn't hold up well either. There were fifty riders competing in that eventing competition and only twenty-seven finished.'

Grace could hardly believe it.

'The Germans, of course, knew about it and had been practising at the fence for weeks. Even the Japanese rider who was the hot favourite foundered there.'

'How dastardly,' said Grace. 'Although, to be fair, I expect any home nation would employ similar tricks if given half a chance.'

'I expect you're right,' smiled Fitz. 'You should know. You were a damn fine rider yourself. Still are. And, in sport, not unknown to employing a few dirty tricks yourself.'

'I have no idea what on earth you're talking about,' said Grace, smiling, as she recalled how when they were young she would often outsmart her brothers at tennis and cricket. 'All is fair in love and war.'

'Hah!' laughed Fitz. 'Well, we definitely know that's not true.'

'Shut up and watch the race,' she said, elbowing him in the ribs.

Jesse Owens had already made history. Today, at the age of twenty-two, he had the once-in-a-lifetime chance to do it all over again. He had already won three Olympic gold medals in the last six days and in doing so had captured the world's imagination. As a black athlete, he had also caused consterna-tion and fury amongst the host nation's political elite. He had almost single-handedly shattered the dream of Aryan white supremacy.

He was now limbering up in the minutes of preparation before the final of the 4 x 100 metres relay.

Less than a week earlier, he had entered a crucible of hate to compete in the 100 metres sprint. As the German dictator had entered the stadium, the German national anthem 'Deutschland Über Alles' had struck up, followed by the Nazi anthem 'Horst Wessel Lied'.

To accompany this, a forest of arms had shot out with the salute of 'Sieg heil, sieg heil'. Such an intimidating and partisan crowd Jesse had never before witnessed.

Yet he had triumphed, and then gone on to win gold in the long jump the following day, and in the 200 metres sprint the day after that in another world record time of 20.7 seconds. In doing so, he had also won over the crowd and the admiration of millions of people listening to broadcasts around the world.

Now, as the expectant 115,000-strong crowd began to hush, he took one last look around the vast Reichssportfeld and the iconic Olympic flame burning brightly in its huge pedestal at the Marathon Gate. Either side of it stood the magnificent twin towers which led to the Maifeld outside, where a quarter of a million men could parade at once. There, at the western end of the Olympiastadion, he could just make out the huge bell at the top of one of the 77 metre high towers on which he knew were boldly emblazoned the five Olympic rings, an imposing eagle, the year 1936, a picture of the Brandenburg Gate, the dates 1–16 August, the number 11 (because these were the games of the XI Olympiad) and finally, between two swastikas, the rather ambiguous words, 'I call the youth of the world.'

Less than 150 yards from where he now stood, in the grandiose stand designed specifically for the Reich Chancellor and his political associates, a shortish man in a brown uniform and black military peaked cap slowly took a seat. The bold black swastika on the band of crimson on his left arm and the iron cross he had been awarded in the last war and which he proudly wore on his chest clearly identified the man as Adolf Hitler himself.

Jesse kicked his spiked shoes out in front of him in the time-honoured manner of a nervous athlete about to perform and then stepped forward, knelt down on the track, every sinew tensed and ready to explode into position. He lifted his eyes from the track and looked ahead 100 metres to where Ralph Metcalfe was standing in his position, ready to grab the baton. He looked as nervous as Jesse felt himself.

Now there was only silence. The official at trackside was counting down in German.

Jesse tightened his hold on the baton in his right hand and took his marks.

In the crowd, Grace and Fitzwilliam leaned forward, holding their breath.

As the starting pistol cracked, the African American athlete in lane 7 sprang forward and the tens of thousands of excited spectators rose to their feet as one.

The American relay team huddled together in a group of unbridled joy. They had achieved a new world record of 39.8 seconds and earned another gold medal for the United States. A hundred and fifteen thousand spectators were still on their feet shouting, yelling and applauding enthusiastically, Grace and Fitz included.

'Wow,' said Fitz.

'An incredible athlete,' said Grace.

The four grinning athletes jogged around the track together in a lap of honour and Jesse Owens passed beneath the Reich Chancellor's stand, where the Führer himself gave a thin smile and a wave.

'He's not going to be happy,' said Fitz.

'It's a rebuke of what he stands for, that's for sure,' said Grace. 'The supremacy of one race.' She lowered her voice. 'How ridiculous.'

'And he's certainly not the only successful African American athlete at the Games by any means. There are eighteen. Eight of them have won gold.'

On the track, Jesse savoured his victory. He tried to ignore the greater context for a moment. He felt that sport and the individuals involved in it were inherently decent and good. Qualities such as fairness, discipline, trust and morality underpinned everything they believed in. Luz Long, his German rival in the long jump, was the epitome of this. Jesse firmly believed that it was Luz's selfless technical advice in the long jump that had allowed him to emerge victorious, even at the man's own expense. They had struck up an immediate friendship.

His heart was bursting with pride as he paused to greet his admirers spilling on to the track. He glimpsed Marty Glickman looking on forlornly from the centre of the field and felt a deep pang of sympathy for the Jewish American man whose place in the team he had taken twenty-four hours previously. As he had been ordered to do.

Jesse was no stranger himself to discrimination. Back home in Ohio, he had been restricted to ordering takeaways or eating at Black-only restaurants whenever travelling with the university team. He'd had to work in a series of part-time jobs to make up for the scholarship he was never awarded. He had even publicly considered boycotting these games six months previously because of the treatment he had heard was being meted out to German minority groups. He had been criticised, however, for being 'an American agitator' by Avery Brundage, President of the American Olympic Committee, so had backed down.

It seemed whatever action he took politically, he could not win. But he had won today at the *Olympische Sommerspiele*. And he had won over the crowd again too. He intended to enjoy the moment. When he stood with his three teammates on the podium to receive his medal, he did what he had already done three times before. He listened to the American national anthem and proudly saluted the American flag.

66

Wandsworth, London, August 1936

Will was at home with Emily, poring over textbooks and former case notes. He had listened to his mentor and believed he knew what was ailing him, but, as he'd been taught, he was making no knee-jerk reaction and instead ensuring he could confirm his instincts.

Daniel was currently visiting Robbie at the Maudsley and had been telling Will about how the conservative doctors there were reluctant to try any radical treatments that perhaps could be helpful for his grandfather, and Will felt bad that he hadn't given that more thought or attention yet, but he was happy his son was so interested and involved with not only Robbie but the other patients there. It reminded Will of when he'd first volunteered in hospitals.

Emily was reading a book beside Will but often would get up and click on the wireless or make a cup of tea or fold some tea towels.

'You are restless, darling,' Will said, looking up from his notes. In fact, her actions echoed his own inner state, tied up with worry about Forrester, about Grace, and finding better answers for Fitz's condition. He'd been able to deduce on the phone that Grace wasn't telling him everything, that something serious was going on. He himself hadn't told her about Dr Forrester, not wanting to worry her when she was so far away. She had to look after herself and the baby growing inside her.

'I am restless, Father,' Emily said, sighing and sitting back down. 'You, Mother, Daniel — you all seem to have a calling. I'm working as a nanny and occasionally being courted by half-decent suitors, but I must admit I feel a tad aimless.'

'Well,' Will said, sitting forward and looking into his daughter's eyes, brown like his father's. She had chestnut hair, close in colour to his own. 'Not everybody knows what they want to do in life until something significant happens that pushes them one way or the other.'

'Uncle Jack keeps making terrible jokes about me ending up an old maid. And he says this in front of Great-Aunt Clara, mind you!'

Will shook his head. 'You're still so young. Uncle Jack is simply frustrated with the way his own life has ended up. But he made his bed and now he has to lie in it.'

No one was quite happy with the situation as it was, Will thought, but Clara insisted on staying at home despite the fact Jack often brought back company, and the only meal he'd mastered was a pork chop and peas. They both convinced themselves they were independent, and in this they were strangely good company for one another.

Emily picked at her fingernails.

'What about the old Brough? You used to love helping me or your mum out, tinkering with it to get it in good shape.' The old motorcycle still lived in their shed by the back gate. 'Why don't we wheel it out?'

Emily's face lit up. 'Yes, I do love a good machine.'

'Just like your mother. Perhaps you could make some extra

money working on your clients' cars? You always did have a knack for it.'

They stood together and walked out to the shed. It was drizzling lightly but not enough to deter them.

Emily was smiling and shaking her head. 'It's very sweet, Father, that you think any of my clients would let me do that. I'm there to handle their soft, delicate children, not their oily, hard machines.'

Will shrugged.

As they wheeled the old beast out, a plane flew high above them across the sky, and Emily shielded her eyes to see glimpses of it between the clouds.

'Now that would be fun,' she said, smiling cheekily at her father.

'Do not even consider it, young lady,' Will said.

Will thought about Grace's brother, James, who worked for Ford in America. He wondered if they hired women. Amy was over there now, too, and had found a niche writing gossip about glamorous movie stars for fan rags. Her columns strangely came across as conservative and somewhat outraged, despite her own wild and free youth. If his daughter chose to go to America, she wouldn't be alone. But for Grace and him it would be difficult to have her so far away.

Emily got to work on the motorbike and Will excused himself to go and phone the hospital lab. His notes had confirmed that Dr Forrester likely had Addison's disease, affecting the adrenal glands. The hospital lab had adrenal glands of cows, pigs and sheep, and Will could administer them orally. Forrester would also have to increase his salt and sugar intake.

After that call, he got through to Dr Forrester.

'Will,' his old friend and mentor said weakly, 'I think it might be too late.'

67

Berlin, August 1936

Hugo's four-door 1.2 litre Opel saloon car turned down the lane leading to Rolf Fischl's handsome country house a few miles north of Oranienburg. Grace had been in the front seat giving directions and Fitz, in the rear seat, frequently peered out the back window to ensure they were not being followed.

It seemed unlikely that Liese would have returned home after her narrow escape from the *Sturmabteilung* at the conference centre as this would be the first place they would likely look for her. But the three of them felt they had to start somewhere.

Hugo slowed the car as it approached the wrought-iron gates at the entrance to the drive. Both had been torn from their hinges and the steel bolts that had been supporting them were bent and hung from the crumbling masonry of the posts on either side. The gates themselves were broken and twisted, lying across the ground as if some heavy vehicle had steamrolled them flat. Belt tracks of the type Grace had seen many times on the battlefields of the Somme led up to the front steps of the house, so she knew that a military vehicle of some kind, possibly even a small armoured tank, had been there.

They moved slowly up the drive, looking to the left and right for any signs of activity. There were none. They pulled up at the bottom of the steps and jumped out of the car. The once beautiful oak front door was splintered and hanging open. Some of the downstairs windows were smashed and, on the right-hand side of the house at the top, black soot stained the brickwork where a fire had raged from within but had not taken hold. Across the outside wall of the house, the word JUDE had been crudely scrawled in 4-foot-high yellow letters.

They climbed the steps and ventured inside. Every picture had been ripped from the walls and slashed. Every piece of furniture, every family heirloom and treasure and artefact lay trampled on and destroyed. Anything of any value had been taken. The kitchen had been ransacked and was devoid of provisions. There was no sign of Liese or her mother, Greta, the bedrooms had not been slept in, and there was no indication that clothes or toiletries had recently been used. The place was deserted. They looked in the attic and in the cellar. In the wood store and shed. They stood outside in a forlorn huddle at the top of the steps, wondering what to do next.

If any of them had any lingering doubt about the extent of Jewish persecution taking place in Nazi Germany, it was now dramatically extinguished.

'She isn't here,' said Hugo. 'Where else might she go?'

Grace was thinking furiously. What had Liese told her in their chats over the last few days? Had she mentioned any other family? Any friends nearby? Was there anyone else she worked with, any medical colleagues she had mentioned who might have volunteered to help? She couldn't think of any. Their conversations had generally been light-hearted, focused on the conference, or had been simple banter exchanged in the rowdy beer halls and hostelries of Berlin's city centre during the Games.

'What about the man you saved from a beating the other night? The one you think might have inadvertently drawn attention to Liese because of it?' asked Fitz.

'Lothar. Lothar Stein, I think his name was,' Grace said.

'But where did you take him?'

'Oh. To a safe house of some kind. We dropped him off where he said his friends would shelter him. Friends who also have relatives in Sachsenhausen and were campaigning to have them released.'

'Could she have gone there? Could you find it again?' Fitz said, frowning again at the smashed front door.

'I . . . I think so . . . It was late. It was dark. But I could try.'

'Let's go,' said Hugo. 'I have a feeling . . . the sooner we find her, the better.'

They piled back into the Opel and slammed the doors. Hugo started the engine and moved off. Grace tried to recall in her mind's eye the route they would have taken when they delivered Lothar to his place of refuge. But she had been paying more attention to his injuries and blood loss than to the road or anything else, so she was not at all confident. The image of his blood on the pristine upholstery of that beautiful car was difficult to forget.

'The car!' cried Grace, putting a hand on Hugo's arm. 'Wait! Liese drove us to the conference in it. It wasn't there when I left, so I'm assuming she took it when she fled the sanatorium. If we can find the car, maybe we can find her too. There's one more place I want to look.'

They drove up to the garage set behind a dense hedge of yew trees and Grace was relieved to see that its brick walls and tiled roof looked as untouched and sturdy as the day Liese had taken her there to borrow her parents' car a week and a half before. The wooden double doors at the front were intact and unlocked and they stepped inside.

The Mercedes W21 Kurz was there, but it was now no more than a sorry pile of scrap metal. Grace was horrified. The large twin headlamps were smashed, the radiator grille had a wooden fence post stuck through it, the windscreen was broken and mangled and every tyre, including the spare, had been slashed. The mudguards, running boards and bonnet were riddled with deep dents and scratches and the convertible hood had been torn from its mountings and sliced into shreds. The engine had been irreparably sabotaged and the exquisite tan leather interior splashed with battery acid and creosote. Grace's increasing nausea from the pregnancy welled up with the smells, the fear and disgust.

'So she must've brought the car back here then,' said Fitz. 'Because why would anyone else bother? Or know how to find the garage?'

'Before the stormtroopers responsible for this got here, you mean?'

'I suppose.'

'So where is she now?' asked Hugo. 'Maybe she came back home and they found her and arrested her . . .'

'Or maybe she got out when she could but was forced to leave the car and make her escape. The second one in as many days,' said Grace, hoping against hope. She cleared her throat. She didn't want to get sick in front of Fitz when they had bigger things to worry about.

'Come on,' said Hugo. 'Let's see if you can find that safe house.'

They drove south towards Oranienburg and passed the grassy bank outside Sachsenhausen where Grace and Liese had witnessed the brutal attack on Lothar a few days before. Grace remembered the first part of the route they had subsequently taken as it was on a wider main road with very few turn-offs or junctions. The further on they went, however, the busier the road network became and the more unfamiliar the buildings and landscape on either side seemed to be. Three or four times, Grace had had to ask Hugo to stop, turn around and retrace his route. Stopping also gave her a brief chance to sip cold tea from a flask and quell the nausea from the movement of the car. On each occasion, she had finally seen something – a road sign, a farm vehicle or a stables – that confirmed they were still going in the right general direction. But it was taking time.

'There!' she said excitedly at one point. 'I distinctly remember that Picea abies.'

'The what?' asked Fitz.

'The Picea abies. It's a tree. A Norway spruce. That one must be about 160 feet high. You remember how I love trees, Fitzy.'

'How could I not? You nearly killed yourself a few times climbing them all on the estate when you were just a baby. Nearly killed Mother, too, for that matter – from the worry of it all. Father was proud as punch, though, wasn't he? Couldn't help tell anyone who'd listen about what a mountaineer you were.'

There was a pause as they both let in the grief for their father, and thoughts of their frail old mother, who now kept her worries much more to herself.

'Well, now it's paying off. Or at least I thought it was. Now we've gone a little further on, I don't remember any of what I can see in either direction. I think I've led us up the garden path.'

Hugo pulled the car over to the side of the road and stopped.

'Look,' he said after a few moments, 'we've driven about twelve kilometres from Sachsenhausen and it's taken us about thirty minutes. We've been stopping and doubling back a little, so let's say that to reach here it normally would've taken us about twenty minutes travelling at about 40 to 50 kilometres an hour.'

'So?'

'Roughly for how long do you think you were driving that night with Lothar before dropping him off?'

'Gosh,' Grace sipped from her thermos, 'I don't really know. Liese was putting her foot down, doing maybe 70 to 80 kilometres per hour whenever she could. We were obviously a bit jittery because of what had happened.'

'Understandably.'

She closed her eyes for a moment to think. Fitz's breathing was loud in the car.

'But I suppose about fifteen minutes or so.'

'So that means you wouldn't have been a million miles from where we are now. Do you remember seeing anything significant *later* in the journey that comes back to you? Forget where we are now and the scenery around us. Do you recall any place or landmark nearer to your destination that night?'

Grace frowned. 'There was a river.'

'What? You crossed a bridge?'

'Yes, a bridge. The place where we dropped Lothar was just on the other side of it.'

Hugo smiled. Now she tells me, he thought. 'Excellent,' he said. 'I've lived in Berlin for long enough to know that there's only one bridge within another few minutes of here

419

and it's at Hennigsdorf on the River Havel. If our timings are right, that should be the one.'

Hugo drove off towards it.

'So why didn't you mention the bridge before?' Hugo asked. He could not help thinking how strange it was that intelligent women like Grace could never seem to understand geography or maps and had never considered mentioning a landmark as important as a bridge. That was the difference between men and women.

'You didn't ask me. A bridge is a bridge is a bridge. There could be hundreds of the bloody things around here, for all I know.'

Hugo grinned and studied Grace's amused yet defiant face more closely. She was really very attractive. If he wasn't already deeply in love with Christel, he might have tried to engineer things in such a way as to spend more time with her.

The block of flats with its central courtyard was dark and eerie. Despite the uncomfortable warmth of the summer night, the shutters were closed on all the windows, and as they drove under the archway and into the yard, a few hunched human shapes disappeared into the shadows. Once they had reached the bridge, the building had been easy enough to find. On Grace's previous journey, Lothar had been giving careful instructions to the two women just before they dropped him off in the early hours and so Grace had remembered this part clearly.

They jumped out of the car and looked around.

In the dim light, they could make out washing drying on a line, a child's bicycle discarded beneath it and some garden tools scattered about on the worn grass. The embers of a recent small bonfire glowed in one corner, charred leather covers of several books cooling at its edge.

'Liese,' called Grace quietly to no place in particular. 'Liese, it's Grace. Are you here?'

There was no answer. Only a deafening silence. But they all felt like many ears within the building were listening.

'Lothar? We brought you here the other day. Do you remember?'

They walked softly on the grass beneath the ground-floor shutters quietly calling out their names. 'Liese? Lothar? Are you here?'

Several minutes later, as they were returning, disappointed and dismayed, to the car, a quiet female voice beckoned them from a partially open doorway.

'Come,' the woman said. 'Your friends are downstairs.'

In the damp, dimly lit cellar in the basement, Liese and Lothar were delighted and relieved to see them and Grace was rewarded with a hug. Lothar's face still looked battered and bruised and his arm was resting in a makeshift sling to support his broken collarbone. They looked tired, haunted and hungry, but at least they were alive. They were not alone either. A dozen or so adults and children were sharing the same accommodation and they looked as if they had not eaten in days.

'Liese, thank God you're safe. I've been so worried. We've been looking for you.'

'Thank you, Grace. Thank you so much. You're so kind. But you're not the only ones looking for me. As you already know.'

She looked warily from Hugo to Fitz in turn.

'It's all right,' said Grace, hurriedly introducing the two men. 'Fitz is my brother and Hugo is an attaché at the British Embassy.'

'And I'm also Jewish.'

Liese seemed to visibly relax.

'I brought food for you just in case,' Grace said. 'It's not much. I hadn't expected to find so many of you, but—'

'Whatever you have, we can share it.'

For the first time, Liese managed a smile. Grace put a hand on each of her shoulders and looked into her eyes.

'I had visions of you being caught outside the hospital last week and taken away like your father.'

'And I had visions of the stormtroopers bursting into your cubicle in the *Damentoilette* and you being caught with your knickers down.'

Grace chuckled. 'Where did you go, Liese? What happened?'

'I looked for my father, but there was no sign of him or his abductors. There were trucks parked outside at the front and when I heard soldiers coming towards me, I ran to the car and got away. I didn't really know what to do or where to go, only that first I had to drive to Oranienburg in the hope of warning my mother. I parked the Mercedes safely in the garage, but just as I was locking up, the fascists drove through the gates and ransacked the house. I didn't know what to do. I hid. I could hear them smashing up the house and taking things. Then they came out with my mother. She was struggling and protesting, but they were relentless. I wanted to run over and protect her. To scream and punch and kick. All my instincts told me to go to her rescue. My own mother, Greta. But I didn't.'

'You couldn't.'

'I knew it was useless, Grace. They would have arrested me too. What good could I have done?'

'None, Liese. You did the right thing. The only sane thing.'

'But I abandoned my mother. I was a coward.'

'No, Liese. No, you weren't. You were sensible. You thought on your feet. Acting recklessly would've achieved nothing. It would've played right into their hands and made matters worse. How do you think your mother would've reacted to see you get yourself arrested needlessly? Or possibly assaulted? It would've made matters so much worse for her. They're bad enough as it is, but you can do more from the outside, with us, with your friends here, to try to find your parents and have them released.'

Liese nodded slowly but did not look at all reassured.

'I feel so bad. So guilty.'

'Don't,' said Grace softly, giving her another hug. 'You did the right thing. The only sensible thing. Ultimately, the most loving thing, too, except I'm sure you don't feel like that now.'

'I don't. I walked here that day and I cried all the way. My feet were bleeding, but the pain was nothing compared to the pain in my heart.'

'Grace?' said Lothar, interrupting the story. 'I'm sorry to say this. I'm glad Lieselotte came here and that I could repay the favour she granted me. But she cannot stay. She is the daughter of an eminent scientist considered to be an undesirable by the Nazi regime. They are actively hunting her and she puts all of us here at increased risk. We too have to protect ourselves and fight for the welfare of our loved ones who are incarcerated at Sachsenhausen.'

'You believe Rolf and Greta were taken to Sachsenhausen?'

'There is no way of telling if they are there or Dachau or any of the dozens of so-called confinement camps springing up like weeds all over Germany. But Liese has to leave.' Lothar's face was drawn, firm.

'Where will she be safe?'

'Nowhere in this godforsaken country. No place where such vile state-organised persecution thrives. With you, however, I think she has a chance.'

Grace gave Liese a questioning gaze as Hugo and Fitz looked on.

'Get her out of the country,' Lothar continued. 'Her papers and passport are useless because they identify her. I imagine they have been confiscated anyway. But new ones can be forged. Or procured officially from your Embassy perhaps?'

Fitz looked hopefully at Hugo, who was deep in thought.

'I can try,' he said. 'But it's become almost impossible already and getting much more difficult with every passing day.'

'I can't leave my parents,' interrupted Liese. 'I won't. If I do nothing to help them, I will never forgive myself. Leaving the country is out of the question.'

'Liese,' implored Lothar, taking her hand. 'To stay is to embrace despair. Your defiance would be like spitting into the wind. You are bright. You are intelligent. You can use these resources from afar to much better purpose.'

'I cannot leave my parents.'

'You must.'

'It's all right for you to say!' she said angrily. 'But you're not leaving, are you? How can you ask me to?'

'Firstly, I know where my brothers are and I suspect my parents too. Here. Not far away, in Sachsenhausen. You don't. Secondly, I can stay and do everything you would do on your behalf while you go and tell the world what is going on here. That I promise you. I will do all I can to find out exactly where your parents have been taken and try to free them. And I will keep you informed.'

'He's right, Liese,' said Fitz. 'It's painful, but it makes sense, and between the three of us, I believe there may be a unique opportunity we can use to help get you out.'

Hugo looked at him with surprise.

'We've just been attending the eleventh Olympiad a few miles down the road from here. There were thousands of international visitors and competitors from all over the world enjoying their farewell parties and preparing to return home. Surely no one would notice one more anonymous individual among the excitable throng returning home?'

Hugo raised an appreciative eyebrow. The plan seemed a half-decent one.

'Good idea, Fitzy,' added Grace. 'I'm sure we can hide her somewhere. And you're meant to be an official part of the British Olympic delegation for goodness' sake! Lothar? Can you grant me twenty-four hours? Wherever we go now, they'll be looking for her. I'll come back tomorrow and will take her with us. You have my word.'

'Tomorrow . . .' he said, turning to look at the dispirited group behind him. He was weighing it up in his mind. He was torn. Eventually, he spoke. 'All right. But please. No longer. For them.'

'I promise,' said Grace, making eye contact with each person in turn. 'Before we go, let me bring you the food from the car. I will bring more with me tomorrow.'

'Please.'

They fetched the provisions and gave them to the woman at the doorway. Then they climbed back into the Opel and left as discreetly as they could. None of them spoke for several minutes. Fitz's breath wheezed in and out. They had twenty-four hours to devise a workable plan.

But then, Grace thought, she had to convince Fitz to go home, too. He was pushing himself far too much. He needed rest. And she hoped desperately that Will had found out something miraculous about a cure.

68

British Embassy, Berlin, August 1936

At the British Embassy on Wilhelmstrasse, Hugo spent over two hours meticulously searching through a database of passport-sized photographs of women roughly the same age as Lieselotte. Finally, he came across one that seemed a reasonable likeness. Same dark, slightly wavy, shoulder-length hair, brown eyes, Roman nose, full lips with a distinctive dimple in the cheeks at the angle of the mouth. It belonged to Gelleh Solomons, aged thirty-five, a dressmaker whom Hugo had already successfully managed to get out of the country using the same documentation. It was far from a perfect match, but time was of the essence and it would have to do.

'Christel, darling,' he said to his clandestine lover sitting beside him. 'Would you please ask our specialist to prepare documentation and a visa for this woman?'

'Of course.'

'And have it expedited. Put it at the top of the pile, will you? I need it ready by lunchtime.'

'By lunchtime? Are you serious? There's no chance Hannes can turn it around in that time. He says three days is the minimum.'

'We haven't got three days, Christel. He's got three hours.'

'But you know how fastidious he is.'

'I know. He'll say it is unsafe and discoverable, but it's a risk we'll have to take. If he doesn't like it, just remind him what we've already done to help his own family.'

'Very well, Hugo. But what's so urgent about this particular woman?'

'Take the photo to Hannes and tell him to hurry up. Then come back and I'll tell you.'

After collecting Liese's new documents from Hugo's apartment, Grace picked Jenny up from the Olympic Village and drove her out to Hennigsdorf. They brought two huge bags of oats down to the cellar, along with a large wooden crate full of carrots and swedes and a carrier bag laden with milk, bread, eggs, ham, potatoes, butter, jam and biscuits.

Lothar could not help thinking that it was a rather bizarre selection of provisions to have brought but reasoned it might have been all that was available at short notice.

It would not last long among the dozen or so hungry souls dependent on it, but it was a thoughtful and welcome gesture.

An older lady in the group, who called herself Revekka, held out a small velvet pouch tied with a purse string and handed it to Liese. It was light and contained what felt like a bunch of small pebbles within it. 'The jewellery inside is not much, but it is all we have. It is of no use to us here and being found with it puts us in greater danger. It will be safer with you and your friends. Would you please safeguard it for us until we can be reunited?'

'But we hardly know you. How can you entrust it to us?'

'Because you are here. Doing this,' she said, pressing the pouch into Liese's palm. 'You will be in touch with Lothar. And he with us.'

'We live in very uncertain times. But I promise to safeguard this until you can reclaim it.'

'And if we can't, for whatever reason, please use whatever it may be worth to support our brethren.'

'Of course. If that is what you wish. We will find each other.'

Liese carefully placed the pouch in her inside pocket.

Lothar took her hand and kissed it. 'Thank you for what you did for me at Sachsenhausen. For intervening. Thank you both. I live to fight another day, Liese, and I promise I will move heaven and earth to find your parents. As if I were your brother. As if I were their own son.'

'Thank you. Then you can write to me here.' She passed him a scribbled note. 'In England at Grace's address.' He put it in his pocket and nodded.

'Now you must go. You serve our cause better from the outside and I know you will. Goodbye and *Leich l'shalom*.'

Lothar hugged both of them and turned away before they could see the tears in his eyes.

Hugo was not usually given to jealousy, but Christel was the love of his life. He could not help feeling overly possessive about her.

The flowers he held in his hand as he crept towards the open door of her office to surprise her would reward her for the effort involved in preparing Lieselotte's papers at record speed.

She was on the telephone. Who was this Altmann she was talking so quietly to? He put his ear closer to the door and listened more intently.

'I'll pass by at the usual time,' she said in a whisper. 'I can't stay. Just a dead-letter drop.'

She replaced the telephone in its cradle on the desk. Hugo paused outside the door and looked down at the bouquet of red roses in his hand. Silently, he retraced his steps down the corridor and returned to his room, puzzled and deep in thought.

The three women shared the driving and only stopped to fill the petrol tank or relieve themselves. Pregnancy hormones meant the urge to do this was more frequent than usual for Grace, but she did her best to hold it. They needed to reach the border as quickly as possible. Liese insisted on doing the lion's share because it took her mind off worrying about her parents and because she was used to driving on the right-hand side of the road.

'But the steering wheel's on the wrong side for you,' Grace had pointed out.

'You saw me throwing the Mercedes around, Grace,' Liese had said, smiling for the first time in days. 'I think I'll manage.'

Grace was convinced. She was also relieved to think of Fitz, halfway back already on a first-class train. She'd managed to convince him he'd done enough. She hoped the travel wouldn't wear him out more and he'd actually rest at the other end.

Liese felt sad at the mention of the car. Perhaps the ruined car was a symbol of what was about to happen to her parents. But she must not dwell on it. The vehicle she was currently driving was very different. She had made her choice.

'Whereabouts are we now?' asked Jenny.

'About 2 miles from the border at Enschede.'

The 3-ton Vincent horsebox was the Reading manufacturer's most recent design for horse transportation and just like the horse ambulances which had been used by the British

429

army in 1914, it had been adapted so that the body could be rotated on the chassis, allowing horses to walk forwards both on to and off the vehicle.

Jackson, the horse which Alec Scott had ridden to the bronze medal in the Olympic eventing competition a few days before, was swaying about in the back and seemed to have become more used to the bumping and cornering of the ungainly machine. Grace asked Liese to pull the horsebox over to the side of the road and stop.

'We're nearly there,' Grace said. 'It's time to decide. Plan A or plan B?'

Both she and Jenny thought plan B was too risky, and said so. Neither option was particularly attractive, but plan B had the potential to end very badly. It involved an immediate physical threat to their friend's life. Yet Liese now had a deep-rooted distrust in officialdom, administration and third parties and insisted she did not want to be captured and imprisoned. She did not trust the false papers and her ability to sweetly smile at a Nazi as she handed them over to be checked. She also thought she risked her friends' lives much more that way. Besides, it was precisely because plan B was so risky that they might just have a better chance of getting away with it. Surely no officious border guards would imagine three mere women attempting anything so foolhardy.

'Plan B it is,' said Liese confidently.

69

Royal London Hospital, Whitechapel, London, August 1936

Will was relieved Dr Forrester was beginning to show signs of improvement after he'd administered the adrenal extract and he could finally track down Professor Peter Brewin, said by many to be the most eminent cardiologist in the whole of London. Now he could help out Fitz, and, in turn, Grace.

He followed the busy Dr Brewin on his rounds as he described the symptoms Fitz had been increasingly experiencing, such as breathlessness particularly when lying flat and pitting oedema – swelling – around the ankles. He handed him the notes that Dr Forrester had made after he had kindly examined him last.

'I'll be happy to see him for a proper assessment on his return from Berlin, Dr Burnett,' he said, pausing in the hall. 'Since he's had the symptoms from birth with only slow progression, I would imagine he either has a patent ductus arteriosus or an atrial septal defect. Either way, they'll be a left-right shunt with oxygenated blood mixing with deoxygenated venous blood and a consequent reduction in oxygen supply to the rest of the body. In time, his symptoms are likely to deteriorate as the strain on his heart will inevitably increase.'

431

'Are there any promising treatments on the horizon which might improve his prognosis?' enquired Will.

'Tonics, elixirs, fresh air, rest and gentle exercise!' he said as they began walking again towards another ward. 'All completely useless of course. Surgery? Out of the question. Ludwig Rehn performed a successful repair of a stab wound to the heart for the first time way back in 1896. Since then . . . not much. Theodore Tuffier attempted an aortic valve procedure in 1912 and Elliot Cutler a mitral valve operation in 1923. Good man, Cutler! Neither very successful.'

'I thought Henry Souttar successfully operated on a young woman here in this hospital in 1925?'

'You've done your homework, Dr Burnett. Yes, he poked around – literally – in the appendage of a female patient's left atrium, to correct the mitral valve. She lived several years more, but he wasn't allowed to take the risk again.'

They paused at the entrance to a ward and Dr Brewin ran his eye down a chart by the door. He turned to Will.

'Operating on the heart, you see, is like trying to service a motorcycle engine while the motor is still running. It's best left alone, without us doctors doing more damage. Isn't that what the Hippocratic oath says? Above all do no harm?'

Will felt despondent. He had hoped for more from the top man in his profession. There had been so many promising advances in other fields of medicine in recent years, including orthopaedic surgery, which he most commonly performed. So he had been half expecting at least a chink of light to shine on the improved management of heart disease. What would he tell Grace and Fitz when he had no good news to offer?

Brewin seemed to sense Will's disappointment and decided he could give him more hope after all.

'That's the official view, anyway,' said Brewin.

'And what's the unofficial view?'

Nurses bustled around them as they spoke.

'Have you heard of a man called Forssmann?'

'No, never.'

'Well, there's a reason for that. Which I'll come to. Werner Forssmann carried out the world's first right heart cardiac catheterisation seven years ago. In Germany. And here's the interesting thing. He performed it on himself.'

'He fed a catheter into his own heart?'

'He did. And broke all scientific rules in doing it.'

Will baulked. 'Was it safe?'

'Of course not. Highly dangerous, in fact, but brave at the same time. We've known about the cardiovascular anatomy for decades, the position of the great vessels and the chambers of the heart. Forssmann wanted to discover more. He hypothesised that if we could thread the catheter into the cardiac chambers themselves, we could deliver drugs directly to the heart, measure blood pressure more precisely and use radiopaque dye for more accurate diagnosis.'

'So he proved it.'

Brewin nodded.

'Forssmann is something of a character. I heard him speak once. He is an eccentric and a complete maverick. He knew it could be fatal and wouldn't be condoned by his head of department, but he somehow persuaded his operating room nurse, Gerda Ditzen, to assist him secretly. With local anaesthetic injected in his arm, he introduced a urinary catheter and fed the entire 60-centimetre length of it along the major veins and up into the right side of his heart. God knows what it must've felt like. He then calmly walked over to the X-ray department, where a fluoroscope demonstrated the tip of the catheter in his right ventricle. He had it recorded on the X-ray film for posterity.'

'That's incredible,' said Will.

'It is the future of cardiology, in my opinion,' said Brewin. 'When we refine it, it will give us our first opportunity to examine the dynamic function of the heart without having to open the chest. And it will provide your brother-in-law with a means of determining his exact diagnosis. That done, I fervently believe heart surgery to correct the defect will be available to him and others like him within a few short years.'

'That's good to hear, sir. Thank you. Perhaps we can keep in touch.'

'Indeed.'

Will shook the doctor's hand and turned to leave, but stopped and turned back again.

'Just one more thing, Professor. You said Forssmann's technique would need to be refined. How far has he got with it?'

'Absolutely nowhere! After his pioneering demonstration, his superiors summarily dismissed him from the Hospital Charité Berlin on the basis it was unapproved, dangerous and unscientific. The last I heard is that he is a urologist and a fully paid-up member of the Nazi party.'

Will shook his head. 'And you haven't been tempted to pick up the baton of cardiac catheterisation yourself?'

'Oh no,' said Brewin with a grin. 'Tonics, elixirs, fresh air, rest and gentle exercise remains my mantra. Much safer all round.'

Will left, feeling dejected all over again.

70

Ministry of War, Berlin, August 1936

Hugo followed at a safe distance on the other side of the street. Christel had slipped out the Embassy just before lunchtime and, after one or two backward glances, had walked straight past two of the cafés from where she usually picked up a sandwich for lunch. Five minutes later, he was surprised to see her climb the steps at 76/78 Tirpitzufer, the headquarters of the German Ministry of War, and even more astonished when, at the top of the steps, she furtively handed an envelope to a man pretending to simply pass her by – a man with a massively disfigured face.

Hugo Lowenthal was stunned. It was impossible, he thought. There had to be some other explanation. To even consider his lover could be a Nazi spy who had infiltrated the British Embassy and used him so cynically . . . He felt physically ill. Surely he could not be that stupid. They had worked together and confided in one another. He knew women. He understood their moods and machinations. She loved him, didn't she? He had been so sure of it. His head was in a spin and fighting with his heart. It had to be resolved urgently, one way or another. He would not confront her this afternoon, however. If he accused her wrongly, she would be justifiably insulted. And angry. It might even jeopardise the long lovemaking session scheduled for the following weekend. No. He needed to carefully think this through.

It was a warm evening, but dark now with a slight drizzle. Hugo had watched from the street below, hidden under a beech tree with rain dripping from the leaves above on to the brim of his fedora and the shoulders of his greatcoat. Christel had left her apartment three blocks away two hours after returning home from work. She looked glamorous in a gold and silver dress, silk stockings and heels, with her hair tied up in a bun and her best necklace draped over her elegant décolletage.

Lights were only on in one room of the building, on the first floor to the left of the staircase, so it was a reasonable guess that that was where she had gone. He crossed the street and climbed the stairs. On the landing of the first floor, he listened at the door and examined the name above the doorbell. Ilse Lehmann. He had never heard of her. He also felt intense relief flooding through his body. His worst fears that Christel might be secretly seeing another man had not been realised. But who was this Ilse Lehmann and why had Christel been delivering messages to the Nazi intelligence agency? Why had she bothered to dress up so alluringly just to visit a girlfriend?

He turned the door handle and eased the heavy door open. He heard laughter and female voices coming from another room on the far side of the lounge. He padded silently across the carpet to get nearer. He knew what he was doing was absurd and inexcusable, but he did not seem to be able to help himself. Soft music played on the gramophone and the only light in the room came from the golden glow of the bedside lamp near the door.

Hugo angled his head to one side to peer into the room. Both girls were naked, their lips locked together in a lovers' passionate embrace. Christel lay on the other girl's right side, her right hand buried deep between her legs as it languidly moved to and fro. Ilse moaned quietly, pulling Christel's buttocks towards her with one hand, the other one on Christel's breast. Hugo was aghast. Shocked and stunned. Paralysed. Then he felt an overwhelming rage. She *was* being unfaithful to him. She was taking him for a fool. And no doubt she had been playing him in her role as a spy all along.

He stepped into the bedroom and Christel looked up in surprise. She broke away from Ilse and reached for the bed sheet, pulling it up under her chin. Ilse, horrified, leapt out of bed and raced past Hugo into the lounge.

Christel allowed the silk bed sheet to fall back into her lap, blatantly baring her perfect breasts. She looked at Hugo and a slow smile spread across her face.

'Well, now you know,' she said. 'I have a girlfriend too.'

'You bitch,' he whispered.

'Why? Because I like to play for both teams?'

'No. Because you play for both sides. The British who employed and trusted you and your Nazi paymasters at the same time. Because you're a traitor.'

'Not to Germany.'

'To everyone else. Including me.'

Christel was laughing now and quite unashamed. 'Oh, poor Hugo. Not only have you discovered you're a cuckold, but you've fallen for the oldest trick in the book. The honeytrap. You thought you were so wonderful in bed too, darling, didn't you? But, really, I was just doing my duty. You should take a leaf out of Ilse's book. She could teach you a thing or two.'

437

Hugo struggled to contain himself. 'You've screwed me, but in doing so you've screwed your own career and the entire organisation designed to offer safe passage to thousands of Jews out of Germany.'

'Even now, your precious Lieselotte is heading towards the border with papers I personally flagged for the authorities and tampered with sufficiently to ensure her immediate arrest by officers fully conversant with the name Gelleh Solomons. It was all in vain, Hugo. And you had no idea, did you?'

She threw her head back and laughed again.

Hugo was boiling inside. He had never experienced such fury. He lost all control and flew across the bed to grab her by the throat. He sat astride her, his thumbs pressing down into the notch above her breastbone and his fingers squeezing the arteries at the sides of her neck. Shocked, with wide staring eyes, she thrashed at him with her arms and legs but did not have the strength to dislodge him. His lips were pulled back in a wolverine snarl and as he leaned further forward, all of his weight was thrust down on Christel's dainty neck. Her eyes became bloodshot, her face purple and her lips blue. But Hugo had gone somewhere else in his head. Betrayed, grief-stricken and broken, filled with hate. He could feel her legs in spasm, kicking out and jerking. He could see saliva pooling at the back of her throat and her hugely dilated pupils searching his face. But what he did not see or notice was Ilse running into the room behind him and raising a revolver.

The bullet hit him in the right side of his back, traversing his chest and tearing through his heart, killing him instantly. He slowly pitched forward, hitting his face against the headboard and sliding off Christel's body like a spent lover who had given his all. Ilse ran forward to revive Christel, but it was too late. The woman she had admired so much, looked up to and loved so completely, the woman she had wanted to spend the rest of her life with, was dead.

71

German–Dutch border, August 1936

It was three o'clock in the afternoon when the Vincent horsebox idled to a halt in front of the barrier 5 miles east of Enschede. Two border guards stood outside a gatehouse on either side, brandishing machine guns. They stubbed their cigarettes out with their boots and walked towards it.

Grace and Jenny saw the back end of a tractor passing through the barrier further ahead of them, but apart from that there were no other vehicles in the vicinity. Grace was behind the wheel, with Jenny sitting beside her in the passenger seat. Grace had been in scrapes before and felt calm enough, and although Jenny was scared stiff, she showed no outward sign of it.

They had rehearsed their performance thoroughly, but time was of the essence.

'*Guten Tag, meine Damen,*' said the first man to arrive. He looked in turn from one occupant to the other and smiled. '*Also was haben wir hier?*' What do we have here? His tone was rather overfamiliar. A little patronising. Flirtatious.

'What we have here is our horse, Jackson, a medal-winner at your recent Olympics.'

'*Ah, die Olympische Spiele. Sehr gut.*'

'We are heading home. Back to England. I think he's more used to the grass there.'

The officer studied Grace.

'You think the grass is greener in your country?' The question seemed loaded.

'You'd better ask the horse.'

'*Jawohl, ich werde.* But first your papers.'

Jenny took the passports from the glove compartment and passed them through the window.

'Mrs Jenny Jenks. And Mrs Grace Burnett. I am Hans. You travel alone?'

'No, we travel together.'

'But no male company? Where is the rider?'

'Oh, the rider is far too grand to be driving this contraption halfway across the continent. He's probably drinking schnapps on a train back to England as we speak.'

'So you are?'

'Trainer,' said Jenny. 'And groom,' nodding at Grace.

'So not in fact a nurse and a doctor as it says here.'

'Well, yes, we are. But even professionals love an amateur hobby.'

'Aha. Well, let us see this magnificent beast. I like horses.'

Jenny opened the rear doors of the vehicle and Hans and the other officer stepped inside.

The two women had already discarded all of the now empty 20-litre jerrycans half a mile back, so the interior was sparse. There were bare metal sides over a wooden frame, a layer of hay on the floor, a feeding bag hanging from behind the cab and a deep water trough on the left side over the rear wheel arch. Despite a copious amount of horse manure decorating the edge of the trough, Jackson was drinking quite happily from it.

The second man was running his hand over Jackson's muscular flank and patting his haunches in admiration.

'*Ein wunderbares tier,*' he said. A wonderful beast. 'Yet the German equestrian team made a clean sweep of the gold medals in Berlin. The first time in history,' he boasted. 'We had plenty of time sitting here listening to all of it on the radio.'

'They were incredible,' said Jenny, deliberately trying to flatter them. 'Utterly untouchable.'

'*Jawohl.* Germany is raising the bar in everything, is it not?'

Jackson's head was still in the trough, contentedly licking up more water with his tongue. His smell reminded Hans of the horses he had enjoyed riding as a child. He leaned forward and stroked the long white nose. He was focused entirely on the animal's sleek coat and mesmerised by his huge brown eyes, the long dark lashes and the nictitating membrane – that rather strange pinkish third eyelid unique to all horses. He was taking care to avoid the fresh horseshit on the top of the trough so did not notice the steady stream of air bubbles rising up through the water at the edges at its base.

Both of the women did, however, and they were fearful about what it implied. If air was escaping from the hollow cavity below the trough, it meant water was getting in and replacing it. The bubbles were alarmingly large ones as well. The hidden compartment was small and it would not take long to replace all the air inside it with water. Air which Liese, lying curled up inside, was dependent on. They had to get going urgently. They hoped it was not already too late.

'*Alles ist gut,*' Hans said, slapping Jackson on the shoulder and turning away. 'But you have far to go? Why not stay and have a celebratory drink with my fellow officers? It's not every day you win an Olympic medal.'

'It's very kind of you,' said Grace with a forced smile and a slight tremor in her voice. 'But we really must make a move. We have a rendezvous in Utrecht this evening and in this old banger it will take us several more hours.'

'*Das ist schade*,' said the other man, loitering outside the horsebox. 'We could've had fun.'

Jenny shot Grace a look and indicated with her head.

'Come on then, groom,' she said quickly. 'I'll drive the next bit and you can take over later.'

They bolted the door at the back of the horsebox, jumped into the cab and set off through the raised barrier, taking care not to show their panic by going too fast and spinning the wheels. Getting out of there was now a matter of life or death.

Jenny drove until they were just out of sight and pulled the vehicle on to a farm track behind a hay barn. They raced around the back, prised open the doors and opened the spigot at the side of the trough to drain the water. Jenny bailed out more as fast as she could with her bare hands and Grace used a horse blanket as an improvised water carrier to speed up the process.

Liese had been incarcerated in the coffin-like chamber beneath the trough for around forty-five minutes and they had no way of knowing how much air she had left or if she had any at all. It all seemed such a foolish idea now. Should they have used the forged paperwork after all and hoped for the best? Or was it the right decision to hide beneath three feet of water in a rapidly contracting air pocket barely big enough for Liese to lie flat? They should have gone for plan A, but Liese has insisted, not knowing if she could trust the Embassy paperwork.

Grace asked Jenny to press down with all her weight on the top of the trough while she undid the four metal nuts bolting it to the underneath. Then they each took an end and lifted the trough with its remaining few inches of water from its mounting. Litres more of it gushed out and they saw that Liese lay completely immersed in water, her lips blue and parted and her skin deathly pale. She was not moving. They hauled her out and placed her on the hay on the floor. Grace raised her chin with two fingers and put her mouth over her friend's mouth and nose and breathed into her lungs. Pausing, she thumped her fist down hard on to the middle of Liese's chest and then Jenny took over artificially pumping her heart.

They worked on her desperately like that for several minutes while Jackson whinnied and looked on.

72

Southall, London, August 1936

Fitz had been back in London for just over a day, but the desperate message Hugo had sent via electric telegraph arrived far too late. When the postman had put it into his hand, Fitz had torn it open on the doorstep of his little house in Southall and had to hold on to the door frame to steady himself. It was short but to the point. And shocking. It appeared Christel, Hugo's secretary and lover, might be a spy.

'L's new identity not safe,' it read. 'Repeat: not safe. Door open. Horse bolted.'

Fitz had understood immediately.

Dear God, he'd thought, his heart palpitating. The three women had left Berlin as planned, but the false passport in Lieselotte's possession was almost certain to incriminate and expose her when they were examined. But it had taken Fitz two days to return from Berlin by train and now even if he had any possible way of warning Grace and her companions, it would be too late.

He had taken a taxi straight over to Westminster and, using his employers' office, had telephoned the British Embassy in Berlin to speak to Hugo directly. They were sorry to have to tell him that Hugo had been tragically killed. Two days ago. Apparently caught in the crossfire between enemies of the state and the police, they had said. And no, they had not seen Christel since then, although her desk had been cleared, along with all of her work files and personal belongings. They were looking into it and had thanked him for his call. He was dumbfounded. He had realised the telegram might have been Hugo's last communication before he went to confront the rat in the ranks.

In turmoil, he had brought the news straight over to Will's house and now, three hours later, the mood of the entire group was grim. Kitty had just departed for war-torn Spain. Will was out of his mind with worry about Grace and his anxiety was only matched by that of Reggie, who had raced over as soon as he had heard about Jenny's involvement. Jack was patently failing to calm things down with the offer of cocktails. Emily and Daniel were frowning and lost, and only Clara seemed to be thinking clearly. She could see Will was furious with Fitz for condoning this hazardous and foolhardy plan but also doubted that he would have had much say in it.

'There's no point mulling over why they took their decision to attempt this escape,' Jack said. 'They must've had good reason. You know your sister, Fitz. When Grace makes up her mind to do something, she does it no matter the risks or consequences. Will, you know that as well. It's who she is.'

Daniel and Emily took note of this too — it was strange that once you were older, you saw sides to your parents you'd never really considered before.

'Jenny is no different,' added Reggie. 'Just as impulsive and obstinate. And as for the two of them together . . .' His voice trailed away and he never finished the sentence.

'Why is it worse when they're together?' asked Daniel, always interested in the psychology of pairs, after growing up a twin, but his question was ignored. He looked so much like a mix of both his parents, Clara thought. His mum's auburn hair and his dad's deeply set hazel eyes. As tall as Will, yet, at seventeen, rather gangly.

'When did they leave, Fitz?' asked Will.

'Three days ago, just after I got my train.'

'And what was the route?'

'The shortest possible to the Dutch border. Via Wolfsburg, Hannover and Osnabrück.'

'How far is that?'

'About 250 miles, I suppose.'

'So they should have reached the checkpoint that same evening, knowing how slow Jenny's Vincent horsebox is,' said Reggie.

'But still no word!' said Will. 'Surely we would've heard by now if they had reached Holland safely?'

'Not necessarily,' said Clara. 'Had Grace or Jenny planned to send messages en route? Would they normally?'

'Well, no, but in the circumstances?'

'And worry you half to death? Grace took great pains not to worry you with the twins being born prematurely, didn't she? And it was probably an even more dangerous situation.'

'Thanks, Clara,' said Emily mischievously, twirling a chestnut strand of hair around her finger. 'Nice to know we caused so much trouble.' But Clara could see in her eyes she was just as worried about her mother as her twin brother.

'Would you have heard anything at all from the Embassy in Berlin or from Westminster if there had been an arrest or any other development, Fitz?'

'Well, no. Officially, I'm nothing to do with the Embassy, remember? I only met Hugo as a so-called administrator for the British Olympic delegation. Knowing what's going on in Germany at present, I'm afraid news travels very slowly, if it travels at all.'

'Christ!' hissed Will, desperately worried about Grace but furious with her at the same time for getting involved in such a hare-brained scheme. She was only meant to be going to Germany for a conference in bacteriology, for God's sake.

'Suppose Lieselotte had been caught with the false papers,' said Reggie. 'A Jewish woman – Jewish at least in the eyes of the current regime – disobeying directives and attempting to escape. Aided and abetted voluntarily by two English women. What actions might the authorities take?'

They mulled the question over, but had no answers. The possibilities, however, were frightening.

Jack came out of the kitchen with a bottle of whisky and several glass tumblers, despite the fact everyone had said no to cocktails. It was getting dark outside and they needed a pick-me-up.

At that moment, Emily looked out of the window at the sunset. As she watched the last shaft of summer sun play through the leaves on the trees, she saw the horsebox pull up.

'They're here!' she cried.

Jack stopped pouring the whisky and followed the others as they raced out of the door into the street. Emily jumped into her mother's arms and Daniel and Will quickly joined them in a family embrace. Reggie was smothering Jenny in kisses as Jack watched on from the doorway.

Suddenly they all realised only two of them had jumped out of the cab.

'And Lieselotte?' Fitz asked Grace after a few seconds. 'I'm so sorry. I couldn't get the message to you in time . . . I . . .' He panted.

'What message?' she said.

'About her papers. The false identity. Gelleh Solomons.'

'Well, we knew they might be unreliable, so we didn't use them in the end.'

'So what happened? Where is Lieselotte?'

'Someone asking for me?' said a female voice behind him, stepping out from the back of the horsebox. She looked a little bedraggled and smelled slightly of horse, but her clothes had dried off and she was alive. 'Hello again, Fitz! Jackson was getting a little restless after three days in the van, so I spent the last few miles travelling in the back with him.'

Back inside the house, the telephone began to ring. Will, too astounded and relieved by Grace's presence, at first ignored it. Daniel ran inside to pick it up. He returned, face sombre, and walked over to his embracing parents.

'Dad? It's the hospital. It's Dr Forrester . . .'

In Berlin, the Nazi propaganda machine was in full swing, broadcasting the messages it wanted heard and suppressing those it did not. The loss of one of their top agents would never be shared except in the most esoteric of secret intelligence circles. The courageous action of the secret police, however, in a street fight at a hideout in Hennigsdorf resulting in the killing of a dozen or more heavily armed dissidents, was widely reported as a triumph of German nationalism and the rule of law.

Altmann attended the scene, wishing he'd been present for the action. Apart from those of the children, the bullet-riddled bodies of the undesirables had been deliberately displayed propped up against the wall outside their refuge to serve as a warning to others. Within days, stray dogs and foxes had reduced the corpses to bare carcasses. The chief of police delayed their disposal as he preferred them highly visible. Altmann thought it was a smart move. But some of the Brownshirts under the chief's command had questioned this macabre tactic. Would it really have the desired effect on the local community? they had asked.

'Remains to be seen,' he had joked sadistically to Altmann as they stood over the decaying flesh.

Revekka, Martha, Otto, Jorgi and the others would never now discover the fate of their relatives last seen being taken to Sachsenhausen and Lothar would never be able to fulfil his promise to Lieselotte of finding her parents and forwarding the information.

Altmann felt the blood pulsing through his body. He felt strong, and he vibrated with new purpose. A shift was occurring, and fast. And he knew, with every fibre of his being, he had a role to play, as Germany reasserted its superiority.

73

St Andrew's Chapel, London, August 1936

This was one of the saddest days of Will's life. There had been so much loss, but standing in the packed chapel surrounded by colleagues and former patients of Dr Gordon Forrester, he could not hold back the tears. Grace clasped his hand. He couldn't help but feel – if he had only seen the earlier signs. Forrester had been reluctant to let him help, but he should have insisted.

And he had seemed to be getting better. When Will last saw him, he'd smiled at him, sitting up in his hospital bed, colour in his cheeks beneath his smudged bifocals, and said, 'You did everything right, Will. Everything I taught you. Thank you, son. For your faith in me.'

Perhaps he had known that he didn't have long after all.

Will remembered other times when he and Forrester had done everything they could and had still lost a patient. Forrester would place a hand on Will's heavy shoulder and say, 'Sometimes nature is simply destined to take its course. We are men, not gods.'

Grace, in her usual way, sensed the thoughts playing across his mind.

'Will,' she whispered, 'he was an old man who lived a rich life doing what he loved. Just look around you. So many people would not be here if not for him, and many if not for you helping him. He loved you like a son.'

Tears slid down Will's cheeks as a sob burned in his throat. He swallowed it down. He looped his arm in Grace's. He knew she was right. To think of his own mistakes was to be self-absorbed and self-pitying on a day that should be devoted to celebrating the life of a great man. He needed to push back these thoughts for now and be grateful — so grateful — for everything Forrester had given him, and others.

Oh, how he would miss him.

Will had helped arrange the funeral as Dr Forrester, of course, had seemingly believed he'd live forever and had made no plans or provisions. A rough will drawn up ten years ago existed, with everything going to hospitals and charities. But no wishes stated on how he'd like arrangements to go. He and Will had never spoken of it. Will knew Forrester wasn't overly religious, but many doctors were seen off in this beautiful chapel, and it was big enough to fit the crowd.

It was coming up to Will's time to speak.

Grace patted Will's arm and gave him a reassuring look as he cleared his throat and moved towards the pulpit.

Just then, Grace felt a strong pressure in her lower back. This morning she had seen some dots of red in her underwear, but knew that this could sometimes happen in a normal pregnancy. Now, though, as she sat back down, she felt damp beneath her skirt. She wasn't far along in her pregnancy. She knew that miscarriages were quite common. Nonetheless, another layer of sadness slid in and settled over her.

As Will spoke — strong, sure and loving — about Dr Forrester, Grace let her own tears come.

Epilogue

The Eagle and Child public house, Oxford, December 1936

'Which one are you on now?' called Grace from the kitchen.

'Number eighteen out of fifty-two,' Will replied from halfway up the stairs. 'How's my little scrubber getting on?'

'Not funny.'

Will was beginning to wonder whether they had taken too much on. He had been thrilled to accept the appointment as general surgeon at the John Radcliffe Hospital in Oxford, his first ever consultancy post. But the big, dilapidated Victorian house which he and Grace thought they would do up and restore themselves was proving a bigger job than they had ever imagined. Still, they shared the determination and drive to get it done and had all the time in the world in which to do it.

Right now, Will's surgeon's hands were red and sore from rubbing down the paint-peeling bannisters with wire wool, and without any heating in the house due to the unserviceable boiler, he felt suddenly cold, weary and in need of sustenance. He descended the creaky oak staircase, turned back along the hall and leaned against the door frame of the kitchen, where Grace was on her hands and knees scrubbing thirty years of ingrained dirt and grime from the tiled floor.

'Can I interest you in a winter warmer?'

'You certainly can. But we'll have to venture out into the freezing cold as the cupboard's bare and there's nothing to be had here in the house.'

A few minutes later, they were strolling along the banks of the River Iffley towards the town centre, sleet in their faces and the icy wind biting at their noses and cheeks.

How handsome Will looked, thought Grace, in his dark blue ulster with his hands thrust deeply into his pockets. She threaded a sleeve of her own quilted coat under his arm and buried her hand into one of them. Huddled together like that, she leaned her head against his shoulder and they wended their way towards the twinkly Christmas lights and illuminated spires ahead of them.

The move to Oxford meant they would be able to enjoy the luxury of a bigger house and a lovely garden, but, prestigious as it was, they both knew they were an integral part of a larger family and felt a degree of responsibility for it.

'You're still worried about Jack, aren't you?' Grace said.

'I suppose. But at least he is happier now that things have picked up further in the construction industry and he's always been less likely to get himself into trouble when he's busy.'

'He'll be fine. Jack could fall into a sewer and come out smelling of roses.'

'And Dad is faring better lately too. The hospital Daniel got him into that's open to different types of treatment really seems to be helping.'

'It does. And Clara is still as sharp as a pin. Her arthritis might be slowing her down, but if she was worried about either of them, she'd be sure to let us know.'

'But she can't tell me about Kitty, can she?'

Kitty was somewhere in war-torn Spain still working with the Red Cross and the International Brigades and lately her letters home had become few and far between.

'Kitty is quite capable of looking after herself, Will. I know she's your little sister, but she is intelligent and determined and doing nothing different to what you and I did when we signed up during the Great War. You should stop worrying.'

'You can talk. Fitz is never far from your mind and nor is Dorothy.'

'Fitz is currently holding his own among the likes of Baldwin and Mosley. Though I'm not sure his colleagues know of his temporary bohemian accommodation.'

'Well, when we told him he needed a rest cure, he said he knew of a place right in London. Apparently Gandhi stayed there.'

'He's loving it.'

'Well, I'm glad about that. But I still feel guilty that my decision to up sticks to Oxford has left you with that long journey back and forth to London every day.'

'But there are benefits too, Will. My mother has the company of Henry and his wife at Bishop's Cleeve and I can get there and back in a day if I want to see her.'

'Good. But your commute? It must be so tedious.'

'Rubbish. The train service is good and I can get quite a lot of work done on the way. Besides, I can enjoy a decent breakfast en route. Talking of which, I'm famished.'

The Eagle and Child public house at 49 St Giles was smaller and narrower than they had imagined, but they had heard it was a well-known meeting place for a literary circle which included a number of Oxford academics like J. R. R. Tolkien and C. S. Lewis and went by the name of The Inklings.

Hungry and chilled to the marrow by the icy wind, they took one look at the warm yellow light emanating from its windows and went in. It was packed. Loud conversations at the bar were competing with the insistent but accomplished efforts of the pianist and Will pushed his way forward to order the drinks, leaving Grace to search for somewhere to sit while attracting admiring looks. All seats around the blazing log fire were taken and so, it seemed, were all the tables. But no. There in the far corner was a small, cushioned bench seat with just enough room for them both.

'Is anyone sitting here?' she asked a tall, bespectacled man at the table opposite.

'No. You go right ahead,' he answered with a slight Antipodean accent. Grace tried to place it. Australia or New Zealand? Australia, she thought, but she never could be sure. Kitty would have known in an instant.

Will looked back from the bar at his beautiful wife. He tried not to think about how far along she would have been by now. At least she was healthy and well, and she'd been so strong afterwards – helping him through his own grief while she suffered hers. 'We have two incredible children,' she'd said to Will. And, 'We can get through anything.' Those two children were currently with their grandmother at Bishop's Cleeve, where Will and Grace would join them for Christmas. They'd come back to Oxford once their parents got the boiler working. Daniel was looking at where to study to follow his interest in psychiatry, and Emily would work as a nanny and help around the house until her 'calling' announced itself.

Grace looked around the pub. A sea of red, happy faces of people engaged in animated conversations about their work, current affairs, Oxford itself or preparations for Christmas. Now she could see Will carefully pushing his way through a jostling group of revellers, keeping the tray of drinks and potato crisps out of harm's way.

He set them down on the table where the Australian was sitting.

'Would you mind?' Will asked.

'Not at all.'

'I'm gasping,' said Grace, taking a long gulp of her beer. 'And the crisps will fill a hole too.'

'That's all they've got left, I'm afraid. But we'll find something on the way home, I'm sure.'

'Take Salvarsan, for example, James,' said the man sitting opposite his younger companion.

Will's ears pricked up; he knew all about Salvarsan as Gordon Forrester had used it, or rather neosalvarsan, to treat Jack's syphilis.

'If a simple colouring dye can enter the cells of bacteria that cause disease in humans and prevent serious infection, who knows what other chemicals might be useful to cure such illnesses?'

Grace looked at Will and raised an eyebrow. She felt slightly awkward about eavesdropping, but she could not help herself. This was her life's work after all.

'Well, look what Domagk has done with Prontosil at Farbenindustrie,' replied the young man, setting down his pint. 'First he demonstrates that mice can be protected from the effects of streptococcal infection, and then he uses it successfully in humans.'

'Proving it to be a remarkably powerful treatment for infection in about 1 per cent of new mothers who otherwise have a 25 per cent mortality rate.'

Will could hardly believe what he was hearing. It was only twenty-six years since his own mother's untimely death from the same disease.

Despite knowing about Prontosil and the aminobenzenesulfonamide active ingredient that killed certain bacteria, Grace wanted to hear more. She was curious to know who the two men were. What other work might they be involved in and what was their level of expertise? Were they doctors, too? Or researchers or academics? Perhaps they were biochemists or pathologists? For all she knew, they could simply be journalists looking into a promising story. She was desperate to introduce herself and join in.

'And according to my sources, it's proving to be surprisingly effective against meningitis and gonorrhoea as well, by all accounts,' added the Australian, polishing his spectacles.

'But not where an infection is complicated by the presence of pus,' said Grace boldly.

The two men fell silent in astonishment and looked at Grace.

'And not without staining the unfortunate patient's skin bright red.'

Will looked at her too. He knew she could be direct, but she never usually butted in on other people's conversations.

'Am I sitting next to a fellow pathologist?' enquired the older man amiably.

'You are. Please excuse me, but I couldn't help overhearing. You're both pathologists yourselves then, I take it? Here in Oxford?'

'My name is Howard Florey. Chair of Pathology at the university. This is my assistant James Kent.'

Grace thought, Of course it's Florey! She knew she'd recognised him.

'I know your name very well. I'm Grace. Grace Burnett. And this is my husband, Will.'

'How do you do, Will. And Grace,' he said, shaking their hands. 'Are you at Oxford as well?'

'We just moved up from London,' said Grace. 'Will recently took up a job as surgeon at the Radcliffe and I'm currently travelling back and forth to the research department at St Mary's — for my sins.'

'Are you indeed? That's quite a trek.'

'Needs must, I suppose.'

Grace flashed a quick smile and glanced fleetingly at her husband. Florey thought he detected a slight awkwardness about the subject.

'What's your special interest in antibacterial chemicals?'

'Up until now I've mainly been researching vaccines. The work is encouraging, but, as you know, there are only so many microorganisms amenable to the immunisation approach. The potential for active treatment rather than prevention seems unlimited.'

'That's what we believe,' chipped in Kent. 'But it's not our main focus at present. People like Ehrlich and Domagk have been tinkering about with hundreds of different dyes for years, but finding ones that work is like panning for gold. Time-consuming, back-breaking and generally disappointing.'

'We're currently working on lysozymes, tetanus, lymphatic vessels, gastrointestinal secretions and the mechanisms whereby antibodies can agglutinate bacteria and destroy them.'

'Grace is hell-bent on treating established infections,' said Will. 'As a surgeon, so am I. We both saw the results of rampant sepsis in the war, and ever since then, Grace has devoted her life to asepsis and sterile techniques. But sometimes it's not enough.'

At that moment, the spare chair at the table was pulled back and a smaller man with a thick head of hair and a well-trimmed moustache planted himself down on it.

'What's not enough?' he asked in a distinct German accent.

'Trying to prevent disease by relying on asepsis and vaccination alone,' said Will.

'Quite right,' he said confidently. 'We need much more in our medical armamentarium if we are ever going to kill bacteria before they kill us. I'm Chain, by the way. Ernst Chain. I'm a colleague of Howard here, whom you've obviously met.'

'Ernst is a biochemist working with me, Grace. And a very gifted one. Nearly as gifted as he is on the piano. That was him playing in the other corner just now.'

'A favourite composition by Alexander Scriabin,' he said. 'But I'm not convinced his search for the mystery of life so evident in his themes is always fully appreciated by the half-drunk clientele of a middle-class pub like the Eagle and Child.'

'You're very talented,' said Will.

'So they say,' replied Chain rather immodestly. 'Are you a musician yourself?'

'Far from it,' he answered as Grace nearly choked on her beer with amusement before enlightening him briefly about their respective careers.

Nodding, Chain reverted to the subject of music.

'I could not exist without music. I might still abandon science and devote myself to its magical allure.'

'You certainly could,' said Florey, 'but you won't. And anyway, I won't let you.'

The two men smiled and clinked their glasses.

'Ernst is currently working on enzymes and proteins. Important and interesting work.'

460

'And unravelling the mechanism whereby tiny amounts of snake venom can paralyse the central nervous system and kill within minutes.'

'Even more important and interesting if you ask me,' added Kent. 'But then I'm fascinated by anything to do with animals.'

'So if, as you say, vaccination and asepsis are only part of the answer, where do your other interests lie, Grace?'

'Recently I've been investigating phages. Viruses that can penetrate bacterial cells and destroy them from within. In fact, I returned not long ago from Berlin from a conference on the subject. During the Games. Are you from Berlin, Ernst?'

Chain had suddenly frozen at the mere mention of the name of his capital city. It reminded him of the heartbreaking news he had recently received by letter from Hennigsdorf about his mother and his cousin Anna.

Initially, Grace thought he had not heard her because of the cacophony of noise in the pub. So she asked him the same question again.

'Yes,' he said eventually. 'I received my PhD from the prestigious Charité Hospital there. How did you find Berlin?'

It seemed like a loaded question. She did not know this man nor his political affiliations or background.

'A city not altogether at ease with itself,' she said diplomatically.

'A city run by Nazi thugs trying to hide their true colours from the rest of the world would be more accurate,' he said flatly.

'Germany's loss is Oxford's gain,' said Florey, jumping in. 'The situation there forced him to get out while he could. And we are pleased to have him.'

Grace looked down and reddened slightly. 'I'm sorry.'

'No need. I'm Jewish. The main reason I'm still here.'

461

Grace hoped Liese was settling well in Edinburgh. She'd said she wanted to start afresh, but somewhere smaller, where she could carve out a new life. All letters to Will and Grace's old address would be forwarded to them in Oxford, so they wouldn't miss any news from those left behind in Berlin.

'So, Grace,' said Florey, again changing the subject, 'how would you like to forego your daily commuting to London and come and work for me? At the Dunn Institute?'

'What?' gasped Grace, not quite believing what she had heard. 'You've only just met me in a pub.'

'So? I only met James because he was sweeping the floor of my lab in Sheffield when he was fourteen years old. Gave him a job as a researcher the first day I met him. Bloody good at it, too.'

James blushed slightly and picked up his glass.

'This is rather expeditious,' countered Chain, feeling aggrieved as a leading member of the team who had not been included in such a snap decision. 'Perhaps we should reflect on this. Ask the rest of the team. Take up references?'

'It's my team, Ernst. One of the perquisites of being a leader is that I can choose whomever I want. I chose you and I chose James. I'm not one for all this regimented protocol and the very British reliance on the formal interview process. I like to think I'm not a bad judge of character and I listen to my gut.'

Chain looked a little put out by the rebuff, but Will thought Florey's attitude was both surprising and refreshing in an academic and, based on Will's own awful interview experiences, he was rather impressed.

'I don't know what to say,' Grace stuttered. 'Will?'

'I think it depends on what work you want to be involved in. It's a wonderful opportunity, Grace, but it's not just about finding a job here in Oxford.'

'You said you're interested in antibacterial chemicals,' said Florey. 'So am I. We just haven't had much joy with them. And the relative success of Prontosil has rather diverted attention away from another substance whose potential we are having difficulty in unlocking. That's the research role I would like to offer you.'

'Well, I'm very flattered,' she said. 'Really, I am. This substance you're referring to. What is it exactly?'

'It's a mould,' said Chain, 'called penicillium notatum.'

'It somehow seems to have the capacity to kill off pathogenic bacteria,' said Florey, looking at his colleague. 'But we don't yet know how, and we don't know the implications. Perhaps you can help us find out?'

'Perhaps I can,' she replied. 'I'd certainly like to try.'

'And?' said Will.

'So, yes . . . If you're serious. I'd love to accept your offer.'

'We can't pay you much,' said Florey. 'I've only just banned my people in the department from using the lift in order to save twenty-five pounds per year from the research grant. But I'll talk to the MRC people and see what we can do.'

'That doesn't surprise me,' said Grace. 'But the salary is less important than the work.'

She glanced at Will. This was true, but they also did have a budget to consider. He nodded, meaning: we will work it out.

'Well, let me get the next round,' said Will, standing and grabbing the tray of empty glasses. 'It's not every day your wife gets offered the job of her dreams just around the corner from where she lives. And who knows,' he added, without a hint of irony or presage, 'you lot might even end up changing the course of medical history.'

'Well, I wouldn't go that far,' said Florey. 'I think we could make a difference. But I doubt we'll ever be able to cure every human being of infectious disease.'

'Even so,' said Grace. 'If our work could find a cure for just one contagious disease or save the lives of even a few . . .'

'It would certainly make a difference to those few,' said Will with a smile on his face as he turned on his heel and made off towards the bar, imagining the possibilities.

Acknowledgements

Every generation faces its social challenges. But whatever the latest one faces, the challenges must have been many times harder during the interwar years and in the build-up to that terrible conflagration that was the Second World War.

After the first great conflict, the war that was supposed to have been 'the war to end all wars', many people were dealing with the tragic loss of their loved ones while experiencing hunger, rationing, unemployment and a particularly uncertain future. There was no NHS and few could afford the inflated fees of private doctors working in their inaccessible surgeries. For those who could, not many were guaranteed treatments that were proven to be effective or even safe.

It was a time of massive social upheaval and change. While the bright young things from the privileged classes flouted their good fortune and profligately spent their money on sex, drugs and outrageous parties, the suffragettes marched under the watchful – and sometimes unforgiving – gaze of the constabulary; workers who could no longer afford to feed their families and whose pay had fallen while prices and rents soared went on strike and the poor died in their thousands from malnutrition, infection, disease and neglect.

On top of all this, political upheaval and military conflict were never far away.

Ireland was locked in a bloody battle for independence, the Great Depression crippled global trade for years and the Spanish Civil War tore that country apart and further fuelled the flames for the inexorable rise of fascist dictatorships in Germany and Italy.

These years truly represented the eye of the storm.

Yet, like most ordinary people living during those two decades, my characters, Dr William Burnett and his wife Grace, just got on with the task in hand, striving against all the odds to overcome hardship and discrimination and to try, in their own small way, to make a difference. This book is really about them, and the people in the background like them, who nobody thinks very much about until they are needed but who remain dedicated to what they do and whose love for each other, their children and the people they care for knows no bounds.

So I would like to thank all those ordinary people who actually, in times of hardship, turn out to be rather extraordinary. This book is really dedicated to them. I have thoroughly enjoyed writing it, but I could not have done it without the help which I acknowledge here.

I'd like to think my literary agent, Kerr MacRae, for his original suggestion that I try my hand at writing novels and for his guidance and support ever since. My editor, Angela Meyer, has been unswervingly patient and has brilliantly provided excellent feedback and ideas.

Jon Elek and his entire team at Welbeck have all been amazing and I would especially like to thank James Horobin, Rosa Schierenberg, Alexandra Allden, Nico Poilblanc, Rob Cox, Maddie Dunne Kirby, Rachel Hart, Angie Willocks, Carrie-Ann Pitt, Sophie Leeds, Annabel Robinson and Sam Matthews.

A special word of thanks to my wife, Dee, who has done the lion's share of the household chores while I've been engrossed at my desk, and my mother, Noreen, who has provided wise counsel and been my greatest supporter throughout.

I have drawn on various sources of research for historical detail but would like to extend particular thanks to Margaret Dangoor, Chair of the Archives and Museum Group at Queen Mary's Hospital Roehampton. I can heartily recommend their illustrated Blue Book, *A History of Queen Mary's University Hospital Roehampton* by Brenda Weedon and others, for anybody wishing to learn more about this incredible institution.

I am grateful too to Colonel Jeremy Pughe-Morgan, British Forces Cyprus, for his insight into disciplinary and court-martial procedures in the British Army, and also to Alexandra Riverol-Brown, The Worshipful Society of Apothecaries and Mr John Watkinson FRCS, for their additional help and research.

About the Author

DR HILARY JONES is a General
Practitioner and regular contributor
to multiple newspapers and television
shows. He is a well-known and
trusted face to millions in the UK.
His first novel, *Frontline*, was
published in 2021 and was praised
by readers and critics alike.

@DrHilaryJones

www.drhilaryjones.com

WELBECK

PUBLISHING GROUP

Love books? Join the club.

Sign up and choose your preferred genres to receive tailored news, deals, extracts, author interviews and more about your next favourite read.

From heart-racing thrillers to award-winning historical fiction, through to must-read music tomes, beautiful picture books and delightful gift ideas, Welbeck is proud to publish titles that suit every taste.

bit.ly/welbeckpublishing

WELBECK

ANDRE DEUTSCH

MORTIMER

MORTIMER

WELBECK

OH!